Pontiac

on a ball, and my brothers and I have always been invited. You have been to it?"

"No, I did not know of this," Herr Schmidt said, chastened.

"Just this past year," Yusupov said. "I found myself at the Firm ball, cornered by a group of fellows who were once or students there, all very Etonesque, if you know what I mean.

"One of them, a short fat fellow with black mustache asked me if I had ever visited Moscow. I told I had not, and I asked why. He said he had always wanted to go there. And asked if it was true there is a town there called Monte Haute.

"They all had a very nice little Etonesque fashion over that. I told the little blousy fellow the place he really should visit is Arkansas. I said the moment he gets off the train in Arkansas, he will be seized by the locals and serially butt-fucked, which I assured he would probably enjoy."

We all exploded laughing, and Yusupov stuck his nose even higher in the air as if he didn't know how funny he was. Yusupov could be funny...

"Yusupov?"

"Herr..."

Pontiac

A NOVEL

Jim Schutze

DEEP VELLUM PUBLISHING

DALLAS, TEXAS

Deep Vellum Publishing
3000 Commerce Street, Dallas, Texas 75226
deepvellum.org · @deepvellum

Deep Vellum is a 501c3 nonprofit literary arts organization founded in 2013 with the mission to bring the world into conversation through literature.

Support for this publication has been provided in part by grants from the National Endowment for the Arts, the Texas Commission on the Arts, the City of Dallas Office of Arts and Culture, the Communities Foundation of Texas, and the Addy Foundation.

Paperback ISBN: 9781646053483 | Ebook ISBN: 9781646053605

LIBRARY OF CONGRESS CATALOGING-IN-PUBLICATION DATA:

Names: Schutze, Jim, author.
Title: Pontiac : a novel / Jim Schutze.
Description: [Dallas] : Deep Vellum, 2024.
Identifiers: LCCN 2024010362 (print) | LCCN 2024010363 (ebook) | ISBN
9781646053483 (trade paperback) | ISBN 9781646053605 (ebook)
Subjects: LCGFT: School fiction. | Novels.
Classification: LCC PS3619.C4836 P66 2024 (print) | LCC PS3619.C4836
(ebook) | DDC 813/.6--dc23/eng/20240311
LC record available at https://lccn.loc.gov/2024010362
LC ebook record available at https://lccn.loc.gov/2024010363

Cover art and design by Daniel Benneworth-Gray
Interior layout and typesetting by KGT

PRINTED IN THE UNITED STATES OF AMERICA

CONTENTS

CONTENTS

PONTIAC

"Where are you from?"

"Little Rock."

"What is little rock?"

"Little Rock is a city."

"Arkansas."

"You are from Arkansas?"

PONTIAC

Chapter One

THIS IS THE KIND OF PARTY music that puts a bounce in the old WASPs—silly brass, screechy strings, and a twinkly vibraphone playing some variation on "The Teddy Bears' Picnic." With one hand in the air to signal both intention and apology, I wend my way through swirling pastel, past dusty tuxedos and a few white dinner jackets foxed at the lapels.

Two tribes are present, one I know too well, the other unfamiliar. The old people, the ones my age, are the WASPs gathered in from the four corners to attend Compton's fête. The younger people must be underlings, probably employees at one or more of his hospitals. I don't know how many he owns in Chicago. The underlings look self-conscious but pleased with themselves to be here. The WASPs, of course, would dance right over them if they got in the way.

The old men prance painfully on cracked patent leather pumps, their ancient countenances stretched taut over yellowed grins as they bear down on female captives clutched in wrestling holds, perhaps from affection but more likely for balance. All of them shuffle to this daffy orchestra whose name I must get close enough to make

9

out on the head of the kick drum, just to be sure. And, yes, finally, lo and behold and sure enough, even though we are here at our informal reunion at the Onwentsia Club on the North Shore of Chicago in the first part of the twenty-first century, it's the same one—the indefatigable Lester Lanin, who played all the big shenanigans on Long Island in the middle of the previous century. Absolutely amazing how a terrible outfit like this could have held it together all these decades, greatly assisted, I am sure, by its audience's fear of improvement.

Outside, a howling winter storm races up off the black reaches of Lake Michigan to pummel the ballroom's soaring windows with fists of snow. If this is Mother Nature's way of protesting the inanity within, no one hears or cares. Mother Nature can go screw herself. Within this heavy-timbered cathedral, the summer of '62 presses on regardless, except that, instead of teenagers swept along heedless on a happy flood of libido and booze, we are now crones and geezers circling the drain.

Compton whirls by with a decent-looking dowager coiled in his arms, not half dead, and gives me the elbow: "Still a wallflower, eh?"

"Guess so."

"Get a look at that blonde by the bar." He gives his bushy white eyebrows a suggestive waggle, then whirls away, cackling to his dame.

I do make my way over to the bar at the ballroom's far end, more for nothing else to do than interest, and I do see her. But it's absurd. I am in my seventies, certainly not in the market in any way, shape, or form for this child who can't be a day over forty. She is stand-out beautiful, a platinum blonde with huge brown eyes and sinuous legs, a shape and cleavage that might turn a younger man's knees to jelly but not mine. Mine already are. She does notice my enfeebled approach, a surprise at this point. Most young women who look like this not only do not see me, but, sitting next to me at dinner and reaching to pass the butter, could put the butter right through my chest. She does definitely spot me, however, and even seems to be angling for an eye. I am of iron, which is to say, no flutters. I smile and give her a very small nod, as if to a child. But my God, what a child. One heavenly hip against the bar, she is alone except for the liveried and mustachioed bartender already lurching forward to hear my whim.

"Champagne."

He pours and hands over. I turn to her with a sip. We are far enough away from the bunny band and the soft din of senescent shuffling to be heard.

"You are an unlikely wallflower," I say to her, smiling hugely, of course.

"Hump," she says, unsmiling. "Ditched."

"I'm sorry?"

"My boyfriend's a brain surgeon. On call. He does trauma. Had to go in. I'm supposed to Uber."

"And?"

"Fucking Uber won't come out here, because of the storm."

"So, ditched and forlorn."

"Ditched and fucked."

The half-forgotten word spawns a thought. I have been yearning to escape for the last two hours. My intentions certainly are not lascivious. Please. At my age? I just want to get away from here. Something about her seems interesting, and, well, I don't really have to spell it out for you, do I? And anyway, the witching hour is at hand. They've been pouring down the hooch by the bucket all night, exactly as they did when we were young and could handle it. At any moment now, the masks will come cracking off and the convulsive pairing will begin.

"Oh, KuKu!"

"Oh, Chubby!"

I know from long practice that this is my cue to make tracks. The more out of control they get, the keener their noses become for caste, and I will soon become a potted palm. Staggering, falling into chairs, they will pair perfectly as if by computer according to their relative degrees of WASPdom. It was a little less clear what was going on when we were young and reasonably good-looking. Then, at least theoretically, KuKu, once drunk, might have gone straight for Chubby because she thought he was sexy. But now that we are all hideous, there can be no doubt. Like insects sniffing each other's pheromones, nothing turns them on like WASPiness.

I only attended one of these things during my years at the school, but it helped to cement the difference. With my thirteen-year-old chin in hand, sitting on a service stoop at the back of a robber baron's castle on Cove Road, I gazed out at neat ranks of whitecaps marching in from the harbor and knew that I was a proper son of the nation's grimy industrial midsection. Even if I tried, I never could trade the values of Pontiac, Michigan, for Oyster Bay, New York.

"I can give you a lift," I say. "I have my car. I was about to leave."

"I'm downtown."

"You're on my way."

Now suddenly dubious, she asks, "Are you by any chance shit-faced?"

"I sincerely hope you mean drunk."

"Yes."

12

"No," holding up the champagne, "this is it. I never get drunk with these people."

She pushes from the bar, lifting a pearl-encrusted purse on silken strings, and we're off.

And, of course, wouldn't you know, just my luck, the snow is driving down so thick and sky so black I can barely noodle and nose my way along to Townline Road. While my rented rear-wheel drive car tries to turn into a carnival ride, I fight to maintain a false appearance of competence. We have been silent for about ten minutes.

"I can see you're not shit-faced," she says.

"Faint praise."

"Tell me you're not a creep."

"I'm not a creep. Well, wait. What kind of creep?"

"The kind who chases women half his age."

"I do not chase women half my age. And in fact, I can think of nothing more disastrous than catching one."

"OK, sorry. But you were hanging out back there with all of those people, and a lot of them sort of are. Or seem to be."

"Creeps?"

"Maybe not creeps but drunks. Jesus. Old drunks."

"Nothing worse," I say.

"I got ditched. It wasn't my boyfriend's fault. He's a brain surgeon."

"You said."

"The guy who was the host is the CEO of the hospital where he works."

"Not exactly," I say as decorously as possible. "He is the founder, chairman of the board, and majority shareholder in an international holding company that owns multiple chains of hospitals, one chain of which is the chain to which your boyfriend's hospital belongs."

"Whatever. The practice calls, he's gone. I told him I'd Uber. Not to worry. But Jesus."

I am trying to make my way to the tollway. The car shoves through the snow like an egg-laden turtle up the beach. We lapse into another ten-minute silence. Then she tells me her boyfriend loves to go to events like these.

"He's a star fucker. We went to one last year at this same place, and that guy was there who was running for president. Tonight he said there was also supposed to be a guy who's Ernest Hemingway's son, plus some Russian oligarch who owns all the gas in Europe."

"All true."

"Is that why you go?"

"No. The host tonight is an old friend."

For the first time, I hazard a quick but direct glance at the cleavage.

She catches me. "You're not even partially a creep, right?"

"No. I'm just old. Harmless. Disarmed but still disarming."

"I'll be the judge of that."

"What's your name?"

"Ellen. What's yours?"

"Woodrow."

We're on the freeway at last, creeping glacially toward the Loop. I am prepared to remain silent all the way there, to the tomb if necessary. And I really am not a creep, by the way. Not now. It's amazing how much moral improvement comes with impotence. Equally amazing how far that goes to explain the rest of life.

"Every time I go to one of these things up here," she says, "they do the same thing. They walk around with these mummy faces half the night, pour down the booze like no tomorrow, then it's all senior citizen grab-ass. I didn't grow up around old people who acted like that."

14

"Did you grow up around WASPs?"

"Jews."

"There you have it. The old people tonight were all old-school WASPs. When they get together, they behave exactly as they did when we were kids."

"So you're one of them."

"A WASP? No. Not at all. Not a bit."

"If you're not one of them, how do you know them?"

Fair question.

In 1952 when I was six years old, my parents moved us from Quitman County, Georgia ("Where the Fish Don't Stop Jumpin'"), on the banks of the Chattahoochee River where it forms the border with the ever-mysterious Alabama, to Pontiac, Michigan ("Where they make the Pontiacs"), in the heart of the American Ruhr. The automobile industry was exploding in a postwar geyser of smoke and money that must have been visible from space.

When we arrived, it was a place of seventy-five thousand inhabitants just outside Detroit, a thin, sprawling warren of shoe-box houses, most of them brand-new and solidly built under the unblinking eye of a national government still military by custom and practice. The endless rows of tidy structures knelt at the boot of the great roaring, burning stinking Pontiac Motors, more city than factory, a gray duchy of dirty brick and stained tin that yawned out over the land, impossibly huge, insanely complex, and always, day and night, emitting a supernatural symphony of howl, flame, screech, smoke, thunder and random great gushes of air.

Pontiac Motors was a division of General Motors, which was never called that by anyone in Pontiac or Detroit. General Motors was always GM, an entity stitched together from all the great swashbuckling names of Detroit—the Fisher brothers, who made fine horse-drawn coaches, the French bicycle-racers Chevrolet and Champion, who were the fastest human beings on earth. Pontiac's namesake was Chief Pontiac, Obwandiyag, the great Ottawa warrior who in the 1760s led a confederacy of tribes against the English at Fort Detroit. Pontiac's warriors stood outside the fort and chopped open the chests of captive English soldiers, eating their still-quivering blood-slimed hearts while the English looked on hapless from the palisades.

My father told me and my brother that the dream of working in the car plants was what got him through the Battle of the Bulge, and this from a man descended from the greatest hunting guide in the history of the South, Henry Skaggs, a peer and business partner of Daniel Boone himself. What drew our father forward through war, he told us, was never any vision of returning to guns and blood in the red clay hills of Quitman County, but the silver dream of one day going to Detroit, working on the assembly line, breathing grit and grease all day long and making so much money that his wife would never again set a rich man's table and he would never tote another rich man's gun or pour his whiskey. His dream was that one day, he would buy his own brick house and his own brand-new automobile, send his sons to college and, in his final years, enjoy retirement, a thing no one in Quitman County had ever even heard of.

Our father's dream was shared by the soldiers who had known penury and want before enlistment and who now, having survived the rich man's game of war, had come home to pursue the workingman's mission of family. Like my father, many of them came to

Pontiac with a fierce appetite for doing better. And they did. They worked. Pontiac worked. It worked.

For me and my younger brother, David, Pontiac was the most impossibly exciting place on earth. The schools, like the town, were bursting at the seams with too many kids, all of them from everywhere else, shoveled in from the hollers of Kentucky and Tennessee, boated over from Ireland and Poland, hauled North on trains and buses from the dark void of Alabama. In those first years after the war, the transplanted children of the factory workers communicated in the same crude patois their parents spoke when away from home, mainly shouts and the sign language of exasperation. To be unable to shout loudly and wave your hands in Pontiac in 1952 was to be mute.

The kindergarten classes were run in double shifts, one from 6:00 AM to 10:00 AM and the second from 10:30 AM to 2:30 PM. I attended the early rotation. I believe some part of me remembers every single bus ride in the morning on a rattling vehicle painted olive drab instead of yellow, probably military surplus. Those of us who lived on the city's semirural outskirts gathered in small knots on dirt roads, bundled against the cold with lunch boxes gripped in our frozen mittens, craning out from snow-filled ditches to see the first faint approach of the bus's warm lights. Every morning in the gray dawn, the bus brought us down Baldwin Avenue past the west gate of the Fisher Body Plant just as the midnight shift was getting off. Workers released from ten hours of monotonous toil came rushing out into the newborn day full of victory, men bouncing like boys with their lunch pails aloft, and always a few wonderful women in piratical head scarves who walked hard like men, all of them surrounding the bus on all sides in a roiling flood as they hurried across Baldwin to the massive saloons for their end-of-shift beer.

17

The bars were industrial-sized drinking barns with tin roofs and long crank windows the length of the second level. Men and women leaned out of the open upstairs windows with sloppy schooners, cheering the mob in the street to hurry and join, and the mob cheered back. In no sporting event or election that I have witnessed since have I seen or felt anything so raucously happy as that unfailing daily celebration that happened on my way to kindergarten. We had no idea what they were celebrating, but when we came down Baldwin Avenue in the morning, we stood on our seats and hung on the middle sills, waiting with bated breath. We pulled down the windows even in winter and cheered the workers. I distinctly remember them cheering back at us with toothy grins, some hailing with their lunch pails, others with frothy glasses of beer.

The only thing that stood in the way of my father's dream of a new brick house was his and my mother's extreme thrift. Eight years after moving up from Georgia, we still lived outside the city in the somewhat tumbledown informal settlement usually called Little Ottawa. I learned later that my father had paid off our house mortgage in Little Ottawa in those first eight years, and he and my mother had resolved never to borrow another nickel.

By then we were no longer hillbillies, a term which meant newcomer, hick, or outlander. Our meticulous little frame cottage was never even faintly tumbledown, never missing a lick of paint or a fresh trim of the grass. I'm not sure there was a term for people like my family who had assimilated quickly into the culture of the nation's great Middle Western manufacturing region. The only name we ever heard the Michigan natives apply to themselves was Michigander, and I think we newcomers deserved a bit of respect for eschewing it.

Anyway, Pontiac was a place where no accent or physical

appearance disqualified you from belonging, because everyone came from some equally unpronounceable place in Ukraine, Finland, or Quitman County. All it took to be fully installed was learning the ropes—something my father was intensely committed to seeing all of us do as immediately as possible.

My memories of childhood in Little Ottawa are Elysian, mainly, even though I was not a popular boy. I spent a lot of time alone, reading in the cramped attic bedroom I shared with David, who was never there.

When David and I were still little boys, I don't know if rock and roll had brought us the word, cool, yet, but he definitely was cool, and I definitely was not. David was always gone, getting up to mischief with a gang of little buddies, while I had only two friends with whom I played infrequently. Most of the time I was up there in the room by myself reading.

My reading indulged two competing interests. One was the early history of Michigan, especially the eighteenth century and anything to do with Native Americans. My other early intellectual passion was for a satirical magazine called *MAD*, specifically and cleverly aimed, I think, at lonely adolescents. My two companions were Jimmy Shirtlift, whom my father always referred to as "that tree monkey," and Warren Truckman, whom my father called, "the weirdo." Jimmy was short and unnaturally burly, with stringy brown hair cut in a bowl and fierce eyes deep-set beneath a comically beetled brow. He was given to temper over small slights and could be violent, but Warren and I learned early to recognize the warning signals and knew to step aside in time. When something caught Jimmy's interest, he had a way of standing stock-still with his arms clutched up and head turned slightly sideways, peering intently out of the corner of his eye like a parrot.

He was by far the most hillbilly kid in Little Ottawa. Only when we were a little older, approaching adolescence, did I understand that Jimmy and his family were actually too hillbilly even for the hillbillies, either because they had failed to assimilate or because they brought with them some curse from the hollers.

Jimmy spoke with an indelibly Elizabethan accent unsoftened by contact. When he was excited and talking fast, Warren and I only understood every third word. His mother worked for the Pontiac school system. His father had been not merely fired from Pontiac Motors, twice, but permanently banned from the grounds subject to arrest. We were all abjectly terrified of Old Man Shirtlift, a tall, gaunt, ragged rascal out of Faulkner who stitched together an income selling guns and bootleg ammo and breeding hunting dogs. The rear wall of the Shirtlift garage was covered from top to bottom with red-brown splotches where he had hurled pups culled from his litters. In spring, when the ground began to thaw, the Shirtlift backyard stank of rotting dog.

Jimmy was feral. When he wasn't in a rage trying to kill us, he was a source of absolute delight. The school principal once made the serious mistake of leaving him locked inside her office as a form of detention. Jimmy leapt through a closed window in an explosion of shattered glass. While we crowed exultantly from the classroom windows above, a wild, angry, and bloody Jimmy Shirtlift danced a demonic jig on the school lawn, pumping two middle fingers at the building and screaming something we couldn't begin to make out except for an oft-repeated phrase: "You fuckin' Yankee bitch!" If we children had been allowed to choose our own Savior, Jimmy Shirtlift would have been the guy.

I regret deeply that Warren and I lost touch with him after he went to prison the second time. We've agreed that he is either dead or living under an assumed name and president of a Bible college in Arkansas.

Neither Jimmy nor I considered Warren to be weird because he was black. We had plenty of other reasons. His family were the only black people in Little Ottawa, drawn there by their membership in a racially integrated Pentecostal church.

Warren was very funny in ways that adults weren't smart enough to get. He was tall and skinny, light-skinned and wore thick rimless spectacles. His hair stood out from his skull in a helmet. He was an only child who almost never left the house. In fact, he rarely left the basement where his parents, who were indulgent to the point of default and whom Warren called "the Jesus-oids," served him oven-warmed frozen television dinners to eat by himself on a folding tray.

Warren's realm, which was in fact the entire basement including the coal-fired furnace room, was dimly lighted by flickering bulbs suspended on extension cords dangling from overhead steam pipes. The entire space was a maze of model train tracks mounted on rickety, waist-high trestles made entirely of wood strips split from packing crates. His toy trains were not the larger, more expensive models made by the Lionel company, which we considered to be the trains of rich boys, but half that size in the new HO-gauge made by a company called Marx. He had many trains, financed with money easily wheedled from his parents.

Long before toys became digital and programmable, when everything was done by hand with switches and dials, all of Warren's trains operated on a meticulously measured and sequenced timetable. He was able to operate as many as seven trains at once, all of them starting, pausing, starting up again, and crisscrossing over the same tracks without collision according to a pattern that Warren, flying around the room from switch to switch like an alarmed egret, was able to govern with a handful of cheap stopwatches and notes on a clipboard. His notes were recorded in a squiggle code he had devised for reasons he never divulged. The whole thing running at full tilt boogie was a marvel that Jimmy and I never tired of witnessing. I can still see it.

When his mother called down the stairs to offer snacks, Warren always said blandly, "No, thank you, ma'am, we're fine," then wagged a finger at us and whispered, "Jesus food." In a box at the back of the basement, he kept a larder of candy bars and Coca-Colas, which he shared generously. I have no doubt if Warren were a little boy today, he would be diagnosed, drugged and destined for a life of therapy. As it happened, he was mainly ignored by our school because the school mainly ignored all of us. He met a lovely girl in high school who dragged him out of the basement, pushed him into General Motors Technical School and turned him into a handsomely compensated engineer. He's retired now, of course, and has returned full-time to his trains in the much larger basement of a very handsome home in Grosse Pointe Shores.

My mother seemed to want no part of Pontiac. She had no friends, went to church only grudgingly and spent long winter days alone in our house. In the spring and summer, she labored in meticulous backyard flower beds.

She was very beautiful, with the delicate bones and willowy figure that some Scots-Irish women took with them into the forests of North America. Her father, a foreman on a turpentine plantation in Georgia, died in a tree fall when she was nine. At twelve she left school and went to work to support her mother, an alcoholic. She was trained as a household servant in the grand house of an immense and prosperous tobacco plantation on the river road outside the town of Tobanana.

There, as a hard-working, virtually unparented child, she absorbed the poor person's version of rich people's manners and speech, at once proper and subservient. My father spoke the vernacular of the rural south, but my mother spoke two languages, the country vulgate when she was angry and excited at home and a formally correct grammar and diction in front of her betters. She tried to impose the latter version on me and David. He rebelled and talked like my father. But I spoke properly, the way my mother taught. Only as an adult did I grasp that David's redneck speech and manner probably had something to do with my mother's deep love for him, not to mention his success in life, and my own stilted speech probably was why my only friends in Little Ottawa were outcasts.

My father was almost ten years her senior when they married. I arrived soon after. Very soon. I know or think I know now that the rector of the Episcopal church that my father attended at the time introduced my mother to my father. When the rector introduced them, my mother was already pregnant by a member of the rich family for whom she worked. No one ever told me that. But I knew it. Of course, it was never uttered, let alone discussed in the family. I don't remember thinking about it. My father was tough but warm and always attentive—all the father any boy ever needed.

I called my mother Ma or Mother depending on her mood. She was not inclined toward tête-à-têtes with children. Her most frequent admonition to us was, "Don't get on my goddamn nerves." She worried what other people might think of us and then cursed them for thinking of us at all. I steered clear of her. She and David were close, though. One year younger than me, he was the shard that cut her heart. By the age of eleven, he was already becoming what was commonly called a "hood." He wasn't really a hoodlum at all at that point, but he did have the haircut.

The legendary hunting guide at the root of our family tree was Henry Skaggs, a type of man called "long hunter" in the eighteenth century—a freelance explorer whom no one had especially asked or commissioned to explore but who did anyway. My brother and I learned a little of this tale from our father. When I was only seven or eight, a young Ph.D. candidate from Murray State University in Kentucky came to Little Ottawa to interview my father about his lineage. It was from this man my father first heard the story of the business relationship between Henry Skaggs and Daniel Boone.

In my subsequent career as a student of Native American languages, I have learned that the Skaggs story is complex, if that is not too much of a euphemism. He was revered as a fearless hunter, intrepid pathfinder, and fierce warrior who led famished settlers to game and salvation. I think he, like Boone, may have been taken in by the Indians for a while and lived among them. One story suggests he had an Indian wife and child.

Later, I have reason to believe, his role in helping the white settlers decimate the indigenous peoples and steal their land was entirely reprehensible. He was a man of multiple loyalties. The scholar from Murray State told my father that Henry Skaggs almost certainly fought on both sides of the Revolutionary War. At the very end of his long life, he emerged again as Boone's partner in a land company.

I have wondered how any man could survive so long and unlikely a career—courageous and heinous, a saga of valor and duplicity—and come out of it a real estate agent. My conclusion has been that such a man must be born with an unerring instinct for when to duck, a trait I believe I possess as well.

After Henry Skaggs, my father's forebears moved solidly into the sporting version of the hunt, serving as guides who bounded over silver streams on sure-footed mounts, nipping through blue forests ahead of packs of pudgy planters dressed in whites and pith helmets, ostensibly in pursuit of a bear or other hapless creature but just as often seeking and always finding that bottle of fine whiskey cached ahead of time beneath a mossy log. The family seems to have stayed at the top of the hunting guide profession until my grandfather came along. By that time, the hunting camps were a cross between the Arabian Nights and a Barnum & Bailey Circus, with sleeping tents the size of houses, dining tents set with silver and bone china, a kitchen exuding delicious aromas night and day, an infirmary tent, a tent for the hands and a large corral—all to the tune of wandering minstrels. My grandfather slept in the woods in his own pup tent, keeping a proper social distance between himself and his clients as any good guide must know to do.

But the drink almost did him in. By early manhood, my grandfather's career as a guide was already in tatters, and his personal life was imploding because he couldn't get sober. A young planter from an aristocratic family, who had grown to respect him for his prowess in the hunt, was unable to stand by and watch him kill himself with booze. He led him to a program that sounds as if it may have been a precursor of Alcoholics Anonymous, with an entirely unlikely connection to the tiny rural Episcopal mission church just outside the town of Tobanana. I still can't imagine any association with Episcopalians that would do anything for a drinking problem but make it worse, but in my grandfather's case the pledge took hold. He dried out in time to enjoy life as a sober man.

The little gray stone Episcopal chapel with a river-rock steeple, set at the back of a deep green dale, looked for all the world like a postcard from the English countryside. It started as a place where planters worshipped away from home, but over the decades the town grew slowly toward it. The year-round congregation may have grown modestly, but the church never expanded beyond its mission status and always struggled to make ends meet. My grandfather was on the vestry and for a brief time toward the end of his life was senior warden. My father, in spite of a Celtic heritage that should have made him the sworn foe of all things Anglican, grew up as part of that congregation. When he moved us to Pontiac, he sought out an Episcopal Church and found the same sort of small mission chapel on the outskirts that Anglicans afford their lesser co-religionists. Called St. Mary's in the Hills (I saw no hills), that church was another over-darling Episcopal incarnation of the English countryside. My father was a committed and involved parishioner. He carried power tools to the church on Saturdays and worked with other men on repairs like rebuilding the wooden steeple. He was elected to the vestry and eventually, like his father, served as senior warden. At some point along the way, he became involved in diocesan affairs through a system of committees. He made frequent trips down Woodward Avenue to St. Paul Cathedral near Wayne State University in Detroit, sometimes taking me with him. He liked to walk me over to the campus so I could see what a university looked like. He reminded me that the cathedral was where Henry Ford's funeral had taken place not many years prior. My mother, very anomalously, was eager to accompany him on these journeys, though she skipped the campus tours and stayed visiting with the cathedral staff. I also accompanied him when he visited other big Episcopal churches in some connection with his duties.

The fact that we were Episcopalians rather than Baptists conspired with another social factor to create awkwardness for us in Little Ottawa. Not more than a few years after going to work at Pontiac Motors, my father, whom everyone addressed as Bill, rose in the ranks. He was made an assembly line foreman, taking him out of labor union membership and rendering him a part of management, although at the very bottom rung. He was required to wear a white shirt and tie as emblems of his new rank and fealty.

Normally, a man who left the union to become management was expected to move his family out of a union neighborhood in keeping with the company's military culture of rank. But my parents had their own idiosyncrasies. My mother, in her youthful employment as a domestic, and my father, from his family's legacy of hunting with and for the wealthy, had both developed a skepticism for rich powerful people. They knew far better than most working people how to get along with the rich and how to avoid ruffling delicate feathers. But my parents also took rich people with a grain of salt. My father said it was a waste of money to move out of a perfectly serviceable house only to borrow more money for a longer mortgage. My mother said we'd be better off in the end with the money saved than with the extra pittance some folks earn by sucking up. But by staying in Little Ottawa, my father had set a potentially difficult path for us. Our failure to move up to the proper level of neighborhood was a heresy. He was able to smooth all of that over with deer hunting—a thing of near religious importance to auto workers. Most had come to Detroit from places where hunting was either a rich man's province or the poor man's poaching.

A legacy of thin sandy soil and hard winters in northern Michigan had left vast tracts of timber and farmland in state ownership for unpaid taxes—more public land than any other state east

27

of the Mississippi River. In the years right after the war, Michigan discovered that rough-hewn outdoor leisure activity could be both remunerative to the state in the form of hunting and fishing license fees and also a good thing for the fragile northern economy, dependent as it was on cabin rentals and liquor sales. Vast tracts of public forest suitable only for logging, an albatross until then, became a profit center for state government as deer farms.

The idea that working men could be sport hunters was new. In Michigan, a working man didn't have to sneak or wheedle to get out onto a forest full of deer. He went proudly, license in hand, ammo packed, guns cleaned and oiled, to claim his rightful place in the woods, in worlds gone by a privilege only for barons.

But deer hunting was not always a pretty picture. The great armada driving north bumper-to-bumper on two-lane highways the day before the opening of deer season was a mingle of hunters, whores, poker hustlers, bootleggers, ammo smugglers, loan sharks, and counterfeiters. All of them gathered together at crossroads bars and gas stations, the hunters, the whores, and the rest of the hustlers furiously excited about the fun and profit ahead, thrilled to be headed to the woods.

In this world, my father was of ancient lineage. He knew hunting as he knew his own breath and heartbeat. As a child long before he had ever hunted himself among men, he listened rapt to wry stories of the hunt at the Thanksgiving Day table, to whispered anecdotes and raucous dirty jokes. He was capable of killing every whitetail deer within three miles of camp on the first day but knew not only how to mark and leave deer for his fellow hunters but also how to lead the others to the deer without domineering. He had grown up to the thrill and dread of men drunk in the woods with guns. He knew the importance of getting drunk with them, plunging with them into that dark distance of blood, fire, whores and booze in the forest where social rank melted away at least for the week, where men were stitched together by the stink of their firearms. It was in those Michigan hunting woods that my father preserved his status as Bill, the regular guy, the man who could be trusted even in a white shirt and tie, and it was there he carved out a social channel by which the rest of the family could navigate Little Ottawa. I don't remember ever thinking that we were better than the people around us, but I do remember knowing we needed to behave as if we didn't think so.

In this somewhat precarious status, and given my mother's occasional anxiety about respectability, it galled me that my brother, the nascent hoodlum, was more the object of her affection than I. I wanted to be the special one, the one who stood out.

Then suddenly I was. I was in the eighth grade. One evening, my father called me down to the kitchen. He was already seated at his end of the table, and my mother, looking very grave, stood behind him with a hand on his shoulder. David was not present, probably off somewhere stealing cigarettes or drinking beer behind a barn. I knew right away that I was the defendant in this proceeding. I did a quick inventory of my entire life so far. I always got top grades. I did not steal cigarettes or drink behind barns. I did not bully David.

Something unfamiliar was in my mother's eyes, a profound sadness and regret commingled with anger, a quivering indecision, as if she might bolt from the room at any moment. My father's face, on the other hand, wore an expression of excitement and pride. I wondered if they were getting a divorce. My mother took a seat at his side and stared down at her folded hands.

"You remember Johnny Wilson," my father said.

"Yes."

"Of course he does," my mother snapped. "Johnny's only been gone two years."

My father ignored her.

"Mr. Wilson is teaching at a school in New Hampshire. You know that he left the diocese, right?"

I did know about Johnny Wilson's departure from Detroit. I knew more about him than about anyone else at diocesan headquarters. He was the only black person I knew other than Warren. My father told me once that Mr. Wilson was an orphan adopted by the bishop from the streets of Detroit. The bishop sent him to Cranbrook, an exclusive Episcopal day school for boys in the affluent suburb of Bloomfield Hills, and then to Harvard. He attended the Virginia Seminary in Alexandria and was ordained an Episcopal minister. The bishop brought him back to Detroit as his special assistant. Both of my parents were very close to him, especially my mother. I had the feeling he served as a kind of bridge between my parents and the rich people involved in diocesan affairs.

I had no idea yet what they were talking about that day at the table, but I was already excited. It sounded like something far away. My mother crossed her arms and gazed at me, chin in the air.

"Do you want to go to New Hampshire to go to school?" she asked.

"What do you mean, go to New Hampshire to go to school?"

My father said, "That's what this is about, Woodrow. Johnny Wilson says if you can pass the entrance test, you can go to the school where he's teaching now in New Hampshire. For free."

My mother watched me shrewdly. "Pick up and leave your family? Leave your little brother? Leave Warren and Jimmy?"

I sensed danger. Whatever this grand adventure might be, she could nip it in the bud with one harsh look at my father.

30

I said, "It seems like there's more places in the world than just Pontiac." It was the most positive thing I could think to say, given that I still didn't really know what they were talking about.

She clicked her tongue and turned to my father.

"You hear that, Bill? He can't wait. And your idea is send him off to a snot-nose school halfway across the world so he can come home even more of a snot-nose than he is already."

"Susan, that's wrong, and you know it."

"Go ahead. Send him. And when he comes back more son of a bitch than he was before and turns it agin us, don't come bawling to me."

My father chewed his lower lip and said nothing.

She shrugged. "I just wisht I knew," she said. "Why him?"

It was a good question. I certainly had no inkling at the time why this fate had befallen me. I was thirteen years old then, standing at the shore of a new universe ordained but not explained by adults.

Six months later I ran into Ellen entirely by accident at the Pacific-Union Club in San Francisco. Some colleague of the brain surgeon had invited her to lunch. She was walking in to meet her host in the little side dining room where women were allowed, and I couldn't resist sneaking up behind and snagging her sleeve.

"Please stay in your assigned area," I said.

She wheeled around furious, looking like she wanted to kick my ass, then remembered who I was.

"Oh, Woodrow from Chicago," she said, laughing. She seemed glad to see me. "Do you know that women are not allowed in the main dining room in this joint?"

"I am very aware," I said. "That's why I like this place. I am headed into the main dining room now. Please do not try to follow me."

I invited her to dinner two evenings later and was amazed when she accepted. I took her to a dockside restaurant where we ate lobster washed down with cold beer. It turned out she was in San Francisco on unhappy family business and was only too glad to get away. I also divined not too far into the meal that she had become informed about St. Philip's School, which puzzled me.

"I'm so glad we ran into each other," she said. "I can't stop thinking about you and the funny group you were with at the Onwentsia. I must have started half a dozen times to try to find you. I guess I'm just that curious. I'm so glad you asked me out."

"Invited you to dinner."

We ordered, and, while we waited, we talked a little about her family issue. A brother was struggling financially, and the family had gathered to set things straight. I listened closely. I liked the way she spoke—smart but not brittle. The lights of Treasure Island behind her made a twinkling halo of her hair. I had not forgotten how beautiful she was.

"What was it about the Onwentsia crowd that captured your curiosity?"

"It's just such a foreign world to me, with these British-seeming boarding schools and all the little tribal rituals and so on. I've never known anyone from that background. I Googled your school. St. Philip's, right? I take it it's very different now."

"Unrecognizable. And a pretty cool place, I think."

"I found some old pieces in *Fortune* from the fifties and one even farther back in the *New Yorker*, a few other hints here and there in the *New York Times*. I gather the school's main claim to fame back

32

then was that it was the one place that would never admit any boy who wasn't a blueblood."

I gave her the same thumbnail version Johnny Wilson had provided me but didn't go into detail. I was more interested in her.

"Where do you live?" I asked.

"Right now we're in Evanston. What about you? You don't live in Chicago, do you?"

"No. I live in Michigan some of the time. I move around a bit."

"But you said you're not a WASP."

"Oh no, not at all. Son of a factory worker."

"Really. So was it strange for you, going to a hoity-toity school like that?"

I said that it was very strange at first. She wanted to know if my going to the school was the reason I knew all of the WASPs at Compton's fête, and I said the school certainly was where those associations began. Harvard didn't hurt, and then there was my business career afterward. Ellen said she supposed my arrival at the school must have been a little strange for the school as well. Her remark triggered a memory I had either forgotten or suppressed.

—

At the end of the 1960 spring term before the first scholarship boys, including me, were to show up in the fall, the rector of St. Philip's, a tall, stiff Georgian with flamboyant white eyebrows and a British manner, called the entire student body and faculty together on the rolling lawn outside the towering Gothic church called the New Chapel. He warned the assembled 480 students that "a new type of boy" would be arriving at the school in the fall.

I only knew about the speech from eavesdropped gossip.

Some sort of admonition seems to have been given against telling me the details. The only portion I was ever able to get anyone to recount in detail was the part about table manners. The rector warned that the new boys would be "quite unlike" other boys at the school, perhaps with strange ways of speaking and odd clothing. Our manners might be quite different, or we might not have any manners at all. None. At the table, for example, we might even eat with our hands. The rector was very firm in telling the boys that no one was to remark upon or call attention to our appearance or behavior.

The business about eating with our hands was a real concern. I learned that the senior student supervisors, who were stationed at long tables with the younger boys in the Lower School dining room, were told in a separate meeting that, if a scholarship boy were to begin eating with his hands, the supervisors were to eat with their hands, too. Needless to say, they awaited our arrival in a state of high consternation.

The irony in this for me was my mother's special obsession with table manners. She had drilled me and my brother on knives, forks, spoons, soupspoons, fish knives and finger bowls from birth. Now that I was being sent to dine among the wealthy, her greatest fear was that I would embarrass the family in front of them, an anxiety greatly heightened when I came home from junior high school in Pontiac at the end of the 1960 school year with a bleeding knife wound over one eye.

A hillbilly kid named Kelvin had called me a pussy. If there had been no witnesses, I might have weaseled out of it with a devastating wisecrack and a twenty-yard dash, but he called me a pussy in front of the entire wood shop. I was skinny and not at all a good fighter. I could throw a basic punch and block a slow one, but only

34

because a boy in Pontiac, Michigan, who couldn't throw or block a punch at all would be dead by the fourth grade.

Unfortunately for me that day, the word, pussy, was the one thing from which one could never retreat. I have no idea why. But if someone called you a pussy in Pontiac, there was no way out. You fought, or you died.

I don't even remember why Kelvin called me a pussy. We were in the center of the vast, barracks-like woodshop, surrounded by lathes, drill presses, and workbenches, where we were training for our destiny as factory workers. Kelvin, who had recently arrived from Kentucky, was long and lean with a hawk nose and flashing dark eyes. People were afraid of him. He was snake-mean and carried a gaudy imitation pearl handle switchblade knife that he liked to take out to show how quick he was.

He and I were surrounded by a dense ring of boys in blue denim smocks and dust-smeared safety goggles pushed up on their sweaty foreheads. We all carried in our hands heavy wood-handled chisels with long steel blades. When he called me a pussy, I had my chisel in my left hand, my off hand, but I hit him with it anyway, landing a weak glancing blow on the right side of his head. He produced the switchblade as if it were part of his hand, and time popped like a soap bubble. We stood facing each other in a dimension of silence and fate. The blade came glinting to my jugular like a trail of stars rushing down from the sky. I ducked to my right. The knife went high just above my left ear. His head and hand were extended forward over his balance point. As I pulled my head back up left, Kelvin made a sloppy after-plunge to his left and caught me a deep gash above my right eye. But in that silence out of time I threw the chisel to my right hand. Gripping it hard with both hands and before he could get up square again, I cut the air and landed a shivering crunch with the chisel's long steel blade against his left temple. He stood up stiff, stopped moving, dropped both arms to his sides and stared at me with wide, unseeing eyes. The knife clattered to the floor. His knees folded like a church chair, and he collapsed backward in a hump, eyes clamped shut like a baby. A disembodied voice behind me whispered, "Woodrow done kilt that hillbilly son of a bitch."

And suddenly, time and sound returned, boys hooting and hollering, jumping up and down, the woodshop instructor, Mr. Betka, rushing forward in his gray pinstripe coveralls, throwing boys out of the way like laundry. He wrenched a red fire extinguisher from a post, aimed it at Kelvin's head, pulled the trigger and covered his slumbering face with white foam.

Kelvin's eyes opened and his head snapped up. He sat akimbo on the floor, wiping foam from his face and spitting it from his mouth. He spotted the knife next to him on the floor, snatched it up and leapt to his feet in a shower of white flecks, ready to go again but this time against Mr. Betka, who was standing in front of him with the extinguisher. Kelvin started to lift the knife, but Mr. Betka shot foam into his eyes. Kelvin stopped, wiped his eyes clear with his left hand and came at Mr. Betka again. Mr. Betka shot foam into his eyes and mouth again. Every time Kelvin tried to wipe his face and mouth, Mr. Betka shot him full of foam again.

Mr. Betka danced around him, shooting him with foam, making him turn and turn, until finally Kelvin began to miss steps and stagger. Boys laughed uproariously. Mr. Betka took the fire extinguisher with both hands and swung it hard like a homerun baseball bat against Kelvin's knife hand. The knife went to the floor. Mr. Betka snatched it up, closed it deftly with one hand and dropped it into the breast pocket of his coveralls. Kelvin held up his wrecked hand like the foot of a mangled bird.

He cried, "You done broke all my fingers you goddamn Yankee son of a bitch."

Mr. Betka said to a boy standing nearby, "Go to the office and tell them to call the cops."

Kelvin grasped the injured right hand at the wrist, looked around the room sharply like a cornered wolf, then lowered his head and snarled roughly through the crowd. He ran out a back door to an open storage yard. We could barely see him in the distance, climbing a low steel fence with his left hand, the mangled claw dangling painfully to his right. He dropped to the far side of the fence, gave us all a left-handed middle finger, turned, and ran. We never saw him again.

Mr. Betka called me to him with a gesture. He pushed my wound open with a hard thumb.

"You see out of both them eyes, Woodrow?"

"Yes, sir."

He plucked a dirty orange machine rag off my lathe and snapped off the sawdust.

"Shove this up in that cut, hold it there, stop that blood coming down your neck."

He turned to the gawping boys, who looked back and forth from him to me and to the empty fence in the distance.

"I told you men oncet, I told you a hundert times, don't never hit a man with a tool. This time, that dumb hillbilly took after young Woodrow here with a knife, so I guess that about evens it out. More's amazing, it looks like Woodrow done won it for oncet."

After a moment, my name went up in a sudden cheer: "Wood! Row!" It was the best day of my life to that point. It may still be.

Mr. Betka sent me to the school nurse, who called my mother and said I would need stitches. My father was home from work and came to get me. He consulted with the nurse and Mr. Betka, then drove wordless all the way home. I knew not to break his silence. When I walked into the house, my mother cried out, not in pity but shame.

"You had to go and get your face cut up, didn't you? Just in time so you can go off to that rich people's school and make us all look like white trash."

She wanted my father to take me into Pontiac to the hospital to have it sewn up properly, but he said I'd have to go to the country sawbones up the road who tended to the farm families and factory workers of Little Ottawa.

My mother said, "He'll stitch him up like a goddamn barn cat."

My father said, "It's what we can afford, and it's what he deserves."

On the way to the sawbones, he said to me, "Betka told me you knocked that hillbilly down with a hammer."

"No, sir. Chisel."

"Jesus, Woodrow, you are one problem."

"Yes, sir."

"Never again take a weapon to a man's head. I mean never. You hear me, boy? A fight is a fight. A weapon is prison."

"Yes, sir."

"So you won it then?"

"Yes, sir."

He turned toward me twice without speaking. Finally, he said, "Woodrow, you are one problem. I am going to miss hell out of you up there in that school."

"Yes, sir. I will miss you and Ma and David."

"It's the chancet of a lifetime, Woodrow. It's such a big chancet, I cain't hardly believe it come to us. Don't go and mess it up."

"No, sir."

He reached over and tousled my hair as he had not done since I was little. I thought I saw the glint of a tear.

"But boy, you promise your old daddy from Quitman County, Georgia, one goddamn thing, you hear?"

"Yes, sir."

"Don't take no shit off nobody."

"No, sir."

"Jesus Christ, Woodrow, you are one problem. Just don't get kicked out."

"No, sir."

"But I mean it, don't take no shit either."

"No, sir."

•

For the rest of the spring and summer, my mother never looked at my face without turning a sharp eye to the scar above my right eye. I know she hoped with each passing day she would see it fade, and it did a little, but never enough. A week before I was to take the sixteen-hour Greyhound bus ride by myself to Boston, she even briefly proposed makeup, an idea my father quickly killed. She punished me by subjecting me to a merciless Saturday-long refresher course on rich people's table manners, along with relentless corrections of grammar, diction, and usage.

On one important point, she remained adamant.

"Don't be envious, Woodrow. An envious man is lower than a drunk." She said it over and over again, in case the admonition slipped my mind.

I never understood her. She felt revulsion, almost horror of anything that might smack of envy or, worse, being what she called a "mooch." Since the avenues of envy and mooching were closed, the alternative was work. That summer, I worked pretty hard in the peach orchard of a rich man who belonged to the church, and I saved every penny for a wardrobe to wear among the wealthy. When I had accumulated what I thought should be more than enough money, I bought a ticket on the express bus from Pontiac to downtown Detroit.

I knew Detroit a little. My father had taken us many times for picnics on a beautiful island in the Detroit River called Belle Isle Park, where we rented canoes and paddled through a maze of narrow canals walled by trees and birdsong.

For my shopping trip, my father had armed me with detailed directions. I walked directly from the bus stop to Hudson's Department Store and asked for the boys' department. The school had sent my mother a letter saying I would need three wool sport coats or two sport coats and a blazer. A saleswoman in the boys' department of Hudson's told me I didn't have nearly enough money for all that. She picked out a shiny, silver-gray suit with very narrow lapels, a bright-red blazer made of some kind of synthetic material, a few white shirts, some neckties so narrow they looked almost like shoestrings, and a pair of gray, lace-up shoes made of a fuzzy material I thought she called "foeswade." With her help, I located a barbershop near the store. There, I studied a photographic rogue's gallery of hairstyles on the wall while I waited. I found one—almost a butch haircut with a forward fringe of short upswept bangs—called "The Princeton." I knew Princeton was an eastern school, so I instructed the barber to give me that one.

•

A few days before I was to leave, my father took David and me to a drive-in movie theater near the Pontiac city limits for a farewell outing. One of his great delights in life, ever since we were little boys, was taking us to the drive-in, where he loved western and cowboy action movies much more than we did. What little I remember now of most of the movies themselves is overshadowed by my memory of my father muttering from the first to the last scene: "You son of a bitch, that ain't your ranch;" "You tell 'em, sheriff;" "Now watch this, boys, they're gonna catch them bastards red-handed." But on that last visit to the drive-in, the movie itself made a more indelible impression. My father told David and me ahead of time that the movie was called, *Daniel Boone, Trailblazer*. He said it would be instructive because of our family's personal connection with Boone.

Whenever our father got going on the names of our forebears, his voice fell into the tone and cadence of the Bible. The ancient names had been etched deep in his memory at a young age, as tends to be the case with people descended from the early Southern settlers. As he chanted our antecedents one "beget" and "begat" at a time, we could hear whispers of the old people long gone, muttering the ladder of names in flickering candlelight within their own chinked cabin walls. And they begat, and she wed, and they begat, and she died in infancy, and he lived, and he wed—a trail carrying us back to the ship and the water and the shores of our departure. The chanted names were a coal blown live by each generation, marking the way we had come, proof to doubters that we were not random creatures of the forest but people who came from people.

We loved the movie, and so did everybody else at the drive-in that night, judging by the raucous hoots and hollers erupting from shiny new sedans and hopped-up pickup trucks all around us. In the film, Blackfish, leader of the Shawnee, is played by the same actor who had played a deranged swamp-dwelling hermit in another film called *The Alligator People* that most of us in the audience had seen just a few weeks prior. When he showed up again clad in an elaborate feathered headdress and buckskins, everyone immediately recognized him. We booed and jeered him the moment he came on screen, as if he should have learned by now to stay the hell away from Pontiac.

My father's eyes were locked in rapture. He beamed and shouted, his left fist pumping wildly outside the open window every time Daniel Boone pushed a ladder off the stockade walls of Fort Boonesborough and sent another squalling heathen to his everlasting reward. At other moments, my father gazed up at the screen in beatific awe as Boone yielded yet another Mosaic pronouncement on the need for courage, the value of perseverance, the importance of loyalty, and, most wonderful of all, the destiny of the white man. I was moved almost to tears by my father's openhearted embrace of this third-rate Hollywood fare.

The film's penultimate exultation was provided by a character—I think he was a merchant—a pudgy, irritable man rendered un-masculine by a long white shopkeeper's apron. First, he established himself as reprehensible by threatening Boone with a court martial. The next thing we knew, the vile bourgeois had noodled his way past Boone and was running out the front gate of the fort waving a white flag of surrender. The savages, being savages, ignored universal protocol and began firing musket balls into the aproned man.

Whatever else may be said for him, no other man under such a fusillade took longer to die. He threw up his hands as if waving goodbye, crooked his elbows and flapped his arms like a chicken, bent first at one knee and then the other, waddled under a hail of musketry thick enough to chop down a tree, until finally he fell down good and dead. With every shot that struck him, the audience at the drive-in, including my father, screamed delight, honked horns and flashed headlights in exuberant celebration. The entire evening was one glorious unbroken orgy of chauvinistic joy as only a bunch of homesick, displaced Pontiac hillbillies could have managed.

•

The sixteen-hour Greyhound bus ride from Detroit to Boston was a blur of groggy half-sleep, noxious odors, anxiety, and aching loneliness. The bathroom at the back of the bus backed up and smelled terrible, which did not discourage a sailor and a girl from having sex next to it on the back bench of the bus. An elderly couple bickered loudly for sixteen hours. In the morning when we arrived in Boston, the sailor was asleep on the floor of the bus and had to be awakened by the driver.

When I arrived in Boston, I somehow accomplished the unfamiliar task of hailing a cab and found my way across town to North Station as I had been directed. It was a more vast and intimidating public space than any I had ever set foot in. I swallowed down panic and stepped through the door dragging in my huge seaman's chest and two battered suitcases. A short, wiry man in a yellow vest appeared suddenly and shouted that he was taking everything from me. His red cap was my clue. My father told me that a man in a red cap would insist on carrying my bags through the station and that I was not to be alarmed. I read the man my father's note telling me where I was to wait for the train that would take me to school. He whirled before I was done pronouncing and danced off through the dense crowd with all my earthly possessions. I skittered behind, digging furiously in my pocket for the coin I had been instructed to give him when we got to our destination. Once at the proper place with my things, I sat down on a hard bench, looked at a wall clock and calculated I would need to wait six hours for the train to New Hampshire.

The stinky bus ride and anxious trip across town had left me temporarily un-hungry. I walked a few yards to a kiosk and bought a paper cup of black coffee to clear my head. Then I returned to my bench to study this planet on which I somehow had landed. Everything was foreign. The people spoke in a kind of quack. The men all wore the same dark suit and gray hat. The women wore belts cinched tight at skinny waists and walked on clickety-clack high-heels.

Then, beginning about forty-five minutes before my train was to depart, a new and very distinct tribe of persons began to gather around me. Boys of all ages appeared, some stiffly well-behaved with mothers who wore white gloves and stooped from a distance to kiss their foreheads, others unattended and a little rowdy, pushing and shoving each other as if there were no one there to see them. They were all of a kind. While my hair was cut short with fringy bangs waxed straight up above my forehead, their hair was long and soft, combed over their foreheads. I was wearing my new red blazer, my very thin black tie, and my foeswade shoes. They wore thick tweed sport coats or dark blue blazers and long-eared shirt collars that closed around fat striped neckties. Their pants were baggy, made of dark gray woolen material or stiff brown khaki that looked almost like pleated cardboard. What I noticed more than anything was their shoes. Some wore lace-ups, and some wore loafers with little leather ribbons on top, but all of their shoes shared an uncanny characteristic: whether black, brown, or reddish oxblood, they shone to a jeweled gloss, glowing in the overhead station lights.

They all spoke with the same accent, not at all the sharp quacky speech I had been hearing all day but a round gliding tone, long open vowels softly fluted in perfect expression of indifference and superiority. None of them even looked at me. As I watched and listened, I hoped against hope these would not be the boys with whom I was expected to live and go to school.

But they all boarded my train. A very few gave me sidelong glances, but most seemed not to see me. I tried to sit separately at the far end of a car, but the train was fairly full, and several of them came and sat near enough to me that I could hear their happy gossip while we clattered out of Boston and into the Massachusetts countryside.

Things I had only read of in novels, places and experiences I had never taken as real—these boys chatted about them all amiably and casually as if they were nothing special. They spoke of summers mountain climbing in Switzerland, sailing in the Caribbean, even meeting famous movie stars and sports heroes on tennis courts and golf courses. I would have taken it all for bullshit had it not been for the tone, the gliding speech and nonchalant chuckle, as if these impossible accomplishments were not only easily achieved but even, in some inexplicable way, a bit of a bore.

At the small depot in Rumney, New Hampshire, they all piled

into taxicabs together. I stood alone at the baggage check having collected my seaman's trunk and suitcases. A tall boy with a long jaw and deep-hooded eyes peered at me for a while from across the depot, then came over.

"Are you headed out to St. Philip's?" he asked kindly.

I told him I was. He said his name was Barry and that I could share a cab with him and another guy his age. I sat in front with the driver. On the way out of town, Barry asked me where I was from, and I said Pontiac.

The other guy in back said, "Is that your home or your car?"

"It's a place," I said. "A city."

They chatted with each other. The cab turned at a small white sign swinging from a post that said "St. Philip's School" above a coat of arms. I have no memory what I saw on the drive down into the campus on that first evening. I'm not sure I saw anything.

Barry directed the driver to stop in front of a wooden building the size and shape of Noah's Ark.

"This is you," he said.

Inside, the lobby was a roaring hell of boys in coats and ties, some with their parents, all of them swarming noisily up and down a broad switch-backed staircase. Adults I took to be teachers were posted in the lobby with lists of names, giving directions. The ascending staircase spiraled into gloom above. As directed, I hauled my luggage up the stairs, dodging boys and their fathers. I dragged first the bigger suitcase to a middle landing, then the trunk, then the smaller suitcase until finally I arrived with my cargo in a large open lobby on the second floor. I was directed through a broad door beneath a sign that said "Dormitory Four." The space inside was long and narrow, lined on both sides with two dozen cots set apart by wooden partitions about eight feet tall. The spaces between the partitions, called alcoves, were closed at their outer ends by cloth curtains. I was told that we would choose our own alcoves after dinner. Until then, we were to pile our baggage on a rough wooden bench covering a steam radiator that ran the length of the center aisle.

I followed the others out of the dorm through a racket of boys in the lobby to a long gloomy hallway at the far corner. Large double doors stood open at the end of the corridor. The noise of the crowd subsided as boys passed through the doorway, as if they were entering church. A big athletic-looking older boy stopped me at the door and asked my name.

"Woodrow Skaggs, sir," I said.

He looked me up and down coolly, consulted a clipboard, and said, "Don't call me sir. You sit at the near table over there on the right side. You can sit anywhere toward the middle of the table on the outside facing the wall. Your table master is Herr Schmitz. You call him Herr and his wife Frau. They're German or Austrian or something. In you go."

The room was dimly lit by high chandeliers and a faint early evening glow from the tall stained-glass windows. I found my table and put a hand to the back of a chair facing the windows as instructed, but a big kid with red hair came up to my right side and, without looking at me or otherwise acknowledging my existence, bumped me so hard with his hip that I stumbled into the boy to my left. The boy with whom I collided, another big kid with thick horn-rimmed glasses, leaned around behind my back to address the red-haired kid.

"Watch your ass, carrot-top."

"Oh," the carrot-top muttered to himself with an amused nod. "Carrot-top. Very original. I suggest you watch my ass, four-eyes."

Four-eyes and I moved down a peg to the left to make room for Carrot-Top. We all three took our seats and sat scowling at each other.

I was in the middle of the table. Barry, the older boy who had given me a ride from the station, appeared and ordered the boys directly across from me to move to other chairs. He was accompanied by another boy about his age but shorter and stockier. Both sat facing me. Barry's face, mournful at rest, broke into an easy grin.

"Doing OK so far, Pontiac?"

"Yes, sir."

"Don't call me sir. I'm Barry."

Carrot-Top turned to me.

"What's your real name?" he demanded.

"Woodrow Skaggs."

"Woodrow Skaggs," he repeated to himself, as if carefully considering. "Sounds like a character from Tom Sawyer."

A few boys smiled on the other side of the table.

"What's your name?" I asked.

"Who wants to know?"

Barry said, "Tell him your name."

Carrot-Top muttered something indistinct.

"I didn't get that," Barry said. "What is your name?"

"Tom Compton," he said with sullen emphasis.

I said, "You on a wanted poster or something? Afraid to say your name?"

He flashed me an angry challenge. Barry said, "Enough of that." But a few boys across from me had already smiled at my jab, which I found gratifying.

"All right," the stockier older boy next to Barry said, "My name is Adams. This is Barry. Now each of you will introduce yourself to the table." He nodded to a mop-headed boy with his nose in the air to begin. Never lowering the nose, the boy said, "I am Feodor Sergeiovitch Yusupov. You may call me Sergeiovitch."

Barry said, "We will call you Yusupov."

We went around the table. A tough-looking kid named Granger let us know he was Canadian, not American. A guy with bushy black eyebrows and a strong accent named Aubert was French. A boy who looked as if he had never smiled in his entire life said his name was Smiley. A little guy who did smile a lot and seemed inexhaustibly cheerful was named Davidson. A huge kid with the deep barrel-chested voice of a man was already known to several at the table as Tweetie, which made no sense at all. A short fireplug of a kid with albino-white hair was named Roosevelt. The big boy with glasses next to me seemed to stumble on his own name, which, when he coughed it out, was Gellhorn. There was me, and there was Compton, whom we all knew already was an asshole. We were in what was called the Third Form, which I took to be comparable to the ninth grade in public school. I had the impression most or all of us were new to St. Philip's, but several boys at the table already knew each other from other schools. We all lived in Dorm Four, representing a little under half the population of the dorm.

All the boys at the table, including Barry and Adams, stood suddenly, so I did too. A small, somewhat hunched man with a narrow nose and pointed chin came to the end of the table. His thinning dark hair was combed back, and his bulbous eyeballs swam behind thick rimless spectacles. I immediately disliked and feared him. He was followed by a skinny woman with lips bitten tight and tiny dark eyes peering from beneath thin black tented eyebrows.

"Herr Schmitz," Barry said with his head tipped forward in the tiniest hint of a bow. "Frau Schmitz."

Herr Schmitz bowed, a bit more demonstratively.

"Barry," he said. Then, "Adams."

He seated his wife to his left, then sat down primly at the head of the table. We all sat down, and the room fell silent. Behind me, an old man's voice, loud and slurring, called out, "Mr. Rutledge, would you say the prayer for us this evening, please?"

I turned to see. At the far end, a raised platform like a stage carried one very long table from wall to wall, a length of at least forty feet. In the center and facing the room, a fat man with white hair and a red face appeared to be the person who had just spoken. A tall older boy with shiny blonde hair slicked to his skull, wearing pink-framed glasses and an almost comically bored expression, rose and barely mumbled the same grace I had heard my father say all my life, except that when my father said it, he meant it. This guy could have been reading the small print on a can of beans:

"Bless, O Lord, this food to our use and us to Thy loving and faithful service; In Christ's name, Amen."

Across from me, Barry whispered to Adams, "The great Rutledge bestirs."

Adams whispered back, "I wish he'd bestir himself to pay me."

Herr Schmitz looked at them both sternly, and they nodded acquiescence. Barry said to me, Compton, and Gellhorn, "The man at the head table is Rockwell Frick, Head of the Lower School. We call him Beetle, but obviously not to his face."

Compton said, "Who's the zombie guy who said the grace?"

Barry and Adams smiled.

"That was the great Rutledge," Adams said, "a legend in his own mind."

Herr Schmitz cleared his throat and looked at us for silence. Speaking with a very slight foreign accent that I was not competent to identify, he addressed the table: "These two gentlemen to my right (indicating with a nod Barry and Adams) are Sixth Formers who are supervisors. You boys will call them supes. They are also the supes in Dorm Four where all of you reside. Your dorm master is Mr. Fell, and decorum within your dorm is his purview. At this table, you will regard the supes as superior to you in rank and in every other regard, and you will obey their directions as if they were masters."

Barry and Adams gave us small waves and embarrassed grins.

"Every week," Herr Schmitz went on, now droning, "two boys from the table will be assigned to be waiters. I have already made those assignments and given directions to the boys who are waiters this week."

Gellhorn, the one with the glasses, and Roosevelt, the white-haired fireplug, rose from the table, disappeared, and then reappeared a few minutes later with covered serving trays. On the table before me lay a bristling array of silverware, which I was able to navigate pretty well, thanks to my mother's exacting instruction. I stole glances at the others. In dress and appearance, they all looked remarkably similar, as if in uniform. They seemed tough and self-assured, speaking in the same confident tones I had heard at North Station and on the train.

At a point not far into the meal, I discovered that Barry and Adams were scouring me intently, watching my every stroke of the knife, sip of water, transfer of fork, touch of napkin to lips. I began glancing sideways to watch others at the table, worried I was doing something wrong. As far as I could tell, everyone was eating pretty much the same way I was except for Compton, who had both elbows on the table, shoveling food into his mouth. My mother would have told him, "That's a spoon, not a coal scoop, soldier."

I had noticed already that no second serving of food was to be requested or touched by a boy until the boy had first offered it to Frau Schmitz. I complied by not seeking second helpings of anything. The savagely hashed eyebrows over her green eyes were enough to make me starve to death.

Compton was raucous, teasing Davidson at the other end of the table. They had known each other before in a place called the far hills or just Far Hills—I wasn't sure. Davidson was a small frail boy with curly hair that looped over his brow in question marks. Compton ridiculed him for having shown up for school a week early. I gathered Davidson had made a mistake. Rather than return home, he had spent the intervening week in a spare bedroom in one of the masters' homes.

Davidson, unfailingly chipper and impervious to Compton's taunts, fended him off with smiles, nods, and cheerful shrugs. I was puzzled. I knew if Compton had been speaking to me this same way, at some point I would have been obligated to punch him.

"Jesus, did your parents not know when First Day was?"

Adams told Compton, "Don't curse at the table."

Davidson shrugged and laughed. "Nope."

"Christ, how'd you get here?"

"I said don't curse."

"Car," Davidson said with a little shake of the shoulders.

"You drive yourself?"

"Nooo," Davidson said, laughing again.

"Fucking idiot."

"Do not curse again," Adams told him, "or I will send you away from the table."

Herr and Frau Schmitz seemed unaware of the exchange.

"Do you understand me?" Adams asked Compton.

Compton did not reply.

"Do you understand me?"

"Yes," he muttered, face darkening.

"Good."

Stuffing meat into his mouth, Compton barked a loud fake laugh. Frau Schmitz winced and whispered into her husband's ear. Herr Schmitz nodded to Adams, tipping his meat knife gruesomely toward Compton.

"My wife and I find this boy common and unpleasant," he said. "Please speak to him."

Adams leaned forward across the table to Compton and said, "Shut up."

Compton's face flashed hot, but Adams cocked a cold eye back at him. Compton stopped eating and glared down into his plate.

Desert was flan in a little white china bowl. It was very good. The delicious jolt of flavor in the flan made me suddenly ravenous, but I controlled myself, did as my mother had taught, and tipped the bowl away to scoop out the last morsel daintily with a tiny silver spoon.

Barry said to Adams, "His table manners might be better than mine."

Compton looked up quickly from his plate with a malevolent grin. "Must be talking about me."

"Hardly," Barry said. He nodded toward me. "Him. He's impeccable. You're far from it."

Compton gave me an angry purple stare, brown eyes flaring.

"Yes, his manners are quite good, aren't they?" Herr Schmitz said to Adams. Before Adams could respond, Herr Schmitz turned to me.

"Your name is Skaggs, is it not?"

"Yes, sir."

Speaking in the same faintly foreign accent, his wife said, "A very rugged name, I think." She and her husband traded amused expressions.

"And tell me," she said, "where you are from."

"Michigan."

"Aha. The West."

"The Middle West," I said.

Frau Schmitz stiffened, her empty fork suspended in air. "Oh, I see. Do forgive me, then. You live in the middle of the West."

A soft titter went up around the table.

"Well, Skaggs," she said, "Herr Schmitz and I have only traveled as far west as the eastern bank of the Hudson River, and that is quite west enough for us."

I wasn't sure where that was, so I said nothing.

After the table had been cleared by Roosevelt and Gellhorn, a silence fell, broken when Rutledge at the head table picked up a small silver bell and gave it a quick ting-a-ling. All of the boys rose and stood behind their chairs. The Schmitzes remained seated, as did the masters and their wives at the other tables, until Beetle and his wife had left the dining room via a door behind the dais. It was their own private door, I later learned, leading to their own private staircase, which took them down to their apartment directly below Dorm Four and the dining room. When they were gone, the masters and their wives rose and filed out through the swinging doors. A hubbub revived among the boys, and I followed the crowd out into the second-floor lobby.

Little First and Second Form boys flew up the massive spiral staircase to Dorms One and Two on the third level. They were mostly eleven and twelve years old, I learned, although a few were only ten. We Third Formers were thirteen and fourteen years old. Older boys in the fourth through sixth forms, most of whom were fifteen to eighteen years old, had their own rooms in other buildings on the campus. A few sixth formers were nineteen years old, because they were repeating years they had spent in foreign schools.

After dinner the third formers divided themselves in half, some to the left into Dorm Three and the rest of us to the right into Dorm Four. Just inside Dorm Four, a tall genial young man in a tweed jacket stood waiting for us. He looked athletic, with smooth blonde hair and hazel eyes in a handsome face. He seemed barely older than Barry and Adams, who were standing just behind him. We fell into loosely gathered attention before him, and he introduced himself as Louie Fell.

"Mr. Fell to you," he said with a grin.

He said he would be our dorm master. He lived in an apartment attached to our barracks of alcoves. Barry and Adams, he said, would share an apartment next to his. He pointed to a small wooden box on the wall behind him filled with markers of various colors.

"Mark all of your laundry with your dorm number, which is four, and your alcove number, which is above your alcove. Only use the blue markers. Please also mark all of your clothing, skates, other possessions so we won't have any problems about ownership. It's very important to get your clothes marked right away with the blue markers so they'll come back to you each week from the laundry. I don't believe in assigning alcoves. You may now choose your own."

Compton shoved through the crowd of boys, ripped two suitcases off the radiator bench and plunged down to the far end of the room. We all stood dumbstruck as he slashed open a curtain at the farthest alcove and hurled his bags onto the narrow bed inside.

Then boys sprang into action, rushing all over the dorm, staking claims, calling to comrades to move in next door. I was still paralyzed at the near end of the room, standing next to Mr. Fell, the supervisors, and Aubert, the French boy with the eyebrows.

Aubert turned to Mr. Fell and said, "Je ne comprends pas. Qu'est-ce qui se passe?"

"Aubert, tu droit choisir ton lit," Mr. Fell said. "Et c'est toujours mieux de parler Anglais quand tu peux."

"Oui, monsieur," Aubert said.

Adams corrected from behind Mr. Fell, "Yes, sir."

"Yes, sir," Aubert said to Adams.

"Pas lui," Mr. Fell said, smiling. "Il est etudiant comme toi. You don't have to 'sir' these guys. Just do what they tell you."

Barry and Adams tipped their heads subserviently to Mr. Fell.

"Alors," Aubert said to me, "on what do we attend?"

He and I grabbed our bags and surveyed the dorm. Up and down the length of the long room, boys stood in their half-curtained doorways, already defending their territory. Only at the far end were two alcoves open—one directly across from Compton and the other right next to him. Compton's curtain was drawn closed, and he was not to be seen. Aubert looked to me with a deeply baleful expression. In his heavily accented English, he said, "Which do you prefer?"

"No," I said, "which do you prefer?"

"I suppose," he said slowly, "if I were perfectly free to choose, I would choose to be across from him rather than juste à côté de."

"Juste à côté de means right next to?"

"Oui."

"OK, I'll take the côté de."

I threw my suitcase on the bed in the alcove next to Compton's, then dragged in my dented chest and sat on it with my curtain open. I heard Compton's curtain fly open, then saw him burst into the aisle and come glowering into the narrow opening of my alcove. He posted one hand up on the partition insolently, as if at a bus stop.

"The Tom Sawyer boy who wants to know if I'm a wanted man," he sneered. "Why did you ask that, Tom Sawyer? Any particular reason? You think you know something, do you?"

I was still sitting on my seaman's chest and did not rise. He looked much bigger than he had sitting next to me at the table. He was muscular, like an older boy, with a cruel swagger that ran to the bone.

"No reason," I said. "You just took a while to spit it out. Seemed a little odd to me."

"I seemed odd. To you? That's a good one. Where did you get that jacket?"

"What about it?"

"Nothing, but I've never seen a jacket like that before that wasn't on a Puerto Rican."

"Maybe I'm Puerto Rican."

Behind Compton's mass I could see a circle of faces gathering, all watching intently.

"You look a little pale for a Puerto Rican," he said. "What are those shoes made out of?"

"They're shoes."

"They look like mouse-skin to me."

I heard tittering from the faces.

"Fuck you," I said. I stood up and faced him.

"Oh, 'fuck you,' says the witty boy. Very witty boy. And what's

57

with the haircut? What's that supposed to be, with the little girly bangs?"

I said nothing.

"You know what you look like to me?"

In a terrible flash, I saw it coming. I hoped desperately I was wrong. I was not.

"A pussy," he said.

I flew forward and punched him in the nose as hard as I could. He fell back, speckling my alcove curtain with blood, then lunged at me. I kicked for his balls, but he stabbed out a hand with bullet reflexes, caught my foot and flipped me to the floor. On my knees, I punched straight for his nuts again with my fist and connected hard. He let out a quick groan and collapsed backward, stooping and holding his groin with both hands. By the time I regained my feet, he was already upright and grinning, two fists churning at his sides, head nodding sideways like a bull pawing.

A shout went up from the crowd, and the faces fell away. Adams flew into Compton with a full football tackle, knocking him down hard, banging his head against the steel radiator with a sickening thud that opened a flowing cut above his right temple. Barry grabbed Compton's arms and pinned him. Mr. Fell appeared above the tangle, shaking his head and smiling ruefully.

"Well, well, well, I guess I know which end of the dorm to watch for trouble. I'm not going to have any more of this. Do you two understand me?"

They let Compton up. He nodded yes, mopping his temple with a bloody shirt cuff. I nodded. Mr. Fell motioned with a finger for me to follow him to the far end of the dorm.

"Who started this?" he asked.

"Nobody, sir. I guess we both kind of did."

"Compton!" he shouted. "Up here on the double. Who started this?"

"I don't know, sir," Compton said. "I guess we both did."

"All right, boys," he said, nodding approvingly, "there may be some accidental drop of gentleman in you two after all. But you had damned well better learn not to go to fists in my dorm. I will not have it."

We nodded.

"Next time, pistols."

We nodded.

"That's a joke."

"Yes, sir," we said in unison.

The supervisors led Compton into the immense group bathroom at their end of the dorm. When they reappeared with him, his hair was sticking wet to his head, and a clean white bandage was wrapped around the cut on his temple.

I returned to my alcove and sat on my cot, wondering if this was what it was going to be like every minute of every day and night. Compton stayed at the other end of the dorm with Mr. Fell and the supervisors. I watched from the opening of my alcove, as did all the other boys from theirs.

Beetle appeared, his face redder than at dinner, his bouncing girth now covered by an over-generous white silk bathrobe. He was a gouty man with a blue-veined nose, thinning white hair, blue eyes, and an unsmiling mouth that showed points of yellow teeth. He wore white cotton pajamas, leather slippers, and a drooping red nightcap.

"What kind of preposterous poppycock is this?" he bellowed.

"A fight, that's all," Mr. Fell said quietly.

Beetle and Mr. Fell conferred long and morosely in quiet voices.

Then Beetle spoke with the supervisors and finally with Compton. I couldn't hear from that distance. Mr. Fell seemed to be minimizing the situation. Compton was sullen and unresponsive.

Beetle reached with a fat hand and examined Compton's bandage, speaking in low tones. Compton stared at the floor and shook his head no repeatedly. Beetle turned, looked down the dorm and found me with a long cold stare. He said something to Mr. Fell then marched from the dorm to a tattoo of loudly flapping slippers.

Mr. Fell put both hands to his mouth and shouted down the room: "You have one hour to unpack your things for tomorrow and to use the bathroom. I strongly suggest you shower tonight, because you will not have much time for it in the morning. Have a jacket and tie ready for breakfast. There will be athletics in the afternoon. You will be issued athletic clothing at the gym. When I say, 'Lights out,' I mean lights out. First night, and you've already got me in hot water."

The bathroom was long and wide, with toilet stalls behind swinging doors along one wall, sinks along the other, and a large communal shower at the far end. We wore pajamas and bathrobes to the bathroom, hung them on hooks, and showered naked in the big open space, examining each other minutely to see who was strong and who was weak.

An hour after our fight, Mr. Fell popped back out of the door at the end of the dorm and shouted, "Lights out!" He snapped a switch on the wall, plunging the vast room into darkness. "Get in bed, all of you. Shut up and get a good night's sleep. Good night, boys."

He moved to the center of the room and stood turning his head expectantly one way and the other.

"Boys," he called amiably, "are we forgetting something? I believe that I told you good night."

"Good night, Mr. Fell," a reedy voice called from behind a drawn curtain at the far end. Then a slow ragged chorus arose from behind other curtains: "Good night, Mr. Fell. Good night."

Aubert called out across from me, "Bonne nuit, monsieur."

I said, "Good night, Mr. Fell."

He did not move from his post. "Compton?"

After a silence, Compton's voice came up grim and ragged. "Good night, for Christ's sake."

My bed was made with crisp white sheets, a nice fat pillow, and a thin blanket. I had already surveyed my alcove and found more blankets stacked on a shelf along the wall above my seaman's chest. Beneath the shelf was a short rod with wooden hangers, on which I put my clothes from Hudson's.

My rust-streaked seaman's chest held my winter things: a heavy wool coat, galoshes, scarf, knit cap, gloves, and two sweaters. At the far wall of the alcove, squeezed between the partition and the head of the bed, was a tall narrow dresser. The clothing from my suitcase filled only the top two of seven drawers.

Darkness was a mercy. Even though the night was warm, I burrowed into my bed and made a cocoon with my nose out for air. Not asking for seconds at dinner had left me hungry, but I found that nesting tightly in the bed relieved a weight of apprehension pressing on my chest since I had boarded the bus two days earlier in Detroit.

I had no idea where I was. Adults had deposited me on the surface of the moon. This great yawning hangar, where apparently I was intended to live, felt less like a home than a mausoleum, my alcove less a room than a crypt. But when I curled myself inside the thin blanket and shut my eyes, I was in a place that was somehow snug and safe. Alone.

Ragged fragments of the bus ride from Detroit floated up from my unconscious, jumbled out of sequence. I tried to order them. Which had come first, the man sitting next to me who smoked a cigar that smelled like a burning car tire and set my stomach to somersaults? Or the even more evil odor coming from the backed up toilet?

I sorted the moments, trying to put them in line like breadcrumbs to take me back to Pontiac, to Little Ottawa and my parents' Formica-topped kitchen table, my father telling me I might be going away. I needed to make sense of it, but a profound exhaustion kept dragging me down and down, deeper into slumber and trance.

Chapter Two

"JESUS CHRIST!" A VOICE DECLARED FROM above my bed. "What the fuck are you? A Puerto Rican?"

I popped my head out of my cocoon and looked straight up. Above me was only empty black wall for at least two stories, washed at the top by a haze of moonlight.

Another voice that I recognized as Aubert whispered hoarsely from across the way, "Tais toi!"

"Have you got a fucking switchblade, you Puerto Rican son of a bitch?"

"Ferme là!" Aubert called again from his bed.

I rose to my elbows and looked up to the very tall window above Compton's alcove. He was seated high above me on a stone sill, leaning out with one hand up against the deep-set jamb like a chimpanzee on a branch. The bandage on his head had slipped down, partially covering one eye with an insouciant piratical air.

"Shut up," I said. "You'll get us in trouble again."

"Don't be such a . . . " He paused and watched me.

I threw back the cover and jumped to my feet on the bed. I stood glaring up at him with fists at my sides.

"Such a . . . "

I arched my back and made ready to climb.

"Is it the word?" he whispered softly. "If I say that one word, you have to kill me?"

"Just don't say it."

He swung around and let his bare feet dangle. "Let me just say the word for discussion," he whispered. "But it won't be about you, OK? But the word is 'pussy,' right? If somebody calls you a pussy, you have to kill him?"

I shrugged.

He gazed at me intently. He shoved a box to the edge of the sill so I could see it.

"My mother gave me this box of treats as a bribe so they could dump me. Lot of good stuff from the best store in New York. Come on up and have a bite."

I was starving.

"If I go up there, are you going to start a fight?"

"If you come up here, are you going to bring your switchblade, you Puerto Rican son of a bitch?"

I went out of my alcove and into his, stepped onto his bed, climbed up on his chest of drawers and then to the other end of the sill. The box was full to the brim with little wrapped sandwiches and cakes, dried fruit, candy, cheese, and crackers. The packaged treats were fascinating, with an unfamiliar quality I recognized as fancy.

"Eat up," he said.

I took two miniature cream sandwiches and wolfed them down, then a piece of cheese and a piece of candy. It was all delicious.

"So do you?" he asked.

"Do I what?" I asked with a full mouth.

"Have a switchblade?"

"No, asshole. Why would you ask me that?"

"Beetle asked me if you did. He also asked if you had a gun."

"Oh, that's bullshit, and you know it. He did not ask you if I had a gun."

"He fucking asked me if you had a knife or a gun or any other weapon of any kind."

"Jesus. No. Of course not."

"What's that scar on your face?"

"It's a scar."

"From what?"

I hesitated, seeing the trap but not knowing how to avoid it.

"A switchblade," I said.

"Let me guess. Somebody with a switchblade called you a pussy."

"Yes."

"Oh . . . my . . . God. You are a fucking Puerto Rican. How in the fuck did you get into this school?"

"I am not from Puerto Rico. And by the way, you're the one that kraut called . . . what was it? 'Common and unpleasant,' I believe. I never heard anybody called that before."

"Of course not, because that's what you are." He nodded up and down, snorting. "And believe me, the kraut is going to pay a price for it."

"Oh, right."

"Just watch. Where are you from, anyway?"

"Pontiac."

"I didn't ask how you got here."

"Pontiac is the name of my town, asshole. It's a town in Michigan. It's called Pontiac."

"You named your town after a car?"

"No, dumb shit, they didn't name the town after the car. The town and the car are both named after Chief Pontiac. Obwandiyag. He was a great Ottawa chieftain who led a rebellion against the white man in the eighteenth century."

"What was so great about him?"

"He was a badass. Sometimes he stood outside the fort at Detroit and ate the hearts of soldiers he had captured so the English guys inside the fort could see him doing it. Other times he made them eat their own shit."

"Lovely. Did he offer them a choice?"

"I don't think so."

He reached out very slowly to hand me a piece of cheese, eyeing me. "I ask again. How did you get into this school?"

"I don't know," I said, snatching the cheese. "I have no clue. I don't even know where I am. How did you get in?"

He nodded thoughtfully. "Not sure. My mother, I guess. She's a big social climber. I think she got me in on hockey. I'm pretty good. I didn't want to come. This is a fucking gentry school."

"A what?"

"A gentry school. It's a blue-blood school. Philadelphia Main Line, Beacon Hill, Upper East Side, that sort of thing. Do you not even know what I'm talking about?"

"No."

"Really? You have no idea?"

"No."

"That's amazing. How could you not know this stuff? I'll tell you what, Pontiac, you are a bigger mystery than that fucking frog across the aisle. He's just from France. You must be from outer space. Michigan. What in the fuck is Michigan? Is that the same thing as Minnesota?"

"No, they're two different states, for Christ's sake. Jesus."

"And your town is called Pontiac? Do they have a town in Michigan called Plymouth?"

"Yes."

"Oh . . . my . . . God." He nodded thoughtfully, munching. "So you have no idea how you got here. Well, I know one thing for sure. You're not going to last."

"Why not?"

"You're going to flunk out or get kicked out or something. But you're not going to last."

"Fuck you."

He looked more closely into my face. "I'm not trying to be a shit. I'm just telling you the facts. You're too different. You're from some place with a car name. You have a scar from a switchblade. You have a weird accent."

"I do not have a weird accent. You do."

"You have weird hair."

"It's not my actual hair. I just got it cut like this because I was coming here."

"Well, don't do that again."

"Fine. What else do I need to change?"

"You can't. You're too different. You could get kicked out just for your mouse-skins."

"They're not mouse-skins. It's called foeswade."

"That's not a real thing."

"Fuck you."

I thanked him for the food and said good night. When I got back down to the floor, he leaned forward from the sill and said, "Sorry about beating the shit out of you."

67

"Yeah, I'm sorry about beating the shit out of you, too. What's your name again?"

"Compton."

"Skaggs."

"I'll call you Pontiac, like Barry does."

"I'll call you Asshole."

"Then I'll have to kick the shit out of you again."

"Then I'll have to kick the shit out of you again, too."

"Deal."

•

The next morning, the same boys ate breakfast at the same long table in the dining room, seated in the same places except for the two boys who had given up their seats so Adams and Barry could sit across from me to see if I was going to eat with my hands. Barry took the seat at the far end of the table from the hunch-backed Kraut's seat. To my great relief, the Kraut and his frightening wife did not reappear. Adams sat just to the right of the Kraut's place, across from the ugly wife's empty chair. From these posts at the extreme poles of the table, Adams and Barry kept eyes on us and also on Roosevelt and Gellhorn, who were serving as waiters. Beetle and his wife were not at the long table. No grace was said before the meal, and there was no conversation while we ate. Compton and I ignored each other.

After breakfast, we poured out of the Lower School building like rats from a ship. Only then did I recognize the place around me as Episcopalian. My early universe had contained two galaxies, the one dominated by Pontiac Motors and the other ruled by Episcopalians, and this was definitely an exaggerated, all-encompassing expression of the latter.

I followed the crowd into the New Chapel, which reminded me of large Episcopal churches I had seen in Detroit, except that the pews were turned the wrong way. Instead of facing the altar, they ran in long ranks the length of the sanctuary facing the center aisle, raised in steps like theater seats. The youngest boys sat at the bottom, with the older, bigger boys in tiers above them, so that we all sat looking over the tops of the heads of boys before us, facing boys our same age across the way. In the very top pews on both sides were the masters, glowering from deep shadow. Multiple clergy appeared at the altar in white and black vestments, but they were too far away from me to make out faces. Prayers were mumbled, a couple of hymns droned in the autistic fashion of Episcopalians. Then we filed out and found ourselves standing on a massive lawn nipped smooth as a baby's cheek and bright green in the white morning sun. The air was astringent with pine.

Supervisors shooed us forward to form a tightly packed scrum beneath a high stone promontory just outside the chapel door, which I recognized as a kind of outdoor lectern. The boys' soft muttering stopped cold, and silence fell like a rock. A tall, gaunt man in vestments, with a hard face and translucent eyes, appeared at the promontory, staring down on us with a cold, tiny smile. A light breeze rippling his white cotta made him look as if he might float up into the sky but for his firm grip on the lectern. I knew immediately this was the rector.

"Good morning," he called. His ice-blue eyes jumped out of his face like sparks.

A few boys mumbled greetings. He waited, stone-faced. We called back again, this time in half-hearted unison. His face did not move.

"Many of you are new boys," he said. "I don't know if you all made it to the welcome tea that Mrs. Holden and I hosted yesterday evening at the rectory. If not, then please allow me to introduce myself. I am Matthew Holden, the rector of the school."

He spoke a few more words of greeting and with that the ordered part of the morning ended. We new boys were led off on a succession of tours, some led by supervisors, some by masters. As we left the chapel lawn and shuffled toward the library, which was my group's first objective, I caught my breath at my first comprehensive look at the school in daylight.

Nothing seemed real. Everything was unnaturally beautiful, as if I had walked into one of the paintings my mother had shown me in her big coffee table book of the works of Winslow Homer. The belching smokestacks and screeching train wheels of Pontiac were lost in some other dimension entirely. Here, I walked in a world brushed, imagined, and perfect.

We marched across a stone bridge above a softly murmuring creek flowing to a glassy pond surrounded by conifers soaring up into scudding white rags of cloud. In the distance, I made out what looked like small castles, each with its own ceremonial paved path winding to a porch and massive door. The master leading us was an old man with a foreign accent who told us he was the head of the modern languages department. He called out the names and purposes of the castles we passed, but not a single name stayed with me for even an instant. The fine buildings surrounded by a grand green wall of forest all faded into one, more a feeling than a place, while my mind whirred, working a puzzle I could not quickly resolve. I couldn't work out how or why any of this was happening, why I was here, what I was supposed to do, what was to become of me, or what had happened to the boy I had been before. Some powerful magic had transported me not to a school, not to a town or a state in America but to another way of being alive, a painted and beautiful way that felt stone-cold inside and deeply frightening. A sudden yearning for din and grit stung my heart like the stab of a knife.

"Pontiac," a voice whispered behind me, calling me back to this place. It was Compton. I was glad to be spoken to.

"Asshole," I whispered back.

"Where are we going?"

"The library, I think."

Gellhorn, the broad-shouldered boy with thick horn-rimmed glasses who sat to my left at the table, turned back toward us.

"Your names are Pontiac and Asshole?"

"That's about it, Mr. Magoo," Compton said.

Gellhorn's face flushed. He turned his back on us and marched forward, showing with squared shoulders that we were beneath his contempt.

The library was a yellow stone edifice rising next to another pond, this one smaller, shinier and more closely contained than the one we had passed earlier. We had been pared down to a group of about a dozen boys. We waited on the steep steps at the front until the librarian appeared in the doorway and introduced himself as Mr. Althorpe. There was something immediately sweet about him, a kindness that shone through his tweed. He was middle-aged and clearly a member of the striped tie and button-down collar species, but he seemed more avuncular than authoritarian.

He led us inside and showed us the reading room and the large card catalog in burnished brown oaken cabinets on black tables. Through tall leaded windows across one end of the reading room, a flight of Canada geese drifted down to the surface of the pond.

Mr. Althorpe spoke first to Gellhorn.

71

"We have all of your father's published works here," he said, "many of them in first edition, although those do not circulate, of course."

"I see," Gellhorn said in a high nervous tremolo. He fidgeted, shoving his hands in and out of the pockets of his tweed jacket, adjusting his glasses with a finger and turning away from the librarian.

Compton spoke from the back of the crowd. "Who's his father?"

Mr. Althorpe was suddenly taken aback. "Oh, I'm sorry," he said to Gellhorn. "I just assumed it was generally known."

Gellhorn said, "That's perfectly all right, sir."

We toured the gymnasium next. Our tour guide was a short thick-legged gray-haired man in a blue T-shirt and tight-fitting knee-length shorts over lace-up sneakers. His accent was musical and alive, not the controlled monotone of the other masters. He told us he was the boxing coach.

"I can teach you boys to box," he said. "I can sure do that. The boys call me Frenchie, but don't call me that. I don't like it. I ain't French. I'm American. I'm Coach Mack to you. I can sure teach you how to box."

Coach Mack poked Gellhorn playfully in the chest. "They tell me your daddy is Turk Ambrose."

"Yes, sir."

"He was one heckuva boxer up here. I coached him."

Gellhorn said, "I've always heard a lot about you."

Coach Mack beamed.

After our tour of the gym, Coach Mack pointed the way back to the Lower School and told us we had ten minutes to get there for lunch or we would be shut out of the dining room. We hurried along in a tight little mob. As soon as we were away from the gym, Compton drew up next to Gellhorn and grabbed his sleeve.

"I asked you who your old man is, Magoo."

Gellhorn snatched his arm free. Roosevelt pushed ahead of me, came up to Compton, and shoved his shoulder hard.

"Leave him alone."

Compton's face flashed purple, and he began milling his fists.

"What did you just say to me, you fucking midget?"

"Hey," I said. "C'mon. We're going to miss lunch."

Roosevelt signaled with a finger for Compton to come close, but it wasn't a dare. Compton approached warily.

"Turk Ambrose is his adoptive father," the boy said. "He was a big deal here. But his real father is Ernest Hemingway."

"No shit," Compton said.

"Let's go," Roosevelt said. "We don't want to miss lunch."

The three of us formed a little knot as we walked along. Gellhorn stumped out far ahead.

"What's his problem?" Compton asked.

"I guess he's ashamed of the Hemingway business," Roosevelt said.

"Why would anyone be ashamed of that?" I asked.

Roosevelt stopped for an instant and scanned me up and down as if I had stepped from behind a tree. Nodding toward me, he asked Compton, "Who is he?"

"Pontiac."

"That guy's real father is not Ernest Hemingway," I said.

"Yes he is," Roosevelt said. "That guy is Tim Gellhorn. Ernest Hemingway is his real father. But his adoptive father is Turk Ambrose. He was Golden Gloves at Yale." He stuck out a hand to shake. "My name is Montgomery Roosevelt."

I shrugged and shook his hand. "I'm Skaggs."

"Nice to meet you, Skaggs."

"Nice to meet you, too, Roosevelt. Why isn't Gellhorn's name Hemingway? Or Ambrose?"

"His mother gave him her name."

"That's weird."

"Yes."

"How do you know all this stuff?"

"I'm a little bit related to the Ambroses through Turk's first wife. My family knows his family. And there was a big article about Hemingway's wives in a magazine this summer. It was pretty shocking. My mother knew Gellhorn was going to be here, and she showed me the article. It had a picture of him when he was a little boy. The article said he was Hemingway's son, but they never knew each other. My mother knew all about Gellhorn, but she always thought his name was Ambrose."

"Damn. And he doesn't even know his real father?"

"I guess not. I mean, I guess he must have known it was Hemingway, but the article said he never met him. He grew up an Ambrose."

"So why isn't his name Ambrose?"

"The article didn't say why exactly."

"And that's how the library guy knew? From the magazine?"

"Maybe."

I said, "I still don't get how anybody could be ashamed of being Ernest Hemingway's son."

"Well, you know," Roosevelt said. "He's a writer."

•

The Schmitzes returned to our table for dinner. Rutledge said his numb-lipped version of grace again, and we sat down. Gellhorn and Roosevelt came to the table with platters carrying big blue and white china soup tureens with ladles. They had already set out straw baskets filled with dinner rolls and two pewter dishes with butter and knives. With what I thought was kind of an overdone bow, Gellhorn placed a tureen and ladle in front of Herr Schmitz. Roosevelt put down the other tureen at the far end of the table in front of Barry.

Boys passed their soup bowls down, each to his right, and Herr Schmitz and Barry served from both ends. Compton, who was seated at Frau Schmitz's left elbow, offered her rolls and butter, of which she took one roll and a thin slice of butter. Herr Schmitz took two rolls and a fatter hunk of butter. We were all hungrily slurping soup when a sharp tone rang out. We looked up and saw Herr Schmitz strike his water glass again with his knife. We sat back with our hands in our laps and looked to him.

"Mr. Twitchell," he said crisply to the boy called Tweetie, "did I just now see you take a roll and butter without first offering to Mr. Barry?"

Tweetie was midway down the table between me and Roosevelt.

"You did, sir," he said in his booming baritone. "I apologize. I did not know we had that rule at our end of the table."

Barry laughed genially. "It's all right, sir," he called down the table. "We actually don't have that rule at our end. No offense taken."

Herr Schmitz stiffened. "I'm sorry, when you say 'we,' whom do you intend? Who is this 'we' who make rules at your end of the table, Barry?"

Barry pushed back from his plate. "I apologize, sir. It is my mistake. I misunderstood. Of course, I agree that things at your end should be offered first to Frau Schmitz and then to you. I guess I just didn't see myself as that important."

"Oh, I assure you, you are not important at all. What is important is the rule, and the rule, to be sensible, must be consistent for the entire table."

"Of course, sir," Barry said. "All right, men," he said, turning to us, "from now on you will offer all dishes to me before partaking."

We shifted our collective gaze back to Herr Schmitz, who clearly was not done.

"Twitchell," he said, "you will take your rolls and butter back to the kitchen and throw them into the waste bin. There will be no rolls or butter for you at this meal."

Twitchell almost leapt to his feet smiling broadly.

"Yes, sir," he boomed. On his plate were two untouched dinner rolls and a thick blob of butter. He crushed the rolls into a wad in his left hand, then scraped up the butter with his dinner knife and pasted it on top of the squashed dough with slow ostentation so that the whole concoction looked like an ice cream cone.

Our entire end of the dining room had gone silent, and boys were watching from other tables. Tweetie spun on a heel and marched out of the dining room with the rolls and butter aloft like the Olympic torch. Not a minute later, he marched back into the dining room, theatrically chewing a massive wad of dough, some of which leaked from the corners of his mouth, with butter smeared wetly across his nose and chin. Laughter went up from nearby tables. Tweetie was still standing by his chair chewing when the room went dead.

Beetle had left his post on the dais and was paddling slowly toward our table, flapping his napkin at his side in a rowing motion.

When he arrived at last, breathing noisily, he said, "Is there an issue here, Herr Schmitz?"

Herr Schmitz rose, wiping his lips daintily. "Not at all, Mr. Frick. Twitchell has been entertaining the boys with his antics. He's very amusing."

"Is he?" Beetle asked. He put his beady eyes close to Twitchell's face, boring in. "It looks to me as if Twitchell needs to wipe his chin."

"Wipe your chin, Twitchell," Herr Schmitz said.

"Yes, sir!" Twitchell said in a voice so loud that Beetle snapped his head back in alarm.

Beetle turned to Herr Schmitz. "Does he always talk like that?"

"He speaks in a very loud voice."

"He certainly does. A very loud voice. I had not heard it before."

"I will ask him to be more soft-spoken at the table."

"Yes," Beetle said. "By all means." He turned back to Twitchell. "Keep your voice down in the dining room, Twitchell. In fact, with a voice like that, you can keep it down everywhere you go in my Lower School."

"Yes, sir," Twitchell said at megaphone volume, causing Beetle to jerk his head back again.

"Herr Schmitz," Beetle said, "I believe you have things well under control. Carry on then."

Beetle steamed serenely back up to his seat at the dais, the napkin making a small wake behind him.

Herr Schmitz hissed at Tweetie, "Sit down, you ass, and don't make a sound above a whisper or I will expel you from the dining room."

"Yes, sir," Tweetie whispered a bit too hoarsely.

We were back at our soup, quietly, when the knife rang again against the glass, this time with a more subdued ting. We looked again toward the end of the table.

"Twitchell," Herr Schmitz said evenly, "I am about to speak to you, but you will not speak a word in response."

Tweetie nodded that he understood.

"Twitchell, Frau Schmitz and I have agreed that dinner rolls do not seem to agree with you. Therefore, for the rest of your time at my table, you will not take rolls or butter again. Do you understand me?"

Tweetie nodded.

"Good. Don't forget it, and don't let me catch you cheating, or you will be very, very unhappy with the outcome."

Tweetie nodded again.

"And for all of you," Herr Schmitz said to us, "this is a matter that will stay at this table. You will not discuss this matter with any other boy or master. Expect harsh consequences if you do. Do you understand me?"

"Yes, sir," we said in unison, returning to our now cold soup.

"You, Skaggs," Herr Schmitz said to me, "some of the rules and customs here will be quite new to you, I suspect."

I looked at him but did not speak.

His eyes went dead, and he turned slightly away. "I suggest you consult with your tablemates just how serious a mistake it would be to bruit something about after I have specifically instructed you not to."

"Brute, sir?"

"Jesus Christ," Compton muttered.

"Jesus Christ, indeed, Compton," Herr Schmitz said, smiling unpleasantly. "Perhaps you will exert some of your energetic

Christian conviction by assisting Skaggs here with his deficient vocabulary, no doubt a result of growing up in the middle of the West."

A few boys laughed. Compton grinned at me malevolently. "Glad to help, sir."

Immediately after dinner when we returned to Dorm Four, all the boys from our table, representing a little under half of the dorm's total population, gathered in front of Compton's alcove.

Tweetie bellowed like a ship's horn, "Why did he warn us not to tell anyone?"

Yusupov, standing a little apart from us with his mop of hair thrown back and his blade-like nose vertical, said loftily, "Clearly the man is an asshole."

Compton stood in the entrance of his alcove, listening intently.

"Tell people what?" I asked. "That some guy at our table can't eat rolls and butter?"

"Jesus," Compton interrupted brusquely, shaking his head in disgust. "How stupid can you guys be?"

Davidson looked stricken. "What did we say that was stupid?"

Compton scuffed a heel on the floor and surveyed us all with a caustic eye. "Jesus. He's afraid of our parents. They're all afraid of our parents. The guy is a wog. He's a weird Nazi foreigner. You can't withhold kids' food. It's not American. It's some kind of European Kraut shit they do to kids over there, like caning. He's afraid we'll tell on him to our parents."

We were all silent, considering it.

Yusupov said to me, "Pontiac, if you were to inform your parents back in Minneapolis . . . "

"Michigan," I said.

"Exactly," he said, his nose so vertical I could barely see his

79

eyes. "If you were to tell your parents in Michigan that a boy here was being deprived of rolls and butter, what would they say?"

"They would probably tell me to shut up."

"Nobody's afraid of his parents," Compton spat derisively. "He's poor. Schmitz is afraid of the parents who are rich. He doesn't want word getting back to them that some foreign ex-Nazi master up here in New Hampshire is starving rich kids to death."

"By depriving us of rolls and butter?" Tweetie boomed.

"Well, you know, whatever," Compton said, "taking food away."

"Oh, I don't know about that," Roosevelt said. "My parents are rich, and they wouldn't care."

"That's not the point," Compton said. "Herr Schmitz is afraid of our parents."

Yusupov said to Compton, "You say the Schmitzes are afraid of our parents. Why aren't they afraid of Pontiac's parents?"

"Because they're low-class."

"So, given what one reads in the newspaper of your own parents, Compton, why would the Schmitzes worry about them?"

Compton pulled a shoulder back and threw a short punch straight onto Yusupov's mouth. Yusupov took the punch, danced back, and got some air. When Compton charged him, Yusupov punched him in the forehead with a strong right that snapped Compton's head back, then popped him on the chin with a left. Compton tried to get his feet square again, but Yusupov hit him hard in the gut with a right. Compton stooped forward deeply to the blow, and it looked as if the fight might be over. Yusupov backed off with both fists in front of his face, watching Compton closely. Compton rushed straight at him through a rain of punches. He grabbed Yusupov's neck and arm and hurled him like a bag of dirty laundry over the radiator bench to the floor on the other side.

Yusupov was on his face on the floor and Compton was about to do a one-handed hurdle over the bench when Barry and Adams came charging down the dorm, heads low, arms pumping. Adams put his right shoulder square into Compton's gut and plowed him down. Barry took a position between Yusupov, who was still prostrate on the floor, and Compton, who was now sitting with his back against the radiator bench. Barry pointed his finger at Compton.

"Don't get up."

Yusupov was struggling to his feet when Mr. Fell appeared, relaxed and bemused with his tie removed and cuffs rolled up for the evening.

"Campfire stories again, boys?"

"Yes, sir," they both said.

"You know what to do."

Compton got up and approached Yusupov with a hand outstretched. Yusupov extended his hand gingerly.

"Good fight," Compton said.

"Good fight," Yusupov said.

They returned solemnly to their alcoves and drew shut their curtains.

•

The following night, between dinner and study hall, a number of us enjoyed a feast of rolls and butter at Compton's end of the dorm. Several guys had smuggled them out wrapped up in napkins, apparently without knowledge of each other, and two boys had managed somehow to get back to Dorm Four with knives and big gobs of butter. We gathered around the radiator bench and made a party of it.

"Very good," Tweetie said, hoisting a heavily slathered roll skyward, then taking a massive bite and reenacting his horrendous chewing act of the previous night, met by gales of laughter and cheers. We all took massive bites and competed to see who could best ape Tweetie's slobbery chewing.

Gellhorn stood off at a distance, frowning with his arms folded, one finger pushing at his glasses. Compton looked as if he was about to say something to him, but I pushed him lightly on a shoulder.

"Give it a rest, asshole."

He shrugged.

Yusupov disappeared and came back with a stack of small paper cups and a plastic pitcher of water from the bathroom. He poured cups for us all, then lifted his own and proposed a toast.

"To Herr Schmitz," he said loftily. "A dumb Nazi bastard!"

All of us but Gellhorn and Aubert sang it out in lusty unison: "Herr Schmitz, a dumb Nazi bastard!" Then we quaffed our cups. Yusupov marched to the big window at the end of the dorm, lifted it open with a grimace and tossed out his cup. We all went to the window and dashed our cups into the evening air.

We turned as one and found Mr. Fell standing behind us, puffing a pipe clenched in his jaw.

"You have ten minutes to get to study hall," he said. "And on your way, get out there and pick up those damn cups. I don't want to see a single paper cup out there tomorrow."

Gellhorn said, "Sir, I had nothing to do with this."

"Nor I," said Aubert.

"Just don't let me find any cups out there," Mr. Fell said, turning away. "Any of you. Or you'll all be sorry."

•

During morning chapel every day, we sat with small book bags shoved up under the pews in front of us, just out of the way of the raised kneeling bench. At the end of the service, we retrieved the bags and assembled on the lawn to listen to the rector's reports. From there, we repaired to the school building, almost always entering our classrooms just ahead of the masters. We took our assigned seats around the table, sorted out our books and notepads and waited in strictly observed silence.

It was in the classrooms that my new life began to settle into sharper focus. The rooms were small but not cramped, with large leaded windows looking out over a rolling green expanse. At the center of each room was a massive oval table with a green inlaid surface. Each table was surrounded by twelve St. Philip's School captain's chairs bearing the school's coat of arms. There were no maps on walls, no bookcases or other idiosyncratic furnishings, because each room was to be occupied by different masters at various hours of the day.

The masters, all men, seemed to share with each other a certain style of entering a room, as if they had drilled on it. We rose when they came in and said, "Good morning, sir." The master said hello, waited for us to be seated, then took his own chair at the head of the table and arranged his things before him tidily. Then he began teaching.

And teaching. And teaching. It was nonstop. They taught for an hour and a half, usually with their heads in their notes much of the time. We kept our heads down, too, scribbling our own notes. I wasn't sure what any of my own notes meant, but asking questions did not seem to be part of the protocol. As I scribbled away, energetically covering pages with inscrutable hieroglyphics, it came home to me that Compton was exactly correct. I did not belong here, nor did I understand even a little bit of what was going on or what I was supposed to do about it.

None of what any of the droning masters said at the head of the tables made the slightest sense to me. Nor did scribbling things down on notepads help in the least bit. I felt as if I was taking part in some ritual farce that would end with them all laughing hysterically and then chucking me out a window.

When it was my turn to translate Caesar's *Gallic Wars* aloud in class, I stumbled and muttered, unable to recall the vocabulary or figure out the sentence structure. French class was worse. When the math teacher sent two of us to the blackboard to solve problems, I stood staring at my chalk while the other boy's hand flew across the board,

I wanted to tell someone I was aware they were making a fool of me, as if saying it aloud might salvage some morsel of dignity, but there was no moment, margin, pause, or opportunity to complain. The masters droned, and I scribbled as fast as I could, and every page that I filled with inscrutable gibberish became one more stone tied to my ankle for the day when they would finally heave my corpse into the library pond.

Every time I crossed paths with Johnny Wilson, I thought briefly of telling him how badly things were going for me, but I never did, because I wasn't sure how he would react. I couldn't be certain what he would tell my parents, my mother especially. He always asked me how I was doing, and I always said, "Fine." Then on one occasion when we passed on the bridge over the library pond, he stopped, put a hand on my shoulder, looked carefully into my face and said, "You don't look fine, Woodrow. You look worried."

"I'm OK."

"Come see me if you want to talk."

•

Athletics were even worse than class. Everyone participated in a sport. There may have been some system or unspoken knowledge by which boys who knew the drill were able to choose their own sport, but I was assigned peremptorily to something called rowing, a thing I thought you did only if you couldn't afford a motor.

We were supplied with rowing clothes at the gymnasium— shorts, slipper-like training shoes, and silky T-shirts with spaghetti strap arms. On the first day we were instructed to get dressed quickly, then go outside and form up in three straight lines according to our assigned rowing clubs. As we stood waiting in long parallel ranks, a large, three-bench golf cart appeared carrying a half dozen masters.

Just ahead of me in my own line was Davidson. Immediately to my right was Roosevelt. To my left was Yusupov. It was mid-August, and the day was hot. The road rose ahead like a ladder to the sun. After a while at a brisk pace, I began to feel winded. Davidson, just ahead of me, was stumbling. He looked back over his shoulder with an expression of sweaty desperation and choked out, "Hi, Pontiac."

A sharp noise of rat-a-tat-tatting issued from the woods. Roosevelt, bouncing along as if on springs, grinned broadly and called out, "Pileated!"

Yusupov, who was floating effortlessly through the air on the other side of me, his nose vertical, called back, "Oh, I think not. Not a deep enough hammer. Sounds more like a red-headed."

The golf cart was speeding up. I wondered if a person my age could have a heart attack.

"Do you have pileated in Montana?" Yusupov called over

genially to Roosevelt as if I were not between them. I looked at the Russian. My lungs were on fire, and he was cruising like a hawk on a thermal.

"Sure," Roosevelt called back happily. "We've got pileated, downy, hairy, black-backed . . . "

At "black-backed," Davidson stumbled, put his hand to his mouth, turned, and puked on my shorts. We both fell out of line.

"Sorry," he said, wiping his chin.

Roosevelt said, "You guys need to get in better shape."

"I want to," Davidson gasped.

"Fuck you," I said.

My struggle to keep up seemed to fuel Yusupov and Roosevelt to run even more effortlessly. They also become more loquacious across my chest.

"Why aren't you playing lacrosse?" Yusupov asked.

"I probably will," Roosevelt said. "I'm just trying this. My great-grandfather was a big crew guy here. He wasn't as short as I am. I wanted to try it. Not really built for it. Are your family boat people?"

Yusupov, bounding along with his nose in the clouds, said "Not rowing, really, but we were all about boats. Always. Every kind of boat."

"Big ones, I imagine."

"Of course. My great aunt was aboard the *Standart* when they informed the tsar of the February Revolution in 1917. They were roller-skating around the deck at the time to a string quartet, if you can imagine, with the ship pitching in the sea, around and around, pitching and pitching . . . "

I heard Davidson retch again, this time on someone else.

"Sorry," he muttered. "Sorry."

We finally reached Drake Pond. I was still alive but much the worse for wear. Steep wooden stairs descended from a sandy clearing to a deck joining three long barns at the edge of a silver-white sheet of water just visible through the forest. When we got to our boathouse, the interior was gloomy, but another barn door at the far end opened on a blaze of sunlit water. A broad walkway was bordered on both sides by racks of boats stacked thirty feet high, almost to the roof. Half a dozen moveable ladders, hooked at the top and wheeled at the feet, allowed crews to shift boats off the higher shelves onto canvas slings that were lowered on straps with blocks.

The boats were of a dimension and nature I had never glimpsed even in books or movies—incredibly long, narrow, and shallow, varnished and gleaming like fine furniture.

Davidson and I were assigned to sit cross-legged on the floor and out of the way with a group of a dozen boys, while the French master who had led us to the library the first day, Monsieur Pierremarti, called out a series of inscrutable commands. In response, little boys, First and Second formers, stepped forward and seemed to take charge of the older boys. Fourth, Fifth, and even Sixth formers scrambled up ladders to obey commands squeaked at them from below by tiny tyrants.

"Do you know what's going on?" I whispered to Davidson.

"The coxes are commanding the crews to take the shells off the racks and lower them."

I had no idea what he was talking about. Together, the little boys and the bigger ones performed something that was half dance, half drill, lowering the boats meticulously one by one, forming up on both sides of each boat, lifting them at the commands of the diminutive drill sergeants, then marching out over the pier to the water as if boys and boats had fused into gigantic insects emerging from their nests. We craned forward from our dark corner and watched them lower the boats into the water, then gently place gigantic oars into the oarlocks. In response to more commands, the crews sat down on the dock as one, turned in unison, and placed their feet in the boats. In one movement, they lifted their asses and entered the boats, their backs to the bow. Finally, the coxes boarded, taking forward-facing seats in the stern. Each cox wore a flimsy billed cap and had a little megaphone strapped to his face so that they all looked like ducks. Each rower held one very long oar. On the side of the boat against the dock, the oars stood straight up in the air like lances, and on the other side they were extended flat, resting on the water. The coxswains piped out softer, more constrained commands, and the boats eased away magically from the docks. Then, when they were clear, new orders were shrieked. The oars lifted in unison like wings, dipped, and pulled against the water in long smooth hauls. The boats shot out of view, followed by M. Pierremarti in a large Chris-Craft inboard launch with gleaming mahogany decks driven by a Sixth Former.

"Magnificent," Davidson whispered.

Then it was our turn. We were left with M. Pierremarti's assistant, Mr. Zierotin, a math teacher whom I took for a Polack. He was Czech-Bohemian, as it turned out, in his late thirties, diminutive but wiry, graceful of movement, with gleaming brown eyes and long brown hair swept from his brow to the nape of his neck in a knight's helmet.

He paced around our little mob of two dozen boys, asking questions: "Who has row before? You row? Where? You go over there and wait. You row? No? Never? You stay here."

Mr. Zierotin said Davidson and I were assigned to the barge.

"What's the barge?" I asked Davidson.

"It's our boat. This one." He nodded toward an ungainly dark vessel with a thick hull decidedly unlike the graceful shells. "It's the bottom level boat," he said. "Don't worry. We'll work our way up."

"Fuck," I said.

"Don't do that."

"What?"

"Swear in the boathouse. The boathouse is sort of like chapel."

"Oh, Christ. Sorry. Sorry, Davidson."

"Of course."

Mr. Zierotin spent what felt like the next hour choosing a cox for each boat, then drilling the cox on the precise commands for removing the boats from the racks, carrying the boats out, and placing them in the water. The boats, even our fat barge, were never to be placed on the dock, only to go from soft slings to the bosom of the lake without ever touching terra firma. We were all drilled on the coxswains' orders and what to do.

When we finally were told to lift our barge, the heavy boat strained our skinny arms as if made of stone. We staggered a little, and Mr. Zierotin called out in his intimidating accent, "If you drop boat, you will be immediately kilt."

The crew of our barge was a tossed salad of fat boys, skinny boys, tall boys, and tiny boys from the First and Second forms, then myself and Davidson from the Third Form. Our cox was a boy I had noticed already for his manner in the dining room and lobby before meals. Dickie Decherd, a second-former, was elfin in size but of stunning visual impact. He struck me the first time I saw him as a miniaturized version of the leading man in an old black and white movie with top hat and tap-shoe scenes. His shoes sparkled like diamonds. His hair was slicked back in a trim golden cap. His shirts were always crisp, and his necktie was perpetually puffed out like an ascot. He was physically miniscule, but he strutted and preened as if bestriding the Lower School lobby like a colossus, and I could tell that the boys of his age group, the First and Second formers, deferred to him obsequiously, laughing wildly at his every joke and fawning to hear his wisdom.

Later I learned that Dickie had started out during his First Form year as cox on a Fourth-form shell, but he had been demoted this year to the barge because of a problem involving temper. It was assumed by all that he would re-ascend the ranks quickly and surpass his former rank, probably winding up as cox on the varsity crew sent to England each year to compete in the Henley Royal Regatta on the Thames. For now, though, he was the cox on my barge.

We never rowed that day. We took our boat off the racks, splashed it down heavily into the water to Mr. Zierotin's repeated dismay, placed oars in it, boarded, disembarked, carried it back to the racks, and did it all over again several times, all to Dickie's shrieked commands. Just as were stowing the boat for the last time, the motor launch returned to the dock with M. Pierremarti in the stern bearing an electric megaphone in one hand. The launch had barely touched the dock when all of the shells came into view at once, flying toward us silent as herons drifting down from a silver-blue sky.

"Breathtaking," Davidson whispered behind me.

"Get out!" Mr. Zierotin shouted at us. "You are in the ways. Go now."

I was only too happy to take my leave and join the mob of younger boys hurrying up the hill from the boathouses to the road, but Davidson at my side kept stopping to look back over his shoulder.

"I wish we could stay and watch them all come in," he said.

"Christ," I said.

Unlike the death march on the way out, the trip back through the forest was a leisurely stroll, unmolested.

"What do you think?" Davidson asked me as we sauntered along.

"Kind of rough," I said. "Not the most fun I've ever had. Feels kind of like being galley slaves. Plus Dickie Decherd is a punk."

Davidson laughed. "He really is a punk, isn't he? I've always known him. But on Race Day . . . "

"What's that?"

"Race Day is at the end of the year. Parents come, and, you know, the alumni, all the old guys who rowed here. Pomp and circumstance. Quite lovely, actually."

"How do you know?"

"I've always gone. Practically every year of my life."

"Even when you weren't a student here?"

"My father brought me. He rowed here. So did his father. I don't even know how far back we go."

Ahead of us on the narrow road, a gaggle of boys had formed a comet trail behind Dickie Decherd, trotting to keep up and jockeying for his attention.

"Why is he such a deal?" I asked.

Davidson looked at me quizzically. "Well, he's . . . he's a Decherd. You know the Decherds."

"I don't know anybody. I'm from Pontiac."

"What do you mean you're *from* Pontiac? I thought Pontiac was your name."

"No, it's not my name, for Christ's sake. Jeez. It's the name of the town I come from. Compton calls me Pontiac."

"So it's a nickname."

"I guess. My name is Skaggs."

"I knew that. Your family name. But I thought Pontiac was your first name."

I laughed. "Pontiac Skaggs. Might keep it. Put it on my tombstone."

"I don't think you're going to get rid of it anytime soon. As long as you're here."

"Which may not be too long," I said.

"So I gather."

"You gather how? Who told you that?"

"No one told me. I just saw your rank when they posted the grades."

Our weekly grades and class rank were posted on Friday evenings before dinner in the foyer of Aldredge Hall, a place I already hated. In my first two weeks at St. Philip's, my name had appeared dead last in the Third Form rankings. The first time it happened, Compton turned around from the list and muttered to me, "Told you so." The second week he said nothing.

I said to Davidson, "I think I'm at the bottom."

"You don't think you are," he said with concern. "You are."

"What do they do to you if you're at the bottom?"

"I assume it depends on who you are."

"That doesn't sound too good for me."

"I wouldn't think it would be."

•

Compton's prediction of my early demise became more believable every day. My academic performance was a gathering horror.

Instead of being the smartest kid in the class as I had been all my life before, for the first time I was the dumbest. I listened while the teachers droned from their notes, and I continued to scratch out my own notes in growing despair and embarrassment, but nothing stuck. I still couldn't translate Caesar. Other boys laughed at my French. The math teacher seemed to have given up on me entirely.

Every night after dinner, we walked down the road to the Big Study, an enormous neo-Gothic structure with an open study hall, gloomy and huge, on the first level. With its soaring gables and slitty windows, the building reminded me of Frau Schmitz's face. It was the place where my failings and inadequacy were most evident.

But the same building did offer a small corner of respite. In the basement, in an airless and windowless room behind a large steel door, was a candy store called The Tuck Shop, run by a stout, white-haired, ruddy-faced old New Hampshire Yankee named Dan Biggs, always called by both names. Dan Biggs was of a tribe of blue-collar school employees whom the boys called "wombats," a term used only behind their backs. He spoke with a high nasal twang very foreign to my ear, but his frank manner reminded me of home. When he scolded the boys in the store, I couldn't help smiling. He saw me smiling once or twice and winked at me.

I frequented The Tuck Shop even though I never had any money to buy anything. One afternoon when I was there alone, he said, "Jesus Christ kid, why don't you never buy nuthin' from me? You're down here enough to wear out my floor."

"No money."

"No money? You got no money? Don't tell me we got a poor kid at St. Philip's School."

"Yup."

"Jesus Christ, how did that happen? Well, I'm not givin' you nuthin'. I don't give shit away. Why don't you go in town and get a job?'"

I had already explored that possibility in an embarrassing conversation with Mr. Fell. I also had asked if boys got paid for being waiters in the dining room. He had laughed out loud at both propositions. I explained all of that to Dan Biggs.

"They're a bunch of true jackasses, are they not?" he said.

I laughed at that.

"I'll tell you what, kid," he said, "I'm the postmaster. That makes me the guy who hands out the money. The families send it up to the school and it goes into an account that I divvy out. I put envelopes in boys' mailboxes with the cash. But just this year they started giving some kids spending money direct from the school instead of their parents. The rector's wife gives it to them."

"I don't get that."

"You're not the only poor kid to come here this year. There are about six of you."

"Who are the others?"

"Ain't for me to tell. It's confidential. But like I said, some of the other poor kids get money every week from the rector's wife, even if their parents don't send them nothing."

"And?" I was getting worried.

"I'll put you in for the dole."

I was aghast. It seemed like begging. I thought of what my mother would say.

"I don't think you should say anything," I said. "I already go to school here for free. They might get mad."

"Leave it to Dan Biggs," he said. "It won't be no trouble for nobody, and you'll get some money you can spend in my store. Good for you, good for me."

"Are you sure?"

"I am sure."

On one wall of the long, narrow basement corridor outside the Tuck Shop was a rank of small rectangular mailboxes behind bronze-framed windows that swung open on hinges. A week later, when I visited the Tuck Shop, Dan Biggs said, "Don't you never check your mail, boy? I can't stuff no more money in there for you if you don't take some out."

I rushed out and looked. Through the little window of my mailbox I spied what looked like a brown envelope. I had forgotten the combination for the lock. I had to run all the way back to the Lower School and look in a notebook. When I got back to the Big Study basement, I was out of breath. Dan Biggs was in the hallway, locking up his store for the day. I opened the mailbox and withdrew the envelope. It contained a crisp new ten-dollar bill. Dan Biggs saw the wonder on my face.

"They'd rather give you ten bucks a week for free than see you get an honest job."

"Every week?"

"Every week."

"I can't spend that much."

He laughed again. "You'll go through it. In fact, it's not too soon to start putting some of that good green cash into old Dan Biggs's till." He went to the big steel door, swung up a bar that held it closed from the outside and reopened his store. I rushed to the bin of grape balls and filled a small brown bag. I picked out a bar of handmade fudge from the Granite State Candy Shop in Rumney and two packages of chewing gum from Maine made with pine pitch and maple sugar. It all came to $1.75.

"You got a lot left, ain't you?" he said. "Save it up, and maybe someday you can buy my truck."

"How about some whiskey in the meantime?"

He stuck a finger in my face and said sharply, "Now don't go and be like that, son. That'll get you kicked out and me lose my business. Just because I help you out a little don't mean you take me for a fool."

"I'm sorry, Dan Biggs. I apologize."

"Apology accepted."

We chatted for a while. I asked him why he called the store the Tuck Shop. He told me it wasn't his idea. He thought the name was stupid. In fact, he thought everything about the store was stupid. He had visited other boarding schools nearby, and they had big modern stores that sold clothing and all kinds of sporting equipment and memorabilia. One school store even had a soda bar at the back that served hamburgers. None of them used the term, tuck shop.

"I don't even know what that means," he said, "but judging by some of these little thieves around here it must mean tuck and run."

We laughed. I watched him close up the shop. He shut the big door, swung down the bar and turned a key in the lock.

"Why does The Tuck Shop have a door like that?" I asked.

"Used to be a boiler room. That's a fire door. In the navy, we would have called it a blast door."

On the way back to the Lower School with my riches in hand, I felt at once terribly excited about the money, thrilled with the candy but also a little uneasy at the pit of my stomach. I knew what my mother would call this. Mooching. Taking money for nothing.

But what was this whole deal they had put me into, anyway, if not mooching?

•

The Schmitzes had been away from the table for a few nights. Compton suggested they might be visiting a farm to have sex with the animals. It turned out they had been attending a wedding in Boston. When they returned, Herr Schmitz spotted a small cut and some bruising on Yusupov's neck from his fight with Compton.

"You are a thespian, I believe," Herr Schmitz said to Yusupov.

"I am, sir," Yusupov said, turning but not lowering the nose in Herr Schmitz's direction. "I have joined the Auchincloss Thespian Club. The stage is my calling."

"Did you fall off the stage? Is that why you carry these bruises on your neck?"

"In a manner of speaking, yes."

Herr Schmitz exchanged winces with his wife. "I was a guest master at Eton for a year," he said, "and one of the very signal differences I note between that extremely prestigious school in England and this prestigious school in the United States is the much lower incidence of physical brawling at Eton. Frau Schmitz and I have even wondered if physical violence is endemic to the American upper classes."

"Oh, I think so, yes, definitely," Yusupov said. "I think you make an excellent point, sir. I have noticed this same difference between Eton boys and American boys."

"You know Eton, then?"

"In a way, yes. I have never visited the school, but every Christmas season in New York, the ex-pat old boys from Eton put on a ball, and my brothers and I have always been invited. You have been to it?'"

"No. I did not know of this," Herr Schmitz said, chastened.

"Just this past year," Yusupov said, "I found myself at the Eton ball, cornered by a group of fellows who were current students there, all very Etonesque, if you know what I mean.

"One of them, a short fat fellow with thick glasses and an ascot, asked me if I had ever visited Minnesota. I said I had not, and I asked why. He said he had always wanted to go to Minnesota to see if it was true there is a town there named Many-Ha-Ha.

"They all had a very nice little Etonesque ha-ha over that. I told the little blousy fellow the place he really should visit is Arkansas. I said the moment he gets off the train in Arkansas, he will be seized by the locals and serially butt-fucked, which I assumed he would probably enjoy."

We all exploded laughing, and Yusupov stuck his nose even higher in the air as if he didn't have the foggiest notion what we could be laughing at.

"Yusupov!" Adams chided severely.

Herr Schmitz glared at him. "How dare you speak that way in front of Frau Schmitz?"

Frau Schmitz's tiny eyes hurled hot sparks.

"I should give you demerits for this," Herr Schmitz said, "and I shall do so if you ever again speak in this manner in front of Frau Schmitz. In fact, I will banish you to take your meals alone in the pantry."

"The pantry?" Yusupov said. "Is that the large room to the left just outside the double doors? I was not aware it was possible to take one's meals there."

"It is very possible if I say so," Herr Schmitz hissed.

"But this, I gather, would not be a privilege."

Herr Schmitz breathed in little gasps. "Of course it's not a privilege, you dolt."

I glanced up and down the table, wondering what came next. Yusupov's brand of snide insolence would have earned him a sharp slap in the face in my own home, but here it seemed to result in a kind of weird standoff. The boys went back to their meals; the Schmitzes retreated into their secret language of smirks; the supes were silent. I didn't really understand what was going on.

•

At The Big Study we sat on hard wooden benches before a long waist-high shelf that served as a desk, cowering beneath the eagle eye of a proctor who was sometimes a master, usually a supe. The proctor was seated at a high lectern in the center of the room, raised from the floor about four feet and accessed by a small staircase at the back.

In study hall, I read my notes again and again, because I didn't know what else to do. Boys all around me were bent over books and notes spread flat on the shelf, some muttering silently to themselves in an attitude much like prayer. I did the only thing I could think of. I read again.

Every morning, my classes were the same slow-rolling disaster. Each session began with a quiz on what we had been taught the day before—a list of questions followed by blanks for single-word answers. I got some of them right. Some days I got a lot of them right. But never all. On a ten-question quiz, four wrong answers was a flunk. Three wrong was considered a near-flunk. Two wrong was barely respectable. One wrong was all right. None wrong was good. I either flunked all of my quizzes or came away with barely passing grades. Everyone else got either perfect scores or close enough.

My Latin teacher was Beetle, who taught entirely from notes transcribed to a movable chalkboard with much scratching and heavy breathing. He required us to chant back to him whatever he wrote. His method was to have us memorize vast numbers of declensions and conjugations before explaining to us what they meant.

"You've got to know the bones first," he said almost every day. "Then you can put on the meat."

It was like memorizing the exact order and places of pebbles on a beach. Every once in a while, he tossed us a hint of what a verb tense might mean, but that was all done randomly and as an afterthought or casual aside. I did very poorly at these in-class exercises and even worse on the daily quizzes. Not long into the term, I recognized that Beetle was often caustic with any other boy who flunked a daily quiz but never with me, and it wasn't a mercy. If another boy flunked, Beetle singled him out for castigation and humiliation.

"What kind of preposterous poppycock do you call this? Did you even try to learn last night's lesson? What are you doing in study hall, sleeping? I don't want to see another quiz like this from you again, ever."

But never me. When I flunked a quiz, he looked over and around me as if I were not there. He never called on me to recite or answer a question. I seldom knew the answers, anyway, but on those rare occasions when I did and put up my hand with the rest, he acted as if he hadn't seen me.

The only time he spoke to me was when he was collecting our

completed quiz sheets, after we had graded them. When he looked at my paper, with whatever ungodly score I had achieved, he always said, "Ah, the very dapper Mr. Skaggs."

Compton noticed it, too. "He's glad you're flunking out," he told me at lunch. "He hopes you'll do it fast."

I was just beginning to know all of the boys in Dorm Four. The younger boys upstairs in Dorms One and Two were irrelevant. Across the big lobby was Dorm Three, occupied by boys our own age, Third Formers, mainly, and a few Second Formers. I hadn't bothered yet trying to make them out as individuals, but one day, while we waited in the lobby for lunch, a group of Dorm Three boys wandered to our side of the lobby with the intention of picking a fight with Compton.

Compton knew them. He informed us later they were Reid Rensevear, David Colfax, and Reggie Howard. "I went to school with them at Country Day in Far Hills. Davidson went there, too. They live near me. I hate their guts."

The trio approached in a tight pack, all quite different from each other physically. Rensevear was big and muscular. At home I would have taken him for a football player. Colfax was redheaded and puffy. Howard was blonde and wiry.

They were almost perfectly twinned in dress and appearance. All wore their hair in identical brow sweeps. All wore identical pinkish, clear-framed glasses, identical button-down collar shirts and regimental striped ties, identical tweed jackets, gray trousers, and highly polished loafer shoes with little leather bows on top.

I asked Compton later why they dressed so similarly.

"They're regs," he said, shrugging as if he didn't understand my question.

When they got to our side of the lobby, the trio stood a yard or so off from Compton, speaking directly to him as if the rest of us were not present.

"Hey, Compton," one of them said, "where's your flute?"

"It wasn't a flute," the second one said.

"Clarinet," the third one said, and they all giggled.

"Twee!" the first one said.

"Toodle-doo," another said, and they staggered in laughter, pawing at each other's lapels.

Compton turned purple, for which they seemed well prepared. They spread out instantly, fists at the ready, dancing a little for the first punch.

Yusupov and I stepped forward on both sides of Compton, our fists ready, too. We were also joined by Smiley, who, as if giving directions to a stranger who was lost, said matter-of-factly, "I think it would be better if you guys fucked off."

The three of them eyed Smiley up and down scornfully, then Yusupov, then me.

"Compton has friends?" one of them said. "That's a first."

Smiley, holding his sober expression, said quietly, "Friends who will kick your asses."

Tweetie appeared behind us. He said nothing, allowing his sheer bulk to speak. Then a fourth Dorm Three boy appeared behind the three challengers. Something about him registered on my Pontiac radar. He was stocky, with dark hair swept back, and he wore horn-rimmed glasses. He wasn't dressed to match the other three. When he spoke, it was with a smooth southern accent, not like the sharp hillbilly twang I knew from home.

"Do we have a problem?" he asked.

Yusupov seemed especially struck, even alarmed by the boy's accent. "Where are you from?" he demanded.

"From a place where a man introduces himself before he asks questions," the boy said smoothly, stepping around the other three. He didn't have his fists balled, but I could already tell he knew how to use them.

"I am Yusupov," Yusupov said. "And you are?"

"Evers."

"Where are you from?"

"Little Rock."

"What is little rock?"

"Little Rock is a city."

"Where? I've never heard of it."

"Arkansas."

Yusupov stepped back quickly, the color drained from his face. "You are from Arkansas?"

"I am," Evers said, smiling broadly. "Do you know Arkansas?"

"I have heard stories."

The crowd in the lobby suddenly began moving toward the dining room. The three regs turned on their heels and abandoned Evers. Evers looked directly at me, and I nodded. He nodded. We walked to the dining room together.

"You're friends with those guys?" I asked.

"Those three?" he said with a laugh. "I call them the three stooges."

"Why did you take their side then?"

He looked at me, puzzled. "They're in my dorm."

I shook hands with him. "I'm Woodrow Skaggs from Pontiac, Michigan. They call me Pontiac."

"Nice to meet you, Pontiac," he said. "I'm Ashley Evers from Little Rock, Arkansas."

Yusupov walked just ahead, looking back frequently at Evers.

I told Yusupov, "You've got a guy from Arkansas right behind you."

"I am aware," he muttered.

Chapter Three

AFTER LUNCH AND BEFORE ATHLETICS ONE day, I was depressed enough about my grades to need cheering up. I went to look for my money at the post office, but my mailbox was empty. The Tuck Shop normally was closed at that hour, but the big steel door stood open, and voices were arguing within. As soon as I crossed the threshold, Dan Biggs's voice boomed at me: "Your money ain't here yet, Pontiac. It's late this week. Everybody's late. We got issues."

He was standing behind the counter next to the cash register. Rutledge, the bored Sixth Former who said grace at Beetle's table, was standing on the other side of the counter. Rutledge eyed me up and down warily.

"What's his name?" he asked Dan Biggs.

"Ask him."

"Never mind," Rutledge said, turning sharply away from me.

"I'm not broke," I said. "I got plenty saved."

"Maybe you could give this asshole some lessons."

Rutledge stepped back haughtily.

"How dare you?" he said.

Dan Biggs came from behind the counter and stood in front

of him. "How dare me? This is how dare me. I need that fucking money, and I need it yesterday. You said two weeks, you son of a bitch."

"I don't have it," Rutledge said. He stepped away and examined me again. "So," he said to me, "who sends you your money?"

Dan Biggs said, "That's none of your goddamn business."

My father's words about taking shit from people came to me. "The rector's wife," I said.

Dan Biggs shot a finger to his lips. Rutledge saw it.

"The rector's wife?" Rutledge said with an insinuating sneer. "Well, well, well, you must be a very special little fellow indeed to get a stipend from the rector's wife." He turned back to Dan Biggs. "Maybe that's where all your money goes, handing it out to the scholarship boys. One shudders to think what they must do to earn it."

Dan Biggs came forward and grabbed Rutledge's necktie and shirt in a beefy fist.

"You stupid little shit," he said, "I know everything about what you really needed that money for. That poor girl in Rumney is my pretty little great-niece. You don't think I'll use that? You said two weeks. It's been a month. I need that money. Now."

"I don't have it," Rutledge bleated, striving unsuccessfully to back away. "I told you, my aunt is sending it."

Dan Biggs released him. "You better get on your aunt's ass for that money, punk, because if I have to answer to the audit committee, believe me, you're going to answer to the rector and maybe the cops, who also happen to be my relations."

Rutledge brushed his shirt flat and tugged up the knot of his tie.

"The cops are your kin, are they?" he said with his calm quickly restored. "How very proud you must be. How powerful that must make you feel. Perhaps you think that will protect your little racket here, lending other people's money to boys at usurious rates."

Rutledge stepped up confidently and looked Dan Biggs in the eye. "Listen, Dan Biggs, I don't want this to be any worse than it has to be. I am truly sorry about the money being late. Of course I will get it to you as quickly as I can. But you need to understand something. I am a Rutledge. You probably don't even know what that means, but at St. Philip's School, it means that if you ever say one word to damage my reputation or to disparage the Rutledge name, you and all of your inbred, incestuous Down Easter relations will be fired on the spot and will never set foot on these grounds again without being prosecuted."

He walked to the door.

"Keep that in mind," he said. "Keep it very much in mind." He paused long enough to give me a long hard sneer, then wheeled and left.

"Jesus," I said after a suitable pause.

"Forget what you heard," Dan Biggs said. "And I don't charge no rates. Adams asked me to help the shithead bastard out."

"I'm sorry I spoke . . . "

"Yeah, don't talk about the money I give you. I thought I told you that."

"Sorry."

"It's OK. You don't know what lies a guy like that's going to tell somebody to haul his own sorry bacon out of the fire. He's a snake from one end to the other."

"What about what he said about getting you fired?" I asked.

"Getting us all fired. Probably true. He can do it." Dan Biggs returned to his stool behind the counter. "Grape balls on me today," he said, holding out a small brown sack. "Jesus, kid, why the long face? You came in here looking like you was ready to start bawling."

"I got my own worries."

"What the hell about? Goin' to school free, eatin' free, free bed, free pocket money. Free grape balls. I wish I had worries like that."

"Things aren't that good for me," I said.

I slumped onto an empty crate and poured out my heart: the terrible grades, the looming specter of failure, my anguish over disappointing my father. I told Dan Biggs I was thinking of running away.

He said, "I think about doing that most every day."

"But you don't do it."

"No, my old lady would find me." He watched me for a while. "Eat a grape ball," he said.

I popped one in my mouth and began to chew, immediately calmed by the familiar sugary syrup and artificial flavoring.

"Who do you know here?" Dan Biggs asked.

"Johnny Wilson is the only person I know from before I came."

"From the real world."

I laughed.

"This ain't the real world," he said.

"It doesn't feel like it to me."

"I guess it is for them. The Phillies. The rich kids like that shithead Rutledge. They come here from the old families. They leave here, I guess they go home to some place that looks just like this. But that ain't the real world either, not to people like you and me."

We said nothing for a while. I could hear my own chewing.

"How do you know Johnny?" he asked.

His familiar use of Johnny Wilson's first name was faintly jarring.

"He's from where I am," I said. "He was the rector of our church for a while. He and my parents go back a long ways. He got me in here."

"Really?"

"Yeah."

"You should go see him. I got the idea he has an eye out for you. He probably can tell you what to do. And you'll get your money in a couple days. Everybody will. One way or the other."

Two days later, I went back to The Tuck Shop. Dan Biggs was out, but when I looked inside the window of my mailbox, a brown envelope was there with my ten bucks.

●

I took modern literature from Mr. Fell, who was nothing like the rest of the teachers. He sat on top of the table or slouched on one of the deep windowsills, shooting questions at us and cracking jokes about the readings. His class, like the Tuck Shop and Dan Biggs, was a welcome refuge from my grim descent.

In Fell's class, Gellhorn sat directly across from me. Our first reading was Hemingway's *The Sun Also Rises*, which most of the boys in class had already read. I had skimmed the Cliff's Notes version once for an exam at Lincoln Junior High School for which I had received a grade of A-plus-plus.

At first, Gellhorn was on pins and needles, waiting for someone to mention again that he was Hemingway's son. But Mr. Fell must have picked up on this special sensitivity and never allowed it to come to the surface. Later, when Gellhorn was sure he was immune, he opened up. He condemned Hemingway as the worst hack in the entire history of American literature. At several points, boys were just on the verge of objecting that it was outrageous for Gellhorn to speak that way of his own father, but Mr. Fell always cut it short, which only seemed to embolden Gellhorn.

"Tell us, Gellhorn," Mr. Fell asked one day, "why do you harbor such a strong dislike for Jake Barnes?"

Gellhorn had a stiff theatrical way of launching into a rant. After the first few days, the rest of us traded sideways smiles when we saw it coming.

"I am a bit disappointed that a master at a school like St. Philips would even ask such a question," he said, chin up and eyes askance. "Clearly, this Jake Barnes is a drunk, a person of very loose sexual morals, but the even more egregious thing that he is, the thing that forces me to question why you would even ask such a question, Mr. Fell, is the fact that he is an anti-Semite. Is it your intention, Mr. Fell, to inculcate in us an admiration for people who loathe Jews?"

"I have no such intention," Mr. Fell said from his perch on the windowsill, chuckling with his arms folded. "Just shooting the shit."

At the vulgarity, Gellhorn raised one eyebrow and poked at his glasses in dramatic concern.

Mr. Fell turned to Compton, who was gazing out a window.

"You, Compton," he said, "Is Jake Barnes an anti-Semite?"

"Jake who?"

"Jake Barnes, the protagonist of the novel that I assume you are all reading. Gellhorn alleges that he is a man of loose morals and an anti-Semite. Do you agree with him?"

Compton stared back, shrewdly calculating.

"No?"

Mr. Fell turned to me.

"Pontiac, what is your opinion? Jake makes fun of Robert Cohn for being a Jew. But does that necessarily make Hemingway, the author, an anti-Semite?"

"I'm not sure," I said, faltering. "I didn't exactly get that."

"He doesn't get anything," Compton muttered.

Mr. Fell was on the verge of speaking sharply to Compton, so I interrupted: "I couldn't tell if Hemingway was making Jake be like that to expose that Jake is an anti-Semite or if Hemingway is one himself."

"Jake Barnes is Hemingway's hero," Gellhorn said, "his model of *savoir faire*. Why would Hemingway deliberately make him out also to be a Jew-hater if Hemingway weren't one himself?"

Mr. Fell looked to me for a response.

"Gellhorn has a pretty good point there," I said. "It seems if Hemingway thought being an anti-Semite was a bad thing, I don't know . . . " I trailed off.

"It seems the author would have signaled that sentiment in some way," Mr. Fell completed my thought.

"Yes, sir."

"So you and Gellhorn are in agreement."

"Yes, sir."

"Two peas in a pod," Compton said. "Both stupid."

"Two peas in a pod," Gellhorn snapped. "Both can read."

Compton sat up straight and glared across the table at Gellhorn.

"Now, boys," Mr. Fell said. "The point here is less the study of specific works of literature than learning how to engage in spirited debate without caving in each other's skulls."

On the way back to the Lower School for lunch, I crossed paths with Compton on the bridge over the library pond. He asked me if Gellhorn and I were queer for each other, and I asked him why he never learned to read. His face turned purple and his eyes bugged out. He threw down his book bag, grabbed me by the shoulder, and punched for my head. I ducked just enough to make the blow glance off my forehead instead of smashing me in the head. I kicked for his balls, but he pirouetted smoothly out of the way, spun around, and hit me in the ribs with the back of a hand. I snatched his bookbag up off the ground and threatened to toss it off the bridge into the pond. The flame was already dying from his face.

"Fuck you," he said.

"Fuck you," I said.

I tossed him the book bag. We walked the rest of the way together, talking about an upcoming quiz in Latin class.

Sadly, our innocent contretemps had been witnessed by a master walking a distance behind us. The master reported us not for fighting but for use of foul language in a public place. The next morning when the school assembled on the chapel lawn to hear the rector read reports and dole out the demerits from the previous day, I was standing next to Compton.

"Skaggs and Compton," the rector said, "two demerits each, public profanity. You will report to work squad Saturday morning."

I felt Compton's hand clutch my sport coat at the hem.

"You stupid shit," he whispered hoarsely. "Now look what you fucking did."

Barry was standing just behind us. He stepped forward, pushing between us, and Compton released me.

"Compton," he whispered hoarsely, "you just got demerits for public cursing. Going for some more?"

The rector was gazing coolly at us. A shiver ran down my spine. He went back imperturbably to his reports, announcing the other boys who also were assigned to work squad.

The squad was run by Chester Grace, a squat, slightly stooped man probably in his mid-fifties whom we called "The Toad," but only behind his back of course. The exact status of The Toad at the school not only was unclear but also, for some reason, seemed to be off limits as a subject of inquiry. He was unmarried, and he lived in a rather grand house far up the hill from the main campus near the entry gate. He was a privileged and protected person who seemed to lack not only formal rank and title, but any kind of job other than running the work squad. He was rumored to have been the school's varsity hockey coach many years prior and even before that a graduate of St. Philip's. Another rumor said he had attended Yale for five weeks. Another other story about him, and the only one that really made a difference, was that once or twice a year The Toad took a party of his own chosen favorites on expeditions to whorehouses, sometimes in Boston, sometimes in New York or even sometimes in London or Paris. Only boys of the very oldest and most elite lineage were chosen for these adventures. To be selected to go, we were told, was a coveted bragging right good for the rest of your life. A whorehouse trip with The Toad not infrequently was the deciding factor in being admitted later in life to this or that club and even to being accepted as a suitor by certain fathers. All of this Compton and I had already garnered from evening bull sessions in Dorm Four before introducing ourselves to The Toad in person one Saturday morning at the open door of the big barn downhill from the auditorium.

The Toad wore a tweed jacket and khaki trousers stuffed into L.L.Bean boots, the kind that look like someone took a pair of normal boots and dipped them in a tub of melted rubber. He was mild-mannered and greeted us pleasantly, checking our names off a list. In all, there were about a dozen boys from Forms One through Five. Sixth Formers were exempt from work squad.

We were told to grab shovels and rakes from a loose stack just inside the barn door and follow The Toad up the hill toward the power plant, a large round brick building with a rectangular wing protruding from its downhill side. Above a long metal roof, a series of low brick chimneys emitted a steady flow of choking black smoke that tended to blow straight back down against the side of the building and sift through a withered hedgerow. Our mission, The Toad informed us, was to dig up the dead portions of the hedge, pile the plant material on a wagon, and then rake the area smooth.

The function of the work squad, beyond serving as a punishment for demerits, was unclear to me. Wombats did the real work of maintaining the school's facilities. I had even attempted to say hello to some of them when I saw them for the second or third time, but they never returned my gaze. I asked one night in Dorm Four why the wombats wouldn't speak to me.

"They're wombats," Tweetie boomed.

"Why are they called that?" I asked.

"They're wombats."

"Why won't they talk to us?"

"They're wombats."

I was a little uncertain of my own status, wombat-wise. It seemed to me that at least on social terms, I was closer to being a wombat than I was to being one of the other boys. But I did not pursue the matter.

On work squad that day, I saw that most of the hedges around the power plant had already been excavated leaving clean black dirt in the beds, except for a long stretch along a back wall, apparently set aside for us to attack. Compton and I picked up shovels and went to work together on a large plant at hedgerow's far end. The Toad was involved in animated conversation with several other boys about shovels. When Compton and I looked up, we saw some of the other boys chipping away at the ground with their shovels as if trying to spoon up porridge. Rather than planting the point of their shovels into the dirt and pushing down with a foot on the blade's topside, they banged away with them as if they were hammers. One boy was standing off at a distance, trying out different grips, trading his shovel from hand to hand, his head pulled away from it as if it were a snake.

Compton knew how to dig. He lived on a farm in New Jersey. It was a gentleman's farm, of course, but as I learned later his mother made him and his brother do real work. I was thirteen years old and had already dug holes for a living by then. The rest of the boys on work squad that day were hilarious. The Toad spent most of his time trying to teach them to how to dig. To this day, I watch all digging scenes in movies closely, looking for St. Philip's-style diggers.

At one point, Compton and I became aware that The Toad was standing behind us.

"You boys know how to handle a shovel," he said.

"Not really," Compton said quickly. "I'm just copying him."

"Where'd you learn to dig?" The Toad asked me.

"I don't remember," I said. "I just always did. I had a job in an orchard for a couple summers. The farmer had me dig up bad trees."

"He's from Michigan," Compton said.

"You had a job?" The Toad said with something like alarm. "You mean, you were paid?"

"Yes, sir."

"He's from Pontiac," Compton said, leaning on his shovel in an attitude of world-weariness.

"What's Pontiac?" The Toad asked.

"The town he's from. Pontiac. It's in Minnesota."

"Michigan," I said.

"Why is the town called Pontiac?" The Toad asked Compton.

"Ask him."

"Everybody there drives a Pontiac," I said.

"My word," The Toad said. "Minnesota sounds like a very exciting place."

"Thank you," I said.

A shout went up from farther down the hedge where one boy had stabbed another's toe with a shovel, unclear whether or not it was accidental. The Toad hurried off.

"Why did you act like you don't how to dig?" I asked Compton.

"Christ, Skaggs, you're almost bragging what a great digger you are. What the hell do you think that's going to get you?"

I found out what it got me the following Monday after chapel, when the rector solemnly intoned my name at the end of reports: "Skaggs," he said. "Late for dinner. Two demerits. Work squad Saturday."

I had never been a minute late for any meal, but the demerit system did not include appeals.

Compton said, "Told you so."

The next Saturday morning, I was back at the power plant, digging out shrubs again. This time I was alone with The Toad, who was dressed in the same tweed jacket and boots. On the previous Saturday, Compton and I had managed to excavate at least half of the assigned stretch of hedge, but I saw on my return that precious little had been accomplished since. I started back in where we had left off.

"I'm sorry, Skaggs," The Toad said in a surprisingly timid

tone. He looked seriously contrite, almost as if he was afraid of me. "It was me that reported you," he said. "I know you weren't late."

"Well, why did you say it then, sir?" I asked, more baffled than injured.

"Look, Skaggs," he said, "I'm in kind of a jam. I'm supposed to have this hedge out of here by the end of today. They're doing some work on the power plant next week. I needed somebody who could dig. I don't even know how to dig myself. Compton's OK, but you're really good. I just need it finished. If I don't get it done, the wombats will have to do it for me, and that makes me look bad." He stammered, "I just . . . just needed some help."

"Yes, sir," I said.

For the next two hours, I dug harder and faster than I had ever dug in my life. The day was cooler than the previous Saturday, but when it was time to go to lunch, I was bathed in sweat and covered in dirt from head to toe. The hedge was gone.

The Toad shook my hand. "I really owe you one, Skaggs. Someday I'd like to come to Michigan."

"I wish you would, sir."

"Do they really all drive Pontiacs?"

"Every single person."

"I'd love to see that."

I felt the best I had since leaving home.

•

In only one class other than English was I able at least to hold my own—a course called Public Affairs that was taught by an ancient master named Mr. Bueller. He was tiny, made entirely of sinew and bone with clear blue eyes floating behind very thick spectacles. A thin cap of silver hair swept straight back from his brow to his skull as if glued. He spoke softly but clearly with the St. Philip's accent, having been a boy at the school.

Mr. Bueller did not make grand entrances into the classroom like other masters but was always waiting for us at the head of the table, blinking hello like an owl.

Part of our homework was to read the *New York Times* every day, cover to cover. I read the paper faithfully in study hall every night, but I still did poorly on the quizzes. The three regs—Rensevear, Colfax, and Howard—were in the class, as was their fellow Dorm Three resident, Evers of Arkansas.

Another boy in the class of great interest to me was Peter Stickney, who lived in Dorm Four but did not sit at Herr Schmitz's table. Called Stick and known to the boys from New York and New Jersey, Stick was an extreme introvert who almost never ventured out to the radiator bench to take part in our bull sessions. He was the first human being I had ever met who possessed audio earphones, which he plugged into an amplifier and record player stowed beneath his bed. Also under his bed, on his shelf, and stacked in every corner and square inch of his alcove was the largest collection of long-playing 33 1/3 record albums I had ever seen in my life. Stick lay on his bed with his curtain drawn listening to music every spare second of his day. He was tall and thin with wispy blonde hair and pale blue eyes in a long angular face.

The rest of us had learned early on that it was a mistake to draw open his curtain or interrupt him when he was listening to music. If we did, he leapt to his feet, threw the headphones to the bed and confronted us with a tiny, almost undetectable twitch playing at the long boney jaws.

"I cannot talk to you," he said each time. "I am listening to music."

In public affairs one day, we discussed the fact that a presidential election would take place in a few weeks. Mr. Bueller asked us what we thought about the candidates and their chances.

"Nixon is a greaser," Rensevear said.

"But he's our only choice," Colfax said.

"For our kind of people anyway," Howard said.

Evers asked them, "Why wouldn't you like Kennedy? He's a Harvard Yankee. You should love him."

"Harvard hardly," Rensevear said.

"He's the grandson of a Black Irish bootlegger," Colfax said.

"And from what I understand, he's a nigger-lover," Howard said. He added, chortling, "Doesn't stand a ghost of a chance."

Rensevear and Colfax were about to chortle in with him, when Mr. Bueller, pointing a finger at all three, said sternly, "Do not use ethnic pejoratives in my classroom."

"Yes, sir," the three said in unison, smirking to each other.

"What about you, Stickney?" Mr. Bueller asked. "Which one do you think will win the election?"

Stickney had spoken rarely in class. I was curious how he would answer. Staring down at the table and speaking in a robotic monotone, Stickney said, "Mr. Kennedy will win by a very slight margin."

The three regs burst into guffaws.

"He's a mackerel-snapper," Rensevear said.

"I won't warn you again," Mr. Bueller said sharply.

All three exchanged perplexed expressions.

"Oh," Rensevear said with transparent insincerity, "I meant only that Kennedy is a Roman Catholic. So sorry. Slip of the tongue. May I call him a Papist?"

"No."

"Well then, Roman Catholic it shall be. Kennedy would be the first Roman Catholic in history to be elected President of the United States."

"Preposterous," Colfax said.

"Can't happen," Howard sniffed.

Mr. Bueller asked Stickney, "Will Kennedy's Catholic affiliation be a significant factor?"

In the same monotone, Stickney said, "The largest number of people in American history have registered to vote in this election. A substantial number of Protestant Democrats will vote for Nixon because Kennedy is a Catholic. But that number will be almost exactly offset by Catholics who will defect from the Republican fold to vote for Kennedy for the same reason, controlling for the religion issue and rendering it moot."

Mr. Bueller said to Evers, "And what do you think of Kennedy's chances?"

"You know, sir," Evers began in his suave drawl, "although it pains me to say, I think I would have to agree with the three stooges over here . . . "

"Evers," Mr. Bueller said with the finger stabbed toward his face.

"I am so sorry, sir, and I do apologize. I believe that I must agree with my three very amusing classmates here that Nixon would seem to have the lead. I know that he has campaigned in my home state of Arkansas and has pledged to appear in all fifty states, which I think will be very effective. I think he is a very intense competitor."

Rensevear started to make a remark, but Mr. Bueller shot him a warning look.

"Stickney," Mr. Bueller said, "What do you think of Nixon campaigning in all fifty states? Is that a winning strategy?"

"Campaigning in all of the states is wasted effort," Stickney said. "Kennedy is campaigning only in states where the election is close and in states that have substantial numbers of electors in the Electoral College. He will win a scant majority of the popular vote or perhaps even a minority, but he will far surpass Nixon in the Electoral College and thereby capture the office."

"And you, Mr. Skaggs," Mr. Bueller said, "would you share your thoughts with us?"

I tried desperately to think of anything to say, anything I knew. "I know that Kennedy was endorsed by the United Auto Workers," I said.

"Oh, splendid, the united workers!" Rensevear said.

"United Bolsheviks more like it" Colfax said.

"Maybe they'll give him a Pontiac," Howard said, and the three collapsed in happy chortles.

Mr. Bueller looked puzzled. "Why a Pontiac?"

Evers explained, "Skaggs is from a town in Michigan called Pontiac, where they make the cars. The boys in Dorm Four all call him that. These three think that's funny, because they're the three stooges."

Mr. Bueller frowned. "I'm afraid on this occasion I may have to agree with Evers." He turned back to Stickney. "So, Stickney, as Skaggs suggests, do you see labor playing a role?"

"A very substantial role," Stickney said, "because of the recent economic recession."

"What economic recession?" Rensevear demanded abruptly, looking offended.

"America doesn't have a recession," Colfax said, verging on outrage.

"None whatsoever," Howard said, slapping a palm angrily on the smooth green tabletop. "Prosperous as hell."

"Jesus Christ," Evers muttered to himself.

"I believe the confusion here stems from the fact that you three," Mr. Bueller said, nodding toward the three stooges, "probably have not experienced a recession. But in fact, Stickney is quite correct. The nation underwent a rather severe economic recession in 1957 and '58 during President Eisenhower's second term. It hit industry especially hard, and that sort of thing tends to go against the incumbent party, especially among the working classes."

"Working classes," Rensevear sniffed.

"Why don't they do some work?" Colfax asked.

"They need to stop complaining and make more Pontiacs," Howard said.

Evers looked as if he was about to say something to them, but Mr. Bueller nodded no.

"Stickney," Mr. Bueller said, "I am very impressed with your analysis. Tell me, did you come across a particularly good piece in the *Times* or somewhere else that I must have missed?"

"I do not understand, sir," he said, his pale jaws working a little.

"Where did you get all this?"

"From the newspaper, sir. You told us to read it every night. These things were all in the newspaper."

Mr. Bueller looked both amused and pleased. "Yes. Yes, of course, Stickney. Thank you for sharing."

•

A week later in study hall, I was having trouble keeping my eyes in my books, gazing sideways under my shoulder so the proctor in the tower wouldn't catch me. Surrounding me on every side were the bent heads of boys bobbing like lizards on green leaves. Some silently mouthed. Others glowered fiercely. Some looked down unblinking with faces of stone. It was almost as if I could hear the words clicking up out of the books like ore heaped on conveyor belts, in through the eyes to huge bins where all of it would be refined, forged, chopped, pressed, and bolted together on an assembly line of intelligence.

I didn't see how it was possible, but Compton was right. I, who had always been the top-grade-getter without even trying back home, was now the fool, the moron, the flunk-out. Davidson knew all about me. So did they all.

But that was it, wasn't it? The whole thing. The light was beginning to dawn. These were superior people. Superiority was the product churned out like widgets at St. Philip's Motors. All of these bent heads around me in study hall every evening were the sons of superior people. They weren't faking it. It wasn't just arrogance. They were smarter than me. I had foolishly believed I was smart only because I had measured myself against kids at Lincoln Junior High School in Pontiac, Michigan, a place so inferior in every regard that these people could not even say the name of the city without a smug chuckle. If people here thought even the name of my town was a joke, then they thought everything else about me was laughable. And maybe they were right. Certainly, the evidence on the grade postings in the hated Aldredge Hall every Friday argued in their favor.

I was puzzled, however, by a startling anomaly. The haughtiest and most superior of all the boys in Dorm Four was Gellhorn, and

123

yet his name was often near my own at the bottom of the list. Other boys' names visited the bottom but never stayed for long. Gellhorn never fell quite as low as me, but he was always in my neighborhood. I speculated maybe he was so arrogant he couldn't be bothered with grades.

I could be bothered. Over the next few days, I made up my mind that I needed to get out of this place and return home of my own volition before getting kicked out and sent home in even worse ignominy. I used the pay phone in a booth behind the staircase in the first-floor lobby of the Lower School to call the train depot and the bus company to figure out how much it would cost me to escape. I had to be careful with the calls, because the phone booth was right next to the door to Beetle's apartment, and he had an uncanny way of poking his red bulbous nose out through the door whenever anyone made a call. He never failed to ask later to whom the call had been placed. When he asked me, I always said, "My mother."

My calls to the bus and train stations in Rumney revealed that the money Dan Biggs had scored for me from the rector's wife, a fattening wad in my seaman's chest, would soon be more than enough. It was exciting to think that, in just a few more weeks, I would have enough to pay for a breakout from this prison of humiliation and defeat. But I couldn't simply strike out on my own without first preparing my parents. I composed a letter to my father, which I now can remember almost word for word:

Dear Pa.
Hi how are you? This is Woodrow. I am doing pretty bad.
I am the dumbest kid here. I think they are going to throw me out. I keep trying really hard Pa honest. I just keep

staying at the bottom of everybody. These are all rich people. They are really smart. I can't keep up. The only thing I can do that they like here is work on the yard crew. I guess they think I can handle a shovel pretty good. I know Ma will take it bad if I get kicked out in front of all these rich people. Plus Mr. Wilson is here. He will tell everybody back in the diocese I got kicked out, which will make Ma embarrassed. But I think I better get out Pa while the getting is good. I have the money. Is it OK if I come home now?

Sincerely your boy,
Woodrow Skaggs

A few days after I had slipped the letter into the mailbox, a letter arrived for me. On the crinkled face of the small envelope, I recognized my father's crabbed hand. I put the letter under my pillow where I kept my flashlight. After lights out, I made a tent of my blankets and read:

Dear Wooodrow. It's Pa. I am very sorry to tell you your brother David has got his self in real bad trouble. Him and another boy stole a truck and wrecked it. The judge sent the both of them to the juvenile home. They deserved it. I am about heart broke. I hope you don't get into no trouble at that school. I am real proud of you boy. Love. Your father.

So he had not yet received my letter.

•

A group of us were sitting in the lobby outside the dining room on a Saturday after lunch. Mr. Fell came sauntering over with his customary line of easy banter, then leaned to my ear and said softly, "Your mother is here."

My heart stopped. The possibility of my mother's physical presence in this place had never occurred to me. He might as well have told me Abraham Lincoln was here.

"My mother?" I gasped.

"I believe so, unless she's an imposter. But she seems authentic."

"Where?"

"In the common room."

I flew down the steps, popping a hand on and off the rail, skipping steps, light-headed. Somewhere inside, I feared something terrible might have happened to David for her to be here in the flesh in this strange place a million miles from Pontiac. But another more powerful feeling, one I did not recognize in myself, pushed away that fear—a sensation of breaking the surface and gulping for air.

She was there in the very center of the vast empty common room, sitting stiff-spined in her faded cotton coat, fingering the handles of a battered black purse, staring absently out a window to the street. In her lap was a clumsy bundle wrapped in brown paper and twine. A small carpetbag was at her feet. She turned toward me just as I burst into the room, alarm dawning suddenly on her face as she watched me bound toward her. I threw my arms around her neck and buried my head in her shoulder with tears flowing down my cheeks. She pushed me back and examined me with sharpened eyes, as if the tears were blood.

"What kind of trouble are you in, Woodrow?"

"No, I'm just happy, Ma. Why are you here? I'm so happy to see you. How did you get here? Is anything wrong?"

She rose from her chair and stepped away from me.

"There is nothing wrong, Woodrow. I came to see you. I came on a train from Detroit. Two trains. Then I came out here in a taxicab. It was very expensive. They told me you have Saturday afternoons off."

"Yes."

"Do you have time to show me this place?"

"Yes. Of course." I wiped away the tears with a sleeve. "Wow. I was so surprised. I guess I just started crying, because . . . "

She turned away from me.

"I would like to see your school," she said. "Here," handing me her brown bundle. "This is a quilt I made for you from your father's old tore-up hunting coats. It says in the encyclopedia it gets colder here than home."

"Thank you."

"Run it back up to your room."

"Yes, ma'am."

I raced upstairs with the bundle, dropped it on my bed and snatched up my light coat. She was waiting for me by the front door, shrewdly eyeing the traffic of boys in and out. I took her bag, and we walked from the Lower School up the road to the New Chapel, then across the street and up the hill to the school building. We went in, and I showed her an empty classroom.

"You all sit at one table?" she asked.

"Yes."

"How many of you?"

"Twelve. Fourteen. It depends."

"Why so few?"

"I don't know. I don't know anything about this place, Ma. I just do what they tell me."

She put a gloved hand in the air like a traffic cop. "What is the town called again?"

"Here? It's Rumney."

"Do you have time to go into Rumney with me?"

"Yes."

"The cab was very expensive. Over two dollars just to get out here from the train station."

"There's a bus we can take. It's thirty-five cents."

"One way?"

"I think round trip."

"All right."

On the bus, I said, "Pa wrote to me about David."

"That's good, Woodrow. So you know."

"Is he OK?"

She shrugged. That was our only conversation during the twenty-minute ride.

In town, she asked me if there was a store that sold the kind of clothes worn by the boys "at that school." I said there was. I had accompanied Gellhorn to it one Saturday afternoon when we were going into town to the Granite State candy shop.

The clothing store was an airless box, unlike any store I had ever visited in Pontiac or Detroit. My mother stood just inside the door, glaring inward until a young woman with big dark eyes called from behind the counter at the back to ask if we needed help.

My mother said yes and stood her ground, unsmiling, frozen to the spot just inside the door. The young woman did not move for a long moment, then finally dipped her head in amused surrender and came out from behind the counter.

"What would you like to see?"

"School clothes for this boy."

She looked me up and down, decidedly unimpressed. "Is he a new student at Rumney High?"

"No," my mother said.

"St. Philip's," I interjected quickly.

"Oh, really?" the saleswoman said, surprised. "Well, of course, we cater to a number of the young gentlemen at St. Philip's. Do you know Mr. Barry?"

"He needs three wool sport coats or two sport coats and a blazer," my mother said brusquely.

On racks along both sidewalls were tweed sport coats and blue blazers that looked exactly like what the boys and the masters wore. My mother fingered the fabric of a couple of them with one hand, turning up lapels and collars, searching intently.

"What are you looking for?" the saleswoman asked.

"Price tags."

"We don't use those," the woman said. "I have a list behind the counter. Did you want to know the price of a particular garment?"

"This one," my mother said, wrenching it up by the lapel.

The woman searched behind the counter for a very long while. When she finally produced the list and read off the price of the coat, my mother stared at her aghast as if there were some kind of misunderstanding. The woman met her gaze coolly.

"Do you . . . do you have any cheaper?"

The woman said nothing. She returned the list to the counter, then beckoned us with a small nod to a sofa and chair semi-hidden at the back of the shop. She motioned for us to sit down.

"You know," she said, "they used to make all these clothes in the mill towns around here when my parents were young. They worked in the mills. Everybody did. Where are you folks from?"

"Pontiac," I said.

"Pontiac?" the woman said brightly. "Is that where they make the Pontiacs?"

"Yes," I said eagerly.

"Did you ever see where they make them?"

"Yes, sure, all the time" I said. "I rode by it on my school bus."

"Oh, wow," the saleswoman said. "Now most of the mills here are shut down. They make the clothes down south. But people here still kind of know about mill products because they grew up with that."

"People in Pontiac are like that with Pontiacs," I said.

My mother looked at me quizzically. I ignored her.

"My dad owns this store," the young woman said. "His brother kind of has a business he does out of his house, and usually it's just local folks he caters to. It's nothing wrong with it. It's what we call seconds and overstock. It's just up the hill from here.

"These prices," the young woman said, nodding around the shop, "nobody in town pays prices like these for clothes. These are just for St. Philip's boys and some of the teachers out there and some of the students at Dartmouth, University of New Hampshire, St. Anselm, places like that. Rich people. But my uncle, he sells very high-quality clothes, just as well-made as these but for way less money. They have the labels tore out is all. I could call him up, and you could go up there to his house and see."

On the way out of the shop and in the very corner of my eye, I caught a fleeting glimpse of my mother's hand reaching out to press the young woman's arm. I was instantly envious.

The house was in a part of Rumney I had never visited. The homes were small, about the size of our house in Little Ottawa, but made of brick and much older than the houses at home, somehow more rooted and assured. The street was narrow and twisty on a steep slope, with curbs made of long granite blocks instead of poured concrete.

A tall, rakishly handsome man with thick white hair and the air of a rascal was waiting for us in the doorway with a yellow measuring tape slung around his shoulders like a priest's stole. His brass-framed spectacles were pushed up high on his forehead so that his bangs spilled over the frames in wavelets. He led us through a living room and small kitchen to a large closed-in porch at the back. Big windows looked out onto a barren back yard and forlorn garage. A long wooden table at the center of the room was piled with clothing and rolls of fabric. Cardboard boxes, rush baskets, and wooden milk crates were stacked along the walls overflowing with fabric and various garments. At the far end was a rugged bench, homemade, like what I was used to seeing in garage workshops at home, carrying several sewing machines.

The tailor sat on a wheeled stool and bade my mother sit in the only chair. He asked her what she was looking for. After she told him, he said, "I'll tell you what, young lady, about the quickest way we can cut to the chase and get 'er done here is for you to give me a pretty good idea how much money you got to spend."

She told him. He rubbed his chin thoughtfully. "Well, dear one, I can tell you this much right now, it ain't going to be no three sport coats and a blazer and pants out of that much. It's not but one sport coat and one blazer at the most, three pair of pants, some shirts and ties and a decent pair of shoes, which he needs bad." He gazed at my feet quizzically. "What are those things made out of? You go around Rumney much in the wintertime with your feet in shoes like that, you'll wind up getting your toes chopped off for frostbite.

You'll be walking around the rest of your life like a damn penguin." He got up, did a little wobbly penguin walk back and forth in front of my mother. She smiled, which made me angry.

"I did not buy those for him," she said softly. "He did."

"Well, young lady," he said, "you didn't really need to tell me that part." He winked at me. "Them shoes got boy wrote all over 'em. But not a St. Philip's boy, I'd say."

"I want clothes for him just like what they wear out there at that school."

"My niece told me that on the phone, and that's just exactly what we're going to do for you, dear one."

He grinned at my mother in a way that seemed over-friendly to me. I expected her to douse him with her customary bucket of ice water, the one I was accustomed to receiving, but she was oddly passive. I wished my father was there to punch him in the nose.

"Of course," he said, "anything we put on the boy, my sister and me will have to cut on it quite a bit, because he's a skinny kid and tall, a little harder to fit than most."

"Does that cost extra?" she asked.

"Darling, we're going to stay inside your budget."

My mother smiled at him. I was ready to punch him myself.

"What you told me about your money," he said, "that is your real budget, ain't it?"

"To the penny."

"To the penny it shall be, then, sweetheart."

I looked sharply at her, but she turned away. I glowered at the tailor. He grinned.

"Let's get to work here," he said. "Gonna take this nice boy of yours and turn him into a grade-A St. Philip's snot-nose."

My mother's face softened under a girlish blush.

"I'm ready," she said.

I gave up. For the next hour, they pushed me all over the porch, the two of them smothering me with thick wool and scratchy tweed, strangling me with measuring tapes, holding shirts against my chest, cinching pants up on me by both ends of the waistline until I was almost cut in half.

As they worked, a most amazing transformation took place in my mother. The more they threw me around between them like a rag doll, the more she smiled, but not at me, at him, as if I was not even there. Finally, after the tailor made some offhanded comment about the awkward length of my arms, she did something I had never before witnessed in all my life. A long, deep thrilling laughter spilled from her lips in a waterfall of golden notes, and her eyes sparkled like Christmas tree lights. I looked at her and saw someone I had never seen before—a beautiful girl in a small town in Georgia. She caught me gazing and willed herself instantly into a pillar of salt. In twenty minutes, we were out the door with a promise of delivery at the school in two weeks. My mother and I trudged downhill, back to the town's small commercial center, me stumbling a foot or so behind, deeply disconcerted.

"Where are you staying?" I asked.

"I'm not," she said, never slackening her pace. "I have to catch the train to Boston at eight. Then I catch a train to Detroit at 1:00 AM I can take the Woodward Avenue bus out from Detroit. Mrs. Elkind is going to pick me up in Pontiac. Can you eat supper with me?"

The request was jarring, utterly unexpected. I had to think. She said, "Not if it will get you in trouble."

"I can call Mr. Fell and tell him I'm with my mother. But the bus stops going out to the school at 6:00 PM."

"I will give you money for the cab," she said. "Where can we eat?"

I suggested the dime store lunch counter, but she saw a small restaurant on the square with a menu posted in the front window. She studied it closely.

"We'll eat here," she said.

I knew the place. Boys from the school came here with their parents. I had never been inside, but I assumed it was expensive.

"Are you sure?"

"I have something to say to you," she said. She pushed open the door, held it with her foot, and nodded for me to step in ahead of her.

It was the smallest restaurant I had ever seen. Eight tables were draped in white linen glowing beneath soft chandeliers like moonlit snow. The tables sparkled with my mother's favorite and most feared objects in all the world, gleaming silver, crystal, and fine china. A stooped balding man in a black suit moped forward like a funeral director and asked my mother in what name we had made our reservation. She explained that we had none, causing his eyebrows to become permanently lodged above his ears. At two or three tables, people sat whispering as if conversing with the departed. The man examined his watch so carefully I thought he might be timing an egg. Then with a quick and nervous nod, he agreed that we could stay and showed us to a small table at the back by the kitchen door.

"Order what you want, Woodrow," she told me. "Don't mind the prices."

I scanned the menu, which was utterly horrifying, and found what I thought was the cheapest thing—a turkey club sandwich. The menu was still in my hand when my mother ordered a salad and soup. I looked quickly and calculated that she had underbid me by fifty cents.

We waited in silence with our hands folded in our laps until a heavy-set woman brought my mother's soup and my sandwich. My mother lifted her soupspoon, sipped, and looked skyward, skeptically.

I said, "What did you want to talk to me about?"

She put the spoon down and sank back in her chair. She looked into a shadow and spoke.

"Your brother and another boy stole Tom Quinn's truck and wrecked it."

"The plumber?"

"Do you know another Tom Quinn, Woodrow? The truck caught fire. It blew up."

"Was anybody hurt?"

"No."

"Did it burn up his tools?"

"It burned up his whole truck, Woodrow, so I guess it burned up his tools."

"Do we have to pay for that?"

"Tom Quinn has been extremely good to us. He cares about David. He has business insurance, and we think that's going to cover it."

"And David is in juvie. Pa told me."

The story of the juvenile home was difficult for her to convey. It was her ultimate unspoken nightmare—a son phoning twice a day from the jaws of hell. She visited him often, riding the bus into Pontiac and walking a long distance. As she told me about it, her voice began to shake. I didn't press for details, but I did ask who the other kid was.

"Some hood," she said bitterly. "They were drunk."

"So he's guilty."

"Of course he's guilty, Woodrow. But that don't mean he should rot in juvie forever."

"Are you trying to get him out?"

"No. Not now."

"Why?"

"It's done, Woodrow. It's said and done. He's got to pay his price. We ain't going to be the ones to whine about it. He's gonna pay his price and get out and we'll hope he learned his lesson. We don't have lawyer money."

"But you bought me . . . "

She looked keenly into my face. "I bought you what?"

"All those new clothes."

"So why didn't I use that money to get David out is what you're asking me? Well, that's a howdy-do, Woodrow, if I do say so. For your information, it's money I been saving up for years. And I still didn't have but half what that lawyer said it would cost to try and get David out, and even then the lawyer said it wouldn't work and I'd just be throwing good money after bad."

Her voice was rising. I looked around nervously.

"Don't go accusing me, Woodrow," she continued.

"Ma, I never accused you . . . "

"You accused me like I don't care nothing about David. After I come all this way and done for you."

"Ma."

"Just shut up and finish your meal."

We were quiet for a long while. She finished her soup and addressed the salad. I had finished my sandwich long before.

"Is that what you came here for?" I asked. "To tell me about David?"

"You already knew about David, Woodrow. You said your

father told you. Now why would I come all this way just for that?"

"So you came here to buy me the clothes?"

"No, but you could say thank you."

"Thank you, Mother. It's going to make a big difference. Especially the shoes."

"I would think so. You won't be walking around amongst all those rich kids dressed like a Woodward Avenue pimp."

"So why did you come?"

She put down her fork.

"You wrote to your father you wanted to come home."

I made no reply, but my heart flew up. It didn't make sense, her buying me the clothes if I was to leave with her, but sheer hope pushed aside logic.

"Lucky I found your letter before he did," she said. She pulled the letter from her purse, crumpled and stained. "He never got to it. Do you remember what you said in it?"

"Yes, ma'am."

"I got it right here." She smoothed it out on the table with the butt of her palm. "I been reading it the whole way here. Oh, poor little Woodrow, he's got it so bad here at the rich people school. Pity, pity, poor little Woodrow."

"Ma."

"He's got it so bad he's just gotta come home right now. Wrote his pa, not his ma, 'cause he knows right away what his ma would say to him."

"Please, ma."

"You told your pa you might flunk out and get kicked out and embarrass everybody, and Johnny Wilson gonna come back to the diocese and tell everybody what white trash those Skaggses are 'cause their boy flunked out."

"I didn't say that."

"Yes. You did. That's exactly what you said. Here. You want to read it?" She shook the letter at me.

"No."

She leaned forward across the table with a hard jaw and eyes like rocks.

"Don't you never do a stupid thing like this ever again in your whole life."

The blood drained from my head. "Like what?"

"Like write a goddamn letter like that to your father. Don't you never say you're going to fail out and come back home a deadbeat."

I was suddenly dizzy.

"He understands . . . " I stammered.

"You're the one don't understand a goddamn thing," she said. "Your father is sick to his guts just thinking about poor little David, pretty as a damn girl, in there in the juvie fightin' off the queers. All's that keeps your poor daddy going is thinking how proud he is, ready to bust his goddamn buttons thinking about you going to your goddamn New Hampshire Episcopal school so he can tell himself we're up there with the rich people."

"Mother," I stammered, fighting tears.

"Sweet Jesus, Woodrow, you gonna start bawling again? Y'ain't been here two months, they already turned you half-queer."

Death would have filled my mouth with honey.

She wiped her lips primly and sat up stiff in her chair. "Woodrow, I know you think your father is Dan'l Boone himself, the great hunter from Quitman County, but he's not. He's not a strong man. He's a soft man. Almost a sissy . . . "

"Ma!" I blurted. Heads turned toward us from other tables. "Please don't talk like that."

She shook her head. More quietly, she said, "I don't mean he's queer for God's sake, Woodrow. I mean he's soft inside. He is what you call a romantic. He has these ideas, and the biggest idea he's got is you going to this goddamn Episcopal school Johnny Wilson got you into."

"It's hard," I whispered, staring down at the shards of bread on my plate. "I'm stupid here."

"Look at me, Woodrow Skaggs. You look me right in the eye right now. You are the smartest boy I ever saw. You are smarter than most people. If you are failing, it's because you are a lazy-ass who feels sorry for himself. These are just rich people. They ain't geniuses. You got to get that idea right out of your head. They may think they're geniuses, but they ain't. It's just how rich people think about theirselves. They've got ways of talking and ways of holding their nose up in the air that makes them think they're so goddamn much smarter than everybody else, but they ain't. Not one bit.

"Now you listen to me, Woodrow Skaggs, there's nobody smarter than you at that goddamn school. Even if they might be better than you at taking tests and getting good grades, that's just because they've got some trick to it. It's your job to figure out what the trick is.

"You will not fail out of this school and break your father's goddamn heart and just about strike him down dead. You will get in a taxicab with the money I give you and go back out there and figure out a way."

She stared at me for a long while.

"Woodrow," she said softly, gathering herself.

"Yes, ma'am."

"Honey."

"Yes, ma'am."

"If you do fail out, I know you said in your letter they think you're a good hand with a shovel. Is there any chance they might give you a job so you could stay there for a while? Just not tell Pa what happened until he's ready? Until we know how it comes out with David?"

I thought about it very briefly. She intended for me to become a wombat.

"I don't know, mother," I said. "They might not like it."

"Who wouldn't like it?"

"The school."

She eyed me closely.

"When you've been working on these crews, have you not gotten to know any of the people you're working with? It seems to me like you'd be more friends with the working people than with all these rich kids."

"No. It's separated. We don't work together. It's different crews. We don't hang out with them. There's kind of a line."

Her eyes focused tighter. "A line. A line between the rich kids and the people who work there. And which side of that line are you on, Woodrow Skaggs?"

I knew this feeling too well. I had not heard the rattle yet, but the fangs would appear.

"Which side?" she asked again.

"No side. I just try not to draw attention to myself. I told you, I'm not doing very well. I do what everybody else does. I keep my head down."

"So you're on their side. The rich kids. Like them. Too good to get to know the regular people."

"No, Ma, it's not like that. I'm a student here. I just do what the other students do."

"Sure you do. That's how you get up above your raising. Well, Woodrow, I always thought you had it in you. It's just now coming out."

"I don't even know what you mean, Ma. I'm trying to get along and not get kicked out like you said."

"But you know, Woodrow, I'm just thinking about all this money like you said to come here to see you and the money for the clothes and the restaurant and the taxicab and all. It seems a shame to waste it all for nothing. So if you do get kicked out, maybe you could make some of that money back before you come home."

"How?"

"Get the school to hire you on."

"I can ask."

"Good. Can't do no harm."

On the sidewalk in front of the restaurant, my mother asked me where cabs were to be found, and I told her. She gave me money for the fare. She turned to go the other way, to the train station, but I said I had time to carry her carpetbag, and she shrugged consent. It was a six-block walk. Midway, she reached down with a gloved hand and took my hand.

"You go to Johnny Wilson," she said. "He'll know what to do."

Outside the station, she took off her gloves, held my face in her hands and kissed me softly on the forehead. Her tears stung my cheek like stitches.

•

I asked to see Johnny Wilson in his office. I had to wait two days and then go on an afternoon after rowing. The teachers' offices were on the top floor of the school building on a long narrow hallway that made a right turn off the far end of the main corridor of classrooms. His was almost at the end.

He was a small, elegant man, always dressed in a black suit and brilliant white clerical collar, soft-spoken, with every trace of Detroit drained from his voice. I suppose that must have happened at Cranbrook during his years as a ward of the cathedral. I sat in a St. Philip's chair in front of his desk. On a credenza behind him was a framed photograph of St. Paul Episcopal Cathedral in Detroit next to what I thought might be a signed photograph of the great Detroit Red Wings hockey player, Gordie Howe. He saw me looking at it, reached back, and handed it to me.

"Mr. Hockey," he said.

"I thought so."

The penned inscription read, "To Johnny Wilson, the greatest father a guy could have."

"Wow. How did he know you?"

"Knows me. We talk. Long story. Minister stuff."

"Wow."

"What's up, Woodrow? How's your dad?"

"OK, I guess."

"I heard all about David. I am so sorry."

"Yes, sir."

"Your mother was here."

"Yeah. Yes, sir. How did you know? Did you see her?"

"No, not while she was at the school, I am sorry to say. She called me from South Station on her way home. She wanted to talk about your shitty grades."

"What did you say?"

"I told her they were shitty. I said you'd get kicked out at the end of the year if they weren't a lot better. But I said you could do it."

"How?"

He folded his hands before him and looked deeply into my eyes. I remembered in that moment that Johnny Wilson never became impatient, only more intense. He rose and looked out the window.

"Do you know why you're here?"

"No. And I don't know why you're here, either."

He laughed, sat down behind the desk again and gave me the thumbnail version. It had something to do with a change in admissions policies at the Ivy League colleges and universities. He mentioned Sputnik, the Russian satellite that beat us into space. I didn't get that at all. He said American universities were trying to recruit smarter kids, not just rich kids and kids from old families. I had a bit of trouble following that part as well.

A few years ago, he said, St. Philip's decided that, if it was going to keep the Ivy League happy, it would have to swallow hard and do what it had never done before—admit some scholarship boys from lower-class backgrounds. The school didn't know any such boys, nor did it know anyone who knew such boys. The most democratic institution with which the school had any connection was the Episcopal Church.

"They brought me here," he said, "because I was the most democratic Episcopalian they knew. I guess because I'm a Negro. I had already met the rector at some church functions. They wanted me to help them find worthy democratic boys."

"They thought you were democratic, because you're a Negro."

"Exactly."

"Are you going to bring Negro boys here?"

"That is my intention, but I'm having to work my way up to it."

"So that's why I'm here? I'm like a substitute Negro?"

"I wouldn't try to live up to the Negro part, Woodrow, but, yes, you are what I might call an early installment."

"But I'm flunking out. How is that for you?"

"Not good. Not good at all." He paused a moment, then said, "Look at me."

I did.

"Woodrow, you are not stupid. You're smart."

I made a sullen shrug, looked away and asked the wall, "Then what's my problem?"

He shrugged. "I don't know. I keep up with a lot of research about this stuff. It's interesting. We could find out. We could pack you off to some kind of clinic and get you examined. There are boys here who have been put through all of that. But I'm going to share a little Detroit secret with you here, Woodrow, just between the two of us."

"What?"

"It all comes out in the same place. No matter what you call it or how you dress it up, the answer is always the same."

"What?"

He leaned in toward me, looking me right in the eye. "Try harder."

"Johnny . . . " I blurted.

"Mr. Wilson . . . "

"Mr. Wilson, I do try. I try really hard."

"I believe you. That's not what I said."

"Then what did you say?"

"Try. Harder. Woodrow, these kids have a word for studying hard. What do they call it?"

"Grinding."

"Right. They're all grinds. So you have to be the super grind.

There is no trick. There is no magic way you can make it easy on yourself. It's all just very hard work and very uphill from here, for a long time."

I said, "But I don't know how."

"I realize that, Woodrow. But I do. I was in your position for a long time in life. I can tell you how it's done. When you're way behind and everybody else is up ahead of you, there's only one way to catch up, and it's never easy. You have to park your butt in front of a book every single second you can scrounge in the day. Don't go the Saturday movie. Don't do anything fun. Fun will kill you. Never relax. Lock yourself up in an empty classroom. Grind all afternoon 'til dinner. Grind. All the boys say they grind. They use the word. But I don't mean like them. You have to do it way harder. Read harder. Read again. Read another time. Test yourself. See if you can remember. See if you can explain it back to yourself. Write it on the blackboard, turn your back and see if you can call it back. Beat it into your head. Don't stop until you can spit it back like a machine gun."

He got up, walked from behind his desk, gazed out his window, then sat back down.

"You know I love your mother," he said.

"Sure."

"No, I mean from when we were younger and your dad brought her down to the cathedral. God, she was pretty. She still is pretty." He turned quickly toward me. "I don't mean it like that."

"I know you don't, sir." I was shocked that a black man thought he had to explain to me that he was not romantically attracted to my mother.

"She's pretty. Smart. Tough as nails. Hates the church. You do know that?"

"Yes, sir."

"I loved her right away. Not like that. I mean, I just liked her so much. Thought she was so cool for a white woman."

"My mother?"

His laugh reminded me of the one I had heard from my mother on the tailor's porch.

"Yes, Woodrow," he said. "Even mothers can be cool. A few of them."

"Was your mother cool?"

His face went away for a split-second.

"Oh, I don't know. I never met my parents."

I cringed. "Sorry," I said.

"It's OK." He smiled at me. "Did you ever hear her say goddamn?"

"A lot."

He laughed long and hard, a gorgeous rolling laugh like a song. "Oh, I bet that's true. I can just about hear her now. Woodrow, my man, she's right. She was telling you the God's truth. You're smart. You can make it here. You should make it. You don't want to let your family down, but more than that, you don't want to let yourself down. But you're only going to make it one way. You've got to become a goddamn super-grind."

He paused, looked me up and down and said, "She's tough, isn't she? I don't know where they make women like that."

"Pontiac, I guess."

He laughed again. "Yes," he said. "They made me in Detroit, so I understand."

I rose to leave and went to the door, but he put out a hand for me to pause. I stood waiting with the door half open, one hand on the knob.

"Woodrow, there's something you need to know, and I should

tell you now. You're not going home for Christmas. Your mother said she spent too much money coming here, and I guess she bought you a bunch of clothes."

"Yes, sir." My mouth went dry.

"So your parents can't afford to get you all the way back to Pontiac so soon just for the holiday."

"Just for," I repeated. "Is that the only reason?"

He took a while to answer. "No. She doesn't want you coming home a failure. She thinks it will be too much for your dad, especially if David is still in the juvie."

The full impact took a moment. "What do I do, then? Just sit on my bunk in Dorm Four for two weeks?"

He laughed. "It's more like three weeks. She asked me to let you stay with me. We'll have a great time, I promise."

"OK."

"Woodrow."

"What?"

"You can't take time feeling sorry for yourself. You know why?"

"No."

"It will get in the way of grinding."

•

At dinner that night, Yusupov gave Adams a grand histrionic account of the murder of Grigori Yefimovich Rasputin, the holy man who befriended the family of Czar Nicholas II, last emperor of Russia. According to Yusupov, the plot to kill the mad monk was led by his great-uncle, Prince Felix Yusupov."

"I find this a bit fanciful," Herr Schmitz said.

"I believe it is a true story," Barry said.

Yusupov rolled over them: "My great uncle kept feeding the son of a bitch cyanide ... "

"Watch your language," Adams muttered, though he was completely rapt.

"Yes, sorry, and Rasputin was licking his chops, asking for more, so that's when my great uncle went looking for a gun to shoot the bastard."

"Watch your language."

"Yes, sorry."

Frau Schmitz seemed particularly taken with the story.

"So, Yusupov," she said, "You yourself are titled?"

He paused and gave her a long careful look.

"No one is titled in this country, Dear Lady, as I am sure you know."

She tossed her head and gave her husband a sly glance.

"Yes, I am aware. I just wondered if you would have a title if you were still in Europe."

"Do you consider Russia to be Europe?"

"Of course."

"I am not in Europe, so I have no title."

Herr Schmitz snickered. "I think what Frau Schmitz asks is a simple enough question. If there had been no revolution, if you were still in old Russia today, would you be titled?"

"It is perhaps simple for you, Herr Schmitz," he said. "For me, the question of what the world would be without the revolution is over my head."

The Schmitzes tilted their heads toward each other and winced.

She said, "Then should I take your answer to mean that you are not titled?"

"By all means," Yusupov said with a diffident shrug.

"Did your family get here with money?" Herr Schmitz asked him.

Adams dropped his head sharply and scowled at his plate.

"Oh, my God," Yusupov said. "Mountains of money. Have you ever seen the Disney character, Scrooge McDuck? If you have read those comic books, Herr Schmitz, then you know that Scrooge McDuck has a castle crammed to the rafters with gold and silver and precious jewels. Well, that character was actually fashioned on my other great uncle, Skupets McUtka. As a child, we all went sledding on the mountains of money in the family vault at McUtka Castle in Mount Kisco. There was a string quartet, and . . . "

Adams lifted a hand a few inches off the table and made a cutting motion. "That's enough," he said.

"Oh, no, not at all, Adams," Herr Schmitz said, chuckling. "Frau Schmitz and I enjoy these wonderful Russian narrations. We know Mount Kisco, where Yusupov's relation . . . ?"

"Skupets McUtka."

"Yes, where the grand Skupets McUtka resides. We have gone to Kisco for two summers now."

"Aha," Yusupov said smoothly, "you go to Kisco?"

"Oh, yes," she said. "We love it. We rent a cabin there. Many wonderful Russian restaurants in Kisco."

"Yes," Yusupov said. "There are a great many wonderful Russians in Kisco."

"Your people tell such colorful stories."

Yusupov paused, gazing above the crown of her head a little absently.

"My people?"

"The White Russians," she said. "That's whom one sees in

149

upstate New York, is it not? That's what you are. A White Russian. Am I incorrect?"

"Not at all. My family left in the first wave, usually called the White Movement. We were anti-Bolshevik, naturally. We came here via Turkey."

"You were all monarchists, were you not?" Frau Schmitz said.

"My family, yes."

"Then all of you are dukes and duchesses, I think," she said.

"Well," Herr Schmitz corrected her, "not young Yusupov here. As he tells it, I believe he must be a prince, although he's rather shy about it."

"There's nothing to be shy about in being a prince," she snorted. "Every maître d' in Kisco is a prince when he gets his snout in the vodka."

They both laughed heartily.

"Exactly," Yusupov said, laughing with them. "And I suppose you know the cure for that."

Herr Schmitz said, "History would tell us that the cure for princes is Bolshevism."

"But a White Russian in Kisco," Yusupov said, "would tell you that the cure for Bolshevism is vodka."

The three of them laughed while Adams continued to scowl.

Herr Schmitz said to Adams, "You are the fifth of your name, I believe. I assume this means you are a direct descendant of John Adams, the great founding father of the United States and one of the authors of the Federalist Papers?"

"So they tell me," Adams said glumly.

"Do you share his interests?"

Soupspoon in mid-air, Adams stammered, "In . . . uh . . . which of his interests?"

"Well, any of them. The law. Politics. All that he is so famous for."

"Right," Adams said, returning the spoon to his bowl and touching his lips with a napkin. "Well, actually, it's difficult. Not much demand these days for founding fathers."

"Ha ha!" Schmitz laughed sharply, as if this were the wittiest remark anyone had ever made. "I suppose not. We shall have to wait for this country to collapse before it needs founding again."

"In which case I'll be happy to step in," Adams said, "although I think I would serve better as the new nation's ski instructor."

•

Every night after study hall, we had an hour for showering, tooth brushing and visiting. We were expected to be in our pajamas, robes, and slippers, not allowed to leave the dorm but free to visit with one another. I think we were supposed to be doing what is now called bonding. Mr. Fell seldom left his apartment during this period, and the supes didn't leave their own digs to venture out among us unless there was a loud and prolonged disturbance. It was the most dangerous part of the day and the most enjoyable. I thought of it as the witching hour.

One evening, I noticed Stick standing in his alcove with his back to me, not supine with his headphones on listening to music. He appeared to be rearranging albums on the top of his bureau.

"Am I interrupting?" I asked, poking my head through the door very gingerly.

"No."

"May I come in?"

"Yes."

"May I sit on your bed?"

"Yes."

He continued to sort albums arranged between heavy book-ends on the bureau, plucking out one, examining it carefully, then shuffling it back into a different place.

"What are you doing?"

"I have a new system. It makes more sense."

I watched for a while. "What is it?"

"It made no sense to arrange them by artist, as I had done. I am arranging them chronologically by recording date. Easier to keep track of that way. There is a progression in the music that is basically chronological."

"Do you have Bill Haley and the Comets?"

He stopped cold and turned pale blue eyes to me.

"No. I've never heard of Bill Haley and the Comets. Do they play jazz?"

"No. Rock and Roll."

"Oh. I have no rock and roll. I have heard of it. It's related to the blues, is it not?"

"I don't know," I said. "I never heard that. It's just rock and roll."

"And why is it called that?"

"I don't know."

He went back to sorting.

"All these are jazz records?" I asked.

"Yes."

The full length of his shelf was covered by LPs. I rose to my feet and examined them.

"Please take one out if you would like," he said.

I pulled out an LP. On the cover was a photograph of a man

playing a saxophone against a solid black background. The title read *Bye Bye Blackbird*.

"Do you know this one?" I asked, showing it to him.

He barely glanced. In a monotone, he said, "John Coltrane, tenor saxophone, McCoy Tyner, piano, Jimmy Garrison, double bass, Elvin Jones, drums, one cut on each side, *Bye Bye Blackbird*, 17:50 minutes, *Traneing In*, 18:40 minutes."

He was exactly right on all of it. I pulled out three more LPs from different stacks, and he did the same thing with each one. I was beginning to get the picture. I picked up *Bye Bye Blackbird* again.

"Is this any good?" I asked.

"Listen to it."

He fished out the headphones and put the record on for me. I sat down on his bed. At first I thought maybe it was a comedy album. The musicians were all horrible, as if they were playing badly on purpose. But then I heard a melody striking back again and again like a deep river beneath the chaos, and all of a sudden, the mad honking and barking resolved into a wonderful chorus of voices unlike any I had ever heard in my life. The very long saxophone solo carried me deep into myself, screaming and bashing, wolf howling, and trilling. A dam broke. Suddenly, all of the fear and humiliation of this place surged to the surface—my heartache for family and home, my fury and hope and a frozen loneliness locked deep at the bottom of my gut. It all surged upward on this insane music. When the song ended, my eyes were wet, and my hands trembled a little.

"This music made you emotional," Stick said.

"It did," I said, wiping my eyes on a sleeve. "It's very powerful. I've never heard anything like it before. Can I come listen to it again?"

"The same one?"

"Yes."

"Will it make you emotional again?"

"Ah, I may handle it a little better the second time around. Do you ever get emotional when you listen to your music?"

"No," he said, his face a blank page. "I don't have any emotions."

"Oh." I had no idea what to say.

"People here think I'm a psycho," he said.

"Yeah. Well. You know why they think that."

"I do not."

"They're assholes."

He stared at me for a long while. "They're assholes?"

"Yes," I said. "You're not a psycho. You're cool. They're assholes."

"They're assholes, and I'm cool?" A very minor indication of perplexity crept across his smooth, chalky brow.

I told him I thought his collection was very cool. I returned to my alcove, where I drew the curtain and sat down on my bed to shake off the experience of the jazz.

A moment later, my curtain snapped open, and Stick was standing stock-still in the opening, his blank face smooth as marble. For an instant, it occurred to me that I might be wrong. Maybe he really was a psycho and he had come to kill me.

"If my curtain is drawn," he said, "and I'm inside listening to music, you may open it part way and just do this." He pointed to one ear.

"Point to my ear?"

"It's code. It means you want to come in and listen to jazz. I will let you in."

"Thank you."

"You are welcome."

I said, "I have a friend at home who's kind of like you."

"Does he collect jazz?"

"No. He has a different interest."

"What?"

"Model trains."

Stick rushed into my alcove and sat down beside me. The implacable face broke into something like excitement.

"What gauge?"

"HO."

"Yes. My father bought me only O gauge. Lionel. He said HO was common. But HO is vastly superior in many ways. I bought many HO trains for myself, many of the inexpensive but very clever Marx make, and now more of my set-up is HO than O. My father doesn't know that because he never enters my train room."

"You have a train room?"

He bounced to his feet and disappeared. I followed him back to his own alcove where he was rummaging furiously in his seaman's chest. He pulled out a worn, leather-bound photo album and motioned me to the bed. The photographs were difficult for me to understand at first. They showed a vast space beneath huge leaded windows, more like a museum or cathedral than a room in a house.

"It's my train room," he said.

"Oh, my God," I said. "This is the most amazing thing I've ever seen."

"Really?" he said with unfeigned surprise. "Does your friend at home not have a train room?"

"He does, he does. But it's different from yours. Do you have a timetable for your trains?"

He stooped back into the chest, his long white fingers clawing to extract three green and red hardbound ledgers tied together with twine, which he quickly unknotted. Clutching them shyly at first, he opened the books hesitantly and held them forth to show what lay within. Every page was covered with tiny black squiggles.

"What is this?" I asked.

"Code," he said grimly. "For the timetables. Does that seem psycho?"

"No, I get it."

"My father says it's psycho. He gets very angry about it."

"My friend at home uses code too."

"Really?"

"Yes."

"Is he a psycho?"

"No. He's cool."

"Do you think he could be my friend?"

"I'm 100 percent sure he could be your friend. You guys are a lot alike."

"I've never known anyone a lot alike."

"He is like you. A lot."

Stick said, "Good night," indicating it was time for me to leave. He snapped the curtain closed behind me.

———

Ellen and I were having lunch at a great deli on Northwestern in Lake Forest, not far from the Onwentsia where I was staying. She said, "You told me that your little childhood friend with the trains in the basement . . . "

"Warren Truckman."

"Yes, that he met a girl in high school who got him sort of

straightened out. I believe you mentioned at some point that Warren was black."

"Yes."

"Was the girl black?"

"Yes. I think she was the first black person his own age Warren ever knew."

"How could that be?"

Ellen was wearing a white blouse with décolletage and a light pink silk jacket over a very short white knit skirt and stiletto heels. I was dressed in khaki pants, a blue Brooks Brothers shirt open at the collar, and a lightweight blue blazer. She was devastating.

"Little Ottawa was all white except for a couple of black families. And Warren's parents only associated with people in their church, who were all white hillbillies. Sandra was the first person Warren ever met who could help him understand white people, and that wasn't easy, because Warren didn't really understand human beings."

"You kind of gravitated to weird kids, I guess. You hit it off with the other kid at St. Philip's who was on the spectrum. . . "

"Stick. In fact he and Warren met eventually."

"How in the world did that happen?"

"Warren was in New York with his wife for some kind of engineering thing. That was when I was working with Stick. I got them together, and the bond was instantaneous. They shared a deep identical strangeness that transcended race. Here's little Warren Truckman, who grew up in a basement in Little Ottawa, and Stick, who grew up in a castle in Tuxedo Park, and it was like two undercover Martians meeting accidentally."

"Are they still friends?"

"Yes, absolutely. They meet in New York. The wives go to

museums, and Warren and Stick play trains. I think they have shared their timetable codes with each other, but they can't tell me."

"You worked with Stick?"

"Long story. Very long."

"You've never told me how rich you are," she said.

"Pretty damn rich. Very."

"Did you come to Chicago just to see me?"

"Yes."

"Where from?"

"France."

"Oh, my God, Woodrow." She reached across and put a hand on my arm. "Had I known, I would never have allowed you . . . "

"Then you would have broken my heart," I interrupted.

She snatched the hand back and fixed me with a calculating gaze. "You're not going soft on me, are you, old man?"

"In the head, maybe."

"How much time do you spend in France?"

"A good eight months of the year. I speak the language pretty well."

"Are you still friends with Aubert?"

"Very close friends. He's a big deal. Special advisor on Africa to the Premier."

"Why do you like France so much?"

"I don't like France. I like my part of France. Parisians are a race of shitheads. But I really do like the rural people around my farm. Lots of tractors and trucks rattling around and people pouring wine in their empty soup bowls and wiping it up with bits of baguette."

"Fà chabroù," she said with perfect Occitanian inflection.

"Mais oui," I said. "So you know the Midi pretty well."

"Getting to."

"Prettiest girls in all the world, except for you."

She waved me off. "Rascal. Do you go back to Georgia where your family is from? Or Michigan? Do you like those small-town people, too?"

"I go to Michigan for family reasons. Georgia not so much."

"So you just like the country French because they're foreign."

"Well, strictly speaking, Ellen, I'm the one who's foreign."

"Then you like being a foreigner?"

"I do."

"Why?"

"It makes me feel at home."

—

The new waiters for the week were Davidson and Aubert. Davidson was embarrassingly subservient, incapable of setting down a dish without saying "excuse me" and "sorry" four times, whereas Aubert was imperturbable. Their first dinner was complex, a tomato consommé that had to be served chilled to keep the Schmitzes happy, followed by baked chicken, green beans, and mashed potatoes, all of which needed to get to the table piping hot, then finally a dessert of warm apple cobbler to be covered in a thick chilled cream. Herr Schmitz was making no allowance for inexperience, which made Davidson extremely nervous and Aubert only more suave.

The meal went fairly well. At the end, serving dishes of cobbler were placed at each end of the table along with pewter pitchers of heavy cream. Frau Schmitz accepted a tiny scoop of cobbler but declined the cream with an abstemious wince. Five minutes later, she whispered to her husband. He ordered back the cobbler and cream, then gallantly dished out a steam-shovel load into her empty bowl. He lifted the creamer grandly to top her dessert.

As the cream began to pour, Frau Schmitz let out a sharp whimper as if she had been bitten. She raised both tightly clutched fists to her mouth and shoved herself sharply away from the table with her feet, causing her chair to screech on the hardwood floor.

Compton peered into the pitcher of cream.

"Holy shit," he said, "it's fucking moving."

Adams shot forward over the table and snatched the pitcher. "This is . . . this is . . . "

He dropped it suddenly to the table, whirled away, and bent forward in his chair with a hand over his mouth.

Barry called from the other end: "What the hell is going on?"

Herr Schmitz, unblinking and white as snow, put a finger up sharp. "Shut up!" he hissed. "All of you. Be silent." He turned to his wife. "Get back to the table. Now!"

She pulled herself back to the table, the tented eyebrows knocked flat.

"Adams!" Herr Schmitz snapped, "Get back to the table."

Adams turned around, having successfully fought down vomit. By now the creamer had worked its way down the table to Yusupov. He put in a forefinger and thumb and pulled out something white and wriggling. He dropped it into his bowl, where it continued to writhe.

"Opisthopora," he said, leaning over the creamer to peer inside. "Plenty more where that one came from."

"What is it?" Herr Schmitz asked in a whisper.

"The common earthworm," Yusupov said. "Big gobs of them."

"You did this," Herr Schmitz said to Yusupov.

Yusupov's nose shot up as if he had been hit under the chin. Adams bent forward to be heard.

"Sir, it came from the creamer."

"Of course it came from the creamer, idiot."

"But I used the creamer right after Yusupov, then it went back down the table on my side, and then you asked for it back. It never went to Yusupov after I used it."

Yusupov was silent, sitting on his hands and making a close study of the ceiling.

Herr Schmitz looked quickly to the dais. Beetle was peering toward our table, and some boys at other tables were watching. Herr Schmitz gave Beetle a cringing flutter of the fingers and weak smile to communicate that all was well. Both Schmitzes rose from the table.

"Barry," Herr Schmitz said, "and you, also, Adams, I will want the name of the culprit within forty-eight hours. If I do not receive the name by then, there will be no more dessert, no more coffee and sugar, no more bread or rolls, and I believe that we will also forego oatmeal and cereal at breakfast."

Barry rose at the far end and faced him stoically. "I understand the dessert, sir, but the boys need a good breakfast."

"Yes, of course they do. So I suggest the boys produce the name of the villain. All of the villains."

The Schmitzes left the dining room. Barry and Adams stood whispering at the end of the table. Turning toward us, Barry snapped, "You jackasses better come clean on this right away."

After dinner, we assembled around the radiator bench at Compton's end of the dorm. Barry and Adams went to their apartments, then reemerged ten minutes later with Mr. Fell. All three marched back to where we stood quivering like turkeys the day before Thanksgiving.

"Who did the worms?" Mr. Fell asked.

No one spoke.

"I asked who did it. Look at me. Don't look away. Who did the worms?"

We were silent. A few tried to return his gaze but then cast their eyes down immediately. He was angry.

"So this is how it is," he said.

I said, "We really don't know, sir."

He sat down heavily on the radiator bench a few feet from where I was standing. He looked me up and down appraisingly.

"Barry and Adams tell me Schmitz thinks Yusupov did it."

We said nothing. Mr. Fell's tone softened slightly.

"Look, boys, listen to me. Herr Schmitz is very . . . he is a . . . "

Yusupov interjected solemnly: "I believe the word you reach for, sir, is *asshole*."

"No, Yusupov, that was not the word I was searching for. The word I was looking for is European. He and his wife are Europeans."

"Of the worst sort," Yusupov said.

"Be quiet!" Mr. Fell barked with sudden ferocity. He pointed a finger around at all of us. "Shut up and listen to me very closely. Whoever did this, however it happened, dropping an adulterant into food is uncomfortably close to poisoning. It is not funny. It is not a prank.

"Right now, I would guess Herr Schmitz wants to keep this quiet. He knows if it gets to Beetle, then it goes to the rector. Likewise, if it gets to one of your parents, then it goes to the board and then to the rector.

"You can count on a full investigation at that point, and then people will get sacked, expelled. Maybe it will be the responsible parties, maybe not."

Smiley asked, "What effect might it have for our parents to learn that Herr Schmitz is starving us to get his way?"

162

Mr. Fell got up from the bench and paced, shaking his head. "You can't really be that stupid. First of all, don't call it 'his way.' His way is the only way. You don't have a way. He does. Secondly, starving you? Starving you? Really?" He turned to Barry. "What has been taken away? What food?"

Barry said crisply, "Dessert, coffee, sugar, rolls and butter, oatmeal and cereal at breakfast."

"Does this affect the supes?"

"No, sir."

"I don't quite get it," Mr. Fell muttered to himself. "He can't order no dessert to be served without attracting Beetle's attention." He looked up quickly at Smiley, "In any event, being denied cake and biscuits is not exactly a POW-camp atrocity. I don't think you'll have anybody sobbing over your bleached bones for that. I will have to speak to him about breakfast. You have to have that. But if your game is getting Schmitz fired, you'll have to do a lot better than being denied your morning Danish. You do realize that there are children in this world who actually go to bed hungry every night?"

No one said anything.

"You do not realize that," Mr. Fell said half to himself, "because you're a bunch of incredibly spoiled brats, which is the problem."

"Sir, I object . . . " Smiley began.

"Oh, shut up."

Smiley fell back, abashed.

"I am . . . please, listen to me, boys. I am worried about you. I know the Schmitzes are a problem. But I have a feeling this is one of those things that just gets going. A war of nerves. So then you'll take it on yourselves, and you'll keep taking it up a notch to meet Schmitz on his dare. I understand that.

"I want you to know how serious this can become. You are skating on very thin ice here. If you are caught, boys will be expelled. I don't think any of you wants that."

He looked directly at Yusupov.

"Is there some special reason you hate them, Yusupov?"

"None whatsoever, sir. My dislike of them is more or less spontaneous."

Compton snorted. "Except that they made fun of him for being a Mount Kisco maître d'."

"Are you a Mount Kisco maître d', Yusupov?" Mr. Fell asked.

"No, sir. But I would be most honored to become one."

"All right. You have ten minutes to get to study hall."

When Mr. Fell and the supes had returned to their quarters, we gathered around Yusupov. Compton pressed in on him.

"How the hell did you do the worms?" he demanded.

Yusupov backed away and put up both hands. "I admit to nothing."

"Yeah, right, asshole," Compton said. "How'd you do it?"

"You know that I am a thespian."

"An actor," Compton said. "OK."

"As a part of my training in the theater, I am also a magician."

"You mean like at birthday parties?"

"My brother and I have performed magic on the stage and also, yes, at certain very elegant special events such as wedding receptions and the odd birthday party."

Smiley asked, "Why do you do magic at birthday parties?"

"We're not old enough to be maître d's."

"You do it for money?"

"Yes. To be paid."

"So you're not rich?"

"No."

"Are you poor?"

"We are un-rich, which we would not see as the same thing as being poor, but, in your terms, yes, we are poor."

"What about your uncle," Smiley asked, "the one you told Herr Schmitz about with the mountains of money that your family went sledding on? What did you say his name was?"

"Skupets McUtka. Miser McDuck in Russian. A joke. Get it? Scrooge McDuck?"

Smiley was solemn. He thought about it. "Why do you tell jokes about being poor?"

"What would you do if you became poor?" Yusupov asked.

Smiley thought about that, too. "I believe I might kill myself."

"My brother and I would rather do magic than kill ourselves."

Gellhorn asked, "How did you get into St. Philip's?"

"My family has certain connections, I believe, through the American military intelligence community, although no one will tell me for sure."

"You have connections," Gellhorn said, "but you're poor?"

"Un-rich."

"Are you as un-rich as Pontiac?"

"I do not believe so."

"No one is as un-rich as Pontiac," Compton said. "He holds the world record."

"Fuck you," I said.

We gathered up our book bags and trudged off to study hall together, laughing at Compton because he was wearing only one sock.

Chapter Four

I PLUNGED INTO SUPER GRINDING. On weekdays, if I hurried from Drake Pond to the gymnasium after crew and took a very quick shower, I could carve out about an hour and a half before evening classes. Saturday morning classes ended at noon, and the rest of the day was open until the evening meal at seven thirty. On Sundays, the only required events were morning chapel at 7:00 AM, dinner at 7:30 PM, and the evensong chapel service at 8:15 PM.

I found three locations for studying. During the week, I used a small stuffy utility room on the second floor of the gym, empty except for a folding metal table left leaning against a wall, which I always re-folded and returned to its original position, and a folding metal chair that I scavenged from the spectator area outside one of the squash courts.

On weekends, I took my books and notes to the school building, where the back door was never locked. I was able find empty classrooms as Johnny Wilson had directed, always on the second level and toward the end of the corridor farthest from the wing housing the masters' offices.

I stared at my books with hatred. In study hall each evening,

I read what was assigned, but the knowledge I was supposed to acquire stuck stubbornly to the pages. I did what Johnny Wilson told me to do. I went to the utility room or the empty classrooms and read and re-read assignments, fury growing in me as I realized I wasn't getting any more out of the books than I ever had. My grades on quizzes continued to be C-minuses or worse. For weeks on Friday afternoons, I trudged to the hated Aldredge Hall and saw myself again at the bottom of the heap, exactly where I belonged.

Crew didn't help. We rowed the barge up and down the long hot pond with Dickie shrieking Brit-sounding crew commands at us like, "Avast," to which I always muttered, "Your ass." The first month of it left me so exhausted I had a hard time staying awake during my secret study sessions.

•

After study hall one night, I was on my bed with the curtain drawn, grinding, when a hubbub arose out around the radiator bench. I got up to see.

Tweetie, Compton, Smiley, and Granger were gathered outside Yusupov's alcove. Tweetie and Granger were carrying belts in their hands. They waved me over, grinning.

Yusupov's nose protruded from his curtain. "To what do I owe this honor?"

"We want to congratulate you," Granger said.

"For what?"

"The worms."

"Oh, that," Yusupov said, stepping out jauntily into the aisle in his pajamas. "It was nothing. I already told you." He chuckled. "A bit of sleight of hand."

"No, no, it's much more than that," Granger said. "It was a triumph. What you did deserves . . . " He paused and looked around at the others.

They all shouted together, "Red balls!"

Yusupov's face froze. Then his eyes went wide with fear. He tried to leap back into his alcove, but Compton quickly collared him around the neck. Tweetie grabbed his hands from behind and cinched them together at the wrists with a belt. Yusupov kicked violently, but Smiley grabbed his legs. Granger slipped a belt over Yusupov's feet and cinched his ankles.

"You fuckers," Yusupov shouted. "I'll kill you. Supes! Supes! Barry and Adams, get the fuck out here, goddamn it!"

They dragged him down the center aisle, chanting, "Red balls! Red balls!" Boys popped out of their alcoves and looked on, laughing. I followed.

In the bathroom, a large metal trash can had been filled with piping hot water. They pulled Yusupov to the tile floor and stretched him out. Granger pulled down his pajama bottoms, reached into the pocket of his own robe and produced a handful of red laundry markers.

Yusupov cursed angrily, then begged plaintively for mercy as several boys took pens and painted his balls with a thick coat of red marker ink. Together they lifted him, writhing violently, and managed to jam his feet down into the barrel so that only his shoulders and head were above the steaming water.

According to some arcane alchemy known only to the boys of St. Philip's School, the glycol solvent in a marker, mixed with very hot water and applied to the scrotum, causes a burning sensation close to the pain associated with actual flame. Unlike a real flame, however, the harm wrought by the marker goes away as soon as cold water or ice is applied, leaving no forensic trace beyond a certain appearance of self-decoration which few boys would ever want to share with the authorities.

When the astringent ink on Yusupov's balls hit the hot water, he let out an agonized shriek. "You fuckers! You fuckers! My balls! My balls! My dick! You got it on my dick!"

Compton picked up a long push-broom that had been placed at the ready. He rammed the broom handle through the handholds on the barrel. The broom fit just over Yusupov's shoulders, locking him in the water. Then Compton took one end of the broom and Granger the other. By tipping the barrel on an edge, they were able to roll it crazily across the floor, sloshing water everywhere. They rolled Yusupov out of the bathroom and down the center aisle of the dorm.

Boys poured out of their alcoves laughing and dancing. "Red balls!" they cheered in malicious chorus, "Red balls!"

Smiley and Tweetie took turns with Compton and Granger, spinning Yusupov down the dorm and back. As they rolled him, Yusupov's agonized screams morphed into a forced hearty laugh. The boys dancing in the aisle laughed at him, and he laughed back harder. Mr. Fell and the supes never appeared.

•

The following morning, Herr Schmitz clinked his glass to call us to attention. We sat for a long time, waiting. Frau Schmitz fixed her husband with an unshifting furious gaze, her lips entirely swallowed, perhaps never to reappear. Her small dark eyes, the color and shape of coffee beans, peered like pistols from the penciled eyebrows.

Beginning slowly and sententiously, Herr Schmitz said, "Since the incident of two nights previous, I have been informed by the supes that they have not yet learned the name of the culprit or culprits and that no boy has come forward to confess to the provocation. I am saddened. I do not favor this. I fear that one or more of you may be flirting with disaster.

"I also have spoken with Mr. Fell, who has pleaded for a measure of mercy, to which I have temporarily assented. Barring further incident, I will not suspend cereal or oatmeal at breakfast. For now. But rolls and butter, sugar and dessert at dinner, will not be consumed by any boy until I have learned the perpetrator's name. Is this understood?"

We all said yes.

"I had directed you that you were not to discuss this matter away from this table. You already have discussed it with Mr. Fell. How did this happen?"

Adams spoke up: "I'm afraid that was us, sir. Me and Barry. We thought Mr. Fell should know."

"Why?"

"We asked him to order the boys to give up the name."

"And he did so order?"

"He did."

"And did the boys give up the name?"

"They did not."

Herr Schmitz exchanged a meaningful wince with his wife. "So," he said to Barry at the far end of the table, "what we have here is defiance."

Barry returned his direct gaze. "Yes, sir. I believe so. I think that's fair."

Herr Schmitz looked again to his wife, and they both grimaced meaningfully.

"Very well," he said. He leaned into the table and pointed a knife at us. His face was white and taut. "I will not have it. I will not have defiance."

He said to Adams, "Tell them how this works."

Adams turned to us. "Rolls, butter, and dessert will be served at dinner. Each boy will have all of these things set before him at the table, but no boy will touch any of it. At the end of every meal, the waiters will pick up the food and return the untouched food to the kitchen."

Herr Schmitz waited a beat. "You forgot one thing."

Adams looked up quizzically.

"Barry," Herr Schmitz said, "surely you remember the last."

"Yes, sir," Barry said. "If any boy touches the proscribed food at any point, additional foods will be forbidden to all of the boys at the table."

Frau Schmitz smirked at her husband, who bowed his forehead slightly to her. He turned back to us.

"Do you understand?"

We nodded our assent.

"And no boy will discuss any of this with anyone away from this table. Do you understand?"

We nodded again.

That night at dinner, no one touched any of the forbidden food. We sat for a good ten minutes, staring at our dessert, a warm apple pie with soft candied filling beneath a crisp, brown-sugared crust, while the supes and the Schmitzes gobbled theirs down. The Schmitzes waited for Beetle and his wife to exit via their private door at the back of the dais, and then they left the dining room.

Aubert said to Barry, "What does one do with the tart?"

Barry looked to Adams. "What do you think?"

"I think he'd better take all the food back to the kitchen and dump it," Adams said, "because Schmitz might come back in to check."

Tweetie spoke up in his booming baritone: "Can we still have coffee?"

Adams and Barry exchanged long looks.

Barry said, "He didn't mention coffee this morning."

Adams said, "I think he meant coffee. He just forgot."

They gazed at each other in silence.

"He didn't say no coffee," Barry said.

Adams nodded to Barry and then turned to us.

"You may have coffee," he said.

Compton stared at his pie. "So you're just going to throw away our apple pie?"

"Don't touch the goddamned pie," Adams said.

"Jesus," Compton said.

I said, "It seems wasteful."

"Try not to let the wombats see you do it," Adams told Aubert and Davidson as they began collecting the full plates. "Jake won't like this."

"No, he won't," Barry said. "And if he throws a fit, that'll turn this whole thing into another type of drama."

"Don't let Jake see you dump it," Adams said. "Don't let any of the wombats see you."

"Who is Jake?" I asked.

"The head man over the kitchen and the pantry," Adams said. "He rules back there. He can give boys demerits."

172

"I wonder," Davidson whispered meekly.

"You wonder what?" Yusupov asked.

"What if we all confessed? Said we all did the worms? Together. Wouldn't that solve everything?"

"I don't think so," Barry said. "Herr Schmitz wants blood. He wants someone he can go after."

Yusupov said, "Frau Schmitz does, too."

"Exactly," Barry said. "Which makes it that much worse. The Schmitzes are not going to be satisfied until somebody hangs."

"What do you mean, hangs?" I asked.

"Until someone gets kicked out."

"Of school?"

"Yes, Pontiac, for God's sake," Barry said with exasperation. "Did you not get that part? Out. Of. School. Gone. Expelled. You guys have gotten yourselves into a fix. Herr Schmitz is not going to go to Beetle until it's a *fait accompli*. He wants to show he has it under control. He wants to be able to tell Beetle what happened and who did it, then offer Beetle a head on a platter, a boy to expel. So far, Yusupov is their favorite suspect. I wonder how far off the mark they are."

We gazed back at him in silence.

"All right, if that's how it's going to be, you're going to have to stick it. I strongly advise you not to confess to anything unless you want to get somebody kicked out. I wish you could just cut it out, this whole thing with the Schmitzes. It's a bad fight."

"Yes," Adams said. "It's a bad fight."

"Don't let it go any further," Barry said. "Don't let it escalate. If you leave it where it is now, just sit there and stare at your pie every night and look like you're going to cry, maybe even show a little fake remorse, they might even relent at some point."

"Maybe Frau Schmitz will feel sorry for us," Davidson said hopefully.

"Oh sure," Compton said. "Like Hitler would."

•

Back in the dorm before study hall, we went to Compton's end of the radiator bench to discuss what had happened. Yusupov said, "I don't know why we should be afraid of these people. They're just Germans."

Aubert said, "These people are not Germans. They are Belgian. They speak French to each other."

"Oh, bullshit," Compton said. "Their name is Schmitz, for Christ's sake. That's not French."

"Oh, la vache," Aubert said with a frustrated shake of the head. "Do Americans not know anything of the rest of the world? Here, I will show you."

He led us to the area inside the main door of the dorm where there was a battered coffee table and a couple of badly scuffed captain's chairs. Piled on the table were dog-eared copies of the *New York Times Sunday Magazine*, coveted by boys for the lingerie ads, poor solace though they were. Aubert shifted some of the magazines out of the way and came up with a thicker, more rigidly bound volume, almost an oversized book. On the cover was a photograph of the Old Chapel and a title, "Welcome to St. Philip's School."

"What is that?" Yusupov asked.

"I have not an idea," Aubert said. "I think it is made for the ancient students."

"Alumni," Yusupov explained to the rest of us.

Aubert spread it open on the table. Across two pages lay a

splendid portrait of Herr and Frau Schmitz shaking hands with the rector on the lawn in front of the New Chapel. The text explained that Herr Schmitz had come with his wife from their native Belgium to join the language faculty. The story said he had last taught at Odenwaldschule, a boys' boarding school in Heppenheim, Germany. The story seemed to be two or three years old.

"So what is he?" Compton asked, "a German or a Frenchman?"

"It's very complicated in Belgium," Aubert said. "But the Schmitzes are more French and Flemish than they are German."

Granger said, "Then why are they Herr and Frau and not Monsieur and Madame, as they would be in Canada?"

"Because they came to the United States to teach German, and Americans have difficulty distinguishing. They thought Herr and Frau would appear better for their work."

Compton pushed his chest up to Aubert.

"How do you know all this shit?"

"I know the Schmitzes very little," Aubert said, pulling away. "They assisted me with matters when I was first arrived."

"They were nice to you?" I asked.

"I would not say nice. These people are not nice in the American sense. Mr. Fell saw that I needed assistance with some documentaries, and he asked them to help me. The point is, they are Belgian, not French. I am French from Alsace, where there are also many French people who have German names. The Schmitzes are not German."

"They're krauts to me," Compton said.

Aubert's face reddened.

"I do not like this, calling people by dirty names for foreigners. What must you call me when my back is turned?"

"Frog," Compton said.

"Then I will beat you," Aubert said stepping up to Compton with his chest puffed and his fists at his hips.

"I don't think so," Compton said, darkening. "I don't think a frog beats an American."

Aubert stooped as if to jab Compton with a left. Compton turned to it and didn't see the right coming. Aubert speared him hard on the left temple, snapping his head back. Compton shook it off and dove back into Aubert full-body, throwing his right arm to hook Aubert around the neck, but Aubert spun away like a dancer, opened some air and plowed a straight left jab into Compton's right forward ribcage. When Compton bent to the pain, Aubert rushed him, got a hand up under his chin and pushed his head up hard against the outside edge of an alcove wall. Then just as suddenly, Aubert released him and stepped back two paces out of the fight. Compton shook it off again.

"Fuck," Compton said. "Can you skate?"

"Skeet?" Aubert asked.

"Skate, skate," Yusupov said. He made a ludicrous pantomime of skating up and down the floor, flapping his arms like a ballerina. "Ice skating. Faire du patin à glace. Do you do it?"

"Ah, oui, bien sur, le patin à glace. Of course I do this very well. I told you I am from Alsace. I think I can skeet as well as any of you."

"Skate," I said.

"Skite," he said.

"You ever play hockey?" Compton asked.

"Hockey? Oh, you mean with the long paddles and the little black . . . no, of course not, this is a Canuck game, of Quebec, I believe, invented by the sauvages."

Granger stepped forward. "Careful who you call savages."

"I did not say savages," Aubert said, correcting him. "I said sauvages."

"Right," Granger said. "OK."

"You should come try out," Compton said. "I'll tell the coach about you. I think you might have a little sauvage in you."

Aubert smiled in spite of himself. "I will try it if you will not call me . . . "

"Sauvage?"

"No, I would take that word as respect. The other."

"Frog."

"Yes. Grenouille."

Compton came forward to shake. "I won't say it again."

"You give your word?"

"Yes. You have my word."

Aubert held out a hand.

"Good fight," he said.

They shook hands and dipped their heads in very small but distinctly courtly bows.

I was still having a lot of trouble with the "good fight" and the bowing. There were no courtly bows in Pontiac. If someone said, "good fight" at the end of a fight, it would start another fight.

•

The next week was my first as a waiter. I was to work with Yusupov, who already had served a tour of duty and was able to show me the ropes. The tables were set by the kitchen staff before each meal. We were to carry large trays with serving dishes from the kitchen into the dining room. We cleared spent plates and platters after each course. At breakfast and lunch, there two courses, and at dinner, three.

Two doors opened off the long hallway outside the double doors to the dining room. The door on the left, with a small copper plaque, "Pantry," was always closed. The one on the right opened to a serving area and the kitchen.

At breakfast one morning, Herr Schmitz said to Adams, "The porridge is too runny." He meant the oatmeal. "Have Skaggs and Yusupov tell Jake to remake it."

I nodded to Adams to show I had heard and understood the order.

"I still don't know who Jake is," I said.

Herr Schmitz said, "May I suggest that you ask?"

Yusupov and I rose to fetch trays to collect all of the unsatisfactory oatmeal.

"Skaggs and Yusupov," Herr Schmitz said, "this is really your fault. You should have seen that it was over-cooked. You should never have served it. I want you to take this matter in hand. It is an opportunity for you both to learn enterprise, self-sufficiency, and responsibility."

"Yes, sir," we said in unison.

"I want you to speak to Jake only. Don't deal with anyone but Jake. When you talk to him, I want you to tell him he has embarrassed you by cooking this porridge poorly. You want it recooked. And you don't want to see this mistake made again. You are to say all of this precisely as I have told you. Don't leave out a word. And don't put it off on me. These are to be your commands, not mine."

I thought I saw Adams frown, and Herr Schmitz may have seen it, too.

"You, Adams," he said quickly, "will accompany Skaggs and Yusupov and see that they carry out my instructions exactly as I have given them."

Herr and Frau Schmitz exchanged sly smirks. On the way down the hall to the kitchen, Yusupov muttered to me, "This is a set-up."

Behind us, Adams said, "Do as you're told."

Inside the door to the kitchen was a large anteroom separated from the working kitchen by a screened counter that ran the width of the room. A single serving window was at the center of the counter. The anteroom was big enough to allow all of the waiters to wait for each new course in a winding queue. When the three of us entered, the area was empty. The kitchen smoked, billowed and banged on the other side of the screen as a dozen workers in white uniforms prepared a main course of thick succulent fried ham, fluffy scrambled eggs, crisp toast, and fresh squeezed orange juice.

A young man in a toque came to the window and shrugged to see what we wanted. All three of us stood back. Yusupov and I were carrying heavy trays piled with two big pewter serving dishes of oatmeal and stacks of partially empty bowls. Yusupov shoved me forward with his shoulder. I looked back at Adams who nodded for me to proceed.

I stepped to the window and banged my tray on the counter a bit more violently than I had intended, causing the young man in the toque to step back.

"I need to talk to Jake," I said.

"Jake's busy."

I looked back to Adams, who nodded again.

"I need to talk to Jake," I said.

"He's busy."

"Tell Jake I want him to come here."

The young man gave me a searching sidelong examination. He shrugged and disappeared into the din. A moment later, a huge man with a head the size and color of a pumpkin emerged from a white cloud of steam. His face was darkly veined beneath a gleam of sweat, his eyes enormous and unblinking, his teeth set in a voracious growl. Massive forearms covered in tattoos protruded from his white sleeves. From his belt hung a meat cleaver, its clean blade flashing in the overhead light.

My gut told me that if I said one wrong word to this man, he would kill me. But I also believed I was being tested according to the values of this new world and that if I wanted to survive here, I needed to meet the test.

"*Mon jeune ami*," Jake said in a booming French-Canadian baritone, "what can I do for you?"

I cleared my throat and looked down at the tray. Then I lifted my face and said, "The porridge is too cooked. It's runny."

His eyebrows flew up, and the black eyes flashed. He stepped up to the window, reached through it and ripped the lid off the pewter serving bowl.

"This porridge? Too cooked?"

"Yes, sir."

"This porridge does not look too cooked to me."

"I'm sorry. It's too cooked. It's runny."

"This is not runny," he said. He surveyed all three of us. "Who says that this is runny?"

I looked back at Adams. He gave me a signal with a flick of his fingers to do as I had been told.

"I say."

"You say?" Jake said incredulously. "You say my porridge is runny? And what should I do about it?"

"I would like you to make us a fresh batch," I said. "Less runny."

"Less runny?" Jake said. "Less runny. Well, let's see about that."

He reached through the window with his right arm, grabbed my tray with an enormous paw, pulled the tray through the window and sent it crashing down the counter on his side. It sounded like a car wreck. In almost the same movement, he reached out with his other hand and snatched the end of my necktie. With a solid jerk, he pulled my chin down so hard against the wooden surface of the counter I thought my head would snap off.

He waited and held me there until my eyes cleared. When he was sure I could see again, he reached back with his right hand and snatched the cleaver from his belt. When I saw the shiny steel fly up over my head, I shouted and tried to pull free. He pulled down harder on the necktie on the other side of the counter. I tried to push away from the counter with both hands and feet.

"Stop it," Adams shouted behind me. "You'll get your fucking nose chopped off."

I went limp. The cleaver came down like lightning and chopped off my necktie an inch from my nose. I fell backward on my ass on the floor. A roar of laughter erupted from the kitchen.

"I want them kept in the pantry for twenty minutes," Jake shouted to Adams.

"Demerits?" Adams asked.

"Fuck demerits! No oatmeal."

I got up and dusted myself off. The younger man in a toque returned to the window grinning broadly, and Yusupov surrendered his tray to him. Adams led us across the hall to the pantry. He nodded us through the door. "You will stay in here for twenty minutes. I will come to get you. Do not leave for any reason."

Yusupov said, "You're kidding me. That man can punish us? That cook? That wombat?"

"Jake has absolute authority over the kitchen," Adams said.

181

"Did Schmitz know that?" I asked.

"Of course he knew," Adams said. "It has always been that way. Yusupov was right. You were set up."

"Why didn't you tell us?" I demanded hotly.

"Not my place. Stay here. Shut up. I will come and get you." He left us.

The room was about a quarter the size of the dining room. Directly in front of us was a long narrow oak table with simple wooden chairs on either side. We sat staring across the table at each other for a while. Yusupov snickered and shook his head.

"What's funny?" I asked.

"This country."

"What's funny about it? I didn't think Jake was very fucking funny. I thought the fat fucker was going to kill me."

"It's just . . . so American. The bloody cook has authority to punish us. It's even one of the school traditions, obviously. Adams knew. Schmitz knew. The young man behind the window. They all knew he was going to chop your tie off. They were having great fun at our expense."

"My expense."

"Yes, happily."

"Fuck you. Did you know?"

"Of course not. But I knew whatever was going to happen wasn't going to be good. Didn't you see the *sale boche* snickering to his hideous frau?"

"Yes."

"In Russia, they would all be flogged within an inch of their lives, what they deserve."

"I thought it was the other way around. I thought in Russia, the communists did the flogging."

"Same thing."

I drummed my fingertips on the table's oaken surface. Yusupov looked at the ragged stump of my necktie and emitted a delighted chuckle.

"You look ridiculous," he said.

I looked down and fingered the remains of the tie with the other hand.

"I know. I guess I can't go back to the dorm and change."

"I wouldn't. And don't take it off. This game is not over. When we are released, you will have to go back into the dining room looking like a fool with your dick chopped off, and they will be expecting to be entertained."

"They all know?"

"They do now. Adams will have told them."

"And you got nothing."

"Of course not. I sidestepped the noose. You put your head right in it."

"Fuck."

He turned away, scanning the room. He was facing the door. Behind him, the morning's full light streamed in from two tall windows, putting his face in shadow.

"Jesus Christ," I said, half to myself. I rubbed a palm over my chin where I could feel swelling and sore teeth. "Shit. I don't see Schmitz pulling a trick like that on Granger or Smiley or Tweetie or Gellhorn. Or you."

"Maybe on me. Not on them."

"Why on you? Why not on them?"

"Ah," Yusupov said with more groan than sigh. "Pontiac, you really do not know anything at all about the world, do you?"

"How much do you know about Pontiac, asshole?"

"You make a legitimate point."

"Besides, what fucking world are you talking about?"

"This fucking world, obviously. The one where you have alighted and now live, although no one can figure out how or why you are here."

"Least of all me."

"Least of all you."

I twisted to look at the door, wondering when we would be freed.

"They'll let us out soon," Yusupov said.

"How do you know so much?" I asked. "You're a new boy, too."

"We have customs in my culture similar to this. I believe the American term is hazing."

"So why would Schmitz haze me and you but not the other guys?"

He sat back down and leaned across the table on an elbow.

"Pontiac," he said, "I'd like to be your friend. I admire your spirit."

"OK."

He rose and went to the window. Gazing out with his back to me, he said, "You Americans have a very hard time coming to grips with each other because there are certain facts of life you cannot acknowledge." He turned toward me, looming tall and loose-limbed.

"There are words you cannot even say aloud," he continued. "When it comes to social class and rank, you are all pussies."

"Find another word."

"All right. You, for example, are from a place called Pontiac, a city named for an automobile produced in local factories. Pontiac is the asshole of the planet. Your people are robotniks. Urban peasants."

"We don't have peasants in America."

"But you see, Pontiac, that's just the problem. Of course you have peasants. Every country has peasants. You are a peasant. And the four boys you named at the table whom Schmitz would never dream of hazing are aristokrats. Schmitz is a burzhua, a quaking little bourgeois who would never want to earn their enmity, not only because he is afraid of them and their fathers but also because he worships them and hopes one day they will bestow favor upon him."

"Bullshit. That's Russia. I mean, that's not even Russia anymore."

"Pontiac, you are quite wrong. The world I'm talking about is the whole world. It was Russia before the revolution, and I assure you it is Russia now. We White Russians talk about you Americans. You are always itching in your skin because you can't accept the reality of rank. Your constant anxiety about who and what you are and your total inability to speak honestly with each other about class makes all of you obsessed with it. You don't understand that knowing your place makes you strong, while not knowing your place makes you a pussy, a word I use advisedly. When you know who you are, you can keep your cool, which is the main thing. When you don't, you are fragile, thin-skinned, defensive, and flying off the handle, playing the fool and the victim. You are a typical American."

"You're not American?"

"One resists. I suppose I should give in to it. Perhaps you could instruct me."

"You could come visit me in Pontiac some time. They'd knock some of that Russki bullshit out of you."

He looked alarmed. "Is Pontiac in Arkansas?"

I laughed. "We're kind of midway between Boston and Arkansas."

"Oh," he said, sitting back down with a careless toss of the head. "I can handle that."

"Why do you think Schmitz would pull this trick on you? Aren't you an aristocrat?"

"My mother thinks I am. But to these people here, the American gentry, I am a wog. Herr Schmitz and his wife know that because they summer in Kisco. They're very shrewd, as are all Europeans. They know that in this country, I have a wog name. I don't quite count. The American gentry are insular and conflicted. They have summer homes among us in upstate New York. We know them. They like to associate with us, especially with those of us who have titles. They all wish they had titles. But they are like all Americans, all of you. Even your aristocrats are afraid to name their class, even to themselves, especially to themselves."

"Do you have a title?"

"Yes."

"What is it?"

"My full name is Feodor Sergeiovitch I-will-kick-your-pussy-American-ass Yusupov, Esquire."

The door opened and Adams looked in.

"Go back in and clear the table," he said.

Yusupov looked me in the eye gravely. He whispered, "Keep your cool, Pontiac. Know who you are. Don't let them get to you."

When we walked back into the dining room, a slow titter arose among the boys who first saw my truncated tie. The laughter swelled to a boisterous symphony of hoots and hollering that shook the room. I smiled as broadly as I could stretch my mouth, and I did a runway walk, turning this way and that, flipping the remains of my necktie at everyone with one hand. The room laughed louder and louder while I pirouetted and bowed. Gellhorn rose from his chair, then Tweetie and Granger, then the entire dining room except for the masters and supervisors, and gave me an ovation.

Beetle rose from his chair, his face beet-red and swollen. He shouted in a voice that was almost a squeal, "Stop this preposterous poppycock at once! I will not have this in the Lower School dining room!"

The room went silent. Later, as I cleared the dishes of the Schmitzes, I gave them my most transparently insincere smile.

•

The next morning on the walk from reports to the schoolhouse, Compton caught me by the sleeve. "Hey," he muttered softly, "I guess you can come sluicing with us this weekend."

I knew what the sluice was, but I didn't know what he meant by sluicing. Sluice was the nickname given by boys at the school to a New England stream whose topographical name was Frenchie's Creek. Even in warm months, Frenchie's ran white, strong, and cold from the steep dark hills above the school through rocky wooded ground to the campus. Beyond the school, it flowed over sloping, thin-dirt farms and plunged through dense forest for a course of about twenty miles, southeast to the Southern tip of Rumney on the Giizhigokwe River, usually called the Gitch by locals. Where it ran through the school, the sluice was confined by stone walls and ponds that held it flat and quiet, allowing only the hum and chuckle of an English brook. But at the school's southeast end where the stream burst its bonds again, it bounded back to its New

187

England nature, foaming and furious, showering and shouting, a racketing torrent through jagged boulders and tumbled trees. The school, knowing the stream was only civilized against its will and still potentially murderous, long ago declared any part of it outside school grounds to be out of bounds and forbidden to boys, which, of course, only made it more irresistible.

At lunch, I asked Compton what sluicing was. He angrily shushed me. It was a plot, he said. He, Yusupov, Aubert, Smiley, Gellhorn, Tweetie, Roosevelt, and Davidson had chipped in money to purchase two inflatable rubber rafts at the Army-Navy surplus store in town. They had cached the rafts in the woods near the sluice about six or seven miles southeast of the school. Beneath the folded rafts, they had hidden a bicycle pump, matches, two fifths of sloe gin and a box of cigars. Davidson would bring peanut butter and jelly sandwiches wrapped in wax paper on the day of the quest.

They had calculated the reach of the sluice between the place where the rafts were hidden and the Gitch at about one and a half to two hours floating time, plus an hour for lunch, drinking, and naps. The plan was to go into Rumney immediately after Sunday chapel on the bus so as not to arouse suspicion, hire a cab to go out to the hiding place, then float the sluice, go to a gas station they already had scouted near the river, call another cab, hide the rafts, and return to the school in time for dinner. I had a feeling these arrangements, all of which Compton conveyed as fiendishly ingenious, were well known to boys at the school and even a bit of a tradition. I could tell he felt singularly honored to have been included. He didn't say why I was invited, although he gave me the impression that he was only a messenger and did not especially approve.

The only day of the week with a free window long enough for the plan to work was Sunday, because we were allowed to skip lunch. The cost for me, including cab and my share of the rafts and provisions, was twenty dollars.

"That's two weeks allowance," I said.

"It's worth it," Compton said.

And the fact was, I already had saved up a hundred dollars from what the rector's wife was giving me. I was careful not to sound too interested or, God forbid, grateful to be invited, however, because I knew that would only invite some kind of a verbal whacking from Compton. I said, "It sounds sort of weird to me."

"Jesus, Pontiac, it's not weird," he said hotly. "It's one of the coolest things. You're lucky to get to go."

I put him off for a day because I was having genuine trouble making up my mind. Things were getting just barely better for me at the weekly posting of grades. My name was creeping up from the bottom of the ranking list. I knew it wasn't good enough to keep me from getting kicked out, but things were moving in the right direction. For every inch of progress, the cost in sheer effort was great. An entire Sunday afternoon lost to grinding would come at a tangible penalty.

But the idea of being included in something was irresistible—something that was all about boys, only boys, nothing to do with the school, forbidden in fact. I told Compton I guessed I would join.

During chapel that Sunday morning there was so much sly winking, nodding, eye-rolling, and thumbs-upping among the plotters I was convinced we would all be arrested. We returned to the Lower School and Dorm Four without speaking to one another. There, we changed into blue jeans, outdoor shirts, and sneakers. Smiley handed us small identical cloth knapsacks from the Army-Navy store and told us to stock them with whatever we planned to carry. He spoke grimly, as if preparing for trench warfare.

A dozen or so boys were already waiting for the bus, including a couple of sixth formers, one of whom was Rutledge.

"Must be the ornithological society," he snickered.

"Obviously," Yusupov said with a sniff.

"Supposed to be a lot of good species down on the lower sluice this time of year," Rutledge said. "Do you have good glasses?"

With great froideur, Yusupov said, "We are well equipped, thank you."

Rutledge, looking bored, turned away and left us alone.

In town the sidewalks were beginning to populate with locals strolling home in their church clothes from restaurant luncheons. It was a fine New England fall afternoon, just between crisp and sunny. We bumped along Main Street intermingling with the townies.

Yusupov took the lead, as usual. When we had walked a few blocks, Aubert, who was three spots back in formation, called forward, "Yusupov, where do you take us now?"

Without turning or slowing the pace, Yusupov called back, "I really do not have the slightest idea."

"We need to find a taxi," Aubert called up, steamed.

Gellhorn hurried forward and grabbed Yusupov by the shoulder.

"Stop marching, goddamn it. Why do you always strut along like you're leading a parade?"

Yusupov smiled genially and shrugged without turning. "Because I am?"

At the hotel, four rusty Rumney taxicabs sat idling in a disconsolate row, three yellow and one green. The yellow ones were worn-out Checkers from Boston manned by cabbies in shabby matching caps and jackets. They maintained solidarity, unwilling to take all of us in the same cab and noncommittal about taking us out to the woods to our rafts depending on how many of them we hired. The cabbie with the green car, a dark-skinned foreigner, agreed to pack us all in and take us wherever we wished. His car was a Ford the size of a barge, with muddy floorboards and no meter. Roosevelt negotiated the fee. The cabbie complained vociferously at first in broken English, waving an arm at the rest of us to emphasize the favor he was doing, but Roosevelt argued that for only two dollars more, we could split up and take two Checkers. Then Smiley came forward and explained quietly to the driver that there was a guaranteed return trip of some length in the deal and that we would pay double for that part of the day's work. The cabbie liked this idea and changed his tune.

We packed ourselves into the old Ford, six boys in back and three squeezed in tight in front with the driver. Aubert was none too pleased about being in the front seat squeezed next to Yusupov, whom he often accused of body odor. Seizing the offensive, Yusupov immediately rolled down the window and stuck his head out, making loud gagging sounds to signal that Aubert was exuding too much soap scent, which he was. The rest of us and the driver had a good laugh, while Aubert sat sourly with shoulders hunched against his ears, repeating under his breath, "On fait l'andouille ici."

And then the cab left us. We stood at the brink of our great adventure with the rafts tied in long rolls at our feet and packs on our backs. Black forest soared all around in ramparts. Birds and squirrels and sharp-clawed creatures jeered from secrecy as if all the ancestors of the forest had risen from the underworld to watch us make sausage of ourselves.

"Impressive," Yusupov said grandly.

"A bit intimidating," Gellhorn said softly. "What is that roar?"

We all heard it then, an angry music in the distance like a mob chanting.

"Jesus Christ," Compton said. "Tell me that's not the fucking sluice."

We carried the rolled rafts, a boy at each end, down a deer trail, over tangled roots and fallen trees, squeezing between granite boulders and massive pillars of white pine. The solid black-green coniferous forest gradually relented to a stalwart army of ancient hardwoods. Biblical rays pierced the canopy, and azure patches of sky floated by. The leaves of the hardwoods had already turned a Jacob's coat, scattering like yellow and red confetti on the streaming sunbeams. The deeper we penetrated, the less attention the voices of the forest paid us, busy with their own day's work, and every inch of the way the sluice grew louder.

When we arrived at her banks, the stream we knew as a tamed and docile tenant was now an explosion of magic, wrath, and joy, roiling and writhing over rocks and roots, white in her wings, green in her limbs, raucous, feral, shouting and singing, daring us to join her on her bed of stones.

Standing at the bank with slumped shoulders, Aubert asked, "Is it our purpose to die?"

Yusupov said cheerily, "Eventually."

Aubert turned quickly on his heel. "All right then, it is time for the boats to arrange themselves."

We untied the rafts and spent the next forty-five minutes taking turns at the measly bicycle pump we had brought to inflate them. Most of us were ready to declare the job finished at several points, but Aubert insisted on checking the hardness of the rafts with sharp kicks, sending us back to the pump until he was satisfied.

When it was time to board, Aubert said, "I shall be in the boat that does not include Yusupov."

Feigning injury and surprise, Yusupov said, "As you wish, my gallant Gaulois."

That put me in the raft with Compton, Yusupov, and Davidson. The much larger raft carried Aubert, Gellhorn, Roosevelt, Tweetie, and Smiley. In each boat, two boys had wooden paddles. We engaged in a brief conversation about navigation.

Yusupov said, "I assume downstream."

"The question would be how, idiot," Gellhorn snapped.

"We're about to find out."

The rafts were fat ovals made of stout, drab military material. Roosevelt quickly took command of the larger boat. "No matter what happens," he ordered, "do not lose the paddles." The rest of his crew stuffed themselves into the raft, staring at each other over a thicket of bewildered knees. Roosevelt shoved off with his paddle, and his boat went spinning away quickly, propelled by an eddy out into the main current. A short distance away, they crashed directly onto a black boulder. The raft banged around the edges of the boulder and appeared to be taking on water. They were all shouting as they passed from view around a bend. We heard screams, then only the hungry roar.

After a moment, Compton said, "OK, let's call a cab."

"We can't do that," Yusupov said. "This is our grand adventure."

"We have to go see what happened to them," I said.

"I think we know what," Davidson said.

We sat our raft a little differently, with me aft, facing forward with a paddle, Compton on his knees with a paddle at the bow, Yusupov and Davidson on either side. The eddy floated us out into the current and we began to spin. I steered at the stern while Compton dug hard at the bow, and we were able to maintain a sloppy forward course. When we approached the boulder at the bend, Compton shouted, "Let us hit it, we'll bounce," and we did and floated smoothly out around the boulder into a long straight reach barricaded by immense fallen trees. The first tree stopped us dead, pitching Compton out of the boat and into a narrow pocket of water between fallen logs. Ice cold water poured into the raft as if from a firehose. Compton clambered and hoisted himself up onto a fallen tree. Kneeling, he hoisted Yusupov up out of the boat by hand. They were able to stand upright straddling two fallen trees. The two of them pulled Davidson up. I flopped myself over the first tree by embracing it like a lover. I twisted and kicked until I got my feet up on the second tree, then pulled myself up with my hands and got to a standing position somehow on both trees like the other three. Purple and pink blood streamed from Compton's brow. Together, we managed to hoist the raft up over the tree and set it flat on the downstream side. Only at that moment did we see the other five, thirty yards downstream, clawing their way up a bank like mud-caked muskrats, the last two hauling the raft.

Compton and I climbed aboard and held onto the tree to keep the raft in place. Then Davidson got in gingerly. Yusupov was just stepping in when a powerful current bulged up from beneath the tree, broke our grasp and shoved the raft away from the tree. We went spinning, and Yusupov, instead of stepping into the raft, plunged face-first into the sluice. Compton and I dug with the paddles to get back to him but to no avail. As we spun away, the current shoved Yusupov up out of the water as if tossing a twig, then sucked him back under just as we crashed hard into a thick matte of smaller trees and brush.

Yusupov popped up downstream beyond our logjam, then tumbled away like a ball of rags and shot past the other five on the bank. We saw him wave an arm, then disappear farther down, sucked beneath a massive fall of timber. On the bank, Aubert, who had already stripped off his boots, backpack, and jacket, leapt from the bank and sliced into the water like an arrow. He swam a few powerful strokes downstream, then dove beneath the thick dam of timber and brush where Yusupov had disappeared. He popped out beyond the dam, farther downstream.

"He is trapped," he shouted.

Compton was on his feet in our raft, then out in a powerful arc over the entangling branches in all of his clothes and boots. He swam with hard, bashing strokes down to the tree-fall, then dove beneath. Davidson and I watched from our stalled craft while the four on the bank paced with hungry eyes.

There was nothing, only the hiss of the sluice through the branches. Aubert was struggling to climb out. Gellhorn started toward the water but Smiley saw something, caught Gellhorn's wrist, and held him back. I was about to jump out of the raft when Compton and Yusupov popped up just below the logjam, both swimming hard for shore. Compton reached the bank first, climbed halfway out, and extended a hand to Yusupov, who took it and clambered out.

Standing erect on the bank's edge, Yusupov shouted, "He saved me! Almost fucking died! Marvelous!"

Compton sat on the bank gasping for air and giving Yusupov the finger.

Davidson and I somehow wrestled our raft over the branches and floated down to where the others were resting on a grassy knoll bathed in sunlight. We all agreed to stay put until we had dried out some. Yusupov, whose face was red, puffy and bleeding a little, sprawled flat on his back with his arms outstretched. He fell asleep immediately, snoring loudly.

Compton took off his undershirt and cinched it around his forehead to stop the bleeding. Digging in his backpack, he found one of the sloe gin bottles. It had to be rinsed in the sluice to wash away a sticky paste of peanut butter and jelly. He passed it around, and we all took deep pokes, warmed by the half-sweet bite.

"Tastes like licorice," Roosevelt said. "What more could we want?"

"Girls," Tweetie said loudly.

We were all quiet for a long while, passing the bottle slowly. Davidson waved it away. "I don't drink alcohol," he said quietly.

Compton shrugged and said, "Good." He took a deep draught. I took a couple more sips, enough to barely feel it.

Yusupov snorted, stirred, and sat up wide-awake, wiping a cake of blood from his chin with a damp sleeve. "So," he said to Gellhorn. "This is all very Hemingway."

"Is it?" Gellhorn asked.

Yusupov grabbed the bottle from Aubert and gulped. He winced a little where the liqueur stung a cut at the end of his mouth, then took another solid swig. "Why do you persist in this ridiculous affectation of pretending not to know anything about your own father, who is arguably the most famous living novelist in the world?" He swigged again.

Gellhorn shrugged. "Well," he stammered, "I guess I should know. I mean, I guess I will know, soon enough. Apparently he's going to be part of the curriculum wherever I go."

"Of course he is. But why isn't he part of your own curriculum already? You of all people. His own son. It's absurd. How many of us have already read at least some Hemingway?"

One after another, we all put up a hand, except for Gellhorn.

"It's incomprehensible," Yusupov said, perhaps already feeling his alcohol a little.

"No, it's not," Roosevelt said. "It's a family matter. None of our business. To us, Hemingway is a famous man. To Gellhorn, he's family. Perhaps not good family."

"Are you kidding?" Gellhorn said. "How could Hemingway be anybody's good family?"

"Why wouldn't he be?" I asked. "He's the world's most famous author."

Gellhorn shook his head. "So what? He's a drunk, and he was a son of a bitch to my mother."

"Then I feel really sorry for your mother," Davidson said to Gellhorn.

We all turned toward Davidson, who was sitting slumped on an elbow, higher on the slope. When I looked at him—pale, slight, smaller, and younger in appearance than the rest of us with his wet hair pushed back in a pompadour—I suddenly caught a glimpse of my little brother, David.

"Why do you feel sorry for Gellhorn's mother?" I asked.

"It's not easy having a drunk in your family," he said.

"Do you have one?"

"Yes. My mother. She's why nobody else in my family drinks. She drinks for all of us."

No one said a word.

"That's an awful thing to say about my own mother, I know," he said softly, "but I'm just telling the truth."

Compton said, "I know his mother. Everybody in Far Hills does. He's not lying."

"What does she do?" I asked. "When she's drunk?"

"She's always drunk. She's just really mean. Really, really mean. All the time."

"Like what?"

"Like telling me I'm a waste of time and money. Telling me she doesn't know who my real father is. Once she told me my real father was this really bad guy, the son of the old farmer who works our property."

Compton said, "What does your dad say?"

"He's never there. He really doesn't live with us. He has a girlfriend in London. He's over there most of the time. That's why I got up here a week early. She sent me, because she was loaded."

He said it matter-of-factly.

"So she was just drunk," I said, "and she got First Day off a week and sent you up here by mistake? How'd you get here?"

"She had this guy we call William drive me. He's not really a driver. He's a gardener. She just told me to pack my stuff and get in the car. I don't even know if she really got the date wrong or if she just couldn't wait to get rid of me."

"What's William like?" I asked.

"I have no idea. I've never spoken to him."

"You rode all the way from New Jersey to New Hampshire, and you never talked to the guy?"

"He was driving. I was in the back. It's a very long car."

Compton said, "Why didn't the dumbass take you back home when he found out it was a week early?"

"He was gone by then. We were so late. He got lost in Boston. I tried to tell him. I know the way exactly, because my dad and I ride up here for Race Day every year. But he wouldn't listen to me. He's a black man. They don't listen to white kids."

"Rich white kids," I said.

"Yeah," Davidson said, laughing. His eyes lit up when he

laughed. "White rich kids. He never said a word, but he had this look in his eye, like, 'Shut up, kid, and let me do the driving.'"

"My kind of guy," I said.

"Well, sure," Compton said. "You're a Puerto Rican."

I laughed.

Davidson went on as if we hadn't spoken. "He wasted so much time getting lost in Boston, he didn't get me up here until dark, and he was probably scared Mother would fire him. So when we finally got to the school gate, he just dumped me out."

"That's a half mile from the school," I said.

"He got my suitcases from the trunk and dropped them on the grass and took off like a bat out of hell."

"Jesus."

"For all I knew, he was dumping me somewhere out in the country. But then I saw the school sign."

"So what did you do?"

He waited before answering. "You know," he said, "I don't mind talking about this stuff to you guys, because we're out here sluicing . . . "

"You can trust us," Yusupov said. "We can all trust us. So did you cry?"

He threw back his head. "Cry? No! I took a leak. I watched his taillights go out of view. When I saw he was really not coming back, I sat down on my big suitcase and felt the happiest I had ever felt in my whole life. I was so . . . just happy."

"Why?" I asked.

"I got away from her."

"Oh, wow. Oh, damn."

"So you were very pleased to be arrived here," Aubert said.

Davidson gazed at all of us. "I don't know what St. Philip's is to you guys. I love the school. I think of it as my real home."

No one said a word. Then Compton said, "Knowing your mother, I might feel the same way."

Gellhorn said to Compton, "What's your mother like? I don't hear she's so great."

"I don't give a shit what you hear," Compton barked from beneath a darkening brow.

"Oh, God," Yusupov said, "Compton's about to go homicidal again."

"Shut up," Compton shouted at him. "What's your mother like, Russki?"

"My mother," Yusupov said, dropping his head as if to ponder deeply. "My mother is sweet as sugar, kind, childlike, cares deeply for us all, and may possibly be a bit insane. She worries, which is burdensome at times. What about you, Pontiac?"

I was surprised to be asked.

"My mother is very beautiful," I said.

"Yes, she is," Compton said with a sudden leer.

I pointed a warning finger at him.

"Do you miss her?" Yusupov asked me.

I had to think. "Yes. No. She's pretty mean, as well."

"Aubert?" he asked.

Aubert shook his head gravely. "Well, my mother is French. So, of course, that is a difficulty. She is an excellent mother in every regard, but as you yourself have said, Yusupov, sometimes a mother can be a burden."

We were all quiet again for a long time.

"How many people miss their mothers?" I asked.

Everyone but Davidson raised his hand.

"How many people are glad to be away from their mothers?"

We all raised our hands, Davidson a little too eagerly.

"Six of one, half dozen of another," I said.

Just before setting out, I had folded some of Davidson's peanut butter and jelly sandwiches and repacked them in the cannister that held the bicycle pump. They were only slightly moist, with a hint of three-in-one oil. I pulled them out carefully, pinched them into quarters with my fingers and passed around the bits. We wolfed them down with the sloe gin.

"Of course," Aubert said, "We all know of Roosevelt's famous family tree."

"My tree," Roosevelt laughed. "Hah."

"But why this, 'Hah?'" Aubert asked.

"I am, indeed, related to the Roosevelts you're thinking of, though not directly. I come from a different branch of the famous tree."

"Which one?"

"Mining, railroads, and cattle ranching in Nicaragua."

"Nicaragua!" Aubert said. "I have been there. A magnificent country. Very beautiful. Do you still have a home there?"

"No," Roosevelt said. "In fact, my father reminds us every so often that that no member of my family must ever visit Nicaragua."

Aubert looked embarrassed. "Your nation does not have a beautiful history there," he said.

Compton, who had been listening intently, said, "You guys must have done some bad shit if you can't even go back to the whole country now."

"I believe we did," Roosevelt said. "I don't know what it was. I dread the day I find out."

Gellhorn said, "So you have a curriculum problem ahead of you, too."

"Not looking forward to it at all," Roosevelt said.

Aubert took him by the elbow.

"My friend," he said softly, "my own family has a very ugly history in Côte d'Ivoire. I believe that all white people must have a certain reckoning with history one day."

"Meanwhile," Yusupov said to Roosevelt, "you'll just have to comfort yourself spending all that terrible white money."

"My father made his own money," Roosevelt said tartly, "as will I."

We were silent again.

Taking the sloe gin from Aubert, I asked Tweetie, "Why are you called Tweetie?"

"It's from St. Alban's," he said, "the choir school at the National Cathedral in Washington. I went there before I came here."

"You were how old?" I asked.

"I started when I was nine."

"Your parents sent you away to boarding school when you were nine years old? Jesus. Why?"

"I had a very good voice. And they were always away skiing and stuff in places like Gstadt."

"What is goostad?"

Compton said, "It never ends. You have to explain everything to him." He turned to me. "Gstadt is where all the European royals and nobility hang out in the winter. Rich Americans go there to suck up. Tweetie's parents sent him to choir school for the same reason all rich parents send their kids away. To get rid of them so they can play."

Tweetie frowned for an instant. "I was first soprano."

"You're kidding," I said. "How were you a soprano with that voice?"

"I was a little kid!" he bellowed.

Birds and squirrels scrambled for safety.

"So you were the best soprano," Roosevelt said.

"I guess. We all had choir nicknames. Mine was Tweetie. It stuck for a little too long."

"What do you sing now?" Gellhorn asked.

"Baritone."

"Well," Roosevelt said, "it's time for you to get a new name. You can't go through your entire life Tweetie."

"How?" Tweetie asked. "How do you get a new name?"

Roosevelt said, "We'll just change it. Right here. That's what we do. We're schoolmates. We're sluicing. We get to say what your name is. Who do you want to be?"

Tweetie looked genuinely interested. "What about Butch?"

"Fuck you," Compton said. "Everybody wants to be Butch. I should be Butch way before you."

Yusupov, thrusting himself forward into Compton's face, said, "I know a good new nickname for you, Compton. What about, 'Total Asshole?'"

"Stop it, stop it, stop it," I said. "Don't turn this into a fight."

"Well said," Roosevelt said.

Yusupov backed off. Compton looked at me and settled back onto the grass with the bottle.

"Tell you what, Tweetie," Roosevelt said. "They called you Tweetie because you were a soprano. Now you're a baritone. What if we call you Bear?"

"Really?" he gasped, beaming like a baby.

"Sure."

"That would be great."

"Everybody," Roosevelt said. "Meet our new friend, Bear."

"Hi, Bear," we all said in chorus.

203

Bear grinned from ear to ear. "Hi," he said. "Nice to meet you, total assholes."

Everyone laughed, even Compton.

Gellhorn, Yusupov, and Aubert jumped into a discussion in French. At one point, Aubert appeared to gesture toward Compton and all three laughed.

"Hey," Compton barked, "speak English, you fucking frog."

Roosevelt leapt to his feet as if on springs and stepped between Compton and the three French-speakers. In moments like this, Roosevelt suddenly and convincingly became a Montana cowboy with John Wayne swagger.

"Don't use words like that around me," he told Compton. He could have added, "Pilgrim."

"Like what?"

"Frog."

"What's wrong with it?"

"It's like nigger."

"What's wrong with nigger?"

The two of them drew close, and the rest of us tensed. A fight between Compton and Roosevelt would definitely mean a trip to the cooler, maybe even the hospital in town, in which case our grand adventure would be abandoned halfway.

"It's low-class," Roosevelt said.

"I'll say it if I want."

"Then you'll be low-class."

"You're not colored. What's it to you? I don't care if you're a fucking Roosevelt. Kiss my ass."

Roosevelt was a stone. In a tense whisper, he said, "Why do you want to say words like that?"

Gellhorn and Yusupov began speaking excitedly in French,

explaining what was transpiring to Aubert. Aubert put up a hand for silence.

"I comprehend that I have been insulted again by the word, frog. Compton has made a promise to me some time ago that he would not use this word again. I am less injured by the word itself than I am trumped."

"You don't mean trumped," Yusupov said. "You mean betrayed."

"I am betrayed," Aubert said. "I desire an apology."

We all looked to Compton, who was sullen.

I said, "You did promise not to say it again. That night when you fought."

"You call that a fight?" Compton said.

"Compton," Yusupov said. "You gave your word . . . "

"All right, all right," Compton said irritably. "I'm sorry. I'm sorry. I lost my temper. It won't happen again."

Aubert said, "Compton has apologized. I accept. In return, I shall speak only English."

We all nodded.

"But I must say an additional thing that I have noticed on previous times. The French spoken by both Gellhorn and Yusupov is almost without defect or accent. I admire this very much, and it has aided me in my . . . I don't know how to say it in English . . . mal du pays, in French."

"Homesickness," Gellhorn said.

"I wonder how you two have learned to speak French so well."

Yusupov asked Aubert, "Of the two of us, me and Gellhorn, whose French is better?"

Without pause, Aubert said, "Oh, Gellhorn, most certainly."

Compton snickered. "Jesus Crist, Yusupov, way to walk into it.

You ask a guy who's better, you or the other guy, and the other guy is standing right there. Of course he has to say it's the other guy."

Yusupov tilted his head thoughtfully. "You make a good point."

No one said anything for a while.

Then I said, "Yusupov, I've been wondering something. You and I talked once about class. Everybody here says I'm low-class, even though I never thought I was low-class until I came here. But I don't get what you are. Are you an aristocrat or a middle-class guy or what? What is your family?"

"I don't really understand, either," Gellhorn said. "What is your family, Yusupov? Are you aristocrats or poor people like Pontiac? You can't really be both."

Yusupov shrugged. "True. Not in this country. Perhaps not anywhere. My parents are waifs. They were teenagers at the time of the Revolution, children of old-world aristocracy, doves in a gilded cage thrust into the snow without a clue.

"Most of what they've done ever since then is hide. Upstate New York is their latest refuge, but they've hidden all over the globe.

"The old Anglo-Americans in upstate New York have a love-hate relationship with us White Russians. My father is a little bit clever. He's made a bit of money with his charm, a good deal of it from certain rich Anglo-American widows. My mother is completely tolerant, as long as the family has money in the jar.

"My parents love us dearly, almost as if they were our siblings. They don't belong in this world. At one point, we were almost broke, about to lose the house, and my father came into a big wad of dough. He paid off the house, thank God, but then he pulled all of us out of school and took us to Switzerland. I was about ten. My brothers and I knew even then it was crazy. Stalking butterflies and playing guitars in the Alps, when we had just come close to being beggars in the street. But in those few months, we had the most glorious interlude of our lives, a visit to heaven.

"My father is a grand adventurer. He would love this, the sluicing, what we are doing here."

Bear said, "After that, you were rich, right? Because he got all that money. So now you're still rich."

"Hah," Yusupov laughed. "My fucking parents were out of money again as soon as we got home from Switzerland. In fact, we had to sort of scoot out of our hotel in Zurich at midnight. But you know, that's how they are. They're nothing like Americans, always trying to be something. They think they are everything already. Being alive is their great joy. Alive and well. Chasing butterflies in the Alps, playing music.

"I have five brothers and two sisters. We will never be aristocrats. There is no such thing anymore. The Bolsheviks killed the aristocracy. My brothers and I will have to make a lot of money doing shit we hate. But we have to. That's the only way the family can be rich again."

As we dried out in the sun, we finished off our sandwich bits and drained the rest of the first bottle and half of the second. We needed to get back on the sluice in order to keep to our timetable. To everyone's relief, the stream broadened and flattened downstream from our picnic spot, no longer foaming between boulders. The fallen trees were fewer and farther between, and we were able to navigate without disaster. Roosevelt tied the rafts together with a painter. As the stream calmed, the boats orbited each other slowly, spinning on the water through a brilliant red and gold scattering of leaves. We were all half sleepy, heavy-lidded, lulled by the gentle late-day chorus of the creatures.

Aubert reached into his backpack and extracted a tightly taped plastic bag. With some tearing and gnawing, he finally got it open, reached in with fingers and began pulling out, wonder of wonders, a handful of crooked, rum-soaked cigars, several books of matches, and a pint bottle of Courvoisier.

"Where in God's name did you get Courvoisier?" Gellhorn exclaimed.

"I am French," Aubert said.

We lighted the cigars, sickly sweet and therefore delicious, perhaps even designed for boys, and we passed the cognac between boats, happy as Pinocchio and Lampwick before they turned to donkeys.

"Bear," Roosevelt said, "why don't you earn your new name and sing for us?"

"I have to sing for my supper?"

"It would be nice."

Compton said, "Least you could do."

Bear, who had taken Davidson's place in the raft with me and Compton, exhaled a long blue plume of rummy smoke.

"Sing what?"

"What did you sing at St. Alban's?" Roosevelt asked from the other raft.

"Hymns."

"Sing us a hymn then."

"Which one?"

We all groaned.

"God it's pulling teeth with you," Compton said. "Who cares? Just sing a goddamn hymn."

The rafts spun slowly, drifting down white channels of sun across the painted rain of leaves. We savored our swigs deeply and puffed up tiny white clouds of cigar smoke like so many steam engines.

Bear threw back his head, opened his mouth and poured out an enormously deep round voice that made the air quiver and the sunbeams tremble.

"Ein feste Burg ist unser Gott," he sang in notes of trumpets. "Ein gute Wehr und Waffen."

We all stared at each other, reaching for the answer. I got it first.

"A Mighty Fortress," I blurted, not wanting to get beat.

"Shit that's it," Compton said. "But why are you singing it in kraut?"

"It's a German hymn," Bear said. "It was written by Martin Luther. It's the battle hymn of Protestantism."

"Bullshit," Compton said. "Why would Episcopalians sing it if it's Protestant?"

"Because Episcopalians are Protestants," I said. "Jeez, Compton, do I have to explain everything to you?"

I eyed him carefully, ready. But instead of turning purple, he grinned slyly, reached into his backpack, and pulled out a homely, brown ceramic object that looked like a potato with holes in the side.

"That's not a grenade is it?" I asked.

"No, dumbass, it's a sweet potato."

Holding it in both hands with fingers arched, he put one end to his mouth. From this crude fistful of clay flowed a softly fluted rendition of "A Mighty Fortress."

"What surprise," Aubert called to him. "How do you know to play this?"

"I played clarinet," Compton said, looking away. "It's fingered the same."

Yusupov in the other raft laughed broadly.

"Compton, the little clarinetist! The Far Hills regs were telling the truth. You can still sort of see it in him now, can't you? The little boy in his short pants, squeaking away for his tutor."

Darkly furious, Compton began hauling in the painter to tug the other raft up close so he could get at Yusupov. Yusupov, with eyes bugged out, grabbed a paddle and took a seated batting stance as if to chop off Compton's head.

"Stop it!" I shouted. "Jesus Christ. Are you guys going to murder each other?"

"Bear!" Roosevelt yelled. "Sing! Compton! Play!"

Compton sank back slowly into the raft. "All Bear knows is hymns," he said. "I hate fucking hymns."

"Bear," Roosevelt said, "do you know any songs that aren't hymns?"

"Sure," Bear said. "A lot of hymns are just copies of old folk tunes. We weren't allowed to sing the folk versions at St. Alban's, but we learned them anyway."

"Like what?" Compton asked skeptically.

Bear threw back his head again and sang into the shadowed treetops: "Alas my love thou do me wrong to cast me off discourteously; And I have love-ed thee so long, delighting in thine company."

"That's a hymn!" Compton said accusingly. "Christmas. 'What Child is This?'"

No longer shouting and roaring, the sluice had softened to a silver chorus of bells ringing all around us.

Bear sang: "Greensleeves was my delight, Greensleeves my heart of gold, Greensleeves was my heart of joy, and who but my Lady Greensleeves?"

"Who is Lady Greensleeves?" Aubert asked.

"No one knows," Bear said. "There's a lot of mystery about it.

But one version is that the greensleeves were camp followers in the War of the Roses."

"What is a camp follower?" Aubert asked. "Oh, wait. Do you want to say a *cantinière, the women who sell food to the soldiers?*"

Compton snorted. "I think he's singing about women who sell a lot more than sandwiches."

"Oh, you mean whores," Aubert said.

Bear said, "Called greensleeves because their arms were stained from rolling in the grass from having so much sex with the soldiers. That's the version I heard. That's why we weren't allowed to sing it."

"So much sex," Yusupov said with a sigh. "I think a greensleeves is the only thing missing from this otherwise perfect adventure."

We all nodded and sighed except for Compton, who muttered, "We would need more than one."

"Play it," Roosevelt told Compton. "Bear, you sing."

And so, spinning slowly through the gathering gloom of a late afternoon in autumn, Bear sang a booming sweetness while Compton played birdsong harmony in a minor-key complaint of ancient war and doom. In the last minutes of floating, Aubert joined in, then Yusupov in a surprisingly strong voice, then Roosevelt. I fell in behind Roosevelt, and finally to everyone's amazement, even Gellhorn sang in a shy, off-key mutter. Just as the rafts collided with the bank at the take-out a few yards short of the whispering Gitch, we finished together softly: "And who but my Lady Greensleeves?"

•

On Monday, I went to my postal box on the wall outside The Tuck Shop. In addition to the brown money envelope with my money, I found a thin envelope on cheap paper addressed to me in my brother's childish penmanship. The return address was machine-printed and said "Oakland County Juvenile Corrections."

I looked around to make sure I was alone before I opened it. The letter was scrawled in pencil on one almost transparent sheet:

Dear Woodrow.
How are you? I guess Ma told you I'm in juvee. It's not so bad. The food is bad. I only got in one fight. I won. Ma thinks the queers are after me. Theres queers in here because you can see them do it. So far they ant after me. Do you have queers in that school? Pa wishes I was like you. He's proud of you. He ant proud of me I can tell you that. I hope I make it.
David

That night in bed, using my flashlight beneath the quilt of hunting jackets my mother had brought me, I wrote back:

Dear David:
Ma told me you were in juvie. I'm sorry. I guess you deserved it from what she told me. Why did you guys steal Tom Quinn's truck? Pretty strange we both wound up away from home all of a sudden. I feel bad you are in juvie. It's nothing that bad here but I don't like it. I wish I could get out. I bet you do too. Take care of yourself David. I will too.
Woodrow

The next Saturday after lunch, Mr. Fell told me that boxes with my name had arrived in the first-floor lobby. I rushed downstairs, flushed with embarrassment, because I knew the delivery could only be my new clothes. As it happened, the Lower School lobby was in a rare moment of desertion. I was able to lug all three boxes up to my alcove unmolested. I ripped them open and found to my relief that the clothes were already on hangers. I arranged them quickly on my clothes rod and transported the ruined boxes back downstairs to a set of swinging doors next to Beetle's apartment that led to a maintenance area.

Beetle poked his head out.

"What are you up to, Skaggs?"

"Just helping Mr. Fell get rid of some trash."

He waddled over and stooped to examine the boxes. "This trash seems to have your name on it."

"Yes, sir."

"You must tell your parents that they can't just ship you every little bit of business. Our space is very limited here. Be sure they understand that."

"Yes, sir."

He waddled back to his door, muttering, "Preposterous poppycock." As he entered his apartment, he turned back and said, "Put it all inside the white doors."

"Yes, sir."

I did as instructed, then went back upstairs to my alcove. I sat on my bed and stared disconsolately at the new clothes and shoes. I didn't see how I could wear any of it. I cringed at the thought of the ribbing I would take for changing my appearance. It seemed to me that the other boys had become accustomed to me as I was. My appearance, the red blazer, skinny ties, foeswade shoes, and switchblade scar, no longer made them cringe as if they had stumbled on a burglar. I was Pontiac. They knew me. I looked like Pontiac—what

213

they expected me to be. I didn't know what I would look like, to them or to me, wearing their costume instead of my own.

But then I thought of my mother coming all that way and spending her own dearly held savings to buy these clothes for me, money I knew she would rather have spent getting David out of juvie. I ripped off my Hudson's Department store outfit, kicked it under the bed and began putting on the clothes the tailor had made for me: a pair of boxy khaki trousers, a thick scratchy shirt with a high-standing button-down collar, a fat tie and dark socks. The hardest part, the worst stick for some reason, was the shoes. They were second-hand oxblood brogans, shoes the tailor had taken to be re-soled and polished. When I held them up to the light, they shone like glass. In the box with them was a tin of polish, an applicator brush, a buffing brush, and a polish rag. I thought it was funny how accurately the tailor had pegged the St. Philip's boys. I sat on the bed for a long while, staring down at the shoes before I could shove my toes into them and lace them up. Once I had them on, I kicked my mouse-skins under the bed. My hair had already grown out, and without thinking a lot about it I had been combing it over my forehead in the St. Philip's sweep. As I stretched my arms into the tweed sport coat, I made up my mind that the first boy who said one word to me about my new look would get a punch square in the mouth.

All that afternoon and through dinner, I waited, bracing for it. No one said a word. In fact, no one ever said anything about my clothes again.

•

Two days later, I checked my mailbox and found another letter from David and a note from Johnny Wilson asking me to come to his office.

I sat down on a step and read David's letter.

Dear Woodrow.
We was drunk. I didn't even know we done it 'til next day when I woke up in the hospital. We was stupid Woodrow. Man I wish I wasn't in Juvie. It's bad Woodrow. I'm scared. David.

I went to the school building, found an empty classroom and wrote to David.

Dear David.
I'm sorry. I wish you weren't there too. I worry about you pretty bad. Just keep your head down and do what they tell you. Try to stay out of fights. I have quite a bit of fights here so I know it's not easy. Pa told me not to take shit off nobody before I came here. Did he tell you that too? These guys are weird. They're like halfway between hoods and sissies. Some of them are pretty tough. I didn't think rich kids could fight but they can just like us. After you get over how weird they are, they're almost just like us. I wish you had some friends to stick up for you in there. I might have some here. It helps with how lonely it is.
Woodrow.

As soon as I had finished the letter, I went to Johnny Wilson's office. He answered my knock and told me to come in and sit.

"How are you?" he asked from behind the desk.

"Fine."

"Fell tells me you guys are up to some kind of mischief with the Schmitzes in the dining room."

"I'm not really in on it."

"Did you take a Sunday off and go sluicing?"

I said nothing. It was supposed to be a secret.

"Speak up," he said.

"Yes, sir."

"You can't do stuff like that, Woodrow. They can afford it. You cannot. I told you. Why did you do it?"

"I don't know," I said. "I just . . . it felt good to be included."

He sighed and his shoulders slumped. "OK. So you have joined a gang."

"I guess. Sort of."

He shook his head and looked away. "I know the feeling. I'm in a gang."

"Really? Here? At this place?"

"No. In New York. Maybe someday I'll introduce you to them, but you'll have to get a lot smarter first. Look, I understand, Woodrow. I'm just worried about your grades. They're improving a little but nowhere near enough."

I had been pushing it out of my mind. Hearing him say it out loud was like a dousing of cold water. It almost felt good.

"I'm trying really hard."

"Yes. Fell tells me that. He says you're studying regularly."

"I am."

He got up and walked from behind his desk. He took a chair next to me. "The thing is, Woodrow, and I know you can figure this out because you're a kid from Pontiac, you're not one of these hot house flowers, they could get away with the grades you're getting, because they're what's called legacies. Their fathers and great-great-grandfathers went to school here and their families have been supporting the school with money for a hundred years."

"But I can't, because I'm low-class."

He clucked remonstratively. "I wouldn't go there if I were you, Woodrow. There's nothing in feeling sorry for yourself but more failure and worse pain. And there's only one thing that will ever make you feel good, that will make things right."

"What is that?"

"Success."

"So?"

"Try harder."

•

My heart was resolved. I was going to do exactly what Johnny Wilson told me, try so hard I'd either succeed or die. I repeated it over and over to myself. Succeed or die. Succeed or die. But on the following Monday morning my heart went cold when I heard the rector utter my name in reports. Peering down at his list through half-frame glasses, he droned as if counting sheep, "Skaggs, ten demerits for repeated violation of the dress code after two warnings, weekday work squad for two weeks."

I had never been given even a warning for dress code. I dressed exactly like everyone else, down to the fucking shoeshine. At least to outward appearance, I was now a St. Philip's School clone. Work squad would put a serious dent in my grinding routine.

I stood on tiptoe and looked around the chapel lawn for The

Toad. He was in a knot of masters a few yards off from the rector's stone lectern. He caught me searching and gave me a small sheepish shrug. As soon as reports was over, I rushed through the crowd and caught him slinking along a path into the woods by the chapel pond, a shortcut to his house.

"Mr. Grace," I called. "Mr. Grace."

"Sorry, Pontiac," he said, waving a hand behind him but continuing to plunge into the woods. "I need your help. Sorry. The job is just two weeks. It's not going to kill you."

"Mr. Grace, I'm sorry," I said when I caught up with him, "but I'm having a really hard time with my grades, and I need to study."

"Weekday work squad is only in the afternoons after sports," he said. "It's two hours. You don't study afternoons after sports. You study in study hall."

"You don't understand . . . "

"Look," he said brusquely, turning to stop me, "I need your help. I can do a lot for you around here, Skaggs, but you have to do this for me. I'll owe you."

"Sir, normally . . . "

He laughed. "You would 'normally' what? You're not really in a position to tell me what you would do normally, Lord Pontiac. You will show up for weekday work squad this afternoon, or we'll get into some serious triple demerits. Now excuse me." He turned on a heel and heaved himself up the rising path through the pines.

After Mr. Fell's English class, Compton caught me in the hallway and put a hand on my shoulder.

"Ten demerits for dress code? What did you do, go back to the mouse-skins?"

"It's the fucking Toad," I said, shrugging off his hand, "He's got some shovel job he wants me to do for him. I'm screwed. I really needed that time to grind. Johnny Wilson thinks I'll get kicked out if I don't do better."

Compton followed me out of the school building and down the long walk. "OK," he said. "I'll do it."

"Do what?"

"Your work squad."

"You can't do that."

"Sure I can. Anybody can stand in for anybody else on work squad. Why do you think you never see guys like Rensevear, Colfax, or Howard on work squad? Christ, Howard gets a million demerits a week. You don't see him actually doing any work do you? That guy wouldn't know which end of a rake to pick up."

"How does he get people to do it for him?"

"He pays."

"How much would it cost me to get you to do my work squad?"

"How much you got?"

"I've got thirty bucks saved."

"I'll take it."

"Don't you have extra lacrosse?"

"That's voluntary. Besides, I'm the only hammer they've got in Third and Fourth form. I don't need them. They need me."

"I don't know if I could let you do that."

"Pontiac, I'm doing work squad for you. I want the thirty bucks. You can take it or leave it, but I'm about to change my mind. Do you want me to do your work squad for you or not?"

"Yes."

We walked on to the Lower for lunch. I was stupidly dumbfounded.

•

For the next two weeks, our table in the dining room was quiet. With Mr. Fell's intervention, cereal and oatmeal had been restored, so we were able to enjoy a full breakfast. Rolls, butter, and dessert were all served at dinner, but we were not allowed to consume any of it. Herr Schmitz still had not mentioned coffee again, but we didn't touch coffee until the Schmitzes had departed the dining room, not to press the point.

Herr Schmitz insisted that dessert be placed in front of every boy, probably because he didn't want Beetle to notice anything out of the ordinary. Yusupov suggested that Frau Schmitz had a frailty, which he believed he could exploit with his theatrical gifts. He insisted that by staring despondently at his dessert with just the right forlorn expression, he could coax at least the suggestion of a sigh from her cruel lips, perhaps even the beginning of moisture at the eye. None of the rest of us believed there was a single ounce of human frailty, kindness, or mercy anywhere in her withered soul. If her unrelentingly sour expression changed at all, we argued, it was only to suppress sadistic laughter.

Granger, who sat just to Yusupov's right and across the table close to Frau Schmitz, said he would settle the matter by joining in with Yusupov and double-teaming her. That night, both sat with shoulders hunched forward, peering into their apple cobblers as if gazing into the faces of their dying mothers, uttering no syllable during the entire dessert course. It was difficult for me to see Frau Schmitz's expression because we sat on the same side of the table with Compton between us. But Aubert, who sat across from us, began to believe that the pitiful looks might be having an effect.

"What it is exactly, I am not able to say," Aubert said when we gathered back in the dorm. "When Yusupov and Granger do their absurd behavior, I truly believe that she has a response of some kind. But you know, with these terrible people, one cannot really know if they are smiling or . . . what is the word in English?"

"Grimace?" I said.

"Yes, I think it is the same in French." He looked to Yusupov. "Faire une grimace?"

"Oui," Yusupov said, "c'est exact. But I think Granger and I do more than that. I think we are able to cause regret."

"Whatever it is that Madame Schmitz does with her very unpleasing face," Aubert said, "I do believe you have some effect on her. Good or bad I cannot say."

"Theater," Yusupov said, turning toward his alcove, "will carry the day."

•

At the beginning of Modern Literature one day, Mr. Fell asked, "What is existentialism? Mr. Compton, care to give it a whirl?"

"It's like doing nothing except existing," Compton said nonchalantly, "just sort of sitting there. It's mainly for French people who are still depressed about surrendering to the Germans. They smoke a lot, and, uh, you know, they do the shrug, like this." He executed a perfect Gallic shrug with one hand in the air and the proper pursing of the mouth.

"That's absurd," Gellhorn snapped. "Existentialism is a philosophy. It's what Camus is writing about. It's not about smoking and shrugging."

Compton raised his paperback copy of *The Stranger* just high enough to hide his hand from Mr. Fell and shot Gellhorn the bird. Compton's face was purpling, which meant Gellhorn had things to worry about later.

"Then again," Gellhorn mumbled, "the French do smoke a lot."

"So Skaggs," Mr. Fell said. "Existentialism. All smoking and shrugging?"`

I thought I knew the answer, at least better than Compton. We had gone over it once before in class, which I remembered. This was a moment when I might even have done some showing off back in school in Pontiac, but my persistent failure on the tests and my inability so far to turn the tide by studying harder had robbed my confidence. I mumbled that I wasn't really sure what existentialism was.

"Compton?" he asked. "All smoking and shrugging? Really?"

"But they go too far with it," Compton said, "and then they stab somebody."

Mr. Fell put his palms up in the air. "Good Lord, better to keep them smoking and shrugging."

"If they're French, sure."

Gellhorn asked Compton, "Is there any way we could keep you at the shrugging and smoking stage?"

Compton glared angrily, ready to sock him in the face.

"Smoking, as you know, is an expellable offense," Mr. Fell said quickly, "but Mr. Compton is very good at the shrug."

We all laughed. The purple faded slowly from Compton's furrowed brow, and he gave a grudging sneer to acknowledge the joke.

That night during the witching hour, however, the bad blood reappeared. Compton and Yusupov were reliving the worms in the cream again, taking turns recreating the moment when the big one plopped into Frau Schmitz's bowl. I was in a circle of boys at the radiator bench, laughing and applauding. Gellhorn stood ostentatiously apart with his arms folded and face turned half away, watching disdainfully with one eye.

Compton called him out. "What's your problem?"

Gellhorn shrugged and started to walk away, but Compton said, "Something here you don't like?"

Gellhorn turned back. "How can you think putting worms in someone's food is clever? What are you, six years old?"

Compton left Yusupov and walked straight to Gellhorn, his face darkening. "That's better than being a little chickenshit."

Gellhorn snorted. "For God's sake. You really are six years old, aren't you?" He turned on a heel, plunged into his alcove, and snapped the curtain behind him.

Compton stalked into his own alcove and shut his curtain. We kept still, watching Compton's curtain. In less than thirty seconds, he exploded back out and bellowed, "Hey, Gelding, you chickenshit bastard, come on out here and talk to me."

Gellhorn burst from his alcove without the glasses. I wasn't accustomed to seeing his face bare. He looked harder, more pugnacious.

They both wore pajamas, robes, and slippers.

"What did you call me?" Gellhorn said evenly.

"Gelding. You know. No balls."

Gellhorn walked straight down the dorm, got to about a foot and a half from Compton, and hooked a lightning quick punch into his face, a boxer's punch, trained and controlled. Compton, taken by surprise, fell backward. Gellhorn backed off, fists up and arms cocked.

Compton came back square to his feet with a tight-lipped grin. He charged. Gellhorn hit him in the head with two quick pops, but Compton slammed a hip into Gellhorn mid-body and sent him reeling backward. Before Gellhorn could regain his balance, Compton rushed him, grabbed him by the hair, and threw him face-first against the radiator with a sickening wet thud. I expected Gellhorn to be dead.

But he was not. Compton made his customary mistake, turning prematurely to grin victory at the crowd. Gellhorn bounced back to his feet like a dancer, circled part way to Compton's unsuspecting back, and smashed both fists, one after the other, into Compton's lower back. Compton let out a fierce shout, threw both hands in the air, and turned to face Gellhorn. He cocked his right fist for a blow but took too long. Gellhorn smashed a fist into Compton's jaw, knocking a spray of spit and blood from the side of his mouth.

Their pajama buttons had come loose, revealing torsos. We had all seen each other in the shower, but looking at someone's naked body in a fight was different. Gellhorn was wiry and rippled like the boxer his father had trained him to be. Compton's midsection, arms, ass, and legs looked like the trunk and branches of a tree, impervious to pain.

Laughing, blood running over his chin, Compton ran straight into Gellhorn. With one massive backhanded blow to the head, he smashed Gellhorn to the floor, bent down to him with his left hand, yanked him aloft by a handful of shredded pajama top, and smashed him in the head with a right-handed punch. Gellhorn slumped to a sitting position, his back against the radiator bench.

"C'est fini," Aubert shouted, rushing between them. "The fight is over. You stop now. It is satisfied."

Compton was breathing hard. Gellhorn sat quietly looking up at him. Compton walked to Gellhorn and put down a hand. Gellhorn took it. Compton assisted him to his feet.

Mopping blood from his jaw with a bare forearm, Compton said, "Good fight."

Gellhorn nodded. "Good fight."

Adams and Barry appeared at the end of the dorm just outside the hallway to their rooms.

"Is everything all right?" Adams asked.

"Fine," Gellhorn said.

"Rien a voir ici," Aubert said.

Barry came down the dorm, took Gellhorn by the shoulders, and stared into his face and mouth.

"Cooler," he decreed.

Gellhorn turned silently into his alcove and began packing a few things, books and clothes, to take with him for a night in the infirmary with Doc Herter. He would be served breakfast in bed there by the doctor's wife, a not unwelcome thing. The doctor would examine him in time for chapel.

Barry didn't touch Compton but looked him over closely.

"Teeth?" he asked.

Compton ran his tongue around his mouth.

"Good," he said with a cheerful nod.

"Shower," Barry said.

Compton went to his alcove, got his Dopp kit and fresh pajamas, and stalked off to the bathroom.

"Anyone else mangled?" Barry asked.

We shook our heads.

"Lights out then."

At dinner the next night, Herr Schmitz said to Compton, "I am told that you are quite the hoodlum pugilist."

Compton shrugged. "I don't know about hoodlum."

"I believe you do. Quite a lot about it. Mr. Barry, did you not tell me this morning that Compton had attacked someone? I assume it was Gellhorn, who sits here with a black eye and bandages?"

"Yes," Barry said. "He and Gellhorn had a tussle."

"A tussle? Is that what we call it here, when a person is attacked so violently that he must spend the night in the infirmary?" He leaned forward to peer down the table at Gellhorn and made a muttering noise.

"I'm fine," Gellhorn said, his voice a little muffled by a swollen jaw.

"What I heard," Herr Schmitz said, "was that you, Gellhorn, fought like a gentleman, like your father at Yale, but that Compton here fought like a common thug."

"It was fairly even," Gellhorn said.

Barry said to Herr Schmitz, "I did not tell you that Compton fought like a thug."

Herr Schmitz rose up higher in his chair and tapped his water glass with a spoon.

"Silence at this table," he said.

"Stop eating," Adams told us.

In his most Teutonic sangfroid, Herr Schmitz said, "I want to make one thing perfectly clear to all of you. I am fully aware that the school is embarked on a social experiment this year and that there may be boys among us who do not come from the backgrounds traditionally associated with the families of St. Philip's School.

"Know this. I don't care who you are or where you come from. You will behave properly at this table whenever Frau Schmitz and I are present or you will be dealt with severely. This means you in particular, Compton."

Compton flushed purple. "I'm not a god damn scholarship boy." He pointed at me. "He is. He's the Puerto Rican."

Frau Schmitz leaned forward to examine me. "He doesn't look Puerto Rican," she whispered morosely to her husband.

Herr Schmitz touched his face just above one eye with a forefinger. She looked again, saw my scar, and recoiled.

"Oh, my," she said faintly.

Turning to Compton, Herr Schmitz said, "You are just what the hockey team is looking for, I suppose. It is a colored sport, after all."

Frau Schmitz spoke quietly but sharply to her husband in a language none of us recognized.

"I meant only that it is a sport that was invented by the Indians," he said, half to her and partly to the table. "I had no intention of racism."

"'Colored' is a racial pejorative term in American speech," she told him in English.

He shrugged. "The boys at this table will behave as gentlemen," he said with finality, "or they will not sit at this table." He gazed at Compton. "Do you understand me?"

Compton muttered a barely audible yes through tight jaws, his face the colors of an Easter egg. He sat hunched forward in his chair with a fork clutched in one hand and did not spear another bite for the remainder of the meal.

On the way back to the dorm, I walked with him. Aubert caught up with us at the door to the dorm. "What did she say to him?" Compton asked him. "What is that pig Latin that they talk to each other?"

"I did not hear what she said," Aubert said, "but I gather she was accusing him of making a racist remark, for which she is to be applauded. They often speak Walloon to each other. I understand it a little."

"Walloon?" I said. "You just made that up. That's not a real language."

Aubert shook his head with his hands stiffly at his sides. "I am sorry. I am in a rush. I need to prepare my books for study hall. I do not have time to pause here and educate the entire United States populace on the existence of the world beyond your borders."

"Fuck you," I said.

"Yeah," Compton said to him. "Fuck you, f . . . "

Aubert and I could see the word, *frog*, forming on his lips. We glared at him.

"Fuck you, Frenchie," he said.

•

We had known for some time that Compton was planning revenge on the Schmitzes for calling him common, because he showed us the mousetraps he had purchased in Rumney. It took him a week, but he finally caught one. He trapped it appropriately enough, Yusupov said, in the common room. On Wednesday night after study hall when we were in our bathrobes, he showed us the tiny carcass. We stood in a ring and stared down at the pathetic gray corpse, which Compton had stuffed into a drinking glass.

"Looks like your shoes," he said to me.

Yusupov said, "This is a truly terrible idea."

"Oh, right, worse than your worms?"

"Live worms," Smiley said, mulling it seriously. "I'm having a hard time choosing."

"A dead mouse is definitely worse than live worms," Granger said.

"All at once worse," Aubert said. "Because it is dead."

"I will have nothing to do with this," Gellhorn said. "You're all asinine and utterly puerile."

"Good," Compton said. "Nobody asked you, asshole." He turned to me. "What is puerile?"

"Childish," I said.

He shrugged.

That evening, Compton began to lay out his plot. One boy would smuggle the dead mouse into the dining room in his pocket and, after getting a signal, pass it under the table to Yusupov. Two more boys would distract the Schmitzes. Then, using his birthday party magic, Yusupov would slip the mouse under the cover of the pewter meat platter just before it was passed to Frau Schmitz.

"You expect me to hold this mouse in my hands?" Yusupov asked.

"It will be wrapped in a clean handkerchief until you place it on top of the meat."

"Oh," Yusupov said. "OK."

"This is a misadventure," Aubert said, shaking his head.

Yusupov said, "She will scream, you know. Women and elephants are very afraid of mice."

Granger said, "If you really think she'll scream, I'm in."

"As am I," Yusupov said.

"Idiots," Gellhorn said.

Smiley looked stricken even beyond his usual solemnity. He said, "I think this is a dangerous idea, and I believe we could all be found out and very severely punished, possibly ruining our entire lives, but I will go along if you can promise me that Frau Schmitz will scream."

Aubert said, "I stand with Gellhorn. I am no party."

They all turned to me.

"I'm out," I said.

"I'm doing your work squad, asshole," Compton snarled.

I shrugged.

It was agreed that they would not introduce the mouse to Frau

Schmitz until a Saturday night, because Beetle and his wife were seldom present for dinners then. If Beetle were in attendance when Frau Schmitz screamed, he would come to the table, and we didn't want to have to deal with those consequences yet. In the few days left before the trap was to be sprung, Compton and Yusupov would refine and adjust details.

After lunch, I caught up with Compton as we were walking toward the gymnasium. "I appreciate your doing work squad, even though I'm paying you pretty good. I just can't do the mouse. I feel like I'm on too thin ice."

"Got it," he said.

"How's work squad going?"

He shrugged. "Poor Toad. He's not going to finish. He's got me and three other guys—Rensevear, Colfax and Howard from Dorm Three."

"They didn't buy out of it?"

"Not this time. They got the demerits from their supes and the supes wouldn't let them buy out. They're worse than useless. I almost feel sorry for The Toad. You can tell he's sweating it. We're not going to make it."

"What do you have to do?"

"We're digging a ditch behind the powerhouse. The wombats are supposed to put a big pipe in it Saturday for drainage or something, but it's not going to be ready."

That afternoon after crew, I did not go to the utility room, walking instead to the powerhouse where I found The Toad. Compton was knee-deep in a ditch about twenty feet long, ten feet short of the crest of a slope. Behind him were Rensevear, Colfax, and Howard, paddling away harmlessly at the soil with their shovels. The Toad was pacing above the ditch in his tweed jacket, smoking nervously. When he spied me coming near, he called out, "Lord Pontiac, is it? To what do we owe this honor?"

"Compton said you could use a hand."

"Use a hand? Use a hand? What do you mean? You're going to help me?"

"Help Compton," I said.

"We could use a hand, yes," he said. "We could use a hand. Excellent." He bustled over to the open back end of his battered school van and pulled out a shovel for me.

I jumped down into the ditch next to Compton, and right away we fell into a contrapuntal rhythm, Compton's shovel coming out with dirt flying while mine dug in. We got up a good pace, not so fast it would wind us but quick enough to get it done.

"Is this like rowing?" Compton asked.

"Kind of," I said. "Only it has a reason."

We took off our jackets and shirts and worked bare-chested. The Toad beamed. Half an hour before evening classes, the ditch broke through the crest of the rise. Standing at its completion, I looked down and saw how the storm water would pour into the ravine below and hold the erosion away from the power plant. We tossed the shovels into the back of Toad's van. Compton and I were muddy top to bottom. The other three waltzed off spick-and-span as if from a tea dance. The Toad was ecstatic.

"Skaggs," he said, "you made a big difference. I promise to stop giving you demerits. I owe you one."

"That's OK, sir."

"No, I owe you and Compton both. You two won't be forgotten. I honor my debts."

On the way back to the Lower to wash up, Compton said, "I don't know which is scarier, The Toad mad at us or The Toad thinking he owes us one."

"Yeah," I said. "Owes us one what?"

"Exactly."

•

It seemed to me that in Michigan the seasons plodded along reasonably predictably and in sequence, summer fading slowly into fall, winter beginning with a few light introductory snowflakes and then gradually getting down to business, and so on, so that there were no real surprises. But New Hampshire in August made no sense to me at all—hot as hell one day and then the very next day nippy and brisk.

On one suddenly hot day, I found myself sitting behind Davidson in the hated rowing barge, wearing the wrong clothes, the hot sticky long-sleeved jersey instead of the skimpy rowing shirt. We were rowing the length of the hated Drake Pond, a distance of almost two miles, for the fourth time in one afternoon—twice the amount of rowing we normally did in a day's practice. The afternoon was airless and the water hard as glass.

Dickie Decherd had made up his mind that the only way for him to claw his way back up the ranks into one of the upper shells was for our barge to beat a shell in a race under his command, ignoring the fact that the barge weighed three times what a regular shell weighed and that we were generally a weak crew. He carried a stopwatch, and every time we failed to traverse the pond in the time he had hoped to achieve, he threw a fit and ordered us in shrieks and shouts to row it again.

On the fourth trip back down the pond in sweltering heat, a boy behind me muttered, "He's never going to let us go in. We'll die out here."

A boy ahead of me turned his head back, an act that was in and of itself a gross infraction, and said, "Shut up. There's nothing we can do. He's the fucking cox."

Dickie heard the chatter and shrieked, "Take it up! Take it up! Stroke! Stroke, goddamn it!" And we all rowed harder because we had no choice. If most of the oars in a crew row hard and others do not, then all of the oars will collide with each other in a disastrous tangle, and the boat can actually capsize, in which case, if we survived, our coach, Mr. Zierotin, had already warned us that we would all be killed.

I tried to think how this could have happened to me. How did I wind up chained to an ugly boat on a sweltering day in New Hampshire taking orders from a shrieky little sawed-off punk even I could probably knock flat with one hand, and how was it possible that I was helpless to do anything about it? How could I be helpless? Who said I was helpless? Why was I helpless?

A brilliant idea occurred.

"Hey, Decherd!" I shouted. "Go fuck yourself!"

I kept rowing hard, because if I didn't keep up with the others, I would catch a crab as the other boys called it. My oar would lock in the water, slam back suddenly, punch me in the gut and even rip my feet out of the footholds on the slide, lift me up into the air, and drop me in the drink with injury. I had been a little slow to pick up on the exact principle and had already caught a crab three times. It hurt a lot and left bruises, but I had not been catapulted from the boat. Yet.

After a moment, another voice ahead of me called out, "Yeah,

Decherd, fuck yourself. We want to go in." And another. And another. As we rowed, voices cheered and jeered, with more calls of, "Fuck Decherd!" and "Go screw yourself you little shit."

Then I had the most brilliant idea of my entire rowing career.

I called out, "Weigh oars!"

Everyone stopped rowing at once.

Dickie screamed, "Ready all, row! Ready all, row!" But no one moved a muscle.

"We're going in, asshole," someone said. "We've done enough fucking rowing for one day."

"Take it up, starboard," Dickie shrieked, trying to turn the barge away from the docks in the distance. "Take it up starboard goddamn it!"

I called out, "Take it up port!"

All of the oars on the port side made a clean sweep, steering us toward the docks.

"On my call, row all," I said.

We plunged ahead toward the docks, Dickie shrieking like an injured alley cat and yanking the rudder furiously this way and that, trying to turn the boat, but the little rudder alone was no match for the long oars. We heard a sharp splitting sound behind us that meant the rudder had broken free, and then we heard Dickie sobbing.

"You fuckers!" he sobbed. "You fuckers! This is mutiny! Mutiny! I'll get you all kicked out. I'll get every fucking one of you kicked out of this school."

I thought about it. He probably could at least get me kicked out. I knew that mutiny was very bad, sort of like murder. I called out, "Weigh oars," and everyone stopped rowing. I twisted around so that I could see him in the stern three slides behind me.

"Decherd," I said, "if you tell them we mutinied on you, it just means you were too much of a little shit to be a good cox. They'll never let you cox an upper shell. You better say we had an accident with the rudder. Say we hit a log."

The oars were all suspended a foot off the water like wings gliding on a thermal as we drifted ahead on smooth water. No one made a sound. We could hear Dickie sniffling in the stern.

Finally, his tiny voice said, "Will you let me bring it in and not call out any more commands against me?"

"Yes," everyone said in unison.

"OK," he squeaked. "Row all. I guess."

We glided into the dock, lifted out the barge, and carried it into the boathouse, where Mr. Zierotin set about making a very unhappy inspection. "How have you do this, Decherd?" he demanded. "No one has do this."

Dickie looked across the boathouse and caught my eye.

"We hit a log," he peeped.

Mr. Zierotin said, "And break off rudder? I think maybe submarine has attack you."

I was out of the boathouse quickly, hurrying to my grinding session by the squash courts. When I mounted the hill, the road ahead was empty, as was usually the case, because I always hurried ahead of the pack to get back to the gym. I pulled off the clammy jersey and was just settling into an easy jog when I heard a voice behind me. It was Davidson. I waited for him to catch up.

"Mind if I walk with you?" he asked.

"No. But I'm in a hurry."

"Right. Off to your cave."

I slowed to a walk. We sauntered down the tunnel of tall pines into mirage pools of heat rising from the ink-black tarmac. Bird calls swirled out of tall trees in shrill eddies. Our feet slapped the pavement.

"What's up?" I asked.

He kept walking with his face down, looking away from me. He said something in a tremulous whisper too faint for me to make out.

"I can't hear you."

"I don't like what you did," he said.

We both stopped and looked at each other.

"The mutiny?"

"Yes."

I shrugged and began walking briskly again.

"Sorry."

"I don't like what you guys are doing at the table either."

I stopped again.

"I didn't start it. I'm not even in on it. Yet."

"I know," he said. "I get it. The Schmitzes are assholes. But I don't like it. It's against the school."

"Against the school?" I laughed. "Give me a break. I think the school will survive."

"But I don't like what you did to Dickie, either."

Davidson said Dickie Decherd's mother was his aunt. Dickie had a hard time growing up, Davidson said. It was a long story. I said everybody here seemed to have a long story. These people, I said, were starting to remind me of what my father called "all-cousin towns."

"Except you," he said. "Nobody even knows who you are."

I didn't say anything. We were moving along at a decent clip now. He pointed to a fallen tree by the side of the road and asked if we could sit. I said I was in a hurry, but he said it would just take a minute. We took seats on the tree trunk a bit apart from each other.

"What is it?" I asked.

"I want you never to do crew again after this season."

It took me a couple of beats to comprehend what he was saying. "What business is it of yours what sport I do?"

"You're not good for crew," he said solemnly, looking straight into my face.

"Not good for crew? Fuck crew. What if crew's not good for me? Why do you care so much about crew?"

In the distance, a small knot of younger boys approached on the road. It was Dickie's posse, but instead of trailing behind him like a high-stepping marching band, they were all moping around him like bodyguards.

"Speaking of little shits," I said.

When they drew abreast, Dickie glanced over and saw us on the log. He gave me a quick contemptuous snap of the eye but paused briefly and shook his head at Davidson with a ghastly expression of betrayal. Davidson and I did not speak until they were gone.

"Christ," I said. "Let me guess. It's because you love crew."

"I do."

"Because your dad brings you to Race Day."

"And my grandfather."

"You suck at it."

"I know. That's why I have to get better."

"Jesus. OK. You know what? You're absolutely right. I'm terrible for crew. I am shit for crew. You think I'll hurt crew."

"You already have."

"So you don't want me to do crew anymore. I don't belong on crew. In fact, I don't even belong at this fucking school. I should just leave tomorrow."

"No. No. I didn't say that, Pontiac. You're getting a little better in your grades now. Nobody has ever known anybody like you. I like you. I think you're a good guy. I want you to stay. I just don't want you doing crew."

"Christ," I said, getting up. "Jesus. Speaking of my grades, do you mind if we get going? I have a test tomorrow."

We hiked along at a good pace.

"So," he said after a while, "what do you think?"

"Think about what?"

"Crew next season."

"Man," I said and whistled. "You know, Davidson, some guys think you're a weak little kid or something, but I think once you get going on a thing, you're more like a dog with a bone."

He smiled to himself. "My nanny always said that. She said I was bull-headed."

"Was she nice?"

"She was the nicest person I ever knew. I loved her. My mom got drunk and accused her of stealing jewelry and got her arrested and put in jail."

"Jesus. That's really terrible."

"It was."

We walked in silence for a long while. The gym hove into view, framed by the pines at the end of the road.

"So you think I should stay here?" I said.

"Why shouldn't you? You get to go for free, don't you?"

"I do. But I'm too much of an asshole for crew."

"I think maybe."

"OK," I said. I stopped and put my hand out to shake. "No more crew for me after this season." We shook.

As we completed our walk, I asked, "What sport should I do?"

"You could do cross-country. That's just running around in the woods by yourself."

"Sounds about right."

•

That night at dinner, the Compton revenge plot was put into action. Yusupov made a point of lifting the cover of the large serving dish to display the unblemished meatloaf. Herr Schmitz bristled because he thought Yusupov was about to serve himself, but Yusupov said he only wanted to make sure the meat was still warm.

At that moment, Smiley rose part way from his chair, stooped across the table, and grabbed Bear's necktie.

"You stole my necktie," he said. Give it back."

"This is my necktie," Bear bellowed, clutching it operatically to his chest.

I thought they were overdoing it.

Bear's baritone awakened Herr Schmitz.

"What are you two on about down there?" he demanded.

"Are they fighting?" an alarmed Frau Schmitz asked.

"Stop it now," Barry ordered curtly.

Yusupov turned to his right and gave Granger a long, ridiculous wink that looked as if he was having a stroke. I saw Granger's arm dip into his coat pocket. It seemed to me Adams noticed it too. He watched Yusupov closely.

Smiley said, "He's a thief."

Bear flipped his own tie out to show the maker's tag.

"Do you buy your ties at Rogers Peet?" he asked.

Herr Schmitz put a finger to his lips for Bear to tone it down.

"Certainly not," Smiley said. "I buy all mine at Brooks Brothers."

I saw shoulders moving for what I assumed was the mouse handoff.

"Barry," Herr Schmitz said, "are you not able to maintain order?"

"Yes, sir," Barry said. Turning to Smiley, Barry told him, "If it's not your tie, an apology is due."

Smiley hesitated, watching Yusupov. Both Schmitzes peered down the table expectantly.

"Well?" Herr Schmitz said.

Yusupov's hands were hidden by the meat dish. The cover of the meat dish lifted up slightly as if by levitation, then sank again silently. Yusupov moved the dish a few inches across the table closer to Compton, who sat to Frau Schmitz's left.

"I do apologize," Smiley said solemnly, "and I very much regret falsely accusing you."

"Apology accepted!" Bear boomed in a voice to raise the dead. Both Schmitzes winced.

"Compton," Herr Schmitz snapped, "would you please serve the meat to Frau Schmitz."

"With pleasure," Compton said. Smiling directly into Frau Schmitz's eyes with his gaze above the dish, he lifted the cover with his left hand and picked up the pewter serving knife with his right. Frau Schmitz looked down on the mouse, blanched, pushed back from the table and emitted a blood-curdling scream from a horror film. The entire dining room fell silent. Smiley gave Compton a very slight and unsmiling nod. Compton jumped to his feet and pointed to the mouse.

"Oh my God!" he shouted. "Some son of a bitch put a dead mouse on the meatloaf!"

Frau Schmitz had pushed her chair out into the aisle, where she now sat with her hands clasped beneath her chin. "I'm going to be sick," she whispered.

"Thérèse," Herr Schmitz hissed, "come back to the table."

She shook her head no.

He rose. Every eye in the room was on him. He blandished his napkin in the air and gave a forced laugh. "I'm afraid we have an intruder," he said loudly. "A rodent. My wife is very afraid of rodents, as are many women."

A soft titter rippled through the room and died. The other tables all returned their attention to the meal. In a mutter, Herr Schmitz said, "Get back to the table now, Thérèse."

"No," she said. "Not until it's gone."

"Compton," he said, "cover it up and take it back to the kitchen. Tell Jake that I will want him to report to my apartment immediately after dinner to explain this egregious and totally unacceptable circumstance."

He sat back down. Compton covered the dish and was about to carry it away when Adams said, "Sir, Yusupov uncovered the dish moments ago, and there was no mouse."

Herr Schmitz was suddenly still.

"Is this true?" he asked Adams. "I didn't look."

"I did look," Frau Schmitz said, scraping her chair back to the table. "There was no mouse when Yusupov looked."

"I see," Herr Schmitz said. "I see. I see." He looked around the table. "So now we have a magic show. The mouse was made to appear as if from thin air. Then I must suppose that you boys must have grown tired of meat. All right. I understand. There will be no more meat for you, not at any meal, breakfast, lunch or dinner. Do you understand?"

We all said, "Yes, sir."

"Very well, then. We will make wog vegetarians of you yet."

•

On the way back from study hall, Bear caught up with me and showed a fistful of markers in his pocket.

"What are those for?" I asked.

"Compton."

"Oh, shit," I said. "Red balls?"

"White balls."

I was torn between pity for Compton and a certain pride at being included in the ritual. Bear, Smiley, Granger, Yusupov, and I met in the bathroom. It was Smiley's job to fill the trashcan with piping hot water and secure the broom. Smiley and I were the belt men. Granger, Yusupov, and Bear would wrestle him down. We agreed that luring him out of his alcove wouldn't work—he was too wary—so we decided to wait until after lights out when he might be asleep.

As it happened, Compton was in bed but awake and wary. The instant Bear parted his curtain, Compton leaped for the window ledge and began shouting for Mr. Fell and the supes. Bear and Yusupov pulled him off the wall by the legs, which caused him to bounce hard on his bed and then the floor. Smiley and I shackled his legs together. Getting him to the bathroom was another story. He writhed violently. Yusupov jammed a pillow over his mouth to dampen the shouting, while the rest of us pulled and tugged him. He kicked the entire length of the dorm.

We painted his balls with a solid coat of white marker ink, muffling his screams with the pillow. Getting him into the barrel of hot water and then jamming the broom handle through the handholds was a messy business in which everyone got soaked, and there was some blood. When his balls hit the hot water, Compton screamed. As they rolled him down the dorm, Gellhorn poked his nose out of his curtain and said, "Scum! All of you!"

We danced in the aisle, laughing and chanting, "White balls! White balls!"

Compton laughed back at us even harder.

Chapter Five

"HOW DID YOU GET RICH?" ELLEN asked me. "I thought you were a professor of indigenous languages or something. There can't be much money in that."

We were at the port of Nice, sipping warm limonade at an outdoor table next to an excellent sausage stand across the street from Notre-Dame du Port on a noisy traffic island. The port is a perfect square, open at one end, long since given over to smaller yachts and pleasure craft, surrounded on three sides by shops, bars, and restaurants. We were at the inland end looking out over a thicket of masts.

"Not a professor. A teacher. There isn't any money at all in that. I made all my money before I was thirty-nine. Before linguistics."

"How?"

"I was still pretty fucked up after Harvard. Lotta drugs, booze, bad luck with girls on Long Island. I still hate Long Island. I got a job in Greenwich Village doing bicycle deliveries for a Chinese restaurant, but I got run over by a bus. Early retirement."

"Doesn't sound like a great way to make a fortune."

"I ran into Stick. We had been roommates for one unhappy

semester at Harvard before he moved into a run-down rooming house on Brattle Street. I hadn't seen him in four years."

"Stickney? The boy with the jazz LPs?"

"Yes. The brainy guy. His prediction of Kennedy's election, by the way, if you can remember that story, turned out to be true to a T, down to the exact percentages."

"He was brilliant, then."

"Brilliant but extremely non-functional socially."

"Why did he stop being your roommate at Harvard?"

"I kicked him out because he smelled bad. When we worked together, I forced him to take showers. After my bus wreck, which I got some decent money from, I ran into him in a Coney Island hotdog place in the Village. It was just before I got married the first time. He was painting apartments. The village was having a big re-do boom. A guy he grew up with in Tuxedo Park got him all his work. The guy let Stick sleep in the apartments while he was painting them. Stick took me on as his community relations department."

"Why does an apartment painter need a community relations department?"

"Stick couldn't deal with the people at the paint store. So that was my job. I was his outside man. He would scan around a new apartment for the first time for about two minutes and then tell me to go to the paint store and get eleven and a half gallons of a color, and he would spit out the paint formula faster than I could write. He would say the job would take three ten-hour days and one two-hour day. When we were done painting three days and two hours later, we would be down to the last drop in the last can."

"Did you sleep in the apartments, too?"

"Sure. Saved $125 a month rent. We slept on air mattresses. The fumes were so bad, we had to leave the windows open in February.

Used to wake up high from the fumes and not able to feel my toes."

"And you got rich that way?"

"Stick had this ability to soak up and integrate incredible amounts of information. He was a computer before computers. He listened to the BBC on a shortwave radio while we painted, and he filched all kinds of newspapers and magazines out of trash bins and sat up all night scanning them."

"Why?"

"He would tell me stuff I didn't even listen to at first because it made no sense. Like one night, we were eating hotdogs at our Coney Island, and he said, 'Hot dogs will go up twenty cents in two weeks.' Two weeks later, hotdogs went up twenty cents. When I asked him how he did it, he got impatient. He said, 'You were listening to the BBC when I was, so you know about the drought in Argentina, and you surely heard what's going on with diesel fuel, and obviously you know about the political upheaval in Mexico, plus the changes in U.S. strategic storage policy, and of course we both know that onions are 15 percent of the cost of a chili dog, so how could you not know that the hotdogs at the Coney Island were going to go up by twenty cents in two weeks?'"

Ellen said, "Oh, my God,"

"Yeah. He was crazy brilliant. I took him back to the hot dog place, because the only time I could get through to him was when his mouth was stuffed with Coney Island chili dogs and chopped onions. Watching him eat was not a pleasant experience, but the food put his brain on hold long enough for him to be able to hear me.

"I said, 'Stick, normal people absolutely do not know the shit that you do, and we could make a lot of money.'"

"'We,'" Ellen said.

"Yeah. We. Us. I'm from Pontiac, I'm not a charity. And we

did make money. Shit tons of it. I went to a bunch of guys I knew from Harvard and some guys from St. Philip's, and I raised twenty-five thousand dollars in two weeks. This kid from St. Philip's sent me to his brother who was a commodities broker, but his brother wouldn't take us on. He said we were idiots who didn't know our asses from holes in the ground and we would just lose it all and get him in trouble. I realized then that we had to be a little more street. So I found this discount guy who didn't give a shit who we were or if we won or lost. I placed all Stick's commodities bets through the guy. In eight weeks, we turned twenty-five thousand dollars into two hundred and fifty thousand dollars. In four more months, we turned it into four million dollars."

"And you were the one out there raising the money?"

"I only had to raise money the first month. After that we had to beat people away. They were kicking down the door, throwing money at us. We didn't need it. We had our own. Stick was so good, we got into trouble with the feds accusing us of trying to corner markets."

"Were you?"

"Yes, but it was small plays that nobody would ever have paid any attention to until Dickie Decherd came along."

"Dickie Decherd. Do you mean the guy who was your cock when you were rowing."

"Ellen, the term is 'cox.' Short for coxswain."

"So what did your cocks have to do with it?"

"It's a long story. Dickie was on Wall Street in a white shoe firm half-owned by his family. He was a smart little bastard."

"Still small."

"Diminutive. And very fashionable. He spotted some stuff we were doing, and, of course, he had been waiting for years to get even with me."

"For the mutiny."

"Exactly. So he did. He took what he had to the U.S. Attorney for the Southern District of New York. But we had a great lawyer, and we managed to fend off the feds for the time being. Meanwhile, the discount broker had been selling our bets to other bigger people. Stick found out about it and was convinced it was cutting into our winnings. I never thought it did, but then the broker hired a private eye to spy on us to see how we were doing it. Luckily, the guy was a very stupid private eye and showed his cards right away. Stick went paranoid and insisted we needed an elaborate security system. We wound up with this whole command center in Brooklyn that we worked out of for seventeen years. I came to love it because I came to love Brooklyn. People actually did try to break into our computers later on. That was going on all over Wall Street, all over the world I think, but we were the one place where nobody was ever able to bust the encryption."

"Why?"

"It was based on Stick's model trains."

"Then what happened?"

"Something happened to Stick. He met a wonderful woman, really brilliant, smarter than him but normal. She got him. When he fell in love with her, his brain slowed down or something, and he turned into a quasi-normal person. He became almost charming, in fact, but he started making bad bets. She talked him into taking his winnings, getting out of the market, and buying a company that made railroad cars. The two of them are now internationally huge in logistics. I see them once or twice a year. We're pretty good buddies. We go salmon fishing in Iceland."

"Does he still smell bad?"

"Oh, no, not at all. He smells normal. At least to outward appearance, he's a really normal, really rich guy. And he's also an international rock star in the world of hybridized African violets."

"Is he suave?"

I thought about it. "Nah. She never got him that far. Am I suave?"

"Very."

"Thought so."

"And you?" she asked. "What did you do after he left you?"

"I was stupid. I tried to stay in commodities. I lost a bunch of money fast but realized my mistake. I was still very rich, and later I got much richer because of Compton. But that's a whole other story. Anyway, I took my winnings and settled in as an academic."

"You make getting rich sound easy."

"It's easy if you go to the right school."

She snorted. "Now it comes out."

"What comes out?"

"For all your little woes, it didn't hurt your net worth any to attend the snotty WASP boarding school."

She pissed me off. "Did I ever say it did?"

"I guess not."

"Did I ever say I had more woes than anybody else there?"

"I don't think so. I meant all of you. Poor little waifs, condemned to lives of wealth and privilege."

"Heartbreaking isn't it? Hey, what do you do for a living anyway? You told me once you were a journalist. I Googled you a couple times. I don't find your name in connection with any profession, business, or occupation."

"Oh. Quite the detective."

"Looking somebody up on Google does not make me a detective," I said.

"I told you I was no longer working as a journalist. For the last couple of years, I have been working on a novel."

I waited a beat.

"I wondered," I said.

"Wondered what?"

"Your novel. It doesn't have anything to do, does it, with some old coot who was a scholarship boy at a snooty boy's boarding school in the middle of the last century?"

She laughed.

"What's funny?"

"You know," she said, "I actually considered that at first. But I ran your story by my agent. He said if I was serious about writing a novel based on your story, I'd have to get another agent."

"Because?"

"Apparently, Woodrow, your personal saga, fascinating as I have found it myself, lacks commercial appeal. I think your privacy is quite safe."

"Why didn't you tell me you were thinking about it, though? Would have been nice to know."

"Oh, God, Woodrow, as it is, I am well aware you sort of cook things up a bit to keep me on the hook. If I had even hinted you might be the protagonist in a novel, you'd have had yourself on the winning side of sword fights and parliamentary debates all over the planet."

"That's unfair," I said, even more pissed off. "It's shitty. Very unfair. Everything I've told you is the truth."

"And I believe you."

"So why have you kept listening all this time, if you couldn't even peck a novel out of me?"

She watched an old man on a bicycle drift by with groceries in a wicker basket hanging from the handlebars.

"I suppose some of it is the story itself," she said. "It's a window on a very strange little tribe of people I knew nothing about. But the other part, Woodrow, is that I have come to love you. I care about you deeply, old man."

I couldn't stay angry at that.

"The world is full of literary agents," I said. "I don't think you should have given up so easily."

"I haven't given up. I told you I'm working on a novel."

"About?"

"About a young woman married to a successful brain surgeon, trying to find her own way in the world."

I said, "Let me guess. All the male characters in the end turn out to be perverts and losers, and the women all win Olympic gold medals. Right?"

"How'd you know?"

"If you had written the novel about me, would I have been at all good-looking?"

"Absolutely dashing. A knock-out."

"I'd stick with that. That's where the money is. I think women have had their day. People have gotten tired of them. I predicted it several years ago."

"I'll take it under consideration."

•

In late November the weather turned sharply cooler, and the trees began to go barren. By mid-December the school was blanketed with snow, and suddenly it was time for the Christmas vacation.

I hadn't told anyone I wasn't going home, because I was embarrassed. On departure day, Johnny Wilson snagged me after reports and suggested I take my things to his apartment and wait out the day there. He said the door would be unlocked. I stuffed pajamas, my robe and toothbrush into my book bag and went behind buildings to get to his apartment. His rooms occupied the second floor of a large brick house with dormer windows and chimneys at both ends of a wood-shingled roof. A spacious living room was lined with books. Chintz-covered chairs and a sofa were arranged around a fireplace with a tall white mantel at the far end of the room. I found my way to a small guest bedroom with a single bed, a desk and chair. I spent the day at the desk studying Latin, trying not to hear the chorus of laughter and insults outside the window as boys made their way into Rumney or piled into shiny black limousines.

Johnny Wilson showed up at the end of the day and cooked us a delicious meal of red beans and rice with a salad. The next morning at a hearty breakfast of fried ham and eggs, I asked what I was supposed to do all day.

"I can't believe you asked that," he said. "You're going to study. And I'm going to help you."

And study we did, as I had never studied in my life. He put a book before me and then timed me as I studied a set number of pages. The moment my time was up, he snatched the book back and began peppering me with questions. When I failed to come up with the answers, he put the book back in front of me and told me to study harder and faster.

On the first day of this and after my third failed attempt, I complained. I said I was studying as hard and as fast as I could. I couldn't do what he wanted. Instead of being short-tempered or exasperated, he was genial and funny.

"Just what I thought," he said with a laugh. "Young Woodrow Skaggs here has no idea how smart he is. That is great. That means we've got lots of running room."

Over the next few days, he gave me much longer assignments. While I studied he disappeared into a small office off his bedroom and worked there until it was time to come back and test me. I made very gradual but measurable progress. We seldom left the apartment. He was a wonderful cook, and he taught me how to cook.

On the day before Christmas Eve, Johnny Wilson stayed on my case all day long. He gave me long difficult study assignments, and rather than go to his own desk to work while I read he hovered over me, knowing it would make me nervous, which it did. I muffed a few answers when he first tested me in the morning, but for the rest of the day I hit 100 percent on all his quizzes. Finally in late afternoon, when it was time for us to go to the kitchen and begin cooking, I scored one hundred on an especially tough test. He snatched up my paper and began dancing around the room flapping it in the air and singing a line from a popular Broadway musical in a hilarious British accent: "By George, he's got it! By George, he's got it!"

On the day before Christmas Eve he took me by train down to Grand Central Station in New York, then by subway to Harlem. We were guests in a grand brownstone in a neighborhood called Mount Morris Park. Our hosts were a middle-aged black couple, both doctors. The wife was very genteel and went out of her way to treat me with kindness. They didn't ask why I hadn't gone home, either from delicacy or because Johnny Wilson had asked them not to. Or both. I could have answered. Because my mother was too cheap.

We ate dinner at a very long table, all of us bunched at one end. A maid served a delicious meal of salmon, rice and green beans.

They drank wine and offered me some, which I accepted. They kidded Johnny Wilson about not getting married yet. The wife explained to me that they were all from Detroit and had known each other for a long time. I slept on the softest most gigantic bed I had ever seen in my life, in a huge bedroom with tall windows.

On Christmas Eve morning we ate breakfast in another smaller dining room just off the kitchen. There were no servants in the house. The wife served us. At the center of the table was a small green and white ceramic Christmas tree, lighted from within by a red electric bulb.

When Johnny Wilson failed to appear, I asked where he was, and the man told me he was at church. He finally showed up at about eleven thirty and announced he was taking me to a special Christmas dinner.

Our hosts explained to me that they would not be joining us. They were flying to Detroit that evening to do Christmas with their son, a pediatric neurology resident at Henry Ford Hospital. I thanked them for letting me stay with them and told them their bed was the nicest I had ever slept on. Johnny Wilson went up to his room and came back down wearing blue jeans and a maroon Harvard sweatshirt. I had never before seen him not in his dark suit and clerical collar. The transformation was jarring. He donned his ankle-length blue cashmere overcoat and yellow silk scarf, and we took a cab to a place called Frank's Famous Restaurant. On the way, he thanked me for thanking our hosts. "Both of your parents have lovely manners," he said, "and they have passed that on to you. That's half the battle in life." He pointed out the Apollo Theater. "Someday I might take you there," he said, "but you'll have to get a lot smarter."

When we got to the door, he said, "Time to meet my gang."

The restaurant was cavernous, elegant, softly lighted and humming with subdued chatter. In a long narrow room at the back Johnny Wilson was welcomed warmly by a crowd of fifteen to twenty adults. I immediately scouted the room and determined I was one of three white people. Johnny Wilson took me around and introduced me to his friends with quick labels: "a young student at my school," "teaches English Lit at Yale," "one of New York's finest eye surgeons," "the best jazz pianist in the city." They all hugged him warmly, delighted to see him.

Johnny Wilson sat at the head of a long table where over the next three hours we slowly but relentlessly devoured a feast of pasta, perfectly cooked steaks, and wonderful desserts. I sat next to the man who taught English literature at Yale. Midway through the meal he asked me where I lived and why I was not at home. I said my parents couldn't afford to pay for me to go all the way to Detroit and back just for Christmas. He nodded, and then with his head turned slightly away whispered as if to himself, "The school is not quite deserted. A solitary child, neglected by his friends, is left there still."

Johnny Wilson heard it. He gestured around the table and said to me but for everyone to hear, "These are the happy orphans of Detroit."

A woman at the far end rose with lifted champagne and said, "Merry Christmas to the happy orphans of Detroit."

Then they all rose and made a loud toast that was just, "Detroit!"

Seated to Johnny Wilson's right was a beautiful dark-skinned young woman with long eyelashes and a slow dignified smile. She and he spoke fast Spanish to each other. I already knew he was fluent in French and could even speak classical Latin as if it were a modern language, but the fluent Spanish was a surprise. After the meal and before we left, she and he lingered alone in a corner a long while speaking earnestly.

On the way back to the brownstone in early evening, our cab was a schooner plowing the twinkling lights of New York. I said, "That woman next to you that you were talking to in Spanish so much was pretty great looking."

He gave me a coolly appraising glance. "Don't get out over your skis, young man."

"Sorry. Sir."

"But you're right. She's very beautiful. She's Nicaraguan, from a wealthy cultured family."

"Are your friends trying to fix you up?"

He gave me the glance again.

"Sorry," I said. "Sir."

"But yes, I believe they are. They also want me to become a bishop, be president of Harvard and get elected president of the United States. So one must have a plan. Do you have a plan, Woodrow?"

"I don't think so."

"What I thought."

On Christmas morning we were alone in the house. He brought a tray with pastries and coffee to the small dining room, where I was waiting at the table. He reached over and snapped on the little electric tree.

"Merry Christmas," he said.

I said, "Merry Christmas."

•

Back at school, winter seemed to draw a more aggressive venom from the Schmitzes. Maybe extreme cold was just their natural element. Fortunately, I found that I was a little better at fending them off.

At dinner one night, Herr Schmitz said to me, "Skaggs, I am curious why the boys call you by the name of an automobile. Why are you called Pontiac?"

"I don't think it's about the cars, sir," I said. "The town I come from is called Pontiac. I think that's why they call me that."

"Your town is named after an automobile."

"Yes, sir."

"How interesting. And why is that?"

"It's where they make them."

"The Pontiac."

"Yes, sir."

"And so was this town created for the express purpose of producing Pontiacs?"

"Yes, sir."

Yusupov gave me an approving nod.

"But your surname is Skaggs," Herr Schmitz said.

"Yes, sir."

"What kind of name is that?"

I shrugged. "I think it's an OK name. I've always liked it."

Another nod from Yusupov.

Herr Schmitz winced, but Frau Schmitz put a hand to his arm and whispered, "The name is very American but originally English."

"Are you an Englishman, then?" Herr Schmitz asked me with a broad smile.

"No, sir. American. Way back."

"Way back, is it? How far back do you Skaggses go?"

Now everyone was listening.

"There was a Skaggs many generations back, Henry Skaggs, who was a long hunter with Daniel Boone."

"A long what? With whom?"

"Long hunter. It's what they were called. I'm not sure. They were a kind of explorer."

"The long poachers," Frau Schmitz muttered with a chuckle.

"Oh, no, not a poacher at all," Adams interjected quickly. "A long hunter was a leatherstocking, like Natty Bumppo."

I had not yet read Cooper or heard the name, Natty Bumppo, so I kept silent.

"If your forebear was that far back," Adams said, nodding encouragingly, "then he was a contemporary of my own famous forebear."

"The founder!" Herr Schmitz said thunderously. "And so, Adams, tell me. Do you put this Skaggs, the long poacher, on the same level with your progenitor who went arm in arm with Hamilton and Madison?"

"Yes, of course," Adams said. "An associate of Daniel Boone? I would think so."

"Who is this Boone?" Herr Schmitz asked his wife.

"A famous poacher," she said.

Adams coughed. "That's a bit harsh."

"Yes, it is," she said. "I was only making a joke. Herr Schmitz asks me these questions because he has not been a student of your history, and I have. I find it fascinating. I do know who your famous Boone was, of course. But I also may have a different perspective on your frontier progenitors than the popular American view."

"Oh, I see," Adams said, his enthusiasm waning. "How does your view differ?"

She put down her knife and fork.

"I have read a number of New World travel journals going back to the Jesuits," she told Adams. "One can almost mark the decline, from the very first encounters with the Indians, who were a rather noble people. It begins with the eventual appearance in the forests and on the frontiers of large numbers of English scum."

"Scum," Adams whispered to his dinner plate.

"Yes," she said. "Well, you know, the people they brought in the transportation ships, the human offal scraped up out of the prisons and alleyways of London, the beggars, prostitutes, and pickpockets. And then there were the Irish and Scots, people who were never really civilized in the first place. The English brought their social detritus to the New World and dumped it like garbage. America was their human ash heap. Not for people like your forebear, of course. The founding fathers were gentlemen. But I speak of people like the progenitor of young Skaggs here, though I do give them credit for having survived at all."

Smiley looked around the table morosely. Bear caught his glance and shook his head in open dismay. Barry aimed a frozen stare at his plate.

Their disapproval seemed to quicken her pace. "They were brought here to die," she said, "to spare the over-delicate homosexual British aristocracy the nasty task of mass gibbeting and the attendant challenges of disposal. But instead of obediently dying, young Skaggs's forebears jumped out of those rotten ships, took one good look at the forests of North America, and said 'Poaching! We know how to do that!'"

"A dark view," Adams said.

"Not always. Much of your national origin story is quite inspiring, even heroic. But you Americans do have a tendency to shrink from the darker side of the tale."

Adams nodded, obviously trying to end it. "I think we all take your point, Frau Schmitz," he said. "Perhaps we should talk about something else."

"You know," she went on blithely, "one of the most interesting travel journals I read was written by Frederick Law Olmsted, the architect who designed Central Park in Manhattan and Prospect Park in Brooklyn. A few years before your Civil War, Olmsted traveled by mule and horseback through the American South. I was struck by a particular passage in which he comes across a group of white hunter gatherers. Perhaps they were long hunters. I believe, he found them in Arkansas . . . "

Yusupov looked up from his plate, suddenly interested.

"They were descendants," she said, "of the people brought over on transportation ships. Olmsted's disgust fairly drips off the page. He describes them as so vile that he cannot bring himself to record their depravity in writing. He remarks that the Indians, who were commonly called savages at the time, were far more civilized than these white denizens of the jungle. It is clear that their passage over time and across the terrain from the ships to the forests of Arkansas served only to enable and worsen their natural depravity."

"Not a sanguine view," Adams said.

"Oh, it's certainly not your own history, Adams!" Frau Schmitz assured him.

My father's words came back to me. "It's not my history either," I blurted. "It's bullshit."

She turned to her husband. "I want him to apologize for this insolence."

Schmitz said to Adams, "Tell him to apologize."

Adams said to me, "Apologize."

I said, "I apologize."

On the walk across the lobby to Dorm Four after dinner, Compton hurried to my side.

"Why in the fuck did you apologize to that bitch?"

"I don't want to get into it with them," I said. "They're just ass-holes. I have other fish to fry."

"Sure," he said as we entered the dorm. "Or you don't have the balls."

Barry came from behind and tapped me on the shoulder.

"I would like to see you before study hall."

I followed him down the narrow corridor and into his cramped apartment. He motioned for me to sit on a ragged chintz love seat in front of a coffee table. He sat down heavily on a captain's chair. Nodding to a hot plate on an unkempt side table, he offered to make tea, which I declined. I had my head down for a scolding.

"I heard what Compton said to you," he said, "He's quite wrong. You handled yourself very well. I just wanted you to know that. I admire your aplomb."

It took a moment for the compliment to sink in. No one had ever told me I possessed something called aplomb, and I had to make sure it was a good thing.

"I cannot in any way answer for the Schmitzes," he said. "I know Europeans well. I went to school with them at Le Rosey. They're not all like the Schmitzes. There's something wrong with these people. Something very mean-spirited. I really don't know how you handled yourself so well tonight."

"Thank you."

"The story of your relative and Daniel Boone is fascinating. And you have a proud nickname of course, Pontiac, the white man's name for Obwandiyag."

"You know Obwandiyag?" I was astonished.

"Yes, of course. Pontiac's Rebellion. As important to who and what we are as a people as the revolution against the English, although people who only know the white jingo version of our history wouldn't know a thing about Obwandiyag."

We were both quiet for a while.

"Can I still have a cup of tea?" I asked.

"Of course." He rose to make it. With his back to me, he said, "Are you in on the food poisoning?"

"Not yet."

"Well, don't touch it, Pontiac. Resist temptation. I know how these things go. You're probably already being pressured to join the insurgents. I assume that's why Compton is on your case."

"I don't know anything about it," I lied.

He sat back down while we waited for the teapot to boil. "The Schmitzes already have their eyes on Compton and Yusupov. Now you've baited the bear, and they will be only too happy to add you to the hunt.

"Many of us want you to succeed, because we want the experiment to succeed. Mr. Fell, Adams, myself, Johnny Wilson, others— we're on your side. The rector, I don't know. I can't tell. Maybe on the fence. But some, the Schmitzes, Beetle, would like to see you fail and do so quickly. They don't want you here or anyone else like you."

Adams poked his head in the door. Barry asked him to wait a few minutes, and he ducked out quickly, closing the door behind him.

"I just had a few more things," Barry said. "Some of what happens from here on out will not be fair. The Schmitzes will scour you for any grounds or excuse, especially now that, in their distorted view, you have sort of dared them. None of it will be fair, Pontiac. I'm telling you that. I am telling you, because, when a deal is not fair and you know ahead of time that it's not going to be fair, then it's up to you."

"Up to me to do what?"

"Keep your neck out of the noose."

"Is that how fair works?"

"That's how fair works at St. Philip's School."

•

I was almost asleep when I heard Compton's raspy whisper above.

"Puertorac."

"What?"

"I got another bribery box."

I threw back my covers, slipped on my robe, went into his alcove, and mounted the now familiar path from bed to bureau to window ledge. Compton's bribery boxes were no trifling matter. So far, I was the only one invited to share, I assumed because my alcove was next to his. I certainly didn't want to do anything that might shift invitations elsewhere.

This box, wrapped in tinted foil and ribbons, was a pirate's chest of delicious chocolate, nuts, and candied fruit. I reached in and partook without speaking. We sat for a long while with a wind of moonlight from the great leaded window at our backs, sailing into a black sea. Our munching made the sound of water gently slapping the hull.

"Why do you let those krauts talk to you that way?" he whispered.

"I don't know. Barry told me not to let them get me into trouble."

"Get him into trouble, more like it. Put a black mark on his precious perfect record."

The idea was absurd. "What do you mean? How could the Schmitzes do anything to Barry?"

"He's worried something bad will happen at the table on his watch. It might blow up and put a black mark on his record, which he can't have."

"Why?"

"He wants to be president."

I paused with a candied orange peel in midair.

"I didn't know we had a student government," I said.

"We don't, dumbass. I don't even know what a student government is. Is that something they have in Puerto Rico?"

"Yes."

"Well, we don't."

"So what does Barry want to be president of?"

Compton shook his head. He put his hands on his knees and looked down on the bed below.

"Jesus, Pontiac, you still just have no idea where you are."

"I don't know what you're talking about."

"He wants to be president of the United States."

"So what? Everybody does."

"Right, but most people can't. He can."

"So what does any of that have to do with me?"

"You're a special case. You're the new scholarship kid, and you were assigned to his dorm. They've never had anything like

264

you here before. And he doesn't want to have a scandal with you."

"Bullshit. Man, you just make this shit up, don't you?"

He didn't become angry or red-eyed. Instead, he looked out the window thoughtfully.

"If I didn't have any money," he asked hesitantly, "like if something really bad happened to my parents and they all of a sudden didn't have any money, could I get a scholarship?"

"How would I know?"

"Because you've got one. You're like the head mooch."

The word was a punch in the nose.

"What's the matter?" he asked.

"That's a shitty thing to say. Mooch."

"Christ, I didn't mean anything by it. I was kidding."

"Just don't use that word, OK? Mooch. Why would you even say that?"

"Christ, I already told you I didn't mean anything by it. I just meant your family doesn't have any money. Mooch is just a word I know for poor people."

"We're not poor. We're working people. You think everybody who's not rich is poor. But you don't know shit. You think everybody who's not rich is a mooch? If they're mooches, why do they work so hard?"

"I don't know why. Because they're stupid, I guess. OK, not stupid maybe. Not your family. Sorry. Just kind of dumb. Why else would somebody work hard at a job where they can't get rich?"

I dangled my feet and sighed. "Compton, I feel like you and me are friends now. Maybe it's better if we just don't try to talk about shit like this."

"Fine. I don't give a shit. I don't have to talk about it. All I did was call you a mooch."

"Don't use that word, OK?"

"OK. OK. So that's another word I can never say. I can't call you the word that starts with p, and now I also can't call you the word that starts with m. Jesus, I can't even call Aubert a frog, and he is one. You know, you just wonder where it ends, how long the list of words is going to be."

"And if you remember all of them, you might even turn into a decent human being."

He stiffened his shoulders and started to color, then relaxed suddenly. A very small smile crept across his face. "You think?"

"Stranger things have happened."

———

Ellen stopped me.

"Is Barry the one who ran for president? Is he the guy the brain surgeon met at a party?"

"The same."

"You went to school with him?"

"He was our supe at the table and in the dorm. I've been telling you that."

"You didn't make it plain that it was the same guy. So now do you know John Barry?"

"Not really."

"Do you ever run into him? I think you told me once you go to class reunions at St. Philip's, which confuses me. Do you ever run into him there?"

"Not anymore. He stopped going back. But I saw him a year ago at a Harvard thing. He went back there to speak. We said hello, how are you doing, that kind of thing."

"Why doesn't he go back to St. Philip's?"

"Certain members of his class at St. Philip's have been quite unkind to him during his political career. They have been quoted prominently saying some very petty stuff."

"Why? Is he too liberal?"

"Oh, maybe, but they were never nice to him, anyway, even at the school. They looked down on him because he was ambitious."

Ellen looked perplexed.

"Ambition is middle class," I told her. "It's not aristocratic."

She gazed at me a long moment. "OK, I think we'll just let that one ride. Whatever happened to Rutledge?"

"Come on," I said. "You know what happened to Rutledge."

"No. I do not."

"Sure you do. He was Bush I's Secretary of Health and Human Services."

"That Rutledge? Oh my God. Isn't he the one who went Evangelical or something?"

"Yeah, that was all political theater. He's a hood."

I tried to go back to telling the story about me and Compton on the windowsill.

"Wait," she said. "What about Adams? Is he Adams like John Adams, that kind of Adams?"

"I told you that already."

"Sorry, I wasn't taking notes."

"The same."

"Who else was there? I mean people I might have heard of."

"All of them, if you took American history. That's who they are. The Phillies, anyway."

"Fillies?"

"Yes."

"Anybody else I might know? Any other fillies?"

"Lots. I don't remember. Raven Pell."

"Who?"

"Pell. He was director of the FBI and then a special prosecutor."

"You mean the same guy as the Pell Report?"

"Same guy."

"Do you know him?"

"A little bit. He's a good guy."

"Who else?"

"I'll name some more, if you'll let me get back to my story."

"Please," she said.

I thought that might work.

•

I got a puzzling letter from David. He said things were much better for him in the juvie, and he wanted to tell me about it, but he didn't want to tell me in a letter. He said that my mother had given him money for a long distance phone call. She had calculated how much money would be enough for him to talk to me in New Hampshire for about ten minutes. He wanted me to send him a phone number and a time when he could reach me. He said he could call me between four and five in the afternoon Pontiac time, which would be five and six my time. I was impressed by how he had worked it out. I wrote him back immediately with the number for the phone booth outside Beetle's apartment and a date and time. In a two-line note a few days later he told me I would have to wait for his call over a three-day window, because he couldn't be sure when he would be allowed to go to the phones. It was inconvenient for me, because it meant giving up valuable hours of grinding at the gym in order to wait by the phone, but I was eager to hear his voice.

Hockey was taking a toll. I figured out that we were allowed to fudge the Episcopal stuff as long as we went through the motions in chapel, but hockey, the school's beloved sport and sacred ritual, was to be honored with solemnity always. I learned years later that hockey was the only surviving element of the original school, before the Gilded Age turned it into a faux-Brit finishing school.

The original Rumney Industrial Academy, as it was called, was founded in 1828 by the Rev. Elmer Hudnut, an eccentric Universalist minister and poet who sought to instill rugged heroic qualities in working class boys rescued from the teeming mill cities of New England. Hudnut believed he could pull off this miracle by exposing his boys to a mixture of farm life and what he took for Native American culture.

Games like ice hockey had been played in England for at least a century, but the version adopted by Hudnut was based directly on the raucous, often brutal game the indigenous peoples of North America played, which they called baggataway, kabocha-toli, or tewaarathon—in English, the creator's game. Most European onlookers took these Native American stick games, played on both ice and field, as expressions of savagery and debauch, but Hudnut, who was fluent in several Algonquian languages, understood the games to be the opposite. The stick games of North America were rituals of purification whose purpose was to please the creator with displays of courage and tenacity.

Hudnut's game, played on ice by urban hoodlums at the academy, was the object of derision and disgust among the few townsfolk of Rumney who had witnessed it. The school's hockey games even played a part in the ultimate court trial of the Rev. Mr. Hudnut, sentenced to five years in prison for the crime of corrupting minors, later commuted to a lifetime banishment from New Hampshire. I did a little research on Hudnut at one point and concluded there may have been better evidence against him than hockey alone. He showed up later in some terrible chapters involving Indian schools in Arizona.

In 1880, a consortium of new-rich families of New York, Philadelphia and Boston took over the dwindling remains of Hudnut's school to make it into their own, apparently because they were unable to get their sons admitted to older boarding schools. They immediately rebranded the school as St. Philip's, after the Greek apostle whose punishment for converting the wife of a proconsul behind the proconsul's back was crucifixion upside down at Hierapolis.

The school's proud new proprietors ripped out root and branch every trace of Hudnut, with the single curious exception of ice hockey, which seemed to give their sons a much-needed respite from the burdens of impersonating English aristocrats all day and night. Hockey persisted at the school and eventually was adopted by other schools, first the boarding schools and then at Ivy League colleges and universities, eventually spreading wherever there was ice. St. Philip's claims now to be the progenitor of modern ice hockey in America, which appears to be true, for better or for worse.

That was all OK with me at the time, even though I didn't absolutely love hockey and was barely an average player. At least I was better at hockey than I had been at rowing, not saying much, having grown up playing pick-up games on scratchy little ponds all around Little Ottawa. I was a competent skater. On a good day with some luck I could hit a slap shot into the net without falling down. My shortcomings were slightness of build and lack of speed.

Almost everyone played. The hockey coaches divided us into four clubs of three teams each, except for the top level, varsity, for which there was one team only. The varsity played a few boarding schools, but, because the school was so much better at hockey than the other boarding schools, the varsity team played mainly junior varsity college teams. I was in the second tier down from varsity. It could have been worse. At least most of the other players at my level were about my age. The three teams at our level played only against each other.

A crew of school workers with brooms and shovels maintained ten rinks on the pond, each fenced within low wooden walls we called "the boards," anchored by ice bolts. The biggest and best rink, where varsity practiced and played other schools, was kept glass-smooth by a team of eight expert workers. One man drove a tractor that pulled a blade across the ice, shaving it smooth. Three men followed the tractor with brooms to sweep up the shavings. Another pair followed with hoses, spraying a fine mist, and the last two brought up the rear with long squeegees to clear away the excess water. While the ice team worked, boys of all ages stood on their skates with their sticks against the boards watching reverently as if at a communion service in chapel.

I might even have had fun at hockey, but it took too much time—going to the skate house, putting on skates, taping up sticks, strapping the hard white plastic cups to our groins under our pants to protect our balls, then shin guards and gloves for the other extremities. After an hour and a half of practice out on the pond, often in bitter cold and blowing snow, we had to reverse the whole process.

Compton played at the level just down from Varsity and was about to be given a very early try-out on the Varsity bench, but he showed up for practice one day with his cup outside his pants, complaining he was in a hurry. The boys couldn't stop laughing as he did some quite graceful figure-skating pirouettes on the ice with his protective device in full view. Even the Varsity players laughed, and Compton was a bit of a hero on the pond for a few days, but the coaches were outraged at this insult to the sport, and his promotion was delayed.

Every day as soon as we were dismissed, I raced across campus to the gymnasium, jumped through an ineffectual shower, dressed half wet, yanked texts from my locker and repaired to my lair by the squash courts. There, I snapped open the folding table, set it upright, unfolded my pilfered chair and sat down with elbows pinned so hard to the table they hurt, glowering down on the open text. I was determined to replicate the intense study technique that Johnny Wilson had taught me in his apartment, but it was not to be, at least not at first.

Without Johnny Wilson standing over me with a stopwatch, I was unable to reproduce the intense concentration he had evinced. My grades on quizzes, especially in Latin, were no better. I imagined failure, getting kicked out and becoming a wombat, looking up from my broom or snow shovel as Compton and the others passed by pretending not to know me. I thought it would be better to run away to Boston or New York, get some kind of menial job and live alone forever.

But toward the end of the first week after the Christmas break, something began to happen. An ice within me started to melt. There in my monastic cell next to the raucous squash courts, I began to experience very unaccustomed victories. I slammed the Latin declensions and conjugations into my head, then tested myself as Johnny Wilson had taught me. And to my amazement, there it all still was, all kinds of Latin locked up in my head like bullets ready to fire. I could almost spit it out like a machinegun as he had told me to do.

My self-pity faded. Now when I tried to imagine myself as Oliver Twist, apprentice chimney sweep, a small but stubborn spark of optimism got in the way. What if I was actually doing what my mother and Johnny Wilson had commanded me to do? What if I was trying harder?

I was afraid at first to take it for real. Maybe it would last only an hour or so or barely a day, not long enough to carry me through a quiz. I put away the Latin I had learned and left those books alone for a few days to work on algebra and French. To my astonishment when I went back to the Latin days later, it was still there. So was the algebra. Even the French.

Finally one day on the walk from the gymnasium to the school building for evening class, a new thought streaked across my awareness like a comet. Was it not conceivable that I could not only survive here but even do well? Could I not beat the Phillies at their own game? I thought about what Yusupov had said to me that night when we were prisoners in the pantry. The thing that put me off balance, that kept me from having a clear line of attack, was simply not knowing who I was—the difference between me and them. But why should that difference not make me strong instead of weak?

It was a strange idea, utterly foreign, uncomfortable yet irresistible. Could I not beat them? On the one hand, the answer should be no. I wasn't of their species, the gentry, the race of superior beings. They were all smooth as silk, radiant with confidence. They all knew so much more than I did, about academics, of course, but also about the world and the universe. They had been everywhere. They could go wherever they liked and do whatever they wanted.

Money was air to them. They could go to a whorehouse in Paris with The Toad the way I might go to the drive-in with my father.

But as I approached the schoolhouse, its windows glowing yellow in the evening snow, I saw one thing with absolute clarity. I had something going for me that none of them had. Sheer desperation. Why should that spell weakness? Maybe it was my sword.

The next morning, a Friday, with snow outside blowing like smoke against the classroom windows, I had a chance to find out. Beetle's quiz in Latin class was what the boys called a "Jap," named after the surprise attack on Pearl Harbor. It was a double quiz, forty questions instead of twenty, covering not only the previous night's study hall assignment but also past lessons.

I knew the answer to every single question. All of it. The verb forms and declensions flowed like water to the page. I finished early and sat back from the table.

Beetle turned his face toward me. He couldn't have worn a more astonished expression if I had stripped naked. "The dapper Mr. Skaggs," he said, "are we having a rest?"

"No, sir. I'm done."

"Oh," he said with a jocular toss of his fleshy head. "I see."

Compton looked up quizzically from across the table, shook his head and went back to work.

When the allotted fifteen minutes were over, we traded our papers across the table. Compton got mine and I took his. Beetle dictated the correct answers. I put a check mark by only two wrong answers on Compton's quiz.

Compton slid my paper back to me with a squinty-eyed expression of bafflement. My paper was pristine, clean, virginal. Not a single answer had been checked wrong.

Beetle made his usual progress around the room, beginning

with the boy to my right and circling the table away from me, leaving me for last as always.

"And the dapper Mr. Skaggs," he said, taking up my paper. He frowned at it, turned it to a slightly different angle, and frowned again. He went back to his chair and stared down on my quiz for some time.

At the end of class as we were rising to leave, Beetle said, "Skaggs, would you mind waiting?"

Compton came around the table on his way out and leaned to my ear.

"Did you have a pony?" he whispered, referring to a secret list of answers written on my arm or hidden in a wadded note.

"No."

"Beetle thinks you did."

I remained in my chair halfway down the table. Beetle continued to glower at my test paper. When the room was empty, he looked up.

"You did very well today, Skaggs."

"Thank you, sir."

"Much better than you have ever done before in this class. In fact, you are today's only perfect score. Better than some of my top students. And this was a hard quiz. It's quite a surprising turn of events, if I may say so."

And there it was. Compton was right. The old bastard did think I had cheated. My father told me not to take shit off these people. But I also remembered my session with Yusupov in the pantry.

"Yes," I said, smiling directly at him. "I did extremely well."

"Is there an explanation for this sudden improvement? Are you doing something differently?"

"No, sir, not really. In fact, hockey has been kind of wiping me out these last few weeks, so I haven't had much time to study." I sighed heavily. "I'm pretty good at hockey, but it takes a lot out of me."

"You are good at hockey? I had not heard that."

"Yes, sir. Well, you know. I'm from Michigan."

"Yes, I did know that about you. You are indeed from Michigan. And an even greater Michigan miracle seems to have taken place with your Latin. It's quite wonderful. From the bottom of the class last term suddenly to the top after Christmas, in one daily quiz."

"I didn't think the quiz was hard at all, sir. I mean, really, sir, no offense, it was kind of easy."

He looked away and spoke without returning my gaze.

"I have an hour free three Saturdays from now at 1:00 PM. Can you meet me here at that time?"

"Of course, sir. Is it . . . do I need to prepare?"

"Oh, no. Nothing like that," he said, smiling. "Just a review. If you're going to be one of my best students now, I need to be sure I am giving you my very best instruction."

"Thank you, sir. See you then. I mean, see you Monday, too, of course, but I'll see you three Saturdays from now, also. Also at dinner."

"Good, Skaggs. I will look forward to all of these encounters."

That night after dinner, Compton, Gellhorn, and Bear gathered on the radiator outside my alcove to consult.

"He thinks you cheated," Compton explained. "You can't blame him. You've always been the dumbest guy, and now all of a sudden you're the smartest. Go figure."

Bear's usual expression of surprise had expanded to true amazement. He bellowed, "I can't believe you got a hundred on a Jap Latin quiz from Beetle." He was seated on the bench a short distance from the rest of us, turned toward the other side.

"I graded his paper," Compton said. "He got a hundred. He was the only one."

Bear twisted his immense frame around to face me and squeezed his eyes to a shrewd stare. In a loud whisper, he asked, "Did you use a pony?"

"I didn't cheat."

"Well, you can't blame Beetle for thinking you did," Bear said. "You've been at the bottom of the form in every single subject since you got here."

"Especially Latin," Compton said. "He really stinks at Latin."

"Worse than French?" Bear asked.

"Well no. He double-stinks in French."

Gellhorn had his hand stuffed in his sport coat pocket and was flapping it nervously like a wing. He sounded angry. "Why don't you just get it over with, Skaggs, and tell us how you did it?"

"I grinded," I said.

They all stared at me for a long silent moment.

"We all grind," Bear said.

"Not like I do."

"Oh," Compton said, bobbing his head up and down, "a very grinding boy, the most grinding boy of all, all the way from Pontiac, Michigan."

"You bet your ass," I said.

It was agreed by everyone that Herr Schmitz and Beetle were members of a group of masters who were opposed to the presence of scholarship boys at the school. It also was agreed, therefore, that Beetle might attempt to use a charge of cheating, based on my anticipated poor performance on his upcoming test, to get me thrown out. To my surprise—I would say more truthfully my shock—the boys of Dorm Four were on my side.

"If you have some special way of grinding," Gellhorn said, "and that's why you can get a good grade on Beetle's Jap quiz all of a sudden, then that means you're not cheating."

"Right," Bear said, nodding enthusiastically. "And it means Beetle is an asshole."

"How much time do you have to do your special grinding trick for this test?" Compton asked.

It was Friday evening. I had two weeks. Between that moment and my shoot-out with Beetle, we calculated I had two full weekends, ten afternoons and study halls, plus every night under my blankets before the test.

"But Pontiac can't just let everything else slide," Bear announced.

Compton said, "He'll have to use study hall for everything else and afternoons and nights for Latin."

They all turned to me expectantly.

"So?" Gellhorn asked. "What do you intend to do? Meet the challenge or get kicked out and go home in disgrace?"

"Meet the challenge, of course" I said.

They all nodded approval.

After studying Latin in the phone booth outside Beetle's door for two hours the previous day, I finally got David's call on a Friday afternoon. We exchanged awkward greetings, not having spoken in so long. My heart was tugged two ways—warm yearning when I heard his voice and diction, which was now distinctive to my ear, but also a certain dread that hollowed my gut when I heard the metallic roar around him, a clamor of other conversations and a rudely interrupting voice from a loudspeaker.

"Are you OK in there?" I asked.

"That's why I wanted to talk, Woodrow. It's way better. I'm doing better. I'm on top of it."

I asked for a full explanation. He told me that a particular teacher was infamous for tormenting boys, then sexually molesting them. The teacher targeted David and began picking on him mercilessly. After a week or so of torment, the teacher tried to touch David in a corridor. I gathered the teacher was a small man, not formidable. David grabbed him by his shirt collar and thrust him against a wall.

For this, David was sentenced to six days in something called "the box," a form of solitary confinement. He said it was a tiny windowless cell with a reeking toilet that did not flush, filled with his own excrement.

Midway through his term in the box he was more or less all right, surviving on daydreams, naps and push-ups, when the teacher appeared in the cell and demanded that David give him a blow job. The man dropped his trousers and underwear and told David his dick was the only way David was ever getting out of the box.

David made some kind of feint to distract the teacher, dipped behind, clawed up a fistful of shit and shoved it into the teacher's face and mouth.

I was silent to this point.

David said, "That son of bitch run out there so fast it was like lightin' gasoline on a cat. He was screamin' and hollerin' so bad, he forgot to lock my door back up."

I kept my silence. David said he was told that he would be taken back before the judge and sentenced to be removed to the county jail. He had heard nightmare accounts of what happened to boys sentenced to the jail. He told the officials at the juvie that his mother would hire a lawyer and the lawyer would tell the judge about the teacher's sexual attacks on boys. David said he could get half a dozen boys to back him up.

The officials assured him that no judge would believe any of them and that he was headed to the county jail no matter what. But the next day a different man came back and offered David a deal. He would be released from the box, and he would not be sent to the jail, if he agreed to an additional six months' time in the juvie and also agreed to keep his mouth shut about the teacher. When David asked if the teacher was going to keep coming after him, the man said the teacher was no longer employed there.

He took the deal. He went before the judge and was sentenced to the additional six months. "And, man, Woodrow, I swear, ever since I come out of the box, it's like I'm the biggest hero in the whole juvie. Guys don't pick on me. In fact it's more like they look out for me. I don't have to be a slave to nobody. They even offer to make other guys my slaves. I tell them no, I don't go for that shit, but little guys do shit for me anyway, like they're sucking up to me. I'm telling you Woodrow, it's so good now, I think I could do ten years in here."

Finally I could be silent no longer. "David. David. Shut up. Jesus Christ, listen to yourself. Six more months, and you're proud of it. What does Ma say?"

"That's one reason I wanted to talk to you. I was afraid to put this shit in a letter, because I think they read our letters. I got the money from her for the phone call before I told her about the six months. Now she's real pissed. She's so pissed she won't come see me no more. I need you to ask her to come see me. I want to see her, plus I need her to bring me stuff."

"David, I don't blame Ma. You're thinking just like these guys around you, like a hood, a jailbird. You're proud of being a big guy in jail. You're OK with being in there longer."

"So I shoulda gave him a blow job? Is that what you think?" He was angry.

"No. No. I didn't say that for Christ's sake."

"Well what do you think, then? I mean maybe you just can't imagine it, because you're in there with all those rich guys, and shit like that don't happen where you are. Maybe I'm such a piece of shit you just can't understand nothing about me no more. Maybe you should just forget about me and pretend like you never heard of me."

"Don't be such an asshole, David. I just don't want you to be a jailbird all your life."

"Oh yeah? Well maybe that's just what I'm cut out to be."

He hung up.

That was the day before my Saturday test with Beetle. That night I had nothing else to do, so under the covers after lights out, I worked ahead a couple of chapters in the fatter Latin text, mastering lessons we hadn't gone over yet. The next afternoon, at a quarter to one, Compton, Gellhorn, Bear, Yusupov, Smiley, Davidson, and Roosevelt all walked me to the school building.

"He'll search you for a pony," Bear said.

"I'll punch him if he does."

"Brilliant idea," Gellhorn said. "Then you can run into town and rob a bank."

"Keep your cool," Yusupov said.

"Have you really got it all down?" Compton asked.

"Tight as a drum."

"Well," Roosevelt said, "go kick the fat fucker's ass."

Beetle was waiting in the hallway outside the classroom. He opened the door and nodded me in. His concession to Saturday was wearing khaki pants and tassel loafers beneath his tweed jacket and tie rather than gray flannel pants and lace-up shoes. Something about being alone in a room with him made him even more repugnant—the wine nose and ferret eyes, the breathing, the way he waddled and plopped himself. Everything about him made me angry. Before speaking, he took a long while to arrange a stack of what I recognized as the homework papers of other boys, as if to say he was a busy man whose time here could not be wasted.

"It's really only an hour's worth of questions," he said wheezily, "all multiple-choice, but I'm going to give you two hours, because it's an important test I want you to have every chance."

"Thank you, sir."

I put my book bag down and sat. I shot my cuffs several times, exposing my forearms to show that I didn't have wads of paper stuffed up my sleeves or information tattooed on my arms in ballpoint pen. He practically fell out of his chair leaning forward to look for himself, held in place only by his buttery gut.

"Why don't you take off your jacket?" he said. "I think you'll be more comfortable."

I hung my sport coat on the chair behind me, half wondering if he would ask me to take off my shirt next. He rose and waddled over. "I'll just place this fine garment over here where it won't get wrinkled." He dumped my jacket on a chair against the wall on the room's far side. I decided that if he did ask to search me, I would hit him in the nose.

"Did you bring a bluebook?" he asked.

"Oh, yes, sir," I said as brightly as I could. I held up three floppy blue notebooks from the bookstore. "I have three."

"You will only need one, as I believe I instructed you. Did you bring a ruler?"

"Oh, yes, sir. I brought four rulers." I tapped my book bag. It was a lie. I had only one.

"Well then," he said, "with all of those extra bluebooks and rulers, I'm sure you will do very well."

"Oh, I hope just to pass."

He gave me instructions for drawing a line down the center of each page and numbering each answer—exactly the same procedure we used in class. He said he was making sure that all procedures would be observed strictly today.

"I hesitate to ask about pencils."

"A dozen, all freshly sharpened."

I had three.

"Excellent! Well, then, this should be easy for you."

From the pile of papers before him, he pulled a stapled stack of a dozen or so pages, which he sent sailing down the table to me with a careless backhanded whisk. He pulled a stopwatch from the patch pocket of his jacket and placed it down before him.

"I will collect your bluebook at 3:12 PM."

Never lifting his eyes from the homework papers, he reached forward with one hand and punched the watch.

I took up the pages with cold dread. I knew that he was going to Jap me, I just didn't know how. I had boxed the problem every way I knew how, grinding all the way back to the first lesson and moving forward. But I was certain he would still find a way to assassinate me.

I scanned the first page. Nothing. A snap. I knew all of it. Before making a mark in my bluebook, I turned quickly to the second page, the third, the fourth. I thought I caught his ferret eyes turned up to watch me, but when I looked he stared down hard again at his papers. I continued to scan forward.

I fought down a smile when I got to page nine. The questions were from parts of the text that he hadn't taught us yet. I knew every single bit of it. It wasn't even hard. All of the surprise questions were taken from only the next chapter, and I had grinded far ahead of that. I could take this test in twenty minutes and score 100 percent.

I put the test down and let out a great sigh.

"Gee, it's pretty long," I said.

He looked up irritably.

"I told you, it's only an hour's worth, but I'm giving you two hours. I suggest you get going."

"Yes, sir, I will."

I twirled the pages around once, turned, and gazed out the window behind me.

"What are you looking at?" he asked.

"Birds."

"Birds?" He lifted himself up, waddled to the window, and looked out, craning and peering left to right, in the trees and on the ground, hoping to spot a billboard covered with Latin declensions and conjugations.

"Young man, don't stare out the window looking at birds, for God's sake. Take the damn test. Are you unable to take the test? Is there something wrong?"

"No, sir. Nothing at all. It's just such a beautiful day."

"Get on with the test, Skaggs. Stop flipping through pages and gawping about."

I opened my bluebook and began very slowly and methodically drawing lines on the pages and writing down numbers for the questions. I drew the lines so slowly and the room was so quiet that I imagined he could hear the scratch of my pencil rattling down to the bottom of each page. I stopped and admired each finished line before moving on to the next. I must have killed twenty minutes drawing lines.

"In God's name, what are you doing?" Beetle demanded at last, the veins in his nose ready to burst. He came over and stood above me to look down at my bluebook. "You haven't answered a single question."

"No, sir. I've been drawing my lines."

He gazed at me for a long while, then backed away and returned slowly to his chair. A calm came over him. He nodded yes to himself.

"I am so sorry, Skaggs," he said, "for being impatient with you." His voice was controlled. "We still have an hour and a half or more, so just proceed at your own pace and in your own way. You've done a very nice job with the lines."

"Thank you, sir."

For a while, I gazed at the test and whistled softly, until finally he said, "Stop whistling."

A while later, I hummed. I hummed for a good long while, gazing at the test, slowly turning the pages. He did not lift his face from his papers, but I could see color rising in his flabby neck and cheeks.

At last, without raising his face to me, he hissed, "Skaggs, do not make any noise or sound of any kind. Remain absolutely silent. I do not even want to hear you breathe until the test has been completed. Do you understand me?"

"Yes sir. And I apologize."

"Shut up."

"Yes, sir."

I began racing through, ticking the questions off, printing the answers in clear unmistakable block letters. A sensation of flying lifted me, and I soared, blowing out the tiny candle of every question with my mighty wings. I could tell that Beetle had dropped all pretense of working on his papers and was watching me, counting my every breath. I finished with more than an hour to spare, sat back, gave the test pages a little neatening tappety-tap on the tabletop, put my bluebook inside and sent the package sliding into his homework papers with a backhanded flick.

Beetle snapped up my bluebook with both hands. From a leather portfolio at his side, he removed his answer key. For half an hour I sat watching him go through my exam, a process that should have taken two minutes.

He questioned me on a dozen answers, all of which were perfectly clear and exactly correct.

"This is?" he said, pointing with his pencil.

"Pugnemini."

"Spell it."

I did.

"It is?"

"The subjunctive."

Later, "What is this?"

"Caesarem."

"Case?"

"Accusative. I believe that is what the question called for."

"Yes, Skaggs," he said mildly. "Quite correct."

Finally he finished. I sat waiting for at least five minutes while he arranged his papers in his portfolio. I willed myself silent. He stuck his face deep into the portfolio as if hunting for something.

I couldn't see his eyes. When he spoke, his voice was muffled like Jeremiah calling from the cistern.

"Skaggs, are you not at all curious how you did on my test?"

"Yes, sir."

"How do you think you did?"

"I have no idea, sir. It seemed very difficult. And I wasn't able to study much because of hockey. I take hockey very seriously."

He lifted his face out of the portfolio and spoke bitterly to the wall. "Not skating about with your cup outside your pants, I suppose."

"No, sir. Never. And I apologize for Compton doing that."

"We do not make apologies for others at St. Philip's, Skaggs, but, no, you did not do badly."

He turned his purple gaze to me. I kept my face frozen.

"You scored 100 percent," he intoned solemnly.

I said nothing.

"Did you not hear me?"

"Yes, sir. One hundred percent."

He cocked an eye curiously. "Are you surprised by your score?"

"Not too much."

He squinted and leaned over the table toward me. "I believe that I may have misjudged you, Skaggs. I think you are more capable than I expected. I believe you could do well at this school."

I was tempted to allow a tiny incursion of warmth, but instinct held me back an instant longer.

"The problem with you, though, Skaggs . . . "

And I thought, *Thank God I didn't relent.*

"The thing is," he said, "there's more to being a St. Philip's boy than being a grind. Good marks are very commendable, especially for a scholarship boy, because, after all, a boy who accepts a scholarship has a certain moral obligation to work hard and do well, and I find it commendable that you're living up to that debt."

I smiled genially, thinking to myself, *It's a fucking debt?*

"The question of character," he went on, "is central to being a true St. Philip's boy. People talk about manners as if they were a superficiality, but I think manners flow directly from character. I do not believe that a boy of poor character is capable of good manners or true poise."

I was silent, my face as blank as I could make it.

"Would you agree with me, Skaggs?"

"Oh, yes, sir."

"You often say, 'Oh,' before you agree. Is that something you learned before coming here?"

"Oh, yes, sir."

"I see. The thing is, you got off to a rather pugnacious start here, did you not? And I am not exonerating Compton, who has his own problems and deficiencies to care about, problems at home as I understand, but your first night here was rather disconcerting for us all."

"Sir," I said, "I don't have a gun."

He shot back in his chair. "What? A gun? What preposterous poppycock is this? Why would you have a gun, for God's sake? A gun?"

"Compton told me you asked him if I had a gun."

His breathing was labored. "Well . . . do you?"

"Oh, no sir. Not here."

"Do you have a gun somewhere else? Where do you have a gun?"

"In Pontiac."

"You have a gun in a Pontiac?"

"Oh, no sir. Pontiac is the name of my town. It's where I'm from."

"Yes, I know that, for God's sake. Why do you have a gun in Pontiac?"

"For hunting."

"I see. Well, you must never . . . obviously you would never bring a gun to St. Philip's."

"Oh, no sir. The gun stays in Pontiac."

He whisked away eraser dust from the top of the table with the ham of a hand, looked up at me and then back down at the table. His breathing recovered.

"You may go," he muttered.

I left without speaking.

•

The others didn't believe me.

"How could you get a hundred on stuff he hasn't taught yet?" Compton asked. He sang in a falsetto, "Yankee Doodle went to town, riding on a pony."

A few chuckled. Bear said nothing but looked at me balefully.

"No pony," I said. "You guys just don't know a genius when you see one."

Gradually at first, then in a sudden boom, all of my grades began to soar on quizzes in all of my classes, even French. One Friday when class ranks for the week were posted at Aldredge Hall, I was the top student in the third form. The next morning Johnny Wilson caught me by the arm coming out of chapel, gave me a huge wordless smile and a thumbs up. I was exuberant.

Sharing biscuits from a bribery box on Compton's windowsill

that night, I told him about the thumbs up. "Yeah," he said, "guys are talking about you. Everybody says it's not because you're a genius. You just grind all the time. I mean, you don't even stay for after-practice at hockey. You'll never get above third level."

I kept my face still but laughed inside. Third level at hockey seemed like a good trade for not becoming a wombat.

My reputation spread. One night during the witching hour, Gellhorn let himself into my alcove and asked me to come see him. I was already arranging my flashlight and books underneath my quilt-tent for a couple hours of super study. I told him I didn't want to get out of bed.

"I need to talk to you," he said snappishly. "I wonder if you might be willing to help me."

"Help? You? Me?"

He looked over his shoulder and pulled my curtain closed behind him.

"May I sit?"

I pulled up my feet and let him sit at the foot of my bed.

"I've been noticing," he said awkwardly, "that your grades have come up somewhat."

"Everyone notices, Gellhorn, and it's not 'somewhat.' My grades are way up. Way, way up. I'm first in the fucking form some weeks at Aldredge House, for Christ's sake. That's not somewhat."

"My own grades," he stammered with his head lowered, "my grades . . . I grind, but I'm still doing very badly."

"Everybody knows that. Nobody can figure it out."

"What do you mean?"

"You're smart. You're real smart. So why do you get such shitty grades?"

"I have a problem," he said. "I've always had it. I do very badly on tests. I can't . . . I can't remember the things I'm supposed to remember for quizzes. I can't spit it out in time. In fact, I flunk or almost flunk all my tests. My mother had me in a special school in Georgetown, where I did quite well . . . "

"You mean like a retardo school or something?"

He stopped speaking and stared at me for a while, breathing heavily.

"Even here I always get As and A-plusses on my essays," he said evenly, "but it's these fucking Jap quizzes they give us where you have to just spit out all this stupid memorized trivia."

"So this is not the first place you've had trouble."

"No," he said, looking down. "No. I've been held back. I'm a year older than you guys."

"That's why she had you in the mental school."

"It wasn't a mental school, asshole. It was progressive."

"How did you get in here? You didn't have to take the same test I did?"

He muttered, "They weren't even going to let me in, my grade on the test was so bad. St. Philip's wasn't going to admit me even with Turk Ambrose being my so-called adoptive father. My mother bit the bullet and got me in with the Hemingway connection. She told them I was just like him. He has the same problem."

"Then why don't you go get Hemingway to help you if he's really your old man?"

He was breathing hard with his jaw clenched. "Do you think you could possibly find it in your heart, Pontiac, to leave me alone about Hemingway and who my real father is. You wouldn't understand."

I laughed. "You'd be surprised. You said help you. With what? How?"

291

He gathered himself.

"Is there a particular thing that you do? Is there a trick?"

"It's not a pill or a trick, Gellhorn, like I'm cheating or something. Johnny Wilson taught me. It's just really hard. That's what it is really. Hard. Just hard. No tricks, no ponies. I don't think a rich guy like you could do it. You don't have the problems like I do biting me in the ass."

He looked away. He kept swallowing until I thought he might choke. "Your problems aren't any worse than mine. If I flunk out, I'm toast. I might as well just move to Montana and go to work for Roosevelt and be one of the ditch diggers on his ranch for the rest of my life."

For a long while I gazed at him where he sat in shadow with his head hung low at the foot of my bed. It was stunning, even infuriating that he could possibly think his problems with Ernest Hemingway and the Golden Gloves and Turk Whoever-He-Was were equivalent to my own. But then in a moment of moonlight from Compton's window I caught the glimmer of a tear.

"I doubt you're good enough with a shovel to work for Roosevelt," I said.

"Oh, thanks. Thanks a lot. God you're a bastard."

"You don't know the half of it. Hey, Gellhorn. Do you seriously want me to teach you? Me?"

"Yes."

"Meet me behind the squash courts after crew tomorrow."

•

For an hour the next day, Gellhorn and I had a strange session in my secret lair in the athletic building. I had to tell him several times to shut up and do what I said or I would quit. I made him write out Latin phrases and other quiz questions on sheets of paper, turn the paper over, get up, walk away, come back to the table, and write the answers on the back of the page, then turn it back over to see if he got it right, all of which he said was stupid and the kind of thing only a mental defective would have to do. I said maybe that was a good way for him to start thinking of himself, which made him angry, which caused me to have to tell him to shut up again and do what I said. Between the two of us, so much shouting and stomping around the room took place that a sweaty Fifth Former with a squash racket in one hand and a big red lump on his forehead pushed open the door and asked if we could tone it down. Gellhorn asked him if he could try hitting the ball with his racquet instead of his face, and the guy barged in with two more Fifth Formers behind him ready to beat us up, but Adams appeared behind them and told them to leave us alone. Adams seemed to guess what we were doing and nodded approval.

In the last ten minutes of our session, I spot-quizzed Gellhorn in Latin, math, and public affairs. He spat out every answer perfectly before I could finish the question.

On the way to evening classes, he said, "What is that we're doing? You say it's not a trick. But it feels like a trick."

"It's trying really, really hard," I said, "but to do it, you have to be able to admit to yourself that you have to try really hard."

"Why wouldn't I admit that?"

"Because you're a stuck-up gentry rich kid."

He was silent the rest of the way.

Our next session at the gym was even more raucous. Gellhorn came armed with a bunch of crap to tell me about his previous school and how they had taught him to understand things by

293

"envisioning" them. I told him to envision his ass. I was showing him how to get good grades on quizzes, which is what he told me he wanted to do, which meant knocking the stuff into his thick skull so he could spit it back out when he needed it. He gave me some speech they had given him at the retardo school about "our love of knowledge," and I said they should change it to "how to get yourself kicked out of St. Philip's."

Our third and last session went much better. By this point, Gellhorn had already done quite a bit better on several quizzes, which must have whetted his appetite. I wound up teaching him every trick I had taught myself, and he showed me a couple new ones he had invented on his own. The best one was starting a study session by giving his textbook the finger and loudly telling it, "Fuck you!"

In the weeks afterward, Gellhorn's name moved steadily up the list in Aldredge Hall until finally one week he eclipsed me and was number one to my number two. The evening that happened, I turned to him in the scrum before the bulletin board and said a little hotly, "I guess you're happy now, you beat me."

With a finger to my chest, he pushed me out of the crowd of upturned faces and said in a low mutter, "I owe you, Pontiac. You can't even guess how much I owe you."

A week later Gellhorn invited me to come to his house in Washington, D.C. for the winter holiday, a long weekend in early February when we were allowed to leave school. I was doing well enough in all my classes that I decided I could afford a break. I said yes. It was a few weeks away.

Two or three days later, when I was finally falling asleep in my bunk, I awakened with a start, pelted in the forehead by a candied fig. Above me Compton was in his aerie, grinning from ear to ear because he had made such a good hit. I popped the fig into my mouth, climbed up and joined him.

"I heard Gellhorn invited you to his house," he whispered.

"Yeah." I was busy sorting through his open box of goodies. I discovered a trove of chocolate-covered toffee in one corner of the box.

"Take it easy on the toffee asshole," he said loudly.

Across the way, Aubert called, "Tais-toi!"

I shushed Compton with a finger to my lips. He peered over to Aubert's alcove and muttered, "I'll tay twa *you*, Frenchie." I snatched another toffee while he was looking away.

Wetly through a mouthful of the chocolate covered raisins, he whispered, "Gellhorn's house is the hottest ticket in D.C. His mother is a big D.C. hostess. Granger spent the weekend there once, and he met John Glenn. He said the house is just like one huge party all the time. It's a big mansion in Georgetown. Granger said the house was so full of guests and waiters and musicians and shit, Gellhorn's mother didn't even know he and Granger were there. They got there late on a Friday night, and there was a big party going on. Some butler took their bags upstairs, and they went to their rooms. In the morning, they had breakfast in this little separate dining room just for Gellhorn and his sisters."

"Sisters?"

"Two. One is a couple years older than us, another one who's little. The older one is called Sissy. I think she goes to Choate Rosemary Hall. The little one's still at home."

"How did his mother not even know he was there?"

"Granger said it was a huge party at the house all weekend. He and Gellhorn went to a park on Saturday and practiced lacrosse. Granger said they didn't get back to the house until evening. There was already another huge party going on in a ballroom on the third floor with Lester Lannin."

"Who?"

"A society band. Granger said he saw Cary Grant come down the stairs so drunk he almost fell."

I looked him in the eye to see if he was kidding, but he wasn't.

"He even saw Kennedy there. So Granger and Gellhorn go back to the little dining room again, and a maid serves them dinner. Then they go back up to Gellhorn's room and watch TV. He has his own TV. The next day, they have breakfast and go to another park to play lacrosse. They go back to the house to get their bags because it's time to call a cab and go to the train station. They're down in this big foyer at the front door, waiting for the cab, and Gellhorn's mother comes down in some kind of gown or robe or something. She sees Gellhorn and says (in Compton's version of a womanly voice), 'Oh, Timmy, why didn't you tell me you were here? Do you have to run already? Well, I'm so glad I caught you,' and she gives him a big smooch. Gellhorn's reaching his head way back away from her like he's afraid she's going to bite him."

We both snickered and snorted loudly.

"You are both very inconsiderable!" Aubert called in a hoarse whisper.

•

With Compton's version of Gellhorn's house in my head, I began to grow excited. It seemed as if my visit to Washington was going to be a great adventure. I tried to imagine what it would be like to meet the future president. I could not even bring myself to imagine what it would be like to meet John Glenn or Cary Grant.

In the meantime, a very unwanted event was developing. I had attended the school's weekly Saturday evening movie showings in the auditorium only during the fall term, before I learned how to super-grind. Since Christmas I had skipped the movies because it was a period when everyone else was either in the auditorium watching or gathered afterward in the lobby to gabble, allowing me three undisturbed hours when I could sit in my alcove on my cot with my knees up under my chin and load up for some more A-plusses on my Monday morning quizzes. I don't remember ever feeling lonely or left out during those hours. I may remember being excited about how savagely I was going to slay everyone else on the quizzes.

The upcoming movie titles were posted at the beginning of each month in Aldredge Hall in the same niche where our weekly grade averages were displayed. One Friday evening, when I went to admire my marks for the past week, my eyes strayed to the list of upcoming films, and my heart stopped. The next week, according to the notice, the movie was to be *The Alligator People*. The following week would be *Daniel Boone, Trailblazer*, the same movie I had seen in Pontiac with my father and brother.

I couldn't believe it. Of all the movies in the universe, this particular film had to stalk me here. I knew enough by now to realize I had made a terrible mistake by declaring a familial connection with Daniel Boone.

As he was portrayed in a movie, Boone would be viewed here as a toothless shambling woodland wretch who wore animals for hats. This badly made movie had elicited yodeling howls from the hillbillies at the Pontiac drive-in, but I was sure it would excite a very different kind of howl in the auditorium of St. Philip's School.

In the days leading up to the showing, matters grew relentlessly more dire, like the slow closing of a vise. Gellhorn noticed the title on the list of upcoming films and began talking about it at the table.

"It's about Daniel Boone," he said to me. "I would think you'd want to see it."

"Really?" I said. "Are there any good movies about Hemingway?"

Barry picked up on it. "I don't know how good the movie is," he said, "but it deals with an interesting chapter. The Shawnee were trying to stop American settlers from overrunning what is now Kentucky. The royal governors had engaged in lengthy diplomacy with a confederation of tribes and had signed treaties promising that no white settler would cross the Allegheny Appalachians. But white settlers, led by people like Boone, were ignoring the treaties, streaming over the mountains in hordes, and the Shawnee wanted to stop them."

Making things much worse, Frau Schmitz got into it.

"The Shawnee were allied with the crown, were they not?" she asked Barry.

"Well, yes. The Brits had an obligation to honor and enforce their own treaties with the Indian nations, but the crown was stretched thin fighting the American Revolution. So the governors encouraged the Indians to fight off the white settlers themselves. The English provided munitions and logistical backup but not soldiers."

"You know so much more about it than I do," she said demurely. "How intriguing. I believe I shall overcome my misgivings about viewing films in an auditorium full of boys and go to see this one."

My plan, obviously, was not to attend. They could all sit out in the lobby afterward as long as they liked, cackling and snorting about my hillbilly forebears. As long as I did not have to be physically present for it, I was sure I could weather whatever the aftermath might be, even from Frau Schmitz.

But then Mr. Fell climbed into the act. Whenever he thought a film was worthwhile, he turned it into an opportunity for an informal seminar afterward back in the dorm. He usually discussed the movie before lights out for a couple of evenings beforehand, then sat with the boys for the show. Afterward, instead of mingling in the random hubbub out in the second-floor lobby, most of the Dorm Four boys who had seen the movie came back into the dorm for a postmortem led by Mr. Fell, Barry, and Adams.

Mr. Fell was especially interested in *Daniel Boone, Trailblazer*. Seated out on the radiator bench one evening while we were all in our beds behind closed curtains, he talked about it. In summing up, he said, "Perhaps this movie will unveil for us the true origin of this strange creature in our midst who goes by the unlikely moniker of Pontiac."

"We already know where he came from," Compton shouted from his bed. "The city dump!"

Aubert called out angrily, "Compton, you are but an ass!"

I called to no one in particular, "Fuck you."

"Then it's settled," Mr. Fell said. "We'll make an outing of it, and you, Pontiac, will lead the way."

Now there was no way out. I couldn't be a sullen brat and lurk in my alcove. I had to go.

On the night of the movie, the weather was crisp and blustery. None of us wore overcoats, because that was considered sissy, but we wore our sport coats with the lapels folded up around our ears, and we stuffed our hands into our pants pockets.

"Are you going to be able to help us with the background on Boone later?" Mr. Fell asked me.

"Not much," I said. "I don't really know that much about him."

He gave me a quizzical look, shrugged, and moved on.

The walls of the auditorium were a dull white. Dark-stained wooden pews were covered by cushions cut thin lest anyone start feeling comfortable. With the lights on, the place felt more like a Congregational church than a movie theater. Of 480 boys at the school, probably 350 attended the movie most Saturday nights, packing the first level and the front of the balcony.

I was still reasonably certain of my ability to fend off wise-cracks, and I also was resigned to prison or death in the event of unforgiveable insult. But my resolve and courage deserted me just as we arrived on the broad steps of the auditorium. There, wrapped in fur and wool, was Frau Schmitz in the company of three other tightly bundled masters' wives.

"Thérèse," Mr. Fell said, "how nice to see you. Is Gustave not with you?"

"No," she said with a smirk, "I was unable to talk him into coming." Her eye turned toward me, then shot past. "He said I would have to undertake my research into Daniel Boone alone."

"Will you sit with us?"

She put a hand to the crook of his arm. "Thank you, Louie, no. I salute you for sitting with them, but I will sit with my friends."

By the time we were seated in our pews and the lights were going down, my nerves were knotted in fists. I tried desperately to remember how much of a naive hillbilly the Daniel Boone character was in this movie, but, of course, I could not, because I had watched the movie in the exclusive company of naive hillbillies. It would be like Aubert trying to remember how French some actor was in a French film.

Daniel Boone took a while to show up in the movie. None of

the other actors in the early scenes spoke like hillbillies. They all spoke like natives of Los Angeles.

When Boone finally did appear, I was astonished by his diction and affect. If anything, he seemed like a guy straight out of St. Philip's, now that I knew what guys straight out of St. Philip's were like. In fact, he sounded just like Barry, with the same measured elocution and oratorical delivery. It struck me immediately that if the real Boone had actually spoken and behaved like this, the real hillbillies would have killed him.

But the entire auditorium seemed to hang on his every word. The normal ambient buzz of fidgeting and whispering faded and then ceased. I looked around and saw all faces uplifted to drink in Boone's every syllable.

Boone's speeches in the film are all pious soliloquy and pompous pronouncement, going on about the need for courage and patience, salted with no small dose of Manifest Destiny. The director renders Boone as a white American Moses, landlord of the wilderness tasked with the nasty job of evicting a bunch of non-white tenants behind on the rent.

When I rewatched the film as an old man, Boone's speeches struck me as absurd caricatures of all the racist chauvinist tropes that have led America into tragedy and moral dissolution since the movie was made. Of course, I didn't hear any of that in 1960, not in Pontiac, not at St. Philip's. Nor did anyone else in the auditorium that night, with one surprising exception—Frau Schmitz. For the rest of us, the entire movie was a paean to the glory of the American white man.

The previous Saturday, the audience had watched *The Alligator People*, just as we had at the drive-in in Pontiac. As in Pontiac, everyone in the St. Philip's auditorium that night recognized the actor,

Lon Chaney, playing Blackfish, leader of the Shawnee, as the loathsome swamp-dwelling handyman of *The Alligator People*. For his effrontery in daring to return, Chaney was booed and jeered by the audience in the auditorium the moment he appeared, just as he had been at the drive-in.

When the action got going hot and heavy and the Shawnee were assaulting Fort Boonesborough, the boys in the auditorium cheered every time the pioneers pushed off an attacker's ladder and sent another redskin to perdition. I was still tense, and when the cowardly shopkeeper threatened Boone with court-martial and then raced out of the fort with a white flag to offer surrender to the Indians, I may have expected the auditorium to identify with the shopkeeper.

When the Indians began firing musket balls into him, the vile shopkeeper took eons to die again, twirling and flapping, crouching and spinning with each hit in what looked more like a man doing the Charleston than getting killed. At every gross pantomime, the audience cheered and howled exactly as the hillbillies had done that night at the drive-in.

We did not cross paths with Frau Schmitz on our way back to the Lower. The conversation among the boys was lively. Back in Dorm Four, Barry gave us a brief but interesting explanation of the larger context of southern settlement and the role Boone and Fort Boonesborough played.

Finally, he said to me, "Do you really not know anything about all this?"

Challenged, I offered up what little my father had known, gleaned from the visiting Ph.D. candidate who had come to interview him. Boone, I said, formed a land company that subdivided and sold vast tracts of land in the trans-Appalachian south. My own forebear, the long hunter, was Boone's partner in that enterprise.

Mr. Fell, Adams, Barry, and the boys in the dorm listened with attentive nods. Smiley said to me thoughtfully, "But you are not rich."

"Christ," Compton said, "that's an understatement."

"Pontiac's forebear may have been rich, probably was," Adams said. "We're talking about a time that goes back almost to the early days of my own family. People don't just automatically stay rich that long. The Adamses have been up and down. Some branches of the family today are quite poor."

Gellhorn said, "How could rich people turn into poor people?"

Mr. Fell said, "By spending too much money. It's actually quite easy. You boys will learn, if your fathers haven't taught you already, that holding on to money is a lot harder than making it."

"My father hasn't taught me shit," Granger said. "He's too busy moose-hunting and getting laid."

Everyone laughed.

"Well," Adams said, "then you could wind up poor."

Everyone looked stricken.

"I don't see how that could happen," Granger said.

"Anyone can become poor," Mr. Fell said.

After a long silence, Bear said quietly, "Maybe that is why Pontiac was brought to the school. So his family can get rich again."

Adams chuckled. "That's not how it works, Bear. No one cares if you get poor. No one is going to just make you rich again. You have to do that for yourself."

"How?" Bear asked.

"By making more money than you spend. A lot more."

Bear looked aghast. "I think if something happened to make me poor, I might kill myself."

Mr. Fell turned to me.

"What do you think about that?" he asked.

"Nah," I said. "It's not so bad. We poor people just lie around all the time drinking wine and screwing."

"Shit," Compton said, "I'd be poor for that."

Everyone laughed, and we tramped off to get ready for bed.

•

We were spared the presence of the Schmitzes for two full days while Herr Schmitz attended a retreat of some kind at Dartmouth for masters who taught languages. We took advantage of their absence to make gluttonous feasts of our meals, sending the waiters back for seconds and thirds, which seemed only to please Jake in the kitchen. He always had surplus laid by.

The Schmitzes returned on a Friday evening. I hoped that their sojourn at Dartmouth might have been long enough to take Frau Schmitz's mind off the movie, a hope cruelly extinguished almost the moment grace was said and the evening meal began.

"Mr. Barry," she called down the table before Barry could get a generous forkful of green bean casserole all the way into his mouth, "what did you think of the Daniel Boone movie?"

"Oh," he said diffidently, putting the fork to rest on his plate, "I thought it was not as bad as it could have been. It treats an interesting chapter in our history." He started back to the fork.

"Rather inaccurately, wouldn't you say?"

He put the fork down again. "Well, sure, they played hob with some of the history, as with Boone's court-martial."

"Boone wasn't court-martialed," I blurted, immediately regretting allowing myself to get baited in. "The guy just said he was going to get him court-martialed."

Frau Schmitz raised her penciled eyebrows almost to the roof of her head and pursed her lips.

"I think Skaggs is quite wrong, is he not, Barry? During Herr Schmitz's retreat, I did some reading in the library at Dartmouth. Daniel Boone, in fact, was court-martialed, because he was the one who tried to surrender the fort to the Native Americans, not the merchant."

I whispered, "Bullshit," and Herr Schmitz stiffened, but his wife put a hand to his.

"Let Barry answer, Gustave," she said softly. Herr Schmitz shrank back but gave me a glowering eye.

Barry gazed at his fork wistfully. "Boone was court-martialed, which was part of a very complicated story. Years earlier, he had been captured by the Shawnee, and, as they sometimes did, instead of torturing him to death, the Shawnee adopted Boone into their tribe. By a tradition disputed by some historians, Boone was adopted as a son by Chief Blackfish.

"He later escaped or simply left the tribe, returning to live as a white man. He wound up at Fort Boonesborough as the chief agent and organizer of a land company that wanted to launch a colony in Kentucky to be called Transylvania."

Compton said, "Is that why they used the same actor for the Indian chief who played Dracula?"

"It's not the same actor," Gellhorn said derisively. "Blackfish was the son of the guy who played Dracula."

Barry gazed at his congealing green bean casserole. "The whole business about surrender is sort of lost to time. I forget or I never knew why Boone, who presumably was a civilian, could even be court-martialed. This was all during the Revolution, and Boone was accused several times of harboring pro-British sympathies."

"Bullshit," I said.

Herr Schmitz gave Adams a wide-eyed demanding stare.

"Don't swear," Adams told me.

"At any rate," Barry said directly to me, "Daniel Boone was acquitted and went on to become very much the fine type of American hero who was portrayed in the movie."

I gave both Schmitzes a nod of vindication. Barry attacked his plate.

"But that was not the sort of inaccuracy that struck me most meaningfully in the film," Frau Schmitz said. "That sort of thing, the details, the movie people always play hob with that, as you say, Mr. Barry."

He nodded agreement with a full mouth.

Herr Schmitz prompted her: "So you were in the library reading about Boone while I was occupied with my very boring seminar. What did you find?"

"Oh, I don't know that it was much different from what one would learn from any other comprehensive treatment of American history in the period, as long as the history isn't written by an American."

"How so?" Herr Schmitz asked in a theatrical imitation of studious attention.

"I refer to the film's absurd racism."

This time Adams looked up from his plate.

"Perhaps you could offer us an example," Adams said mildly.

"I don't know," Frau Schmitz said with a tiny shrug. "I really wasn't talking about anything specific, more the film's general tenor. But, of course, you might take the scene where Blackfish swears vengeance on 'all white men.' There are a dozen red-coated British soldiers standing at his shoulders when he says it."

"I'm not quite sure I understand," Adams said.

"Is he going to kill the English?"

"No," Adams said, perplexed. "The Brits were his allies."

"And what color were these Brits?"

"White."

"So if he's going to kill all white men, why isn't he going to kill the Brits?"

Adams shook his head in consternation.

"The line, 'kill all white men,' coming from the Indian," she said, "is simply the moviemaker's way of signaling that Boone and the other settlers were engaged in a war to defend white men."

"You're quite right," Barry said. "It's an anomaly, just sloppy screenwriting by some Hollywood hack."

We attacked our food, eager to end it, but Frau Schmitz was having none of that.

"How is it an anomaly, Barry?" she asked. "The entire movie is replete with soliloquies by Boone about the white man's destiny, as if God in Heaven had sent the white man to rid the forests of North America of the hideous non-white Native American."

Aubert spoke up: "I have noticed these same themes, Frau Schmitz, and I think you make a good point. The Americans took their inheritance of English racism and made it worse."

Barry put down his silverware.

"I think you're both quite right," he said. "But I think in telling things that way, the film is honest, for better or worse, about the way Americans saw things in the period treated in the film. The American perspective in that time was regrettably racist and chauvinist. As such, I don't know that our attitudes back then were much different from those of Europeans."

Herr Schmitz looked expectantly to his wife for a rebuttal.

"But Barry," she said amiably, "the period of your history I'm really concerned with is not the late eighteenth century at all. I refer more specifically to the period of two Saturday nights ago, when an entire auditorium filled with the sons of your American aristocracy were cheering and caterwauling for every racist theme in the film, just eating it up, if I may say so."

"You may say so," Barry said, sitting rigidly upright at the far end of the table. "But I think it's painting with a bit of a broad brush . . . "

"Oh, of course," she said quickly, "and I apologize for that. It's just so confusing for us Europeans."

"What's confusing?" Compton asked.

My blood ran cold. I knew Compton getting into this was not at all a good thing.

"Most of you here are of the American upper classes," she said with new purpose. "For you, Herr Schmitz and I have the utmost respect because you are so similar to our own upper classes. And yet you celebrate the history and culture of your own rabble as if they were almost more noble than the men of birth who founded your nation."

"The whores and pickpockets," Compton said.

She made a gesture with a hand. "Well, not to put too fine a point to it. But yes. Exactly. The offal of Europe. It's as if your society's best people are in thrall somehow to the worst of you. The highest are almost obeisant to the lowest. That's what I thought I saw in that auditorium."

"It was weird," Compton said. "Afterward, everybody was talking like Pontiac was a hero or something because he was related to Daniel Boone."

"Ah, well," she said unctuously, "I'm glad Pontiac has something to be proud of."

"I'm not related to Daniel Boone," I said.

I was ignored.

"Frau Schmitz," Compton said, "I remember what you said about those people who came to this country on prison ships and so on, but you never meant to say that Pontiac's mother was a whore."

The table fell deadly still.

"Shut up, Compton," Adams said.

I felt a numbness creeping across my mouth, and my breath came short. I eyed the meat knife next to my plate.

"Oh, no, no, no," she said in a mock-soothing voice, "Compton did not mean to insult me. He was only asking a question."

"About my mother," I said.

"No, no, no, not about your mother, silly," she said. "We're talking about people a very long time ago."

"Yeah, no," Compton said, "I didn't mean Pontiac's mother was a whore. I meant maybe his grandmother was a whore."

"Shut up, Compton," Adams said.

"Of course," Frau Schmitz said, "so very long ago, and a complete absence of records, it would be impossible to know with precision. We do know that a great many of these rather regrettable people who came in the ships, the ones who are forebears of the ignorant racist white people of the American South today, were of the very lowest social orders, including a great many criminals and prostitutes."

"So," Compton said, twisting a palm in the air, "maybe."

"Jesus," Adams said.

"Frau Schmitz," I said, "since we're talking about such a long time ago, is it possible that one of your own relatives way back then could have been a whore?"

Herr Schmitz looked as if he might suffer a brain aneurysm. "I will beat this boy . . . "

"Ah!" Barry said. "The suggestion has been made that Pontiac might have a lady of the night lurking somewhere in the family woodpile. I think it's fair enough for him to ask the same of others."

"Please, Gustave," she said quietly with the hand back on his wrist, "what the boy asks is entirely fair, and perhaps this is a chance to explain."

Turning to me, she said, "My family comes from a commune in northwest France called Saint-Marie-Aux-Mines. There in the church are found records dating to the eleventh century, and in those records are the names and occupations of all my forebears. There is no mystery. The whole story is there. In all that time, we have been engineers and owners of mines and other things of that level. You will not find prostitutes or pickpockets among my forebears but noble persons, bankers, famous artists, and military leaders.

"We say that having this sort of family history is being 'of birth,' because it is a tradition to which we are born. Our traditions are very ancient because the places where we are born are very ancient. But you see, the thing is, we know our history. It is written. It is in the churches.

"Some of you Americans have history already, which is a very commendable thing and something we greatly admire. The people in this country who are of birth tend to come from people in Europe who had some birth to begin with. Here, it is a relatively shallow thing still, compared to our own, but that is no one's fault. It simply is how things have happened and progressed, and here the people of birth are making great strides.

"Others of you," she went on, piercing me with her tiny dark eyes, "have no history at all because you never did. Your forebears arrived here without history because they were never a part of history. Your forebears were nameless and faceless. They were banished from history, so to speak. They have made little progress in all of their time on this continent, I suppose, because they had nothing to begin with, no idea of how to begin."

"Begin what?" I asked.

"Achieving rank."

Compton shrugged and gave me a look. "Whores and pickpockets," he said.

"Goddamn it!" Adams said.

"Shall we talk about something else?" Barry said.

"Please," Herr Schmitz said.

She sank back in her chair, holding her eyes to her plate and barely smiling.

———

Ellen and I were together in a familiar spot but at an unfamiliar time of year, bundled in blankets and scarves against a sharp fall wind coming off Noyack Bay on Long Island Sound, huddled on folding chairs on the long slope between Compton's weekend castle and the sea.

I had been staying with him in his palatial digs at the south end of Central Park when I learned Ellen and the brain surgeon, whom I still had not met, were winding up a visit to the Hamptons and about to return to Chicago. I thought Compton and I were headed to his place on Long Island for the weekend, so I asked if I could add Ellen to the list, hoping I might inveigle her to send the hated brain surgeon home alone and stay behind herself a few days. Compton agreed, and she did too. But then an hour later, Compton called me from his office.

"Is this the same broad you've been telling your life story to?"

"Yes. Ellen. Same one."

"I won't be joining. I just found out my Mandarin class is having a party in Flushing. It might be a wedding. That woman talks so fast on the phone I can't understand half of what she says."

"A Mandarin wedding in Flushing. You know how to live."

"Beats having to hear your life story."

So it was just Ellen and me, which I loved, except for being out on the lawn. Given the weather, my own idea would have been to go inside to the baronial fireplace and partake of the obsequiously served winter toddies. But sitting out here in the salty bluster was her idea, so I happily agreed.

"How did you take it," she asked, "when Frau Schmitz disparaged your lineage?"

"I don't remember. I do remember that Yusupov made a point of telling me later he thought I had handled it very well."

"Because you had aplomb."

"Probably."

"But you were hurt."

"Are you getting cold?" I asked. "I am."

"Listen to me. My family has history. It's called the Holocaust. It's pogroms. The Lower East Side. But it's all kinds of other stuff, too, like being lumberjacks in Lithuania, rabbis, poets, farmers, wonderful things. Probably 75 percent bullshit, but it's all told in the same way . . . "

"Homeric legend," I offered.

"Exactly," she said. "Heroic legend. You're right. The heroic legend of my family. The story of who we are and how we came to be, all of the good things, the strong things, the wonderful things we were. The bad shit is all about what other people did to us, what they thought of us, because they were stupid and ugly. We're not those things. They are. We are our own strength, our legend. Your family has legend, too. Incredible legend. You were related to Daniel Boone, for God's sake."

"Related to one of Boone's associates . . . "

"Oh, fuck you, Woodrow. It's Daniel Boone. Related, associated, who cares? But it could be Jewish lumberjacks. I remember every single word of the stories I was told about our family in Lithuania, even without the pogroms, because family hero stories like that are what give us breath. Those are the stories that provide life its purpose and hope. I have to think your stories were the same."

I gazed out across the bay to where two young men in a white fishing boat were motoring against neatly ranked whitecaps, hunched low against the cold wind, one in the bow and the other at the stern on the arm of the motor, black silhouettes against a gray metal sky.

"Our stories about Georgia and Quitman County and hunting were wonderful," I said. "Larger than life. My father must have told them to us a hundred times, and I cherished every word. Faulkner didn't come close. We didn't need no stinking Faulkner. We were Faulkner. Even the losers in the family tree, the drunks and the ne'er-do-wells, their stories all reached back in a straight line to the long hunter . . . "

"The first Skaggs," she interrupted, "the guy who plunged into the forest. You were proud of him. You felt that pride I always felt when I heard about the Jewish lumberjacks somewhere in fucking Lithuania."

"The same. Yes."

"So how did you feel when this woman took it all down to shit?

313

When she talked about your people as scum, garbage that should have died? You really can't remember how you felt?"

I waited. I watched the boat. The cold wind taunted my ears. Then suddenly at a ridiculously old age, at a point in life when such things should be long gone and forgotten, tears came to my eyes. I caught my breath against an unbelievable pain, as if someone had run a piece of raw steel through my stomach.

"I wanted to die," I said.

She sat up straight. "Why should you want to die? Didn't you want to slap the bitch?"

"No, no," I said. I rose to my feet and shook off the cold. "I wasn't angry with her. I knew she was right."

Ellen got up and took me by the elbows, peering into my face. "How could she be right? Are you fucking crying?"

"It's the wind."

"Bullshit."

"OK, OK." I shook myself free, walked off a few paces, put a finger to one nostril and blew my nose into the grass.

"That's gross," she said.

I motioned for us to sit again.

"Ellen," I said, "don't ever offer to be a grief counselor."

"Don't worry," she said.

"I remember. I do remember. I wanted to die, right there at the table. I hadn't ever cared before if the stories were true. It's as you say, exactly. They breathed life into us. They made us feel we were larger than life, that we could do anything, be anything or anyone. Seeing it all kicked to pieces with such authority was a kind of death. Aren't you cold?"

"I'm freezing my ass off."

We got up to go back into the castle. She came to me and wiped my eyes with her scarf.

"I'm sorry I made you cry, babe."

"I didn't fucking cry."

"We got into some deep shit here I guess."

"We did, indeed. But I also made a very significant discovery just now, with your help. This is the first time in my life I ever really understood why the rest of it happened, why I got into it."

She stopped and turned back. "Got into what?"

"The food stuff at the table with the Schmitzes."

"You got into it yourself?"

"A story for another day," I said.

"Bullshit," she said. "That's a story for right now."

Don't tell me I don't know how to hold onto an audience.

•

On Sunday, the week before I was to visit Gellhorn's home in Washington, I woke with a slight fever. After chapel, I returned to my alcove with the shivers, burrowed under my mother's quilt still clad in clothes and shoes, and fell into a deep tumbling sleep. I awoke three hours later when I heard someone snap open my curtain, snap it closed again and say, "He's not in there," apparently having missed me in my cocoon. I already felt better and was a little hungry. I was just about to rise and go to lunch when I heard my name spoken out on the radiator bench. Smiley was muttering to Gellhorn about something involving me.

"Your mother would never forgive you for the rest of your life," Smiley said.

Gellhorn mumbled and groused. "Pontiac would never do that. He's my friend. He helped me with studying. He knows better than to go after my sister."

I heard Compton snicker. "Pontiac knows better? You're joking."

"She's older than he is," Gellhorn insisted. "Anyway, it's different. He knows that."

"How different?" Compton asked.

A silence ensued. Gellhorn said, "Pontiac knows he's not one of us. He jokes about it. He knows, even if we're friends here, he's not like us away from the school. He wouldn't actually try to go out with one of our sisters, for Christ's sake."

"Suppose he did go after your sister," Smiley said. "How would your mother react?"

"God," Gellhorn moaned, "I mean, she'd never forgive me. And Turk. Damn it. I don't even want to think about that."

Davidson piped up with a giggle. "You would be in so much trouble."

Gellhorn said, "Yes, but Christ, I've already invited him."

Smiley said, "I suppose you could tell your older sister that his father works in a factory."

"She might like that," Gellhorn said. "She's an idiot. She has the brains of a rabbit."

"She doesn't have the body of a rabbit," Compton said.

"Shut up, will you?"

Roosevelt spoke up: "You guys are like a bunch of bitchy girls. Pontiac's our friend, and you talk about him like he's a monkey."

"Guess why," Granger said.

They all laughed. They were walking off toward lunch. I heard Gellhorn ask, "Why couldn't I just tell Pontiac, 'Hey, hands off, don't even think about it?'"

"Because you'd be talking to a monkey," Granger said.

The last thing I heard was Gellhorn moaning, "Oh, Christ."

I flew out of bed, a bit lightheaded but better. I hurried into the dining room behind them. When we were all seated, Gellhorn asked me where I had been.

"Cooler," I said. "Wasn't feeling too good. Doc gave me some aspirin."

The Schmitzes were not present, but the supes were at the table. The mood was so somber that Adams finally said, "What's the matter with you guys? Did you get into another donnybrook?"

We all said no.

After a suitable pause, I said, "Hey, Gellhorn, I'm really sorry, but I'm getting kind of semi-panicked about a bunch of homework assignments I've got, and I really don't think I can go home with you. Sorry for the late notice."

"Oh, that's OK," he said without looking up from his plate. "I understand."

Within minutes, the table was raucous again with the banter and laughter customary at a Sunday lunch with the Schmitzes gone.

After lunch I returned to my alcove, pulled the curtain and sat on the head of my bunk. More than injured, I was bewildered. My confusion grew when I heard Gellhorn's voice outside my curtain.

"May I come in?"

"Sure."

He sat on the foot of my bunk. "Roosevelt says he thinks you heard us, that's why you said you couldn't come to my house. Is that right?"

I was deeply embarrassed. "Yes."

He didn't say anything for a while. "Roosevelt says you are the gentleman and we're the assholes. I think he's right. I think I'm an asshole anyway. I'm really sorry. I didn't want to hurt your feelings."

My head snapped up. "I have my feelings pretty well under control."

"I'm sure you do. But, shit, you know, you did a lot for me. You might have saved my life. I consider us way more than just school chums. I hope we're friends for life. I feel rotten about your hearing us."

"So now you want me to come after all?"

He was silent.

"Aha," I said. "You still don't want me to come. You're afraid I'll rape your sister or something."

"Not rape. Don't be stupid."

"Go out with her."

"Maybe," he whispered.

We sat on the bunk staring at our shoes for a long moment. The usual Sunday afternoon hubbub was brewing up out in the dorm. Compton was loudly accusing Bear of stealing his tassel loafer, threatening to kick his ass if he didn't give it back. Bear was roaring at Compton that he was demented. Smiley was laughing uproariously at both of them.

"I just don't get it," I said. "You say we're friends for life. You say I saved your life. You invited me to your home. I've never even seen your sister. Guys tell me she's really pretty, really smart and nice. So what would happen, why would it be so bad if I did like her?"

He shrugged. "That just couldn't happen. Pontiac, you must know by now. You're fitting in really well here. You're friends with a lot of guys. Nobody even thought that could happen. You're doing great at school. You're a success. But there are limits."

"I get it. I appreciate your coming in here and talking to me. I really do."

I stood up and put my hand out. He took it and we shook.

Chapter Six

ONE NIGHT TWO WEEKS LATER I was almost asleep when I heard Gellhorn speaking quietly next door in Compton's alcove. I sat up and listened.

Gellhorn whispered, "You cannot not invite him. If you invite the rest of us, you have to include Pontiac."

"La vache!" Aubert called from across the aisle. "One sleeps here!"

I got up, went next door, and ripped open the curtain. Compton was in bed, hoarding a handful of snacks with both hands. Gellhorn stood over him, stooped to whisper.

"What is this?" I asked them. "I know you're talking about me again."

Gellhorn said quickly, "Compton's mother will be here Saturday for parents' weekend. She's taking all of us to dinner. You're invited."

"Who says he's invited?" Compton demanded.

"I say," Gellhorn said.

"I don't want to go," I said.

Gellhorn said, "You're going."

"If there is not quiet," Aubert called, "someone will be beaten."

I whispered hoarsely to Compton, "You were going to invite everybody else and not me? Christ. What a shithead, Compton. I can't believe you would do that."

"Shut the hell up," he said. "I was always going to invite you. But you're not going to like my mother much I can tell you that much."

"You think I can't handle her?"

"Nobody can handle her."

•

On Saturday evening, all three of Rumney's ratty Yellow cabs were lined up at the curb in front of the Lower School, puffing gray exhaust into a white driving snow. Compton motioned me to get into the front seat of the first one while he and his mother took the back. The other two cabs were split between Gellhorn, Roosevelt, Aubert, Davidson, and Yusupov. Bear and Smiley had gone into town already to have dinner with Smiley's parents.

The cabs disgorged us in front of the little restaurant where my mother and I had dined. Three tables had been shoved together and set elaborately for us.

"I hope this will be satisfactory," the gloomy proprietor said to Compton's mother with a tip of his pate.

"It's fine," she said coolly.

"So," Compton's mother said when we were standing at the table, not yet seated. "Which one of you is Davidson?"

Davidson stepped forward. "I am Davidson, Mrs. Compton."

"Why don't you sit at the end here with me and Tommie? I went to Smith with your mother."

Davidson, immediately crestfallen at the mention of his mother, tucked his head obediently and took his place across from Compton.

Compton's mother remained standing, looking us over. I mouthed silently to Compton, "Tommie." He flushed purple.

"The rest of you sit where you like, except that, oh, dear, Tommie told me one of you is Ernest Hemingway's son?"

Gellhorn nodded a very reluctant confirmation.

"I absolutely adore your father's work," she said. "Why don't you sit next to Tommie?"

Gellhorn sat down heavily.

"And I understand we have a Roosevelt in our party. Is it you? Oh, there you are. I'm very interested in FDR. My own father had a quite negative view, but I never took it seriously. Would you mind sitting across from Hemingway?"

"Gellhorn, ma'am," Gellhorn whispered.

"Oh," she said, troubled. She looked to Compton. "I thought you said . . . "

"Adopted," Compton said. "Hemingway ditched him."

"Tommie, don't be coarse," she said unconvincingly. "At any rate, Mr. Roosevelt will need to sit somewhere. Mr. Roosevelt, why don't you sit down across from Mr. Hemingway?"

Roosevelt grinned merrily and plopped down.

"There's a French lad among you, is there not?"

Aubert put up a hand.

"Je parle un peut de Francais," she said. "Peut-etre qu'on peut discuter un peu, n'est-ce pas?"

"Bien sur," he said, smiling genially. "Ce sera tres agréable." He sat down next to Gellhorn.

"And last but not least," she said, "Tommie tells me we have Russian nobility among us."

"We do, Madame," Yusupov said with a deep bow. "The noblest." He sat down across from Aubert, leaving one chair open at the far end.

"And please," she said to me with a wave, "do sit."

I did.

"Order whatever you like," she said. "I know what it's like subsisting on boarding school fare. Enjoy yourselves."

I scanned the prices on the menu as I had with my mother. The other boys were nonchalantly ordering full meals, not sandwiches, so I ordered lobster, because it didn't have a price. The menu just said "market," which I thought might mean it was cheaper.

Compton's mother started with Gellhorn. "Are you familiar with your father's work?" she asked. "Have you read all his novels?"

"We're reading some of them in class."

"That's wonderful," she said. "Do you have a favorite?"

"Not yet."

A beautiful French-Canadian girl with raven hair and sparkling eyes served us bread. I couldn't take my eyes off her. She noticed me staring, blushed and retreated into the kitchen. I think I may also have blushed.

Compton's mother turned to Davidson. "Tell me, is your mother still a force of nature? Mischievous as ever?"

"Very mischievous," Davidson said somberly.

"Oh, well," she said, "some people just never change, do they?"

The mother of the girl appeared, sweat-browed in a splotched apron but smiling pleasantly as she pushed a cart bearing the soup course. I made up my mind in that very instant that I would return to Rumney one day on a white steed, rescue the beautiful girl from her fiendish French-Canadian Catholic parents and carry her off to the Anglo-Saxon safety of Little Ottawa.

Compton's mother went after Roosevelt.

"Which branch of your famous family is yours? The communists or the warmongers?"

Roosevelt laughed. "Neither, exactly," he said. "I think we're the pirates."

"I see. Have you ever met Eleanor?"

"Yes. Auntie Eleanor is a wonderful lady. But we don't see them often. We live in Montana."

"You don't really mean live there."

"Yes, absolutely. It's our home."

"Oh, my goodness, why ever would a person live in Montana?"

"I really don't know. Maybe we're exiles."

She exchanged some French with Aubert. Yusupov and Gellhorn joined in. I think they were talking about Gstadt.

"What did your family do in Russia?" she asked Yusupov in English.

"Ah," he said. "Nothing at all, if they could help it."

"I see. But Tommie tells me they had quite a role."

"Well, we assassinated Rasputin. But we didn't do anything before that. Or after. Except leave. My family doesn't believe in doing things."

"And what do you do here? This is a hard country in which to do nothing."

"It's not going well."

"I'm so sorry. Perhaps you could assassinate someone."

"We are open to suggestions."

She laughed and nodded yes for the waiter to refill her wine. Then her eye fell to me, because no one else was left.

"And Tommie tells me your name is Pontiac," she said.

"Yes," I said, forcing down a hot swallow of soup. "It is."

"Well that's quite wonderful. They're excellent automobiles, I believe. I think we've had a few Pontiacs, have we not, Tommie?"

"I'm not sure," he said sullenly. "Either Pontiacs or Fords."

"Yes, both," she said, draining her glass. "We've probably had both, they're both such excellent automobiles. So, Pontiac, is your family still in the automobile business?"

"Yes, very much so," I said. "It's kind of in our blood."

"Marvelous. I really had no idea. That's quite something. It's a very famous name, is it not?"

"I believe so. Yes. Thank you."

—

Ellen asked me what ever happened to Gellhorn.

"Had a hard time. Hemingway denied being his father. I kind of lost track of him. I know he went to law school, and I think he wound up spending his career at his adoptive father's law firm. Somebody told me he was a tax lawyer for rich families."

"Why did you lose track? I thought you were friends for life.

"Yeah, well, you know how that goes."

We were outdoors at a café in a castle town near Nice. The day was hot. The only breeze was from trucks banging by on the cobbled street. Ellen was sipping warm limonade. The purring thrum of the cigales was just beginning to rise in the trees. In those moments, I was almost sure I caught Ellen drifting to some distant preoccupation, then pulling herself back by force, as if her curiosity about me was a tether.

"Were there not boys at the school who were gay?" she asked.

"Oh, sure. But we didn't know it until years later. We found out at reunions."

"How could you not know?"

"Ellen, no one back then knew the truth about anything or anybody sexually. Truth-telling about one's self was a misdemeanor. Wasn't done. You can't even imagine how deep in the closet that stuff was. Most of us straight guys didn't even learn about anal sex until we were in our twenties."

"That's ridiculous," she said. "I don't believe you."

"It's true. You wouldn't believe how much we didn't know. We didn't understand basic female anatomy. We barely understood vaginal sex when we were doing it."

"I do believe that."

She drifted again.

"An all-boys school," she said idly. "It must have been at least a little heavenly for the guys who were gay."

I shrugged. "An all-boys school isn't heaven for anybody. I don't know that the gay kids were any happier than the rest of us. Or any better. I think we were all equally horrible."

"Like what?"

"I believe that there was abuse of the weaker smaller boys. Rape. Probably by both teachers and older bigger guys."

"Why would you think that? Were you aware?"

"We were kind of subliminally aware. There was a first former in the Lower School named Ragsdale. He was very small and weak."

"How old would he have been?"

"He might have been eleven."

"A child."

"Yes."

"What happened?"

"They had to take him into Rumney a few times to have his

anus stitched. We were told that, when he took a shit, he was so weak he ripped himself open. That was the cover story."

Her hand flew to her mouth. "Oh, my God. What did you do? You defended him. Right?"

"No. Not me. I hated him. We all did."

"Hated him? Why?"

"Because he was weak."

"I don't understand."

"Probably we sensed something going on there, something we didn't quite get but knew was horrible. We didn't know whom to blame. It was scary. So we blamed him for being weak. We made fun of him."

"Oh, that's . . . " She stopped to collect herself. "He was someone's little boy."

"Yes."

"What happened to him?"

•

It was an interlude before dinner like every other evening, gangs of boys gathered in the second-level lobby joking and gossiping, a certain amount of pushing and shoving, a few boys seated at tables on the raised platform at the front of the lobby playing chess, the whole mob sending up a certain noise and scent, not high, not low, a flavor just between salty and sweet, a resonance that can be generated only by a hundred or so over-disciplined and entitled adolescent boys with nothing to do. In that moment on every evening, just before dinner, the balance between control and entropy was precarious. To lock things down and keep it all under control, all that was needed was for a master to march purposefully

327

through the mob. That was enough to keep the lid on. But one always sensed it could go the other way, too, that all it would take would be a moment's neglect, a very slight tilt, half a degree or less, an ounce of license or inattention, and the entire scene would ignite into spontaneous mayhem, which I suppose is what happened.

Ragsdale was perched by himself at his usual spot on a narrow bench at the lip of the spiral staircase, fidgeting and worrying his hands, twisting his toes beneath him. He had been absent for a week. A small crowd formed around him. He was terrified. I asked Smiley what was going on.

In his dour deadpan, Smiley reported: "Ragsdale was in the cooler for a week because he strained his sphincter muscles again during defecation."

"That is not possible," I said.

"Apparently it is if you are Ragsdale. The doc sent him into Rumney to have his asshole stitched up again."

"That's disgusting."

The crowd around Ragsdale was growing. He was whimpering for mercy, which only excited the prey instinct.

"So weak he can't take a shit," someone said.

Then another boy called out from the back of the crowd, "Lynch Ragsdale."

It was a joke. Nothing would have happened. It would have stopped right there. It was his fault. Ragsdale froze, stopped whimpering, clutched himself up close, peered through the thicket of arms and legs and made a dive for it. The dive was what set it off.

Hands stabbed for him, but he wriggled out of his tweed sport coat and almost got free. A boy snagged his necktie with one hand and yanked him to the floor. Purple-faced with eyes bulging,

Ragsdale gave the boy a hard bite, scrambled to his feet and raced across the lobby and up the staircase toward the third level.

We all fell in behind him screaming, "Lynch Ragsdale! Lynch Ragsdale!" We were laughing. No one meant it. He flew up the stairs howling, and we surged after him like dogs on a squirrel. "Lynch Ragsdale! Lynch Ragsdale."

Emitting a series of ear-piercing shrieks all the way up the stairs, he managed to put distance between himself and us at the top. Still squealing, he made a hard left turn and raced into his dorm, the one for First Formers. By then I was at the front of the mob. I have no idea what would have happened. Of course, now I want to believe it was still a joke, but I also have a distinct memory of being drunk on frenzy, lost in a seizure of savagery. I believe there was something in him that we all wanted to kill.

The supes in his dorm had not yet come down for dinner. When they heard Ragsdale's alarum, they came bursting out of their tiny apartment at the back of the dorm. One of them, Pillsbury, was a jock. The other, Pell, was master of the Creator's Game, captain of the hockey, lacrosse and soccer teams.

They said not a word. They took one look at us racing into their dorm after Ragsdale and began snatching us off our feet by collars and belts. They hurled us like bales of hay out into the lobby so hard we smacked our chins and balls on the floor. I put my hand to my mouth and found a rich course of blood and two wobbly front teeth. Groans and curses emitted from bodies stacked on top of me like cordwood. The door to the dorm slammed shut from within. We could hear Ragsdale inside sobbing and the supes reassuring him.

—

"What happened?" Ellen asked.

"Nothing."

"What did you do?"

"We cleaned up and went to dinner."

"What was said? What was done?"

"Nothing."

Ellen was silent for a long while, staring into the distance. She wiped a tear from her eye. "The child. The poor child. Someone's baby boy. Did he stay at the school after that?"

"No, they kicked him out."

"Kicked Ragsdale out? For what?"

"Wanted to get rid of him. Rutledge was always going around setting fires, but he was a Philly, a reg, one of the guys The Toad took to whorehouses. He was descended from a signer."

"A signer of what?"

"The constitution. He was protected. They couldn't kick him out. Anyway, he set a trashcan on fire in the athletic building. We all knew Rutledge did it. We saw him there just before it happened. He was always setting fires. They pinned the fire on Ragsdale and used it to kick him out."

"Whatever happened to Ragsdale? Do you have any idea?"

"I do, as a matter of fact. Ragsdale was from a place called Tuxedo Park. Stick, my old roommate, the one I made money with, grew up there. Their families kind of knew each other. Stick kept up with Ragsdale."

"Was he gay?"

"Ragsdale? No. Stick told me Ragsdale went to Princeton and became a hippie and a drug-user, got kicked out."

"Surprise, surprise."

"Yeah. Then he went to UC Santa Barbara for about two weeks and quit again. He became a surfer."

"A surfer?"

"Yes. All muscled up by then apparently. Then his dad got him into the Naval Academy."

"The Naval Academy? After he had already failed at two colleges? How does that work?"

"WASPs. They tend to get what they want. Or did back then. It's a little different now. Now we have a whole new breed of insects. By the time Ragsdale straightened up and got into the Academy, he was too late for Vietnam, but he had a decent Naval career anyway, came out and went to the University of Texas law school in Austin. Then he went down to Houston and got into a law firm that was big in Mideast oil. Made a pile of money. Married a Texas girl. He's still down there. Stick says he's a big hook 'em horns Texas Longhorns booster. Retired now. Adult kids. All Texans."

"Jesus. I can't believe he didn't kill himself."

"Next best thing. Went to Texas."

"Oh, shut up."

"I saw him down there once."

"Really?"

"When I was working with Stick. I went down there on some business about oil. I attended this law firm shindig one evening in a penthouse on top of a brand new glitzy office tower in downtown Houston. Stick and I didn't know Ragsdale was even with that firm. Partner. Ragsdale and I had no idea we were going to run into each other. He recognized me right away. I didn't know who he was until he was standing right in front of me, and then I recognized the eyes. I said, 'Ragsdale?' He threw a glass of booze and ice cubes straight in my face. Hard. It hurt."

"Jesus."

"Some young guy who must not have worked for the firm was standing there. He got all excited. He kept telling Ragsdale, 'Sir, this is not acceptable. This is not acceptable.' I said, 'Young man, believe me, it's acceptable. Stay the fuck out of it.'"

"Did you and Ragsdale reconcile?"

"Me and Ragsdale, you kidding? I jumped on the damn elevator and got the hell out of Dodge before he came after me with his Texas six-shooter."

A beat-up ex-military jeep fashioned into a truck and loaded with battered green window shutters rattled by kicking up dust. She waited for the sound to die, sipping her drink with her face a million miles away. Without turning toward me, she whispered, "I don't want to believe any of this about you, Woodrow. I almost can't stand it."

"Me either."

She faced me. "As an adult . . . "

"Old man . . . "

"As an old man, how do you explain it?"

I shrugged. "Boys will be boys."

•

After our dinner with his mother, Compton was up on his window ledge, swinging his feet.

"Automobiles are in our blood," he whispered down to me. "So full of shit."

It looked like he had a fresh bribery box. I climbed up.

"Are you kidding me?" I said when I got seated. "After that dinner, you're going to give me lessons on pretentiousness?"

He shoved the open box to me, eying me suspiciously.

"What do you mean?"

"Your mother?" I said, harvesting a couple of toffees. "Kind of a social climber, isn't she? I thought she was going to try to tongue kiss Roosevelt."

He was angry but trying to control it. "When did you start calling people social climbers?" he said. "That's a new word for you, isn't it? You didn't know what that was when you were back in Pontiac. You didn't even know what social was."

"Now I do."

"Tell me."

"Your mother is pretentious," I said.

"Oh, yeah? I noticed you let her pay for your meal. In fact you ordered all the most expensive shit on the menu. Lobster. Give me a break. This time of year? Did you even know what it cost? Your tab was twice anybody else's."

I had found more toffee and was clawing it into a pile at my end of the box. I must have been off my game. I did not spy the fist balling up hard behind his right thigh.

I said, "Don't cry because I said something bad about your mommy, Tommie."

"Maybe she is pretentious," he said. "At least she's not a mooch." He jerked the box hard away.

The word surprised me.

I said, "At least I'm not a pussy."

The fist shot out like a bullet and hit me square on the nose—a hot bolt into my brain. I flinched and lost my grip on the ledge. I fell off, missed the bed, and hit my skull on the wooden floor with a sharp crack. I jumped back up and bounded onto the bed. I grabbed him by an ankle with both hands and flung him off the ledge. His face caught the corner of the shelf.

He staggered to his feet.

"Mooch!" he shouted.

"Pussy!" I shouted back.

"Merde!" Aubert shouted.

Compton took me by the hair and hurled me against the steel leg of the radiator, opening a deep cut above my left eye. We grappled, growled and rolled on the floor for a long while at the end of the bench, clawing, punching, each with bloody hands around the other's throat in a mutual choke hold.

"I'll kill you," I screamed when I got breath.

"I'll kill you," Compton spat.

My right eye caught a brief vision of Mr. Fell racing toward us, shirtless in boxer shorts, Barry and Adams behind him in pajamas. Then all went black. When I awoke, I was sitting on the floor in the bathroom with my back against the white-tiled wall. The floor was streaked bright red, and my robe and pajamas were soaked in blood and water. Adams was standing over me with a dripping wastebasket. Compton was halfway down the room, hunched over a sink, breathing hard. His shoulder and one side of his face were dark with blood.

Half a dozen guys were crowded at the entry of the bathroom, staring at us wide-eyed. Mr. Fell, still in his underwear, came to me, leaned down and peered into my face. He touched the place above my eye, and I saw shooting stars of pain.

"Pontiac," he said, "close your left eye and follow my finger. Close your right eye and follow my finger. Open your mouth. Do not bite me." He jammed a forefinger into my mouth and did a quick dental examination. "Make fists. Wiggle your toes." He stood up. "Compton, teeth."

Compton pushed his finger around the inside of his mouth. "A-OK, Doc," he said.

Mr. Fell said to Adams and Barry, "How bad is that cut on Compton's head?"

"Bad," Barry said. "But it's slowing down. Swelling already."

"This cut on Pontiac won't stop. Adams, get a tight wrap on it and then you and Barry walk him up to the cooler right away. I'll call Doc Herter and tell him you're on your way."

Barry and Adams grabbed a towel and twisted it tightly around my head. Mr. Fell started to walk off, then stopped, came back and stooped over me again.

"Pontiac, can you hear me? Do you understand me?"

"Yes."

"You're going to the cooler. You're going to need stitches. You managed to bung up Compton's head pretty bad, so he's going to have bruises, probably a shut eye.

"I just want you to understand one thing. Whatever you tell Doc Herter, that will be what determines what happens to you both. This was a bad fight. Beetle could go to the rector and use it to get you kicked out. And if the rector kicks one of you out, he'll probably kick you both out."

I saw Compton twist painfully from the sink to give me a baleful look.

Barry, a few feet off, shook his head meaningfully. "Think very carefully what you say up there, Obwandiyag."

I went to my alcove and threw clothes and books into my laundry bag while a ring of boys watched me silently from the aisle. As I turned to leave, Aubert stepped forward from the crowd.

"Is it true?" he asked. "Did you stab Compton with a knife?"

"Yeah, I got him with my Puerto Rican switchblade. I was going to shoot him, but I was afraid my .38 would make too much noise."

"Zut alors!"

"Zut you, froggy."

335

Barry told me to put on my winter coat. When we stepped outside, the night was chilly. Our walk from the Lower School uphill to the cooler took about ten minutes. My head was throbbing and my vision a little cloudy. Adams walked just behind me and Barry at my shoulder.

"People have accidents," Barry said softly. "They get hurt in sports. Or they have fights. There are ways to handle it. Just think about what you say. Don't lie. But you don't have to tell Doc Herter everything."

"Is he going to grill me or something?"

"Probably. The more details you give, the deeper it gets."

The cooler was a long, white two-story building above a steep bluff, with vertical wood siding and a steep-pitched tin roof. From below in the moonlit snowfall, the roof glowed silver. Barry and Adams led me down a narrow corridor. Doc Herter, a tall thin man with white hair and twinkling blue eyes, waited for us at the other end in a ratty bathrobe and worn slippers. He pointed to a small examination room, where Barry and Adams steered me.

"Thank you, gentlemen," he said. "I will take it from here."

"Yes, sir, Doctor," they both said and fled.

"All right then," he said to me, shining a pen light into my eyes, "I was told that someone was bringing me a Pontiac. I thought perhaps my lucky day had arrived at last."

"It's a nickname, sir."

"What is your real name?"

I winced as he probed the cut above my eye with a gloved hand. "Woodrow Skaggs, sir."

"Well, we'll have to come up with something better than that for you here. We go by our own names at the cooler. It's a form of record-keeping."

"Yes, sir."

"And how did you incur this rather bad facial cut? It looks like you were hit hard with something blunt. A puck or a stick, perhaps?"

"No, sir. My friend and I were sitting on a window ledge in the dorm eating some snacks, and I lost my balance and fell onto the floor."

"I see. Mr. Fell tells me I will need to examine your friend tomorrow as well. Did he also lose his balance and fall onto the floor?"

"No, sir. He lost his balance and fell into a shelf."

"I see. And did these two falls take place at approximately the same time?"

"Yes, sir. The same time exactly."

"I see. Was there anything in particular, an unanticipated elephant attack perhaps, that might have caused both of you to simultaneously lose your balance?"

I hesitated.

"I can't remember," I said. "I kind of blacked out."

"Kind of blacked out. All right. As good an answer as any. I will pursue the matter further when I am visited by the other half of the tumbling team.

"Now, look, young man, I need to do some scouring and some stitching here, so I'm going to jab a needle into your face in a couple of places to numb you, and it's going to hurt like the dickens at first. Do you think you can handle that?"

"Yes, sir."

"I see you already have a scar above your right eye. Looks rather like a dueling scar."

"More or less."

337

"So for this new one on the other side, which do you prefer? Another dueling scar or more the Frankenstein look?"

"Dueling."

•

I slept on a cot in a large barren room where three more cots were empty. My dreams were bizarre and vivid, visited by motherly figures who dissolved into mist. At some point during the night, I was aware that a real-live motherly person, dressed in white, was holding my head upright while I swallowed large pills. When I finally awoke, sun was streaming through a large louvered window some distance from me, and a tray carrying a congealed breakfast rested just above my chest on a wheeled table. I pushed some dried-up scrambled eggs around on the plate with a finger, tasted the soggy toast and thought better of it. I pushed the table away.

Ten minutes later, a hearty woman's voice at the door sang out, "Somebody needed a good night's rest!" A chubby white-haired lady in a white nurse's uniform came clucking into the room.

"I'm Mrs. Herter, Doc's wife," she said. "It's so close to lunch, I'll just go ahead and get you a sandwich and some soup and see if we can't get some food into that skinny belly."

"Thank you."

She left with my uneaten breakfast. A moment later, a monstrous version of Compton appeared, looming over me at the side of the bed. One eye was blue-black and swollen shut, the other was at half-mast beneath a deep purple bruise across the brow.

"Jesus Christ, Pontiac," he muttered, "you look like the fucking mummy."

I reached up with a finger and found bandages around the top of my head. The stitched area above my eye was painful to touch.

"I'm sorry," I whispered in a feeble monotone, "Do I know you?"

He jolted back. "What the fuck do you mean? What's the matter with you?"

"You say Pontiac," I whispered in the feeble monotone. "What is Pontiac?"

He was a little breathless.

"Shit. Don't kid around, OK, asshole? You're Pontiac. It's your fucking name for Christ's sake."

In a barely audible whisper, I said, "If I am Pontiac, you must be Chevrolet."

He stared hard at me. The faintest suggestion of a smile quivered uncertainly at the ends of his mouth. Just then, Doc Herter came into the room in an immaculate white gown with a stethoscope around his neck and a notebook sticking out of his side pocket.

"Ah, then," the doctor said to Compton, "I'm going to guess you are the other half of the now-infamous Lower School tumbling team. I was told to expect you. You are Compton?"

"Yes, sir."

He took Compton's head in both hands and turned it from side to side. Compton winced. With his thumbs, the doctor pulled Compton's swollen lower eyelids down and upper eyelids up. Compton jerked his head back out of the doctor's grip, which didn't seem to surprise or concern him.

"From the look of you," Doc Herter said, "I'd say I'll be sending you back to class, where I'm sure you will be a sensation. But we'll take a closer look first in the other room in a moment."

Taking out the writing pad, the doctor said, "First, however, we may as well dispense with the investigative portion of this procedure while you are both present to mutually corroborate."

To Compton, he said, "I explained to your confederate when he came in last night with his head wrapped like a Sikh that we use our own nicknames here at the cooler as an aide memoire. It helps us quickly recall each boy's medical history."

He turned to me.

"For the rest of your years here at St. Philip's, assuming it will be years and not days, your name at the cooler shall be Humpty."

"Yes, sir," I said.

Turning to Compton, he said, "And you will be Dumpty."

"Yes, sir."

With pen poised on the pad, he said to Compton, "Now, Dumpty, your confrere Humpty here tells me that he was eating snacks on a window ledge with you last night when an elephant attack caused him to lose his balance and fall off the ledge, striking his head against a shelf. He tells me that you simultaneously lost your own balance and struck your own head against the floor."

"Other way around," Compton said. "He hit the floor, I hit the shelf."

"Good. Thank you for that correction, Dumpty, which, by the way, was a bit of a test. So, Dumpty, you do remember it. Sadly, your comrade Humpty here is unable to tell me what caused both of you to lose your balance and fall off the ledge at exactly the same moment. He said he blacked out and forgot what happened. Would you please share with me your own memory of events." He put the pen to the pad meaningfully. "For the record."

"Yes, of course," Compton said smoothly. "He did lose his balance, sir, and he began to fall. I tried to grab him to save him, but I sort of missed, and we both wound up falling off the ledge."

Doc Herter waited several beats. There was no twinkle in the eye. "And so, Humpty and Dumpty, this was, I am to believe, an accident. There was no intentionality?"

"Oh, no, sir," Compton said. "I was trying to save his life."

"And is that also your memory of events, Humpty?"

"From what I can remember, yes, sir. I guess so."

"You guess so. How about a yes or no?"

"Yes. Sir."

"All right, I believe we are nearing a resolution of the matter."

He sat down on a worn leather-topped rolling stool at the side of the bed and slipped the pad back into the side pocket of his coat.

"Something a lot of boys don't know about me and Mrs. Herter is that we also serve on a part-time basis at Rumney High School. I am called to the high school in particular when there have been bad fights. Rumney High is significantly more up-to-date on questions of discipline and decorum than St. Philip's School and is, in many ways, more civilized."

Compton was taken aback. "Can I quote you on that, Doctor?"

"I wish you would. It's a point I've been trying to make around here for years. May I continue, Dumpty?"

"Yes, sir. Sorry."

"Perfectly all right. At Rumney High, if I ever saw injuries this suggestive of a bad fight, in spite of some very unconvincing stories about snacks and elephant attacks, I would call the police. That, in fact, is why I am called to Rumney High, for cases where evidence may be needed by the police. A matter of that sort would proceed from there to the juvenile justice system, sometimes with quite dire consequences."

"Like what?" Compton asked sullenly.

"Juvie," I said.

"Aha!" the doctor said, surprised, "So, Humpty, you are familiar with juvie?"

"Yes, sir. A little."

Compton looked skeptical. He said, "I think guys at St. Philip's have our own ways of settling things without the police. It's a little bit different from how it goes in public schools."

Doc Herter made a clucking sound and toured around a little on his rolling stool, watching his toes.

"I think St. Philip's may be less unique than you think, Dumpty." He continued to study his shoes and speak to the floor. "Over the holidays, Mrs. Herter and I also do some light duty at the New Hampshire State Prison for Men. We often encounter a culture there that is quite reminiscent of things here at St. Philip's."

He pushed away from us on the rolling stool and folded his arms across his chest, shifting his gaze from one of us to the other.

"But let's talk about the best of St. Philip's, shall we? According to the very best of what this school may offer you for the rest of your lives, this is how the matter of Humpty, Dumpty, and the Dorm Four tumbling team might be resolved right now, here at the cooler, today.

"You can shake hands. Each of you can apologize. And each of you can promise that this will never happen again. I am not telling you that you must do this. It's entirely up to you. If you choose not to, we will go another route. But if you do, you will mean it, and your promise will be your bond for the rest of your lives. Your vow in fact will alter the course of your lives. It will change who and what you are now and what you are to become between now and when you die.

"When you shake hands, each of you will be promising never

342

to cause the other physical, moral, or financial harm and never to allow the other to be harmed if you can help it. You will take this vow not as boys but as gentlemen."

Compton twisted his eyes around awkwardly to examine the doctor through his purple swollen lids.

"That's it?"

"This time," the doctor said. "Next time, you will both be expelled. I will insist, in fact, that you be expelled and sent out of New Hampshire on the first train south, or the police will be called, and I won't care if your father is the Secretary of State and your mother Marilyn Monroe."

He paused and regarded us with the twinkle. "Well, I might amend that if either of your mothers is actually Marilyn Monroe."

"Not mine," Compton said. "Not by a long shot."

The doctor looked at me.

"No, sir. Me neither."

We shook hands, cementing our vow.

•

In early March there was an event for the masters called development days. We boys were allowed to go home for a long weekend. My mother wrote and told me not to come back to Pontiac for so short a visit since I would be coming home soon for the Spring break. To my surprise, I learned several other boys were in the same boat, including Compton, whose parents were busy with some kind of bad legal problem and told him not to come.

I did have enough money and time to go down to Boston, and Compton said he had money as well, so we planned a trip together. We would rent a cheap hotel room near Scollay Square, get some bum to buy us booze, and take in the burlesque shows at the Old Howard Theater.

Two days before development weekend began, Compton came to me in the second-floor lobby, breathless and bug-eyed, while a hundred hungry boys waited for the dining room to open for dinner. He said he had a "huge secret" to share.

"The Toad is taking us to a whorehouse," he said. He stared at me wide-eyed, nostrils quivering. "You and me. Can you believe that?"

"Why would he do that?"

We both knew The Toad's whorehouse trips were reserved for only the most blue of the blue-blooded boys, the guys whose names were in our American history text, descendants of the signers.

"It's weird," Compton said. "I didn't talk to The Toad."

"Who did you talk to?"

"Rutledge."

I was dumbfounded. Since our brief encounter in the Tuck Shop a month earlier, Rutledge had never again spoken to me and had rarely even allowed his eyes to fall upon me. On the few occasions when he and I had been unavoidably thrust together, hurrying into chapel or out of the schoolhouse, he always managed to ignore me so perfectly that I felt we occupied different spheres of reality. I was amazed he had spoken to Compton.

Compton explained that we were to proceed with our plans to go to Boston on Thursday and rent a cheap room near Scollay Square. On Friday, we were to meet The Toad, Rutledge, and unspecified others at the Brattle Book Shop, around the corner from the Godfrey Hotel, where they would be staying in some kind of penthouse suite that The Toad either rented or owned. From there we would be taken to a whorehouse.

Compton got that much across before the dining room doors opened. He grabbed me by the lapel, put his mouth to my ear and hissed, "Don't say shit to anybody."

All through dinner I examined him across the table, trying to gauge if he was pulling a prank, but his face remained blank. After dinner, he rushed into Dorm Four and hurried to the opening of his alcove, where he stood waiting for me. I plunged in quickly behind him, and he snapped closed the curtain. We sat down on his bed. He put a finger to his lips.

"No one can know," he whispered. "This is the biggest secret in our whole lives."

"Why would he take us?" I asked breathlessly. "He only takes regs."

"I think it's that ditch we dug for him. He must be really grateful. Remember, he said we wouldn't be forgotten. That's the only reason I can think of. Besides, he's not letting us stay with him and the regs at the Godfrey. We just get to go to the whorehouse."

We stared at our shoes in silence.

"Holy Mother of God," he whispered. "This is it. The big-time."

We realized that we had only this night and the following one to prepare. Neither Compton nor I possessed any pornography except for the *New York Times Sunday Magazine*, which offered only scary-looking women in their underwear. We looked at each other for a moment and had the same thought simultaneously.

"Granger!" I said a little too loudly.

Compton shushed me but nodded active agreement. He thrust his head out through the curtain, peeked around, and then he and I marched to Granger's alcove.

Granger was cooler than the rest of us. He was Canadian. His father was some kind of oil tycoon. Granger had lived in Texas, Venezuela, and Saudi Arabia. He never bragged about being cooler or worldlier than us, and sometimes he even seemed to hide what he knew. But we both knew instantly that if anyone in Dorm Four had real pornography, not just the *New York Times Sunday Magazine*, it would be Granger.

When we told him what we wanted, he flipped open his seaman's chest, dug beneath blankets and pulled out several copies of *Playboy Magazine*.

"That's the best," he said. "They're the most real. So how come you guys both need porn? You going to jerk off together?"

Compton's face flushed purple, his pupils dilated, and his fist shot forward to grab a wad of Granger's shirt.

"Jesus Christ, Compton," Granger said, "I was just kidding. I know you aren't queer."

"Let him go!" I said.

Compton released his grip and sank back on the bed.

"Sorry, Granger," I said. "Compton's cracked."

Compton said nothing. He was gazing at the four copies of *Playboy* in Granger's hands.

"So?" Granger asked me. "Why now?"

"Just because," I said.

Granger clucked. "I think somebody thinks they're about to get laid."

"You never know," Compton said gamely.

"Well, OK, boys," Granger said. He flipped open a copy, held it up, and allowed the centerfold to dangle to the floor. "This is the map."

A leggy blonde with enormous breasts like twinned sunrises gazed out at us, her index finger to her mouth. She was utterly naked except for a tiny bikini-bottom. Her entire body was hairless and smooth as a pink helium balloon.

"Shit," I said. "What do you do with their tits? Are you allowed to touch them?"

Granger snickered, so Compton did, too. Compton said, "Of course you can touch their tits. You can touch anything. That's the whole point."

"You can suck on their tits," Granger said, his eyes flashing like little green Christmas tree bulbs.

"Oh, shut up," Compton said, suddenly somber. "Why would anybody do that? You're not a baby."

"Why not?" Granger said.

I said, "Where is—you know—it?"

Granger tapped an index finger on the front of the bikini bottom. "X marks the spot, mateys. Home plate. Stick in your thumb, pull out a plum."

Each of us took a magazine to his own alcove. I stayed awake with mine until two in the morning, studying the photographs with my flashlight like topographic charts.

On the way to breakfast, I asked Compton, "Do you know where to stick it?"

His finger flew to his mouth. "Jesus Christ, Pontiac, will you watch it?"

"Sorry," I whispered, "But do you know?"

"It's gotta be in there somewhere," he said. "It's not that big an area."

On the train to Boston the windows were white with blowing snow. We said little to each other. We took a cab from North Station to Scollay Square and found a seedy hotel where we rented a room with twin beds. By the time we got out onto the street, it was already early evening and bitter cold. Compton confidently approached a bum who agreed to buy booze for us for a fee. We paid too much, of course, and wound up with two pints of applejack, a fifth of gin and a large bottle of Mogen David sweet wine, which seemed like a satisfactory inventory. Each of us put a pint of applejack in his sport coat pocket, and we trudged through snow drifts piled up by city plows to a steamy diner, where we ate bright red hotdogs smothered in black chili. Afterward we found rum-sweetened cigars at a shop and pornographic magazines at a newsstand. Then, chugging freely on the applejack and puffing the cigars as we walked, we wended our way unsteadily through crowded sidewalks and snow to the Old Howard, once a great vaudeville house and now a down-at-the-heels burlesque theater. Propped in the window of the ticket office was a handwritten cardboard sign that said, "You must be twenty-one years of age to enter." We were gazing at it in drunken desolation, two boys of thirteen and fourteen, when the woman inside the booth leaned to the opening, her jagged crimson lips limned by wetly caked orange powder.

"You boys want tickets?" she asked in a smoky drawl.

I nodded. The next thing we knew, we were inside the theater. It probably was capable of seating two hundred souls. No more than a dozen customers were present, all older men, some sleeping, some sipping from paper bags as they awaited the opening curtain. In the pit before the stage, three musicians sat muttering to each other, smoking. An odor that will follow me to the grave wafted up from the floor. We sat, lighted our cigars, sipped from our bottles and exchanged grins of conquest.

The curtain came open unevenly, squeaking on a cable, and an elderly man in a straw boater hat came doddering out onto stage. In a choked voice, he muttered rapid-fire remarks that were punctuated by quick tattoos on the snare drum in the orchestra pit. Strangling sounds from the meager audience told us that these were jokes.

The old man carried a fat cane that was striped like a barber pole. He began twisting it in the air in one hand as if preparing to launch it at us, while he waved the boater convulsively in the other and stiffly stomped up and down, which we took to be dance. The musicians were making a noise like the sounds of a harbor.

A man in the audience stood up and shouted, "Fuck you," then pitched straight forward over the seat in front of him. The ruckus caused the man on stage to drop his boater. He stooped arthritically to retrieve it, then yelled back, "Fuck you" to all of us. The saxophonist stood up in the pit and shouted to the man on stage, "That's it, Howdy, thank you very much."

Howdy limped off, grimacing with a hand to his hip. The musician then turned to the house and called out, "The great Howdy Williams, folks!"

The man in the audience, now reseated, called back, "Fuck you!"

Compton poked me in the arm. "Here it comes."

We both chugged deeply on our applejack and puffed hard on the cigars. The band played music that was easier to recognize as music because the bandleader announced it as such. The tune, which I will carry to the grave with the odor, was called "Big Milly from Philly." When the band began bleating and banging it out, an electric thrill vibrated my spine. I knew that a woman was going to appear onstage and possibly, impossibly, unimaginably, expose her breasts to me.

"And here she is at last," the musician announced, "the one you've been waiting for, the one you paid the big bucks to see, the one and only . . . Angel!"

Angel, a girl of no more than twenty, perhaps younger, appeared stage right. She made a choppy entrance with one eye back balefully to the wings. She was pretty, with pale white skin, bright red hair to her shoulders, lurid blue mascara and garish red lipstick. She lurched around the stage in an ungainly fashion at first, perhaps frightened, while the band continued to churn out "Big Milly from Philly."

Then she stood still, frozen, and stared straight out at us. She was full-breasted, with a tiny waist and delicate fawn legs. When she stopped moving, the lines of her body filled my eyes.

The man in the audience rose to his feet, shouted "Take it off," then pitched forward over the seat in front of him.

She began to move, touching the collar of her blouse tentatively.

I poked Compton on the arm. "Jesus Christ."

Her blouse came off, revealing a thickly hemmed and gathered red brassiere. At the top of her right arm bleeding over onto the collarbone was a dark blue and purple bruise, perhaps two days old.

The men in the audience shouted hungrily. Angel's brassiere came off and her breasts came free. The men shouted for her to shake her tits, and she did, stooping forward with a horrible expression on her face. The squawky saxophone played "Big Milly" like an air raid klaxon. The drummer banged hard as gunshots. She shook her tits faster. I heard an odd squishy sound behind me and turned. A fat man behind me was masturbating at a fiendish pace. For an instant I was furious. I wanted to climb over the seat and choke him to death for insulting her incredible beauty in this way, but Compton bumped me hard on the arm, and when I turned back she was gone, the emptiness of the stage an ache in my heart.

When we staggered back out onto the darkened street, bus exhaust and a nearby diner's pungent odors seemed like fresh mountain air compared to what we had been breathing inside.

"That was amazing," I said.

"No shit," Compton slurred. "Did you see those tits?"

"Yup."

"Would you suck on 'em?"

"Yup."

We laughed, bought more cigars, and staggered back to our shitty room, where we polished off the whole half gallon of horrible wine, vomited up the hotdogs and chili and passed out sprawled on the floor.

•

The next day began very late and slowly. For at least an hour, Compton and I sat on the floor with our backs against the walls of the dingy hotel room. For a long while, we communicated only in groans, getting up occasionally to vomit or piss.

In my painful daze, I envisioned Angel, her beautiful white breasts, her frightened expression and the bruise. I imagined myself returning like Daniel Boone, rescuing her from the Howard Theater and marrying her. I would be unfailingly kind to her forever.

By the time we had showered and regained the street, it was already mid-afternoon. We were to meet The Toad, Rutledge, and the others at the bookstore at 5:00 PM. We strolled around Scollay Square, a place already half-demolished in the name of "urban renewal." The gaps between buildings were answered contrapuntally by the missing teeth of the countless beggars who pitched forward from shadows to plead for alms. We gave money to the first few but then inventoried our resources and agreed to become more flint-hearted. Our appetites were in a state of limbo somewhere between lingering nausea and extreme hunger. We spotted a diner with dirty windows and agreed that a breakfast of greasy hamburgers might make the proper cure.

Devouring a delicious burger stacked with tomato, onion and lettuce, I asked Compton, "Do we have to pay for the whores?"

"Jesus, I hope not. You've only got fifteen bucks left. I have twenty."

"What does a whore cost?"

"No idea. But Toad and guys like Rutledge, probably get top whores. It's probably hundreds of dollars. But I think The Toad pays. I think that's the deal. My dad says he's super rich."

"Why did he invite us?"

"The ditch. I told you."

"Did you see anything on Angel, that girl at the Howard," I asked, "about—you know—where to stick it?"

"No. Her panties were huge. That was kind of a rip-off. Plus, I didn't like her."

"Why? She was really pretty."

"She had hair."

"What do you mean?"

"Like down there. It was coming out of her panties."

"Oh, shut up. That's gross. That's bullshit. They don't have hair."

"How the hell would you know? Who are you, Frank Sinatra?"

Rutledge had instructed Compton that we were to be drunk when we showed up. We returned to our room, where each of us obediently choked down a tall glass of straight gin. We took a cab to the Brattle Bookstore, arriving at 4:45 PM. It was a dumpy little place with a giant pencil across the front for a sign. We were not to go inside. Next to the store on a vacant lot were rows and rows of outdoor bookshelves beneath protective tarps and dangling strings of light bulbs, where people bundled in heavy coats and scarves nosed among the volumes. Their breath made a thin cloud of vapor beneath the lights.

We waited on a bench on the sidewalk as instructed. It was very cold. We lighted our crooked cigars to warm us. At about that moment, the gin slammed us, and we sank into lumps on the bench, cigars hanging from numb lips.

At precisely 5:00 PM, a long black limousine of foreign make pulled up at our toes, and The Toad and Rutledge came out of the back doors. Rutledge looked just the least bit tipsy, a little unsure where to step. He was wearing an ankle-length camel hair overcoat and a white silk scarf. His cordovan tassel loafers, polished to the luminescence of jewels, seemed to banish the snow.

"Good God, Toad," Rutledge said, slurring a little. He surveyed us with disgust. "Is this really necessary?"

"Oh, c'mon," The Toad said, not drunk at all. He wore a tuxedo with the tie loose at his neck, hair slicked back. They clearly were coming from somewhere else. "They'll be OK. They won't get in our way."

"Hey, Toad," Compton said, then burped.

Two Sixth-Formers in tuxedos and cashmere overcoats were craning out the open passenger doors of the limo. One called in a reedy voice, "What's the hold-up, Toad?"

"I really do not want these people in the same car with me," Rutledge said.

"Fine," The Toad said. "Fine." He stuck one hand in the air, put two fingers to his lips, and made a shrill whistle. A battered Checker cab veered out of traffic and slumped to a stop behind the limo. The Toad went to the driver, gave him instructions and handed him money.

"You two get in the cab," he said crisply, walking away.

We dredged ourselves up from the bench with some difficulty, scrabbled at the door handles of the cab, and plunged in headfirst.

"We have to follow those guys," Compton told the driver.

"Yeah, I got it, chief," the driver said, not turning his head. "But if you young gentlemen feel sick, do me a big favor and let me stop so you don't toss your cookies in my hack."

"Got it, chief," Compton said with a wave.

No one before had ever called me a gentleman.

Traffic was a blur of headlights and horns. Neither of us was well, our adolescent bodies not equipped to handle the brutal overload of gin, cheap cigars and grease. We rolled around clumsily in the back seat at first but eventually managed to more or less right ourselves.

"You're headed back to Scollay Square," Compton slurred.

"You got it," the driver said. "Follow the leader."

By stooping over the driver's shoulder and hanging on to the seat with both hands, I could make out the ruby glow of The Toad's taillights snaking through traffic ahead of us.

"Phew," the driver said, waving a hand. "Mind backing off a little there, champ?"

I turned and stared at Compton, puzzled.

"He thinks you stink."

"Well," the driver said, a little apologetically.

I dropped back into the seat.

"We're shit-faced," I muttered confidentially to Compton.

"No shit, Sherlock. Hey. Look. We're back at the Howard."

I stuck my head forward again to peer out the windshield. The driver crooked his head away from me and fanned his hand in front of his nose. We were following The Toad's limo around the front of the theater, down an alley at the side, rolling up slowly on a dimly lighted loading dock. A thick man with a big red nose wearing a worn dark-brown trench coat and dirty fedora stood outside, waving us to a stop with a stubby cigar. Ahead of us, The Toad and Rutledge slid out of limo like eels. The other two Sixth-Formers clambered out after them, gangly and drunk.

Compton and I managed to escape the cab, but as soon as we got to our feet, a wave of nausea erupted from the pit of my being. I retched copious amounts poorly digested hamburger onto the tarmac.

The cab driver shook his head and muttered, "Close call."

Rutledge charged at me, his face quivering. In a high bleat he said, "This is exactly what I meant, Toad. Look at this, will you? So disgusting. I knew this would happen."

Compton threw up.

"Oh my goodness," one of the other Sixth Formers said at a distance. "What is wrong with them?"

The cab driver was inching his car backward away from us down the alley, waving goodbye.

"There's nothing wrong with them," The Toad said cheerfully. "They're just young. Very young."

"I don't want those guys anywhere near me," Rutledge said.

"They won't be," The Toad said. "I have something else in mind for them."

The man with the cigar held open a heavy metal door at the back of the dock. Rutledge swept in first, heels clicking and silk scarf sailing, followed by The Toad, who was followed by the other Sixth-Formers, all disappearing into a dark hallway ahead. When Compton and I reached the door, the man dropped an arm to stop us.

"How old are you?" he asked gruffly.

"Thirteen," I said.

"Fourteen," Compton said.

"Fuck Toad," the man said. "OK. In."

His cigar made me consider vomiting again, but I didn't. We caught up with the rest of them where the corridor came to a tee. The man pushed past us and punched a button on a freight elevator. The door opened horizontally like a great mouth, and we stepped inside. The man operated a crank, which caused us to lurch upwards as if yanked by a crane. Compton put a hand to his mouth, and everyone, including the man in the dirty fedora, stared anxiously, but he did not vomit. The elevator shuddered to a stop. The great mouth dropped open again, and we stepped off onto a bizarre planet.

Everything ahead of us—the walls, the carpeting, even the ceiling—was purple and fuzzy. Everything was bathed in purple glow from lights buried in the walls and ceiling like an aquarium. We came out into a large room furnished with soft purple sofas and chairs, purple tables, and most wonderful of all, astonishing and wondrous, a beautiful black-haired, purple woman with enormous dark eyes. She was older, probably The Toad's age. She stood in the middle of the room in a flowing gown like something I might have seen once in a movie, her top open from the waist to reveal a very ample bosom, which also, in the light, was purple.

In a husky voice with an accent a little like Aubert, she said, "Toadie, you stay away too long."

The Toad stepped forward suavely with a small bow, took her hand and kissed her wrist.

"A day away from you is too long, Nadia," he purred. He turned. "I believe you know Rutledge."

356

"Yes, of course. My handsome young Rutledge," she said, offering her hand. "I knew you were coming. You will be pleased to hear that your favorite awaits you."

"Splendid, thank you," Rutledge said. He tipped his head in a little bow and clicked his heels.

"And I have two new men for you," The Toad said, nodding toward the other Sixth-Formers.

"Then we will make them very happy," she said.

They nodded and fumbled.

Then Nadia turned to survey me and Compton.

"Oh, Toadie," she said, scolding, "Oh no, no. What have you brought me? Not again."

The cigar man went to her and whispered loudly into her ear so that we all could heard: "Thirteen and fourteen."

"Toad," she said, "we have discussed this. I don't have any protection for this."

"Ah, but I do," The Toad said quickly. He inserted himself between her and the cigar man and whispered into her ear for a long while.

She frowned, listening, shaking her head skeptically. Toad put a hand on her shoulder and whispered more. She softened and smiled at him.

"You have it covered, then," she said. "It's on you?"

"Totally on me. You have nothing to worry about."

The cigar man shook his head in disgust and walked off toward the elevator.

To me and Compton she said a little brusquely, "All right then, children, after we get The Toad and the others situated, I will find something suitable for you to play with."

The Toad cocked an eye to her curiously.

357

"Young ones for them," she said to him. "Not as young as they are, of course, because I don't want to spend the rest of my life in prison, but I have a couple of new girls."

"Excellent," The Toad said. "I'll check in on them in a bit to make sure things are proceeding properly."

She reached out with long purple nails and chucked him under the chin.

"You naughty, naughty man," she said. "They're very pretty, your little boys."

He chuckled.

We were told to wait in the lounge area while they all disappeared through a heavily flocked purple door.

When we were alone, I said to Compton, "What is this shit, he'll check on us?"

"I don't know."

"She said we were pretty."

Compton said grimly, "We may have to kill somebody."

Nadia returned ten minutes later and held open the door for us. As she led us down another fuzzy purple corridor, I glimpsed Rutledge behind a closing door with a bare-breasted woman. We passed The Toad, who was standing in an open door with an arm up against the jamb, grinning hungrily. Compton was shunted into a room, and then a moment later, I was pushed into another.

Suddenly, I couldn't breathe. I felt faint. Standing before me in the same outfit she had worn on stage the day before was Angel. I staggered in place.

"You OK?" she asked.

"You're Angel," I stammered.

"If you say so. You saw my act?"

"Yes," I whispered.

"Stinks, don't it?"

"I thought it was wonderful."

She stood with her hands clasped against the tiny waist, looking me up and down. This close, her face was even more beautiful.

"How old are you?" she asked. "Ten?"

"Thirteen."

"Oh, Christ." She pushed past me, yanked open the door and shouted down the hall, "Nadia, what the fuck? This kid's thirteen years old."

A moment later Nadia appeared. With the back of a hand, she gave Angel a loud reaching slap across the mouth. With the other hand, she shoved her hard by the shoulder back into the room.

"You can't make me do this," Angel said.

"Can't I? So you want me to send you back to Frank?"

Angel dropped her chin. "No."

"Do as you're told."

Nadia stepped out into the hallway and slammed the door.

Without looking up, Angel said, "Take off your clothes."

To my ear, she spoke with the authority of a cop. I immediately did what she ordered, stripping off all of my clothes onto a pile on the floor, except that, for some reason that's still a mystery to me these many years later, I kept on my long white socks.

"Get on the bed," she said.

I climbed up onto the bed and stood on it, staring into her eyes. She unbuttoned her blouse and dropped her slip. Her breasts were bare. My eyes locked on them and never strayed. I remained standing on the bed. I think she was gazing at me, puzzled, but I'm not sure, because I was staring at her breasts. They weren't smooth and unblemished like the helium breasts in *Playboy* and instead had dark circles of uneven flesh around the nipples.

She stared at me for a long while. I was still standing on the bed. She was standing on the floor before me, almost head-to-head.

She let out a long sigh. "Jesus Christ. Have you ever seen a woman's tits before, kid?"

"Yes."

"Where?"

"Places."

"*Playboy Magazine* places?"

"Right."

"Those are not real tits. Those are like boy's tits pumped up. These are real. Here."

She grabbed my wrist and put my hand against her breast. I felt as if she had placed my hand on the face of God.

She asked me something, but I was too overwhelmed to hear her clearly. I took it to be, "Do you want to do it?" I now believe she must have said, "Do you want to do it against the wall?"

"Yes," I said.

She climbed up on the bed, naked, and posted herself with her elbows against the wall. Her face was red where Nadia had slapped her. Baffled and terrified, I lay down on the bed on my back with my head between her feet. When I looked up, I was shocked by what loomed above me. Her entire upper body and head had disappeared. I could see nothing of her above the waist. I saw only two legs that rose and disappeared into an enormous orb of reddish pubic hair. When she leaned forward to look down at me, her eyes and brow appeared above this hairy horizon like God peering over the rim of life. I must have started, because she jumped and stepped on my ear. I let out a piercing squeal. She shouted, "Holy shit!" and danced a little jig on the bed.

The door opened, and The Toad came in wearing a floor-length terry-cloth bathrobe with a frosted martini glass in one hand. "How are we doing?"

I sat bolt upright, embarrassed because Angel and I were naked. The Toad came over and sat at the end of the bed.

"Good God, girl," he said, staring at her pubic hair, "what a bush. Didn't anyone ever tell you to shave? No wonder our brave little soldier here isn't standing at attention."

Nadia looked in from the hall.

"Nadia," The Toad said, "look at the bush on this girl. She has frightened the boy inside-out I think."

"She's new," Nadia said. "We haven't ironed out the kinks."

"I won't be here that long," Angel said.

"Keep telling yourself that, bitch," Nadia said. "You might be surprised how long you'll be here."

The Toad smiled at Angel.

"The rest of your life, I hope," he told her. "You're very pretty. And you have such lovely big breasts." He reached across me to touch her, and she winced away from his hand. Nadia frowned hard. Angel bit her lip and shoved her breast into The Toad's hand.

"Very nice," he said, fondling her. "You see, Skaggs, you have to let a woman know who's boss. That's what this is all about."

"Yes, sir."

"Do you need my help here, Toad?" Nadia asked.

"No," The Toad said, "I think I've got it under control."

"That I believe," she said, pulling the door shut.

The Toad smiled at me.

"Let me guess. You don't even know where to put it, do you?"

A sudden shiver raced down my spine, and my entire body compressed into a fist of fear.

"It's OK," The Toad said softly. "Everyone has to learn. I can help." He reached for my penis.

Angel's hand shot out and grabbed his wrist. I didn't understand what was going on except that my penis seemed to be at the center of things and Angel was its protector.

"Yeah, I got this," she said.

The Toad shook his wrist free and sat up with rigid shoulders.

"Oh, do you?" He nodded toward my limp dick. "Doesn't look like it to me."

"Just get out," she said. "I'm about to fuck him."

"Are you? Skaggs, what do you think? Would you like me to stay and help?"

Only at that moment did I fully conceive that The Toad had some intention of participating himself in whatever encounter was about to take place, which meant that he intended to touch my dick. I went numb with terror, and for a moment I could not speak.

"No, sir," I blurted. "I'm going to fuck her on my own, thank you, sir, for offering. I'm fine, I'd like to do it alone."

"Very well," he said with exaggerated injury. "Then I will leave you to it. But when I return, you had better be done, or I'll have to step in."

He left. As soon as the door shut, I exhaled, and tears formed in my eyes.

"Jesus Christ," I said, breathing hard.

Angel reached with a finger and stopped a tear streaming down my cheek.

"It's OK, kid," she said.

I said, "You don't have to fuck me."

She shrugged. "Yes, I do."

She nodded toward a big mirror on the far wall.

"What?" I whispered to her.

"They can see us."

"They're watching?"

"Just forget it."

She took me with one hand and made me hard. She pulled me over her and eased me in very slowly. I felt the sea and all of time rushing through me and up into the stars to explode. It took between one and two minutes. When it was over, I heard a vicious hubbub out in the corridor.

Compton burst into the room, dragging his sport coat in one hand and pulling on a shoe with the other.

"We're leaving," he shouted. "Now!"

Angel pushed me off her.

"Better go," she said. "This could get bad."

In the corridor, Compton was ahead of me, plunging toward the exits. I was still pulling on my pants and jacket when The Toad came staggering out of a room with an arm to his face, bleeding. Rutledge was behind him, naked, raging.

"Kill him!" Rutledge screamed. "Kill him, Toad, or I will."

He made a move on Compton, but Compton body-checked him hard. The back of Rutledge's head slammed against a lamp inside the fuzzy purple wall. I heard glass break. Rutledge slumped to the floor with blood and purple fuzz dribbling down his neck. The man in the fedora waved us toward the freight elevator and warned The Toad with a fist to stay back. Moments later, Compton and I were out in the foul open air of Scollay Square on a forced march to our crappy room.

●

The next day, we sat across the aisle from each other on the train back up to New Hampshire, not speaking. Outside the train windows, new snow made the white world glitter. After half an hour, Compton said across the aisle, "Did he touch your dick?"

I almost jumped out of my skin.

"For Christ's sake," I snapped, looking around. A rowdy group of teenage boys, athletes from Manchester High School according to their letter jackets, were seated a few rows behind us. "Will you shut the hell up?"

He shrugged. "Did he?"

"Shh!" I moved across the aisle and sat next to him. "No. He was about to. Angel stopped him."

"Angel?"

"My whore."

"From the Howard?"

"Yes."

"Jeez."

We said nothing while the train clattered through Somerville and Medford. Then Compton said, "Man, it sounds like you were lucky. One more inch, if she hadn't stopped him, you'd be a queer now."

"Oh, fuck you. You don't turn queer because some old guy touches your dick."

"Jesus," he said, shaking his head in disbelief. "Do you just not know anything at all? That's how they do it."

"They touch your dick one time, and that turns you into a queer?"

Compton nodded solemnly.

"So all those guys are queers? The Toad, Rutledge, the other two Sixth Formers?"

"For now."

"What do you mean for now?"

"Well, The Toad is probably a queer for life. But those other guys will get over it when they leave school."

I looked at him, looked away, looked again. "Did he touch your dick?"

"No. He tried. Rutledge did, too. But they didn't get it. I told them I was going to kill them. I cold-cocked The Toad and kicked Rutledge in the gut. Then while they were boo-hooing, I grabbed my shit and jumped the hell out of there."

"Jesus."

"No shit."

"Did you ever get to actually do it?" I asked.

"Yeah. Just before they came in."

"How was it?"

"It was the greatest thing in my whole life. That's all I want to do from here on out. I don't even want to go to college. Did you do it?"

"Yes."

"How long did it take?"

"A couple minutes. How long did yours take?"

"Maybe thirty seconds."

"Oh, fuck you, Compton. It took you longer than that."

"No. In. Out. Done. Thirty seconds max."

I was angry. "Yeah, you know, Compton, everything you do, you have to be the best, the fastest. You have sex one time, and you're already the king of fucking."

"Take it easy will, you, Skaggs," he said. "Look, I happen to be a trained athlete."

"Fuck you."

"No, fuck you."

365

A while later, I asked, "Why do you think those guys will get over being queer when they leave school? How do you know it's not permanent?"

"I don't really know. It's just what I think."

We rode along without speaking for a time, lulled by the lovely tattoo of wheels on the rails and the just barely perceptible womb-sway of the train.

I said, "Man, I'm glad you didn't kill anybody."

"No shit."

We were quiet again for a while.

"Are you sure you didn't kill Rutledge?" I asked. "He looked kind of dead to me."

"I saw that. I was kind of worried. But The Toad came over to the hotel this morning before you got up."

"He did?"

"Yes. He knew where we were. I was already up and coming back from a walk. The Toad told me Rutledge was OK. He just has a big bandage on the back of his head. The Toad said we need to stay away from him for a while. He said Rutledge is crazy."

"What kind of crazy?"

"Like he might try to kill us."

I watched Compton's face.

"That's bullshit, right?" I asked.

"I don't know," Compton said, puzzled. "The Toad said Rutledge isn't right in the head. He was pretty serious about it. And I've heard some shit from other guys. Rutledge is involved in a lot of bad things.

"Christ. What else did The Toad say this morning?"

"He wanted to know if we were going to tell anybody else about what happened."

"What did you say?"

"I said shit no."

"Why?"

"Pontiac, get a grip. We don't want The Toad on our case. It could ruin our whole lives."

I said, "OK." Then I said, "Compton, I still don't get it. If they're queers, why do they want to have sex with whores?"

"I don't know," he said. "I think they may be just sort of temporary queers, like half-queer."

"What about The Toad, then?"

He pondered for a long while, staring out the window. Some small Massachusetts town clotted with brown frozen slush ticked by like a silent movie.

"You know, that's . . . " he started, "I just don't know the answer to that. I think as far as that goes, The Toad is just The Toad."

"The Toad is The Toad," I said.

"Long live The Toad," he said.

•

We didn't speak for a long while, watching the landscape slide from Massachusetts to New Hampshire.

"That was some development weekend," Compton finally said.

"No shit," I agreed. "Best development weekend ever."

"We learned a lot about women."

"No shit."

"At least we know where to stick it."

"Pretty much," I said.

"What do you mean pretty much? Did you not see where to stick it?"

"I got it. I told you already. I did it."

"Right. That's what counts. You did it. Even if you're not as fast as me yet."

"Fuck you," I said.

"And we learned about queers. We learned a lot about them."

"No shit. Amazing."

"Yeah," he agreed.

"Hey," I said. "Do you think they like doing it?"

"Queers?"

"No, women."

"Of course they do. Why else would they be whores?"

"Right. I guess. But there could be other reasons, too, like they're forced to."

"Jesus, Pontiac. First you're not sure where to stick it. Now you're not sure if whores like to fuck. What else are you not sure about? Are you sure you're not queer?"

"Take that back," I said.

"OK, I take it back. You did it. That's proves it. That's what counts. Now you've done it. I've done it. We've both done it. You know what that makes us, right?"

"Yup."

"What?"

"Men."

I extended my hand. Grinning broadly, he seized it, and we shook vigorously.

"Men," we said in unison.

The train stopped in Manchester. A small crowd of older people, parents and maybe some teachers and coaches, waited on the platform for the high school guys in letter jackets. When they got off the train, people cheered, threw confetti, and hugged them.

"Must have won," Compton said.

We gazed at their celebration for a while.

"Do you think they know what we know?" I asked.

"I doubt it," Compton said. "I mean, look at them. They're still with their mommies and daddies. They're like little kids."

"Yeah," I said. "I'd hate to be them."

"No shit."

When the train got rolling again, I returned to my seat across the aisle. Compton fell asleep with his face smashed against the window, snoring loudly. I watched towering blue-green trees pass by outside, sentinels of time, and sang softly to myself.

"And who but my Lady Greensleeves?"

•

I was so confident, I started going to the Saturday night movies. On this night, rather than return to Dorm Four after dinner to wait for the movie to start, I slipped out of the Lower School and raced all the way to the gymnasium, where I retrieved a text I had cached. I ran back to the dorm and slipped the book under my pillow for a late-night grinding session after the movie.

The film, *Shake Hands with the Devil*, starring James Cagney, was a couple of years old at the time, but nobody at the school had seen it. Cagney plays a fanatical IRA commander in Ireland who has gone war mad. It was a great movie, and I was still deep inside it upon leaving the assembly hall afterward.

Outside, I ran into an unmoving mass of boys, masters, and masters' wives, stalled and speechless on the broad porticoed steps.

Every head was craned upward into an arctic sky that was raging red and yellow. A boy with a voice like a bugle screamed, "It's the Big Study." The mob broke and surged forward.

When I got there, the crowd had stopped dead in its tracks across the street from the blaze. The night was nose-biting cold. Fire trucks were just arriving and raising ladders. Great licks of flame clawed up over our heads, the Big Study transmuted by fire into smoke and dust like an immense shrieking ghost. Cascades from the fire hoses froze in midair, forming a lugubrious lens that refracted the fire's intense red.

Someone near me in the crowd shouted, "It's Dan Biggs!"

The firemen were trundling a gurney out of the wreckage. I saw a great lump in the center and a blackened paw hanging down. I broke through the crowd and raced across the street to his side. The firemen tried to push me away, but the hand reached up and grasped mine. His face, a smear of ash, turned to me, and his eyes found mine.

"Hey kid," he growled, "I fucking made it. Crawled out a window."

"What happened, Dan Biggs? What happened?"

"Rutledge."

They folded the wheels of the gurney, lifted it up brusquely into the ambulance and slammed the doors shut on me.

The next morning half an hour before the rest of us woke, Compton came down the dorm in his parka with snow on his shoulders, banging on the radiator bench with his lacrosse stick.

"It was set!" he shouted. "It was set!"

I got on my knees at the foot of my bed to peek outside. Aubert staggered out of his alcove with one leg of his pajamas above his knee and hair plastered to his face.

"Fais pas de bêtises, Compton," he growled.

Compton went to Aubert and said, pleading, "No, no, Aubert, it's true. I was out there. I saw it."

Smiley was behind him, still tying his robe.

"Please clarify," Smiley said.

"The fire's out. It's just ashes. The big fire trucks are gone. I saw a guy pulling burned-up gasoline cans out of the ashes."

"What person?" Aubert demanded.

"I couldn't tell. It was too far away. He saw me. He ran off into the woods. He had gas cans. Three big ones."

Smiley was pacing, staring at the floor. "Were these gas cans red?"

"No," Compton said. "They were all burned up. They were mostly black."

"Then how do you know they were gas cans?"

"Because I know what a fucking five-gallon gas can looks like."

We were all out in the aisle, arrayed around the radiator bench.

I asked, "Was it Rutledge?"

"It could have been," he said. "But he was too far away. I didn't see his face. He had on a parka with the hood up. The guy I saw was about Rutledge's size. Maybe a little smaller."

"Smaller than Rutledge," Smiley repeated.

"I don't know. Maybe the same size. He was too far away."

When we left the Lower for chapel, the sun was white, and the frigid air was spiced with the sharp scent of ash. The wreckage of the Big Study was almost as shocking as the first sight of fire had been the night before. The ruined castle was enclosed in a sepulcher of ice, blurry and out of focus as in a dream. A small crew of firefighters and police were gathered across the street.

That night at the end of dinner, Beetle stood up, and Rutherford rang his little silver bell for silence.

"After dinner," Beetle said gravely, "you will return to your dorms and remain there. When your name is called, you will report to the lobby."

On the way back to Dorm Four, we could see they had pushed two chess tables together on the raised platform at the front of the lobby. Three chairs stood behind the tables, and three were in front.

Back in the dorm, Aubert muttered, "What species of affair is this?"

"Kangaroo court for the pyro," Compton said.

"What does that mean?" I asked.

"They're going to grill us."

Boys were called three at a time. Compton, Gellhorn, and I were first. Herr Schmitz, Beetle, and Mr. Fell sat behind the chess tables. Herr Schmitz asked us questions, while Mr. Fell took notes and Beetle looked on. Herr Schmitz asked if we had attended the movie, next to whom we had sat and what we had done between dinner and the movie. Compton and Gellhorn had gone straight from dinner to Dorm Four where they had waited until time for the show. I explained I had gone to the gym to retrieve a book.

"Why did you have a book at the gymnasium?" Herr Schmitz asked.

"I just forgot it there."

"And why did you need this book so urgently on a Saturday night?"

"I didn't want to lose it."

Herr Schmitz and Beetle exchanged significant looks. Both looked to Mr. Fell, who obediently scratched notes on his legal pad. Herr Schmitz told Gellhorn and Compton to return to the dorm.

When they were gone, Herr Schmitz asked me, "Why was Dan Biggs giving you money?"

I was stunned.

Beetle leaned forward, the veiny nose twitching.

"Herr Schmitz asked you a question."

I was unable to collect my thoughts. "It was from the rector's wife," I stammered.

All three men exchanged looks.

"What was from the rector's wife?" Herr Schmitz asked.

"The money. The rector's wife was giving it to me."

Beetle elbowed out a bit in front of Herr Schmitz.

"Why would the rector's wife give you money, Skaggs?"

"To . . . to help me out, I guess."

They all stared at me blankly.

"Pontiac . . . " Mr. Fell began.

"We will address the boy as Woodrow for these purposes," Beetle interrupted.

"Woodrow," Mr. Fell said, "the rector's wife doesn't really do that."

Herr Schmitz asked, "What did you do for Dan Biggs in exchange for these payments?"

I was aghast, paralyzed with shock and fear. They thought I did something dirty for Dan Biggs to get the money. They thought I set the fire. Or they were going to say I did. I couldn't believe it. I couldn't catch my breath. This was serious. If David went to juvie for wrecking a pickup truck, what would happen to me for burning down an entire building and almost killing a man?

"You can't believe it's . . . you can't think it's me," I stammered. "I wouldn't do something like that. Why would you think that? It's not me. It's Rutledge. He did it to murder Dan Biggs. That door down there only locks from the outside if you lower the bar. The bar has to be swung over and lowered. It isn't possible for it to just fall shut. And he took gas cans."

"Gas cans?" Herr Schmitz whispered. He looked to the other two. "We know nothing about gasoline cans."

They both shook their heads.

"There were no gasoline cans," Herr Schmitz said to me.

"There were gas cans," I said. "It's Rutledge. It's something to do with a girl. An abortion. He borrowed money from Dan Biggs, and he wouldn't pay it back."

Beetle turned to Mr. Fell. "Don't write that down. It's preposterous poppycock. He makes it up as he goes. There has been talk of his having a gun."

Mr. Fell ostentatiously continued taking notes.

"Get out of here," Beetle hissed at me, waggling his eyebrows and flapping his jowls like a rooster. "Go back to your alcove immediately and do not speak of this to anyone. This inquiry will be continued later, perhaps in the company of the police."

I did as he said. When I was seated on my bunk with the curtain closed, I heard Compton telling the dorm, "They're going to pin it on the Puertorac, I guess because he's a scholarship boy. So long, Pontiac."

I heard only silence in response.

Chapter Seven

THE NEXT MORNING I WAS STILL frozen with fear. In chapel I tried to hide a tremble. In class, my quizzes *were a relief.* I knocked out all of them with scores of one hundred but said nothing in class. When morning school was over, I went to Johnny Wilson's office and barged in without knocking. He was behind his desk, blinking at me. To my great astonishment, Dan Biggs also was present, seated in a captain's chair, bandaged and charred but strangely cheerful.

"Ah, here you are," Johnny Wilson said. "We were about to go looking for you. We understand you had a bit of a Motor City meltdown last night with Schmitz and Beetle."

I collapsed into the other captain's chair. I was surprised to find tears forming in my eyes. "Those fuckers think they're going to pin the fire on me. They're going to call the cops on me. I'm going to wind up in the joint worse than David."

Dan Biggs asked, "Did you tell them anything I said last night?"

"No," I stammered. "I don't think ... well I said it was Rutledge. But I didn't say you told me."

Johnny Wilson asked, "Then how did you tell them you knew it was Rutledge?"

"The gas cans. Compton was out this morning, and he saw somebody taking burned up gas cans out of there."

"Did Compton say it was Rutledge?"

"No. He couldn't quite see. He said it could have been. Or not."

Dan Biggs said to me, "So nobody that you know of seen Rutledge for sure."

"You. You said it was Rutledge."

"Excepting for me."

"No. Compton said it could have been Rutledge, but the guy he saw with the cans had a parka on, and he couldn't see his face. The gas cans were all burned up and black, but Compton knew they were five-gallon gas cans."

Johnny Wilson asked Dan Biggs how the firemen could have missed multiple gas cans. Dan Biggs said there was a deep niche at the end of the hallway just outside the Tuck Shop where the cans might have been hard to spot.

The rest of what they told me went by in a blur. Johnny Wilson did most of the talking. He said I would not be blamed for the fire. That was already taken care of and assured. I was never to tell anyone that Dan Biggs had named Rutledge. An arrangement had been struck with the rector's approval. A new modern store would be built, perhaps in its own new building. It would offer a full line of merchandise and would even have a soda bar that served hamburgers.

"Guess what it's gonna be called?" Dan Biggs asked me with a grin. "Biggs Market. I insisted on that. No more Tuck Shop." He chuckled.

When I finally was able to speak, I asked Dam Biggs how he got out. He said he had always considered the building a fire trap and had made sure he had two windows that worked and a door in the back of the store for escape. He couldn't get to the door so he climbed out a window. Rutledge was stupid to think barring the steel door was enough to do him in. He said he got "smudged up" because it took him a while to gather the store's cash and ledgers.

"That place blew like a bomb," he said. "I'm surprised Rutledge didn't burn hisself up. He must have had enough gasoline out there to float a battleship."

"Three five-gallon cans," I said.

"Might have been more," Dan Biggs said. "After I got out, I heard a couple real loud explosions. There might have been some cans he didn't get poured out."

In a tough accent I had never heard before, Johnny Wilson muttered, "Motherfucker."

Dan Biggs laughed and said, 'That'll be ten Hail Mary's, father."

His laughter and light-heartedness stupefied me. I asked what the police would be told about Rutledge. Instead of answering, Dan Biggs told me that several of his relatives would have jobs in the expanded store.

I asked Johnny Wilson, "Did you go along with this crap?"

He shook his head gravely no. "It's not my call."

Dan Biggs leaned close to my face. "Look, kid, I know it don't seem right to you. But there's right, and there's right. This is food on the table, a roof over people's heads. It's tough to find work since the mills left, and . . . "

I interrupted: "They were going to accuse me of it and get me sent to prison."

"That's all took care of, gone, history, never happened."

"It never happened? Never happened? Fuck. I want my name

cleared. I want to shove it in that prick Schmitz's face. I want him to apologize to me in front of the whole Lower School."

Dan Biggs shook his head and laughed again, ruefully this time. "That ain't gonna happen either."

My heart was pounding and my breath came short. "I thought we were friends."

He grasped my arm. "We are friends. We will always be friends, kid. But this is serious business. Me and my folks, we have our own way of doing, and you need to respect that. You and me are friends, but sometimes when it's serious business on the table, friends only goes so far. There has to be limits to it."

Johnny Wilson said, "Louie Fell called me last night. I explained to him where the money comes from."

"You explained it? How did you even know about it?"

"It comes from me."

"What?"

"It's a discretionary fund. It's just called the rector's wife's fund. I have no idea why. She has nothing to do with it. It's a fund of money we found lying around that no one was using. This is all a fairly ad hoc arrangement right now with the new scholarship boys. The school hadn't thought it through. Most people here don't understand that people who don't have any money don't have any money. They didn't think ahead to realize that the new scholarship boys would need spending money. So now I'm using this fund for that. The money is distributed through The Tuck Shop so it looks like everybody else's money that they get from their parents. It was my fault you weren't on the list when you got here. An oversight. I apologize. When Dan Biggs brought it to my attention, I set it up for him to start giving you an allowance. Ten dollars a week, right?"

"Yes."

"You'll still get it."

I rose and went to the door to leave. "Will Rutledge go to prison?"

Johnny Wilson said, "Prison? No. I think Rutledge is going to Yale."

—

I learned Ellen was back in Nice and pushed for a visit. Had I not, I'm not sure she would have seen me again. When we met, she was either sullen or sad, I couldn't tell.

"Is something wrong?"

She said no at first. But then she said, "I've had a lot of trouble coming to grips with the last story you told me."

"The lynching."

"Yes."

"Sorry."

"Woodrow, tell me, when you were all older and you discovered that some guys were gay, what was that like?"

I thought about it.

"We were all old by then, in our late sixties. It was around the time of our fiftieth reunion I guess. That kind of stuff was sort of academic by then. Like finding out a guy you had always assumed was a Republican was actually a Democrat. Interesting but hardly worth an entire dinner-table conversation."

After a long lull, I asked her, "How does it happen that we wind up in the same place again? Why if I want to see you is it always Nice?"

"I told you in my text," she said, "I'm visiting a friend."

"Male or female?"

"Nice try," she said. "You gave me the impression you were already going to be here. Was that not true? Where were you?"

"Just across the way."

"Across what way?"

"My house in the countryside just outside Aix En Provence."

"A house in Aix, eh?"

"Not in Aix. Outside. The boondocks. Countryside. It's a working lavender farm. A commercial farm, not a touristic one. I make a small profit. Have to, to keep the French tax man from eating me alive."

We waited for a bus to pass. The May sun glittered on the harbor, where white yachts barely rose and fell on blue swells subdued by the seawall.

"Is your father living?" she asked.

"No. He died a decade ago."

"Were you still in touch?"

"Yes. We were close."

"Really?"

"Really. He had a little condo in Oakland County. It was where Little Ottawa had been."

"Your mother was gone by then?"

"She died fifteen years ago. My father retired in his mid-fifties with a disability pension. Little Ottawa was gone by then. They tore it down and redeveloped the land as high-end condos for the tech community at Oakland University. My dad was a holdout. He drove a hillbilly bargain and came out of it with a nice unit of his own in the new development. I visited him every winter and stayed for a week or so. Slept on the couch."

"You? Slumming it like that?"

"I did. He liked it. He came out and checked on me to make sure I was covered up."

"Ahh."

"I tried to do fancy stuff for him. I took him salmon fishing in Iceland once. He hated it. Too many snotty Englishmen, not his comfort zone. But he was too good a sport to complain. I built him a really nice log house on a thousand-acre farm in Northern Michigan with two beautiful trout streams running through. He spent all summer up there fishing, hosting his buddies."

"Showing off his riches."

"No, he wasn't like that. Too many years being management in a union neighborhood. He played it down."

"But he was proud of you."

"Christ, was he ever. Made it a little hard sometimes. He asked me over and over again about Harvard and how much money I made in commodities and how much property I own in France and what famous people I know in New York."

"What did you do?"

"I told him, over and over again. He was a good honest, solid, hard-working American man who had a dream for his family. Life kicked him in the balls pretty hard in ways he didn't deserve."

"So you were his reward."

"Jesus, I was practically his religion."

"What did he do when you told him your success stories?"

"He just . . . " I stammered. My eyes went wet, and I didn't answer for a moment. "He had missing teeth that he always tried to hide. He wouldn't let me buy him implants. Thought they were for actors. When I told him how well I was doing, he grinned so broadly you could see all the holes in his mouth."

She turned away to give me a moment to compose myself.

She asked, "What's the rest of the area like now where you grew up?"

"Outside Pontiac? A lot of it's unrecognizable. It was always lovely terrain, woody rolling hills and sparkling lakes, apple orchards, pretty little farms. But when I was growing up there, a lot of it also wore a certain mantle of grit associated with heavy manufacturing. Oh my God, now. You know what they have now instead of hillbillies and machine shops?"

"What?"

"Bed and Breakfasts."

"Quite a change, I imagine."

"Indeed."

"Is it a good thing?"

"I really have no idea. I think the jury is out. Is it bed and breakfasts or beds and breakfast?"

"I'd go with bed and breakfasts. The other one sounds too asshole."

"You're always right."

"No matter what I say?"

"No matter what."

"Even when I'm wrong?"

"Exactly."

•

I woke with a start at about two in the morning, my head burning with thoughts of Rutledge getting away with it, going to Yale instead of prison where any kid from Pontiac would go if he did the same thing. Like my brother. I took my writing pad and flashlight down from my bureau and made a tent under my blankets. I scribbled the letter, writing fast and hard.

Dear David:

I was completely wrong to jump you about the extra six months. I was stupid. I didn't get it for a long time. I do now. I see why the other guys respect you now in the juvie. It's because you're a hero. I respect you a lot. I love you and you are my brother and I will love you as long as we are alive. I think you are cooler than me. I know you are. When you get out, I will be waiting for you, and we will go somewhere and celebrate. I will bring the beer and the smokes. Who knows maybe we can get some girls even. I get what you did. You did right. Sometimes a man has got to do what a man has got to do.

Love, Woodrow

I got out of bed. I knew that if I managed to be silent, I probably would wake no one, and that even if someone did hear me, he would assume I was on my way to the bathroom. I took a pencil from my backpack. Carefully and slowly opening the top drawer of my bureau so not to make a scraping sound, I withdrew a pair of scissors from my box of supplies. I went to the front of the dorm, sat down on the end of the coffee table and dug past rumpled copies of *The New York Times Sunday Magazine* to find that school book. It fell open to the portrait of the Schmitzes. I tried to rip the page from the book as quietly as possible, but midway through I heard a rustling groan from the nearest alcove. I held my breath, then finished tearing. With the page, my scissors, and the pencil in hand, I crept to the double door of the dorm, opened one side a slim crack and slipped through.

The lobby was lighted eerily by a single sconce high on the wall behind me. I followed my own skulking shadow across the open space to the hallway leading to the dining room. I thought I might have to feel my way, but my feet guided me to the big dining room doors. Inside, moonlight streamed from the tall windows illuminating the silver and china on the tables. I knew Jakes's stew was on the menu for the next night's dinner. Large white stew bowls were stacked in preparation on a long credenza at the back of the dining room. I put the photo down on a clear space on the credenza, placed a bowl on top of it and drew the outline of the bowl onto the photo with my pencil.

•

At dinner the following night, Adams reached for the large serving dish near him, removed the cover and dished out steaming ladles of Jake's famous beef stew, first, of course, into the bowl of Frau Schmitz, who smiled wincingly. Herr Schmitz nodded that Adams could serve him a bowl as well. Then Adams served himself and allowed the tureen to begin its tour down the table.

Adams stared at Frau Schmitz with something like alarm.

"Is there a problem, Frau Schmitz?" he asked in a discreet whisper.

"Not a problem," she said. A generous spoonful of stew was halfway to her mouth, but she paused with her nose oddly crinkled. "An odor."

Herr Schmitz immediately began snorting like a horse.

"Thérèse," he ordered, "put it down immediately." Then to

the table, "Send the stew back down here." When it got to him, he stuck his head into the steaming tureen so deeply I thought he might burn his nose. He lifted his head abruptly. "Nothing here. Barry, is there anything wrong with the stew at your end?"

Having already dished out the tureen at his end of the table, Barry was munching a large mouthful and had to swallow to answer.

"No, sir," he said cheerfully. "Tip top. Jake never misses on the stew."

Herr Schmitz snorted mightily. "Goddamn it. One of these louts has tracked something in. Skaggs, look at your shoes."

I looked first at one shoe, then the other, then rose and examined the soles of both.

"No, sir," I said. "It's not me."

"All of you," he snapped, "look at your shoes."

With a great scraping, bumbling, and bumping of shoulders, all of the boys at our end of the table, including Adams, examined our shoes.

Peering forward to see if Beetle was watching, Herr Schmitz snapped at us to sit back down and stop making a spectacle. By then the pungent odor of shit, carried on vapors of the hot stew, wafted to us all. A few boys began to groan and hold their noses. Herr Schmitz snapped at them to be silent.

Staring meaningfully at his wife, Herr Schmitz hissed, "If it's not one of them, it has to be one of us."

She stiffened and fixed him with a lethal stare. They snarled at each other in the strange language Aubert had told us was Walloon. Then they both bent their heads low and scuffed their heels in a frenzied tap dance.

Suddenly, Herr Schmitz sat up stiff and threw back his head as if threatened by a gun. His eyes went wide as silver dollars. He stared at the bottom of Frau Schmitz's stew bowl. He reached forward with the fingers and thumb of one hand and, fretfully as if defusing a bomb, lifted the bowl a half inch. He reached the other hand forward and lifted the bowl straight up. When it was airborne perhaps six inches, the photograph of the Schmitzes fell back to the plate still connected to the bowl by streaming strands of loose human feces.

The boys at the other end had not seen it yet. A collective gasp went up at our end and was just on the verge of becoming a chorus of cries and shouts when Herr Schmitz slapped the bowl down sharply, stuck his finger in all our faces, and, looking toward Beetle, hissed, "Shut up! Shut up all of you! Sit in your places and look at your plates! Right now."

Frau Schmitz had both hands to her mouth, trying not to vomit.

"Stop it!" he said to her. "Stop it right now."

She composed herself in her chair, but I saw oily black tears drizzling down a powdered cheek.

She whispered, "Gustave, I cannot do this. This is a horror."

He put both of his hands flat on the table and stared down at them for a long while.

"Sir," Adams began.

"Shut up," Herr Schmitz said with a finger in the air, not looking up. "You, Skaggs, clear this away from the table."

I was not a waiter that night, but I said nothing and carried the plate and bowl to the kitchen. I first made sure none of Jake's staff was watching, then dumped all of it, china and all, into one of the large steel trashcans at the far end of the pickup area. I washed my hands in the small sink next to the cans and returned to the table. When I got back, the entire scene was preserved in amber, Herr Schmitz still staring at his hands, jaw muscles twitching in waves.

Adams said to me in a subdued voice, "Sit."

By then, everyone at the table was aware. Even Barry was shocked and tense.

"I have a theory," Herr Schmitz said softly, never lifting his gaze from his white knuckles. We all leaned in to listen.

"I have been gathering evidence since this began. I am quite confident that, should it come to it, which I sincerely hope it will not, I will be able to persuade the rector to expel at least four of you, perhaps as many as six. That would be a great tragedy, because we all know that only one boy is truly responsible.

He looked up at us. "What has taken place here tonight proves my point. I suppose you could take the earlier incidents for harmless pranks. I never thought they were harmless because they were a defiance, but I'm sure you did. But what we have just witnessed is proof that these so-called pranks are the work of a coarse and depraved mind, not at all the sort of thing that the kind of boy who traditionally comes to St. Philip's School is even remotely capable of doing but another kind of boy entirely, a kind of boy who does not belong here."

He finally lifted his eyes but looked past me down the length of the table.

"You have always known who this boy is. You have protected him through a very mistaken code of honor. By protecting him, you betray the honor of the school. You must understand that. The boy who did this is your enemy. He is a cuckoo in the nest. He destroys your honor and the honor of our beloved St. Philip's School by his very presence."

He drew a long breath and pushed back from the table.

"We will settle this matter among ourselves because doing so is a lesson that you must all learn now, here, at my table. And you will learn it well.

"Adams, Barry, I speak to you as well, perhaps especially to you. If word of this goes to Mr. Frick, then it goes from there to the rector and the board. I assure you, at that point the matter will be full-blown and quite out of my control. At least four boys will be expelled as conspirators, perhaps more.

"You are the supes responsible for decorum at the table. Such an affair will become a part of your permanent records at the school."

Adams and Barry gazed back at him with faces perfectly and deliberately blank, attentive but without even the most minute gesture or hint of agreement or disagreement.

"The right answer is the simplest one," he droned on. "You will give me the boy's name. It doesn't have to be something you all agree on. If any one of you brings me the boy's name, the culprit will be expelled and the matter ended.

"In the meantime, since some of you seem to believe you are engaged in a game of dare, I will meet your dare. You will eat nothing at this table. Nothing. Your meals will be fully served to you, all courses. You will not touch the food or take a bite. The dishes will be cleared, taken to the kitchen, and dumped."

"Sir," Barry began.

"Shut up. Don't open your mouth again while I am speaking. They will eat nothing. Not at this table. The supervisors may eat, but not the boys. You will take not one bite of food at this table until I have the boy's name.

"And know this. Be very careful. Very careful. Because if one word of this goes to Frick, a single syllable, then the game is truly up, and more than one boy will be expelled from St. Philip's School."

He turned to Frau Schmitz.

"Dear Thérèse," he said, rising and offering an arm. "Will you join me?'" They slipped out of the dining room unnoticed by the head table.

Barry shrugged.

"Better dig in. This may be your last."

We wolfed down prodigious amounts of Jake's excellent beef stew in preparation for the famine ahead. Sputtering with his mouth full, Yusupov said, "It was rather brilliant. Was it a photo of them?"

"From that magazine on the table in Dorm Four, I think," Granger said.

"Oh, yes," Yusupov said, swallowing hard and nodding enthusiastically. "And it was stuck to the bowl with actual shit."

"Be quiet," Barry said.

"Shut up," Adams said.

"It is that," Aubert said. "I can scarcely believe, but my nose is no liar."

"Your nose is too big to lie," Compton said.

Everyone laughed except Aubert, who was looking directly into my eyes.

"Herr Schmitz suspects you," he said.

"Hey! We don't do that," Compton said. "Nobody else has been nailed at the table for what they did."

"No one else has placed the shit of a human onto the table," Aubert said, still looking at me.

"You don't know anything," Compton said. "We don't know if this is one guy or a bunch of guys. What do you want to do, Aubert, find out who it is so you can rat somebody out?"

Aubert asked Smiley to his right, "What is rat out?"

"To rat is to inform," Smiley said.

"I do not inform!" Aubert said hotly. "You Americans, you don't even know what an informant is. You are children."

389

"I've got a pretty fucking good idea what a rat is," Compton said.

Barry rose and dropped his napkin to his chair. "Adams," he said, "Care to join? I think we might visit a more congenial table."

"Great idea," Adams said. They departed for coffee on the far side of the dining room.

"Listen," Smiley said, "I don't want to be a rat, but at least rats get to eat."

"We'll have to figure something out," I said.

"What species of scheme do you have in mind?" Aubert asked me.

"Shit, I don't know," I said.

Gellhorn, wolfing down a spoonful of stew, said, "Mind not using that word just now?"

Compton said, "Pontiac's right. We'll have to figure something out."

Davidson was sitting stiff-backed in his chair, not eating. "Why is it so bad for Herr Schmitz to find out who did it? He's right, isn't he? All of this stuff that's going on at this table is against the school. I don't like it. And my parents wouldn't like it at all if they thought I was in on it."

Speaking in a low growl, Compton said, "You're not in on it, Davidson, unless you rat somebody out. Then you'll wish you'd never come to this school."

Smiley said gravely, "We don't need to be talking to each other like that. We're not gangsters. We're just kids. We need to eat. What he's doing is terrible. We could tell Beetle that Herr Schmitz is starving us to death. I think even he would find that worrisome."

"You heard what Schmitz told us," Bear said. "He says if Beetle finds out, he'll get four of us kicked out."

"He can't get four guys kicked out," Yusupov said. "That's a bluff. He's in over his head, and he knows it. He's terrified Beetle will find out, because he knows if everybody's rich mummies and daddies find out he's starving us, then the whole thing will blow up in his face."

"So, again," Smiley said, "why not just tell Beetle?"

"Won't someone get caught?" Bear asked.

"Nobody will get caught," Yusupov said. "Beetle also will be afraid of the parents and the rector and the trustees. He'll just quash the whole thing."

"Then we can eat," Smiley said.

"Oh, c'mon," Compton said. "I mean, sure, maybe after a few days, we tell Beetle that Herr Schmitz is starving us. But let's not cave in right off the bat. Herr Schmitz is dropping the puck, so let's play, at least for a little while. Then we'll see how it goes."

"Compton," Yusupov said, "I have decided that you are totally insane, and I greatly admire you for this. You are correct. We should play a hand or two." He lifted his water glass in a toast. "Gentlemen, here's to doing some preposterous poppycock."

We all gazed at Yusupov through a long silence. Then we said in ragged unison, "To preposterous poppycock" and clinked glasses.

On the way to our alcoves to retrieve books and coats, Compton walked ahead of me a few paces. With his back to me, he gave me a quick thumbs up.

•

On the first day of the starvation decree, I began my third tour of duty as a waiter. The Schmitzes had ceased showing up at all for breakfast or lunch. They must have known we would partially or totally ignore the decree when they were absent. Adams and Barry didn't try to stop us.

But that still left dinner. On the first evening of the decree, the meal was green salad, sliced baked chicken, green beans, and mashed potatoes, all of which Yusupov and I carried to the table in large serving dishes. In the pickup area of the kitchen, the young man in a toque shoved trays out over the scarred wooden counter to us. Jake stood behind him, watching with arms folded across his huge chest, the cleaver prominently holstered at his waist.

The serving dishes were passed one at a time to Herr Schmitz and to Barry. Herr Schmitz served his wife and then himself. Then the supes served themselves. We all sat on our hands, staring at the steaming dishes.

"Serve yourselves, all of you," Herr Schmitz said crisply, "but do not eat."

Frau Schmitz looked at him from a lowered brow with what was either a quizzical expression or indigestion. He shrugged and muttered something inaudible in Walloon.

We took turns sullenly spooning small amounts to our plates, except for Yusupov, who began slopping out vast portions until Adams saw him and said, "Cut it out." Yusupov nodded a smiling assent and then sat back with his nose in air to count dust motes.

"Speak," Herr Schmitz said. "This is a normal meal. You will carry on your idiotic chatter as always, only you will not touch your food."

When any meal, especially dinner, was well underway in the Lower School dining room, the general hubbub reached a volume that made it difficult for anyone to hear a person seated even two seats away. Almost immediately, we fell into a pattern. We smiled happily at each other as if talking about sports, or we frowned studiously as if discussing algebra or Latin, while we said things like, "I think Frau Schmitz is really a guy," or, "Even Davidson could beat the shit out of that little hunchback bastard."

The Schmitzes made not the slightest effort to hear us, happily trading their own confidences in whispers and sneers and spooning down what seemed like especially copious amounts of food.

Clearing the table was awkward, because the amount of food left on the plates precluded stacking them on top of each other. Herr Schmitz ordered us to get it done quickly without attracting attention.

"If you do draw Jake's attention," he said, "it will be over for you. I know this man. He is not a civilized person."

We made multiple trips to the kitchen, plates loaded with untouched food, and dumped it all into the trash cans before passing the trays to the dishwashers on the other side. On our third trip, the young man in a toque was waiting. He examined us closely while we dumped the untouched food. Before we were even halfway done passing in the trays, he wheeled and marched off into the din and steam.

"Push is about to come to shove," Yusupov whispered.

Indeed, when we returned with the next load, Jake had stationed himself by the washing basins to see what we were doing. Yusupov and I both stood next to the trash cans with our trays, frozen to the spot. With an insinuating nod and shrug, Jake signaled that we were to carry on, so we dumped the food into the trash in front of him.

By then dinner had concluded, and boys and masters and their wives were thronging noisily down the corridor from the dining room to the lobby. Yusupov was about to leave the kitchen ahead of me to finish clearing the table. He was just out the swinging door when a sharp pain in my earlobe startled me so abruptly that I dropped my tray to the floor. I winced and tried to pull away, but Jake had me firmly in his grasp. He pointed to the small metal table and chairs at the far end, and I understood without asking that I was to sit there or risk dismemberment.

He sat down across from me with his huge red fists before him. "What is this shit?"

"What shit?" I stammered.

"Why are you throwing my food in the trash? Is something wrong with it?"

"No, sir," I said.

He stood up from the table and looked down on me over his heavily tattooed arms.

"You're the kid whose mother took him into town and paid to get a bunch of clothes made."

I was astonished that Jake knew anything at all about me, let alone intimate detail. I said, "Yes, sir."

"That guy who made your clothes is my sister-in-law's uncle. I heard about it. So you're not one of these kids. You're not a rich kid from New York."

I said, "No, sir."

"What's your name?"

"Woodrow Skaggs, sir."

He sat down again, leaning on the massive elbows.

"What's that name they call you?"

"Pontiac."

"OK, Pontiac. That's what I'll call you. Like the car. And don't call me sir. My name is Jake. You call me that. Do it."

"Jake."

"Didn't I cut your tie off once?"

"Yes. Jake."

"Good. Now, why the fuck are you throwing my food away?"

"I'm not allowed to say. Jake."

He shook his head. "Fucking Schmitz. Right?"

I balked. I wasn't sure if sharing this much information would be ratting. But something made me trust him. "Yes."

"That son of a bitch. I hate that man's weasel guts."

"Why?"

Jake eyed me cautiously.

"You boys call us wombats. Right?"

I nodded yes, then shook my head no.

"I don't."

"You all do," he said. "We know that. It goes way back. Maybe a hundred years. Maybe longer. We don't care. You only do it behind our backs."

"Right."

"Well, guess what? And this is our secret, OK? Between us. Don't tell them boys. You promise?"

"Yes."

"We call ourselves wombats."

I was startled and almost gasped. I stared at him to gauge whether he was telling the truth or joking. He shook his head and chuckled to show he meant it.

"Just sometimes. It's a joke. We say it behind your backs. Anyway, the wombats all hate Schmitz."

"Why?"

"He called me a wombat. To my face. I was going to punch his lights out, but all my wombat relations would have got fired if I did that."

"Why did he call you that?"

"I had a kid from his table smart off to one of my folks, like you did. This was two years ago, when Schmitz was still kind of new. So I chopped the kid's tie off, like I always done, ever since way back. So Schmitz sees the kid come back to his table all bawling and carrying on about his necktie getting chopped off, and Schmitz comes back in the kitchen like a bull in a China shop. He's ready to get me fired and this and that, and I told him to fuck off. So he calls me a wombat."

I was truly shocked. But then something occurred to me.

"Maybe it was a language thing, because he's a foreigner and he was new and his English wasn't that good yet. Maybe he didn't know what he was saying."

"I don't give a shit if he knew what he was saying. I knew what he was saying."

I thought it over. "I guess you're right."

"That kraut son of a bitch," Jake said, glowering and kneading the great fists. "I've always wanted to get even with his Nazi ass. You tell me what's going on out there now. What's with him telling you to throw my food away?"

I explained the decree. I also explained we were hopeful Herr Schmitz and his wife might stay away from the dining room for breakfasts and lunches.

"No shit," he said, "so they can't be blamed for starving anybody to death. But he thinks you're all going to go to bed hungry every night?"

"Yes."

"Jesus Lord. Why don't you just tell Beetle? He won't want something like this getting back to the parents. He's more afraid of the parents than he is of our Lord and Savior."

"We can't. If we do, Herr Schmitz says he can get a bunch of us expelled."

He got up from the table and paced nervously with his hand

playing over the cleaver. I reached up and loosened my tie. He sat back down, regarding me appraisingly.

"What do your parents do for work?"

"My dad works in a car factory. My mom used to be a house maid, but she doesn't do that work anymore."

He nodded.

"Working people," he said.

"Yes."

"OK, listen to me, Pontiac." He nodded to where a dozen men and women on the other side of the screen were shutting down the kitchen. "All them wombats in there, they're all my kin. Every one of them. I got 'em all jobs. They all work for me. And we don't have no car factories here. They lose these jobs they got now, they all have to move away somewheres else. I lose my job, they lose their jobs. You understand me?"

"Yes."

"All right. Here's the deal. Nobody throws my food away. And nobody makes kids go to bed hungry. I'll kill the bastard first."

I looked down and saw his fingers flicking across the cleaver. I took his word for truth.

"So I'm going to do something. But if you rat me out, I'll get fired, and all them people in there will get fired, too. You're man enough to understand what I'm telling you, right, Pontiac?"

"I do understand, Jake. I got it."

He walked to a small wooden cabinet on the wall by the swinging door. He opened it and plucked out a large darkened old-fashioned door key, which he held aloft.

"I am going to loan you this key. If anyone asks where you got it, you will say you stole it from this cabinet. If you say I give it to you, we all get fired."

He led me across the darkened corridor to the pantry where he had briefly incarcerated me and Yusupov a few weeks previously. Working the key in the lock, he said, "This is locked as soon as we go home." He let me in and turned on a light. "How long do you have after dinner before study hall?"

"Forty-five minutes if we stay at the table until 6:45."

"OK, Pontiac, here's how it goes."

Yusupov and I were to take our busing trays full of uneaten food on trays to the kitchen and push the trays through the dishwashing window. After dinner, we were to wait until the lights had been turned off in the corridor. Then the ten of us from Herr Schmitz's table would return, and I would unlock the pantry. Our food would be re-warmed, waiting for us on the long table. It was up to us not to get caught.

"Mr. Fell will notice," I said, "if that many guys are out of the dorm at once between dinner and study hall."

"Then do it in shifts. Figure it out. But listen to me close, now, Pontiac." He leaned forward with his face close to mine. "Don't take no dishes out of this pantry. You can sneak out food, but not dishes or silverware. And don't make no messes. Keep everything stacked neat so we can grab it all and get it washed first thing we come in in the morning. And you get caught, you better have a story ready. You guys were stashing the food, not me."

I nodded.

"These other boys at your table will wonder how this deal got set up. Let 'em wonder. You don't say my name to nobody. Tell them they don't want to hurt people that are helping them."

"Got it."

He handed me the key and led me back into the corridor.

"Jake," I said, "Why are you doing this?"

He exhaled a heavy sigh. "Boys is boys. These people around

here that run this place, some of them don't have the good sense God gave them."

•

We gorged ourselves so ravenously at breakfast and lunch that I'm sure we all would have been better off not eating any dinner at all. But once we had our system worked out and fine-tuned, dinner became the high point of every day. The appeal of course, was the sense of danger and the thrill of getting over on Herr Schmitz.

I took Jake's advice and divided us into two platoons of five boys each. Platoon One milled and mixed at the far end of the dorm after dinner. Platoon Two, meanwhile, made its way to the pantry to eat. Then the platoons reversed roles.

The timing had to be both precise and lucky. The formal time for dinner to end was 6:45 PM, but the tables were always empty and the dining room deserted fifteen minutes before that. Jake and his crew had the lights turned off and the doors closed by six forty. On even days, Platoon One assembled in the pantry at exactly 6:45 PM and had until 7:00 PM to eat. We allowed five minutes for shift change. Platoon Two ate from 7:05 to 7:20 PM. That left ten minutes for Platoon Two to be at their desks in the study hall at 7:30 PM—barely enough time but feasible. On odd days we reversed the order of eating. That way if there were tardy arrivals at Study Hall, the latecomers would not always be the same faces. Switching the order also allowed us to mix things up in the dorm and avoid creating too obvious a pattern for the supes or Mr. Fell to notice.

It all had to fit like clockwork. Fifteen minutes wasn't much time to consume a full meal, especially the rich feasts we found ourselves enjoying when things got up to speed. Each boy had to do his part in order to maintain a well-oiled machine.

There were hitches, of course. On one occasion, a boy was stuck in the bathroom with constipation and missed his chance to eat. On another, a boy got caught in conversation with a master in the lobby after dinner. Adjustments always had to be made, and to facilitate these, we developed a code.

Saying that someone was "a real asshole" meant that the boy in question had been unavoidably detained. "Tell (somebody) I need my protractor back," meant that a substitution was being made and the person in question would eat with the other platoon.

We quickly developed hand signs and gestures for emergency situations. An early one was shoving one's left hand roughly and demonstrably through one's hair two or three times in quick succession to signal, "Danger, do not go to the pantry." That signal didn't last long because it was too theatrical.

Some of the boys in Dorm Four who did not sit at Herr Schmitz's table were in on what we were doing and joined us occasionally in the pantry. They also smuggled special treats to us like pies and cookies, none of which we needed and all of which we accepted with thanks.

At first Jake did as he promised and simply re-warmed our untouched meals. That meant that by the time the second shift arrived to eat, the food was cold again already, and, anyway, we weren't exactly starving in the first place. Looking back, I think Jake may have felt injured when his people came back from the pantry in the morning carrying trays of uneaten food. But at a certain point, an electric warming oven appeared in a cabinet at the back wall of the pantry where our food was stacked, offering tempting aromas of Jake's still hot beef stew, meatloaf, or baked chicken. A second oven appeared soon after, carrying hot side dishes and rolls. A prodigious amount of cake and pie also awaited us in the cabinets, along with pitchers of iced tea and cool milk. Best of all, on the bench at the far end of the room behind the racks of aprons, we found two large electric coffee pots filled to the brim.

Only I knew whence or how this bounty appeared. My ownership of these secrets at the time lent me an importance and a measure of respect that I found deeply gratifying. In almost every walk of life that I have experienced since, I have encountered one form or another of person who knows how to get things done without a lot of regard for rules and regulations. In Vietnam I fulfilled that role myself as an officer in the Quartermaster Corps, slipping supplies, expensive booze and other comforts to enlisted men and officers from my air-conditioned office hundreds of miles from danger. I always considered the operation in the pantry at St. Philip's to have been my preparation for life.

The meals in the pantry were festivals of whispered gluttony and muffled hilarity, with much mouth blowing of hastily stuffed food when jokes became too funny. Compton and Bear developed a routine we asked them not to perform until we had finished most of a meal because they were too funny. Compton went to the end of the table and played the part of Herr Schmitz. Bear sat next to him as a very large version of Frau Schmitz. Together, without uttering a word they engaged in a symphony of winces, grimaces, and tics that had us all spitting beef stew at each other.

I didn't get to eat often with Yusupov, because we were in different platoons, but whenever I did, it was like going to the funniest movie ever made. Even better than Compton and Bear, Yusupov perfectly captured an impersonation of the Schmitzes.

Playing both parts, he engaged in outlandishly bawdy and scatological dialogues between the two.

By then, Gellhorn was an active and enthusiastic conspirator, but Aubert and Davidson held themselves apart. Aubert ate with us in the pantry, sometimes voraciously, but he objected to our comedy routines mainly on grounds of manners.

The true holdout was Davidson. He would not attend any of our secret meals and attempted instead to survive on packaged snacks purchased from the temporary store Dan Biggs had set up on tables in a corner of the Upper School common room. Yusupov was concerned that Davidson's frequent trips to the Upper to buy abnormal quantities of potato chips, muffins, and soft drinks might attract suspicion.

Yusupov, Compton, and I went to his alcove one night. He looked even more pale and fragile than usual, sipping a bottle of orange soda on his cot. When he saw us coming, he hunched himself over his bag of potato chips like a jealous squirrel.

"We have meals," Yusupov said. "Better than regular meals. Why won't you eat with us?"

"I don't like what you're doing. It's against the school."

Compton sneered. "How does it hurt the school? It's our damn food. Our parents paid for it. We're just taking what we have coming."

"It . . . " Davidson struggled. "It goes against the school. You guys make a joke of everything. You mock St. Philip's. You act like it's bad, but it's . . . "

"What?" Compton demanded.

Davidson hung his head even lower, mumbling, "The school loves us."

Compton was about to bark, but I signaled for silence.

"I think I know what you mean, Davidson. I understand. But, look, we're the school, too, aren't we?"

He looked dubious.

Compton said, "Listen, Davidson, you're not going to keep going to the Upper every other day coming back with your big Santa bag of cookies and Cokes for yourself. Some Sixth Former is going to figure it out, and that's going to get us caught."

Davidson looked to me.

"You don't have to eat with us in the pantry," I said. "But will you let us bring food to you in your alcove? We can't take any dishes out of the pantry, but we can get you some regular food for dinner. You can eat it after lights out."

He shrugged.

"OK, I'll try it. I get pretty hungry."

•

A few nights later during the witching hour, Barry popped out of the supe's door and stood glowering over the dorm like a lighthouse until he spotted me and Compton at the far end. He pointed a finger at us, jerked a thumb to indicate we were to report to his quarters, then disappeared inside the door.

When we entered the apartment, Barry was already seated in a captain's chair. We sat down on the chintz love seat.

"I know all about the table, the pantry, the whole show," he said.

We said nothing.

"You are about to get ratted out. Someone has already spilled the beans to the Dorm Three supes. They're not going anywhere with it yet, but it won't be long before who ever gave it to them takes it to Beetle or Herr Schmitz."

We remained silent.

"It will be very bad for Jake and his family. You will not be able to protect them."

Compton asked, "What does it have to do with Jake?"

"Everything," I said.

"Oh," he said. "OK, well, we'd have to cover for Jake for sure."

Barry shook his head impatiently. "Look, you two, if this gets to the rector, and it will, you will not be able to 'cover' for anybody, least of all yourselves."

We said nothing.

"I don't think you have a very keen appreciation of your position politically," he said, "and if anything kills you, it will be the politics. I give you credit for managing, by some idiotic instinct, to have put your fingers squarely on Herr Schmitz's innermost frailty, which is his near insanity about defiance. But in the process, you've muddled your way into a situation that you have not analyzed well at all. You think Herr Schmitz is afraid of your parents, which is a bit stupid."

I shrugged. "He's on our asses not to tell anybody away from the table that he's starving us. That's why we think he's afraid of our parents finding out."

"He's afraid of some parents, Pontiac. He's not at all afraid of your parents. And the person he's really worried about is Beetle. He won't want Beetle to think he has lost control of the table, and he especially won't want Beetle to think he has been torturing boys who are sons of important families."

"Who are those boys?" I asked.

Compton shook his head and whispered, "Sheesh."

"People like Gellhorn," Barry said, "He's an Ambrose, a very old St. Philip's family. Smiley is another one. He's old Philadelphia Main Line. Granger's family, even though they're Canadian now, originally comes from Boston. Others."

"Not you," Compton said to me.

Barry sat back. "Herr Schmitz may not be afraid of Pontiac's parents, but in his own way, Pontiac is very important to this. If Herr Schmitz can make the case to Beetle that Pontiac is behind all of it, then he'll be singing to the choir. They both think it was a huge mistake to admit scholarship boys to the school. Whoever put the shit on the table gave their case a major boost."

Compton and I stared at our shoes.

"But they seem to have some new caution about you," Barry said to me. "Something about the Big Study fire?"

"I don't know," I said.

"Let's not get off topic," he said. "I get the feeling Herr Schmitz would have gone ahead and accused you of the shit on the table and gotten you expelled with or without evidence, but now, post Big Study fire, he's more cautious. He needs witnesses. But he's made one major miscalculation. He has successfully kept the withholding of food a secret from Beetle. I'm not sure how, exactly. Beetle should have caught wind of it long ago. But I guess you guys also have spread the word about keeping it from him."

"Yes," I said.

"Why?"

"Timing," I said.

Barry smiled.

"Then you're not as stupid as I made you out to be. Timing is everything here. I can tell you that Beetle will not like being surprised by the food business if it comes to him from anyone but Herr Schmitz. If Beetle finds out in some disruptive way before Herr Schmitz has a chance to tell him about it, he will feel that Herr Schmitz has gone off the reservation.

"At any rate, Herr Schmitz is very much on the hunt for

cooperative witnesses. He is working hard on Mr. Fell, Adams, and me for information. He's trying to figure out which boys at the table may be weak links. For example, I think you can expect him soon to start calling Gellhorn and Davidson down to his apartment for cookies and tea."

Compton said, "Shit."

"I shouldn't tell you this," Barry said, his voice trailing off.

"Yes, you should," I said.

"All right. All right." His eyes were distressed beneath the hooded brow. "Here's the thing. If you can get to Beetle before Herr Schmitz does, and if Beetle hears it as a general campaign of starvation aimed at everyone, then I think we can count on him to react with absolute panic. He's already a tad suspicious of Herr Schmitz for being a wog. And if he thinks Herr Schmitz deliberately hid things from him . . . "

"Which he did," Compton said.

". . . and pulled off some kind of starvation routine on the boys from old families," Barry continued, "Beetle will go off like a Roman candle, right out into poppycock land. But you can't just go tell him. He'll smell a rat. You have to let him think he's discovering it.

"Now how you do that, I have nothing to say about and nothing to do with—I want you to remember that. In fact, you and I did not even have this conversation. Do you promise me that?"

"Sure," we said.

"A last thing."

Barry leaned forward and looked at us severely.

"If I learn that you are out hunting for the potential rat or carrying out any kind of vengeance or intimidation, I will go to Beetle myself and turn you all in."

On the way back down the dorm, I asked Compton, "Why is he so goosey about keeping his name out of it?"

"Christ, I already told you that" Compton said. "He wants to be president."

Before we could make our way down to our alcoves, we were besieged by boys from the table. Even though we revealed nothing, everybody guessed what had happened.

"The jig is up," Smiley said. "We are destroyed."

"My experience in America approaches its finale," Aubert said.

Davidson peeked out from his alcove, ducked his head back in and snapped the curtain closed. Yusupov stood in his own doorway, gaping at us as if we were covered in blood.

"Step in here," he snapped, pushing us roughly by our shoulders. He ordered others who tried to follow to get out. He pulled the curtain closed violently.

"What has happened?"

We told him in hoarse whispers. At one point, we looked up and saw the head of Granger, who was standing on the cot in the next alcove to peer over the partition. Yusupov grabbed a hockey stick and menaced him.

"Go on," he told us, hockey stick in hand. "Tell me all of it."

We all agreed immediately that Davidson was the rat.

"That's it," Yusupov said. "We have to kill him."

"No, no, no," I said, "we're not killing anybody. He just loves the school, and he thinks we don't have respect for it. But I don't want to hurt him."

"Fine," Yusupov said, "but I do not wish to be expelled. My family has things at stake."

"I have more at stake than any of you," a voice barked above. We looked up and saw Gellhorn peering over the other partition. "So what are we going to do about it?"

Yuspov waved the hockey stick at him, and Gellhorn withdrew.

"I need time to think," Yusupov said.

"Why you?" Compton asked. "Me and Pontiac are the ones Barry told."

"You're not capable," Yusupov said. "We will meet again in my alcove tomorrow night after study hall."

I followed Compton to his alcove.

"What is this with Yusupov?" I asked. "Who appointed him?"

Compton slumped to his cot and stared at his shoes with his head beneath rounded shoulders. "Well, you know, he's pretty clever. We could use the help."

Neither one of us spoke for a while. The hubbub outside the curtain was more intense than normal by at least two decibels. I stepped out and snagged Granger by the cuff.

"Davidson is off limits," I hissed in his ear.

"But he's the rat?" he whispered in awe.

"We assume so."

"Davidson was never in on it," Granger said. "He hates this. He loves the school."

"Yup."

I stepped back into Compton's alcove and closed the curtain. He was still staring at his shoes. Not lifting his face.

He asked, "Do you blame me for this?"

"Well, I could," I said. "But you didn't put shit under Frau Schmitz's dinner plate."

He looked up. "God, that was so amazing. That was like the greatest thing anybody ever did at St. Philip's School. Even if you get kicked out for it, you'll never be forgotten."

No, I thought to myself. I'll still be here, digging ditches.

•

On a Saturday evening before lights out, I met with Compton and Yusupov in Yusupov's alcove. Aubert and Gellhorn came in and closed the curtain behind them. They stood facing us in their bathrobes and slippers with arms crossed, not to be expelled.

"In for a penny, in for a pound," Gellhorn said.

"I do not understand this colloquy," Aubert said, "but I believe that I agree with it."

Compton went to the curtain and poked his nose out to look for spies. Yusupov went to the inside end of the alcove and struck a statuesque pose with one elbow atop his bureau.

"Let's get going," Compton hissed. "Down to business."

"We go to Davidson," Yusupov said. "He has ratted us out to the Dorm Three supes. But according to what you said last night, they have not ratted us out yet to Beetle and neither has Davidson. We need to be sure he doesn't. We all go. Now."

Gellhorn and Aubert did not object. The five of us marched to Davidson's alcove. The curtain was closed. Yusupov snatched it open, and Davidson sat up brusquely on the bed, dropping a handful of gumdrops to the floor.

"Oh, God," he wheezed.

We crowded inside the alcove and drew the curtain.

"You ratted us out to the Dorm Three supes," Yusupov said.

"I did not."

I said, "You did, too."

"I did not."

Aubert said, "Davidson, you are the only one who was a private to our plot."

"Privy," I said.

"I didn't tell the supes," Davidson said in a whisper, staring at his gumdrops on the floor.

"Davidson," Aubert said, "the supes are aware. How did they make this discovery?"

"I didn't tell them."

After a long silence, I said, "Who did you tell?"

"Friends."

Yusupov looked sharply to the rest of us. "Friends in Dorm Four?" he asked.

"No."

"Friends where, then?"

In an almost inaudible whisper, Davidson said, "Friends in Dorm Three."

A terrible possibility dawned on me.

"Rensevear, Colfax, and Howard?"

Davidson sat silent. Yusupov, gaping at the rest of us in disbelief, said, "Answer the question. Did you tell the three stooges?"

"Yes," he whispered.

"Holy shit," I said. "Why would you do that? Of all the people. They told their supes, Davidson. Why did you tell them?"

"It just came out."

"It didn't just come out," I said. "You ratted us out. To those assholes. Of all people. Why them?"

Compton said, "Davidson went to the Peck School in Morristown with me and those guys. They were his only friends."

"They were not my only friends," Davidson said defensively.

"You didn't have any fucking friends," Compton said. "Kids wouldn't even go to your house because they were so afraid of your drunk mother."

"Well, that was my mother," he said, stiffening his shoulders. "Lots of guys liked me."

We were silent for a long while.

Finally Gellhorn said, "We like you, Davidson. We're your

friends. Or at least we thought we were. Why would you stab us in the back?"

Davidson rose to his feet, his face drained white. "Why would you stab the school in the back? That's all you're doing. You're trying to wreck St. Philip's. Rensevear, Colfax, and Howard are like me. They love the school. I don't like what you're doing."

Yusupov sank to Davidson's bed.

"All right, Davidson, we respect your feelings for the school, even if we do not entirely share them. We are willing to give you a certain dispensation because we understand your sentiments. However, we need some time. I have been coming up with a strategy. We need two weeks. If you rat us out to Beetle before then, if anyone rats us out to Beetle, we will kill you."

"What?"

"We will kill you."

"You can't kill me."

"Yes, we can."

Davidson looked around to each of us. We all nodded yes. I don't know if we meant it.

"OK," Yusupov said to the rest of us, "let's go. We have business to attend to."

"Where are you going?" Davidson demanded.

"Where do you think?" Yusupov said. "Compton, you and Gellhorn will double-team Rensevear. Pontiac and I will take Colfax. Aubert, can you beat up Howard?"

"Emphatically," Aubert said.

"That's not fair," Davidson said. "It wouldn't be a good fight, five guys against three."

"It's your fault," Yusupov said. "And if you do anything to get in our way, it will be the five of us on your head next."

Davidson shrank away. "Oh, God."

Yusupov went back to his alcove and came out with his hockey stick.

I said, "No weapons. That's prison."

He hesitated, then ducked back in and came out unarmed.

It was against the rules for us to be outside our dorm after study hall, so we had to move covertly across the deserted lobby. Yusupov opened the door to Dorm Three a crack, peeked in, and saw that no supes or dorms masters were about. We filed in behind him.

Boys were scattered here and there in small groups up and down their radiator bench, chatting or looking at lingerie ads in *The New York Times Sunday Magazine*. They turned to watch us parade into their domain. Evers came to the opening of his alcove and stood nonchalantly with one hand up on the partition.

"What the fuck, gentlemen?" he asked.

"We're here for the three," Yusupov said.

Evers shrugged.

"Rensevear," Evers barked. "Colfax. Howard. You have visitors."

All three popped their heads out of their alcoves. Rensevear stepped out, followed by the other two who fell in behind him.

"Well, well, well," Rensevear said to us. "Robespierre and company have come to visit. Oh, I apologize, Yusupov. I should have said Lenin and the Bolsheviks. What can we do for you?"

Compton and Gellhorn went straight for him. Compton grabbed him by the front of his pajamas. Gellhorn stepped quickly behind him to pin his arms. Yusupov took Colfax with an elbow around his neck, and I punched him hard in the gut. Aubert backed Howard down the dorm.

"That'll be about it," a loud voice called behind us in a broad southern accent.

We turned our heads. It was Evers, with a lacrosse racket swinging menacingly over his head. He came closer and closer, the racket whistling about our ears. We released our prey and stepped back.

"Jesus Christ, Evers," I said, "Why would you defend these assholes?"

"They're in my dorm."

A dozen boys stood in a ring around us.

"Is your little Puerto Rican mugging squad all done?" Rensevear asked. "One guy from Arkansas with a lacrosse racket, and you're finished?"

"What's this all about?" Evers asked, the racket still looping lazily over his head.

"It's private," Yusupov said.

"Well, I have an idea then," Evers said, lowering the racket. "Instead of you five guys ganging up on our three guys, which wouldn't be a fair fight, why not each side just put their best man forward?"

No one spoke.

Then Rensevear said, "I'm fine with that."

"So am I," Compton said.

"All right," Evers said, "but there's one rule. Fight quiet. No yelling or screaming to wake up the supes or the master. Fight 'til it's over. Quiet. Does everybody agree?"

He looked around the group. Everyone nodded.

Before I had time to blink, Compton bolted forward and body-slammed Rensevear into the radiator bench, leaving him on his knees slumped forward over the bench with both arms hanging on the far side. I desperately hoped Compton would not turn back to us and smile, but he did, and in that split-second, Rensevear threw himself to his feet like a hawk landing, reached with a sweeping backhanded fist and clocked Compton hard across the back of his head. Compton staggered forward, stooped, and then went slowly to his knees. Rensevear got to the side of him and drew his foot back to kick. Yusupov started forward, but I caught his cuff.

Rensevear let fly a goal-making soccer kick at Compton's head, but Compton snapped his head back. Both hands shot forward and caught Rensevear's outstretched foot, and Compton twisted the ankle hard. Rensevear fell backward and cracked his spine on the edge of the bench. A few stifled groans of alarm went up from onlookers, followed by shushing. Rensevear tried to get up but went spastic and fell sprawling to his face on the floor. Compton, gritting his teeth savagely, was on top of him. He snatched up Rensevear's bloody head by the scalp and was preparing to smash it against the floor when a foot shot forward from the crowd and connected hard with Compton's groin. Compton let out a fierce shout, dropped Rensevear's head, sat back, vomited, then wet himself.

"Stop," Davidson shouted.

It was his foot.

Evers put a finger to his lips.

"You're going to kill each other," Davidson said in a hushed voice.

Compton rose slowly, wiping puke and blood from his mouth. Rensevear, groaning, lifted himself slowly to the bench and sat slumped. Colfax threw him a towel.

"Davidson is correct," Aubert said. "It is finished. That suffices."

"You three listen," Davidson said to Rensevear, Colfax, and Howard. "You weren't supposed to tell anybody. You told your supes anyway. That broke your word. You have to make up for that. These guys need two more weeks. You keep your mouths shut until then."

Rensevear, wiping blood, vomit, and urine from his chin and chest, said, "That's a tall order under the circumstances."

"I trusted you," Davidson said to all three. "You said you wouldn't tell anyone. You told the supes."

The three were silent. Then Rensevear, still mopping himself with the towel, said, "Two weeks. That's it. If it's still going on in two weeks, we report your whole stupid thing to Beetle."

Davidson looked to us.

"How do you trust them?" I asked him. "They already broke their word."

"They didn't give their word as gentlemen before," Davidson said. "They just promised." He turned back to them. "Do you give your word as gentlemen?"

They exchanged looks, then nodded to each other. "All right," Rensevear said, "you have our word. Two weeks."

I asked Davidson, "How do you know their word is any good?"

Davidson looked shocked. "They gave it as gentlemen."

"The nerve," Rensevear said.

"Can you imagine?" Colfax asked.

"Only from this guy," Howard said.

Yusupov stepped forward. "I accept your word." He shook hands solemnly with the three.

"Very good," Rensevear said.

"Excellent," Colfax said.

"Exactly right," Howard said.

I looked to Evers. "I suppose you want to know what this is about?"

He shrugged. "Not at all. But thank you for asking."

—

415

We were back in Nice at the end of dinner in a cozy bistro on a cold autumn evening. The visit had begun poorly. Ellen found the story about the fight with Rensevear, Colfax, and Howard ugly and unredeemed. I suppose I was disappointed.

"Why is the brain surgeon never with you?" I asked.

"He's a brain surgeon?"

"You never tell me why it's always Nice now," I said. "Is it a state secret?"

She put down knife and fork and waved for the waiter to take her plate.

"The good thing about you, Woodrow, has always been that you are not nosy."

"We talk about me all the time," I said. "I care about you as well."

"Not the deal," she said, looking over my shoulder for the check.

"Hey, listen, Ellen," I said, "you don't get out of here until I have my say."

"You don't think?"

"Please."

"So, say."

"The brain surgeon is an idiot. I told you that. You're a wonderful person. You're smart and funny. You have a heart, and you're drop-dead gorgeous. I want you to be having long tête-à-têtes with a handsome guy your own age who cares about you, not some geezer like me who always talks about himself."

She fell back into her chair. "I have tête-à-têtes. Don't worry about it."

"There's someone here."

She straightened again. "You know what, Woodrow, that's none of your business. You're getting out over your skis."

"My skis, eh? So what am I to you? Your excuse? Your beard?

You tell the brain surgeon you're going to Nice to see the old geezer again? Does he think you're writing a novel about me? It would have to be an encyclopedia by now. You know what your problem is. Too many men in your life."

"Oh, Woodrow," she said, unsmiling, "that's a little sad. So you see yourself as a rival."

It was sudden, unexpected. It hit home.

"And that's a bit unkind," I mumbled.

She made a small solemn laugh. "My mind is very much at ease." She rose and threw money on the table. "I'm really sorry you feel this way, Woodrow. Like I've been using you or something."

She put out a hand. I rose, took her hand, and bowed. I watched her through the window while the guy hailed a cab for her. I felt like shit.

•

The morning after the big brawl in Dorm Three, I walked back from Sunday morning chapel with Evers. A sparse dry snow swirled like dust. The sky was blanketed in blue-gray haze.

"That was quite a show you and the Russian put on the other night," he said.

"Why did you stick up for those three clowns?"

"What do you expect me to do, turn on my own dorm?"

He had a smooth certainty of speech that was a few years beyond what boys our age possessed.

"You're a southerner," I said.

"So what?"

"Why did you come here?"

"My father did. His father . . . "

We walked without speaking for a while.

I asked, "Do you like it here?"

"Sure. It's all right. It's a good school."

"Did you say you were from Little Rock?"

"I don't remember saying it, but I am."

"Isn't that where they had all that trouble, because people hate the Negroes?"

"Right," he scoffed, "like people here aren't racist. I never heard 'nigger' so much in all my life until I came to St. Philip's. And nobody up here even knows a colored person."

Our breath made frosty clouds as we walked up hill.

"I don't quite get what you are," Evers said. "You seem more like a southerner to me than one of them. But you're not. You don't talk like one of us. You don't talk like one of them, either."

"I'm not," I said. "I mean I am. We were. My people are from the south, but I'm not now. I'm from the middle of the west. You remind me more of my people than of these guys here."

"Well, you remind me more of us than them. You're descended from Daniel Boone, right?"

I laughed and almost stumbled. "No. That's not true. But we have a guy way back in the family who was sort of a partner with him."

"Anyway we're both just tourists here."

I laughed again. He had a funny way of saying serious things. A charm.

"I guess that's right," I said. "But you seem like you like it here?"

He took a while. "I guess so," he said. "It's OK. But the big thing about me, compared to a lot of these guys, I have a really happy family. I miss my mom and dad and my brothers a lot. Some of these guys . . . "

"Yeah," I said, "I notice the same thing. It's almost like being rich makes it worse."

"It doesn't help them much, I'll say that for sure. Man, some of these guys have got some messes at home. Those three you hate so much . . . "

"The stooges."

He laughed.

"Yeah. The stooges. From what I've picked up in the dorm, just listening to them talk to each other, I don't know why those guys would even go home."

•

That night we convened in Yusupov's alcove. "We are vulnerable," Yusupov said. "We must steal the initiative."

"How in the fuck do we do that?" I asked.

"Aha," Yusupov said with a finger in the air. "With theater."

"Oh, Christ," I said.

"I do not have a good feeling about this," Compton said.

Aubert muttered "L'opéra-comique, ça se peut."

Yusupov came closer to stand between us.

"Listen to me," he said. "The one thing that scares the shit out of Beetle is anything that gets to the rich parents or the rector or the trustees, right?"

We agreed.

"So we let him discover the starvation, like Barry said, but in a way that will make him fear a scandal capable of arousing the ire of the parents, the rector and the trustees. We must shock him. We must jar him so he loses all composure. There are two words that we want to hear blubbering from his fat goldfish lips."

We whispered in unison, "Preposterous poppycock."

"Precisely," Yusupov said. "And we want to hear it in the dining room where everyone else will see and hear."

"How?" we all asked.

"I've been thinking. The answer, I think, is Oliver Twist."

We had to convince Beetle, he said, that we were on the verge of starvation, perhaps death, and that it was his fault. Yusupov had already selected Davidson to play the most important part, because of his slight stature and childlike countenance.

"Davidson's not with us," I said.

"I have spoken with him," Yusupov said. "He's come around. He says that we have respected his feelings for the school. He knows it was dishonorable of him to blab. He wants to atone by doing this for us."

Yusupov explained that Davidson would carefully rehearse to deliver his lines without the least stammer or hesitation. The performance was set for Saturday breakfast two weekends from now, with the Schmitzes absent from the table and the supes away at a lacrosse game.

"Davidson is Oliver Twist?" Compton asked.

"Precisely," Yusupov said.

"So Davidson says, 'Please, sir, another bowl of porridge?'" Compton asked.

We all snickered, except for Yusupov, who suddenly tensed.

"That is not the line," he said. "Everyone always says that. It is wrong. Oliver Twist never says anything about a bowl of porridge."

"Yes, he does, asshole," Compton said, his face reddening. "That's the whole point. The kid is starving."

"Wait, wait," Aubert said. "Yusupov, do you have the book?"

"Of course I do." Yusupov whipped a large volume from the

shelf above his clothes rack and flipped it open to a page marked by a scrap of paper. "Please allow." And he began to read us the words of Dickens.

"The line," he said, "is, 'Please, sir, I want some more.'"

He read the entire scene. When he had finished, we sat in silence for a long while. Outside the alcove, boys were teasing and gossiping with each other as usual.

Finally Aubert said, "I consider, Yusupov, that you are a genius."

"It's great," Compton said. "But we're not using those exact words."

"No, no, not at all," Yusupov said. "The words must match the occasion. It is not the words that matter. You see, in Dickens's scene, there is not even a mention of porridge as people suppose. It's the pathetic quality that provides the scene its power. A poor starving orphan is begging for more food."

"And you think that will make Beetle pity us?" I asked.

We all shook our heads no.

"Beetle is a dishonorable asshole," Compton said. "He'll never pity anybody but himself."

"Pontiac," Yusupov said, "pity is not the point. As Compton says, that is an impossibility. The point is to make Beetle fear scandal."

"And we do that how?" I asked.

"The same way one gets to Carnegie Hall. Practice, practice, practice."

We rehearsed in the bathroom. Davidson did a poor job at first, but Yusupov was relentless.

"Davidson," he said, "you must see this role as a chance to achieve greatness. If you do this well, if it works the way we intend, you will be our salvation."

"You'll be a fucking hero," Compton said. "You'll go down in the history of St. Philip's School. Maybe not the official version."

"OK, I am Beetle," Yusupov said, sitting on a toilet in an open stall where he read from notes on his lap. "You come to me."

Davidson approached.

"Eyes downward," Yusupov said. "You are hesitant. You are afraid."

Davidson did a rather melodramatic expression of fear and hesitation, his eyes cast down.

"Now your lines," Yusupov said.

"Mr. Frick," Davidson bleated.

"Too much," Yusupov interrupted. "You sound like a goat. He'll see right through it."

"Sir," Davidson said, taking it down a notch, "several of the boys have games and races today, and the Schmitzes are not at the table. We're all pretty hungry and kind of weak. I just wondered if we could have a bowl of oatmeal."

"Good, good," Yusupov said. "That's a lot closer. Now, I'm Beetle, and I say, 'Blubba blubba, what kind of nonsense, hubba bubba.' And you say . . . "

"If we could just have oatmeal, sir. We're not asking for bacon or eggs."

We all looked at each other.

"Pretty damn good," Compton said.

"By George, I think he's got it," Gellhorn said.

"Très bien," Aubert said.

"All right," Yusupov said, "at this point, Beetle jumps up and starts in with preposterous poppycock, cockerous poppywobble, et cetera, and so on. And you?"

"I what?" Davidson asked. "I used all my lines already."

"Oh my God," Yusupov shouted, leaping from the toilet seat and slapping himself in the forehead. Pacing furiously, he roared, "Am I completely wasting my time on you people? Are you all tone deaf?"

We shushed him and pointed toward the supes' apartment.

"They'll hear you," I said.

He shook his head several times, slapping his pages of notes against a thigh.

Then in a soft mutter of exasperation, he said to Davidson, "At that point, you will have no more lines. We hope you will not need anymore, because when Beetle starts his preposterous poppycock, he's already beginning to panic. You simply step out of his way and gaze back to the table. It's kind of like pointing with your eyes, but you do not really point."

Yusupov told the rest of us to stand in a line by the sinks, facing the wall. Then, in the role of Beetle, he bustled up behind us, waving the notes behind him like Beetle's napkin. "What is this preposterous poppycock that Davidson is nattering on about? I see you all have your bloody oatmeal. Why don't you eat it then? Is there something wrong with it?"

We remained silent, heads bowed as rehearsed.

"I asked you a question, goddamn it. You, Gellhorn, why aren't you eating?"

"Sir," Gellhorn said calmly, "we're not allowed to eat. Someone at our table has misbehaved, and the guilty person refuses to confess, so Herr Schmitz has no choice but to starve us. We haven't eaten any food in a month."

"Blundering poppy wobble!" Yusupov said in an excellent impersonation. "This is absolute hockey pobble! Haven't eaten in a month? This is rubbish-a-bubbish. Of course you've eaten. No boy at St. Philip's School ever goes hungry. I've been sitting right up there at the head table. I would have noticed."

"All right," I said, "this is the part that worries me, where he starts grilling us. He starts getting into what Jake knew and what the supes knew. He's building a case."

Aubert said, "Pontiac makes a point that is evident. If Beetle comes to the table . . . "

"When he comes to the table . . ." Yusupov corrected.

"When he comes to the table," Aubert went on, "he may demand certain evidence that will plunge us in a spiral."

No one said anything for a long while.

"I have asked you . . ." Yusupov began.

"We can't do that," I interrupted. "We can't make ourselves cry. Beetle will see through it. We're too old. We're not cry-babies."

"We're not very old," Yusupov said. "We are still boys."

"Bullshit," Compton said. "I'm not a fucking boy."

"Me either," I said.

"Well," Yusupov said, shrugging, "I never was."

"So what do we say when he comes to the table?" I asked.

"Let me think," Yusupov said. "I may have a plan. In the meantime, I think we're going to have Aubert deliver the longer speech about not being able to eat."

"Why him?" Gellhorn asked.

"Gravitas."

Chapter Eight

ON THE DAY OF THE ASSAULT, we assembled in the bathroom an hour before the rest of the dorm would wake up. Yusupov had a little tin of grease paint he had smuggled out of the theater department that he wanted to smear on our faces. We all objected, but he insisted that painting our faces was a necessary part of the plot. The paint was grayish. It went onto our cheeks in gobs at first. We looked in the mirrors, and Compton whispered, "We look like dead clowns."

Yusupov came around to each of us in turn, smoothing out the blobs of gray with his fingers, leaning back to shrewdly appraise, then going after it again, smoothing and spreading until he had each of us done to his satisfaction. When we looked in the mirrors again, we were all quite impressed. No paint was visible on our faces, yet Yusupov had given us all the convincing appearance of imminent death.

When we entered the dining room, everything looked in order. The Schmitzes were absent, as were the supes. Our table was set with plates and oatmeal bowls. The waiters, Smiley and Bear, were standing by the table with trays under their arms, waiting to fetch the oatmeal from the kitchen after grace had been said.

But Beetle and his wife did not appear. We all looked to Yusupov. He put his nose in the air, shrugged, and said, "Stick to the plan."

Rutledge rose from the head table and chanted the grace like a timetable. Smiley and Davidson stood riveted to the spot, looking wide-eyed at Yusupov with their trays clapped under their arms like penguin wings.

"Get the fucking oatmeal," he muttered menacingly.

They hurried to the kitchen to join the line of other waiters waiting for their porridge. When they brought it back and placed it on the table, Yusupov said, "Serve yourselves your oatmeal." We did so. Then we sat on our hands and stared at our bowls.

Normally, our waiters cleared the untouched bowls when the waiters at the other tables began clearing their empty dishes. But on this occasion, when the process of clearing began at the other tables, Beetle and his wife still had not appeared at the head table. Bear rose to begin taking our full bowls back out to the kitchen to dump them, but Yusupov hissed, "Stop. We need the oatmeal."

Gellhorn leaned toward him and whispered, "If Beetle shows up, we can do it with the ham and eggs."

"No," Yusupov insisted. "It has to be the oatmeal."

We sat staring speechless at our oatmeal for what seemed an eon, and then Smiley whispered, "They're here. Beetle and his wife just came in."

"Don't look," Yusupov snapped. "Smiley, you are in the best position. You watch Beetle and tell us what he's doing. Everyone else continue to stare at your bowls."

Smiley gave us a running commentary through clenched teeth like a bad ventriloquist: "He's seating Mrs. Frick. He hasn't sat down himself yet. He's gone down the table to have a big yuck with

Rutledge. OK, he's back to his chair. He's sitting down. He's down. They've passed the ham and eggs to Mrs. Frick already, and now he's dishing himself up a big fat pile. What a pig. He's eating. He's slopping down coffee. He's surveying the dining room."

"All right, Davidson," Yusupov said. "Go."

Davidson did not move.

"Go," Yusupov said.

Davidson remained motionless in his chair.

"I can't do it," he whispered.

"Fucking do it," Compton hissed.

"He'll see through it," Davidson said in a desperate whisper. "He'll see we have on makeup. We will all be expelled. I don't want to leave St. Philip's and have to go home to my drunk mother."

"Davidson," I said, "you are our one and only hope. It's time for you to be a hero."

He rose very slowly, turned toward the head table as if toward death and walked forward at a near-stumbling half-pace. He was supposed to climb the steps to the dais and stand behind Beetle for his speech, but he made it only as far as the floor in front of the dais so that Beetle, already alarmed by Davidson's shambling approach, had to lean forward to hear what Davidson was saying below him.

"Davidson is staring at his shoes," Smiley reported with his jaw still clenched so that "shoes" came out wetly and more like "chutes."

"Please, sir," Yusupov whispered to himself. "I want some more."

"Beetle is smiling at the others and saying something to Davidson."

"Rubbish dubbish hubba bubba," Yusupov whispered.

The dining room fell silent as everyone, masters, their wives and students turned to watch spellbound the unfolding drama at the head table.

"Now Davidson is talking. I can almost hear him. He said something about the oatmeal. OK, here it comes." Smiley dropped the clenched whisper and spoke plainly, excitedly. "Beetle looks like his eyes are about to pop out of his head. He's grabbing his napkin. He's about to jump up."

We all whispered in unison with Beetle's scream: "Preposterous poppycock!"

We turned to see Davidson execute a balletic pivot, then point with his little chin straight back to our table. Beetle followed his gaze and came thrashing down the steps and across the dining room in our direction, napkin flailing furiously at his helm.

"Steady now," Yusupov whispered.

Beetle pulled up just behind Compton, me, and Gellhorn.

"What is this nonsense about oatmeal?" he demanded. "You all have your oatmeal. Why haven't you eaten? Is there something off about it? What's the matter?"

Aubert, with his back to Beetle, said, "One is not allowed to eat the porridge, sir."

"What? Then eat your ham and eggs. Get on with it. Why are you all sitting here like fenceposts staring at your food? I don't understand. Davidson is up here nattering on like an imbecile about sports today and how you're all weak because you haven't eaten. Preposterous."

"One is unable to eat," Aubert said.

For an agonizingly long while, all I could hear behind me was Beetle wheezing and snuffling. Then, with perfect timing and just as we'd rehearsed, Aubert rose.

"Monsieur Frick," he said with funereal gloom, "I am very

sad to report that a person at our table who is unknown to us has behaved very badly by distempering the food. Herr Schmitz had no choice but to punish us by withholding our meals until this person was made known. We believe that Herr Schmitz is wise and just in imposing this punishment, but it is true that we are somewhat weakened because we have not had regular meals in some weeks . . ."

"Some weeks!" Beetle blurted. "That is absurd. That is a lie."

The room was silent. He wheeled around furiously.

"This is none of your goddamn business!" he shouted to the dining room in general, vigorously snapping and flapping the napkin in all directions as if to ward off evil. He hurried to Herr Schmitz's chair and sat down heavily, peering at us.

"This is a misunderstanding," he muttered. "A mistake has been made. Surely you've had meals . . . "

Leaning out to face him, Yusupov said solemnly, "Not for a month, sir."

Beetle stared at Yusupov's face with wide-eyed shock. We all turned our faces toward him, and he examined each of us for a long, riveted moment, one after the other.

"Are you . . . are you not well?" he whispered almost inaudibly.

"It has not been comforting," Aubert said. "But we again admire Herr Schmitz, and we are pleased to obey him."

Beetle surveyed our faces in silence. His breathing had become even more labored, and his eyes were bright red.

"Who are the waiters here?" he asked. "You!" he said to me brusquely. "Go get these boys their ham and eggs."

"I'm not a waiter, sir."

"Goddamn it!" he shouted, "I said go and get these boys their ham and eggs!"

"Do it," Yusupov whispered.

I departed for the kitchen with Bear stepping along smartly behind me with his tray.

Jake came to the window.

"Beetle knows?" he asked in alarm.

"He thinks we're starving to death," I said. "He's about to shit his brains out."

"Does he know?" Jake asked, nodding back toward the staff, all of whom were listening intently.

"Not a word," I said. "We're not rats."

A rumble of approval went up from the staff while Jake heaped our trays with absurd quantities of ham and eggs. As we returned with Jake's bounty, we saw the entire dining room was pretending not to watch intently. We set down the trays, sat down ourselves, and began the last part of what had been rehearsed.

Beetle was still in Herr Schmitz's place, nattering on almost to himself, something about Herr Schmitz being a fine man but a European with a different sense of decorum and discipline and how mistakes could be made by the best of us and so on. Ignoring him, we did not take the trouble of serving the ham and eggs onto our plates but reached directly into the serving bowls with our hands, smashing great gobs of food into our mouths. Gellhorn reprised his act with the biscuits and chewed so vigorously that rivers of half-masticated ham and egg flowed from the corners of his mouth.

"Stop it!" Beetle shouted. "Good God, you're not dogs!"

We all stopped eating. Gellhorn wiped his face on his forearm and sat back heavily. To our wonder, we saw tears rolling down his cheeks.

"I'm so ashamed," Gellhorn said. "I never thought anything could make me behave like this."

He was wonderful.

Everyone but Smiley started crying. Yusupov was actually sobbing.

Pleading, Beetle said, "Boys, boys, please don't cry. St. Philip's boys do not cry. Now then. You can eat your ham and eggs like civilized human beings, can you not? With knives and forks from your plates, for God's sake? From your plates, please."

Yusupov cleared his throat in an emphatic signal to the rest of us that the crying needed to stop. He served his own plate, indicating that we should do the same. Beetle sat watching, nodding enthusiastic approval.

"Sir," Granger said, "Are we allowed to have milk?"

"Good God," Beetle barked at me, "get back to the kitchen and bring these boys their milk at once." He ordered Smiley and Bear to follow me and fetch more milk.

Jake was hovering anxiously by the window. He put out his palms in impatient question. I gave a thumbs up.

Back at the table, Beetle was questioning the boys about whether any of them had informed a parent of the misunderstanding. Roosevelt explained that Herr Schmitz had warned us not to speak of it to our parents or to anyone else lest the whole thing blow up into something bigger, resulting in multiple expulsions.

"Well," Beetle said, shaking his head, flapping his jowls, nodding his head up and down, "I would, uh . . . yes, I think, even though Herr Schmitz is a European and may be unfamiliar, he is certainly a very wise man for whom I have great respect, and, yes, this is true, exactly. If this were to go to the parents, it might . . . "

"Go to the rector," Roosevelt interrupted.

"Precisely," Beetle said. "Yes. It might. And then, it's the sort of thing, if it went to the rector, who knows, it could even . . . "

"Go to the trustees," Gellhorn said.

Beetle froze to the spot, rigid. For a very long while he did not move a muscle. The noise of his labored breathing washed over us like a cold surf. Finally, he looked up with a shrewd smile and examined us one by one, his eyes resting longer on me.

"You boys have thought this through a bit," he said. "Have you not?"

We said nothing.

"Well, then," he said with prim conviction, "I assume we agree we don't want this business to go any further than it has already. I will speak to Herr Schmitz. After that has been settled, we will not discuss the matter again, none of us with anyone. And I doubt that anyone will be expelled."

"Wow, sir," Compton said, "that's a load off our minds. Even Pontiac won't get kicked out?"

"Pontiac? You mean Skaggs here. Why do you single him out?"

"Well, you know," Compton said. "He's a scholarship boy."

"I said no one would be expelled. That includes the very dapper Mr. Skaggs." Beetle rose very slowly from the table, taking up his napkin. "You will excuse me."

"Yes, sir."

We all rose to see him off.

Instead of returning to the head table, Beetle walked out through the double doors. I followed. He was halfway up the corridor, past the kitchen and pantry, waddling briskly toward the lobby. I went quietly to catch up without being seen. He crossed the lobby to the far side and began descending the staircase. I watched from above. I had never seen him on the main staircase before. Clutching the railing, he stumbled down the stairs so clumsily I thought he might fall.

The fence across the top of the landing was solid with a white wainscoting so that by stooping a bit, I could hide and poke my nose and eyes just over the handrail with a view straight down into the first-floor lobby to the door of Herr Schmitz's apartment.

Beetle went to the door and pounded hard several times. Herr Schmitz appeared in a bathrobe of some kind, his hair sticking out in all directions. He peered over Beetle's shoulders as if hunting for fire. I heard two "preposterous poppycock"s in quick succession, met by Herr Schmitz's pathetic murmuring. Then suddenly Frau Schmitz appeared at her spouse's side. She had no eyebrows. Her eyes were black buttons on an oval void, her mouth a small dark slash like the face of a neglected doll. She emitted a brusque shriek. I made out my own name, Pontiac, and the word "shit."

Her shriek seemed to drive Beetle mad. He bounced up and down like an angry infant, flapping his jowls and gesticulating wildly with an arm.

I heard him say, "Can't bloody starve them to death for Christ's sake."

Frau Schmitz grew even more shrill, her little mouth working like an angry eel, until Beetle seemed suddenly frightened of her. He took a step backward, then another as she pursued him into the lobby clad in something that looked like hastily wrapped window drapery. Then Beetle stood his ground, sucked down a long deep breath, and blew it back out noisily through his gills. With the little fat fists at his sides and braying like a donkey, he bellowed, "They have us over a fucking barrel, you kraut dolts!"

Both Schmitzes went abruptly silent. Frau Schmitz stared at Beetle, stupefied. Then, as if manipulated by an autonomic force, the little black button eyes began to drift very slowly upward, until finally, like sparks leaping the universe, they met mine. I lifted three fingers and gave a tiny wave, then withdrew.

As I raced back down the corridor, I heard a raucous roar erupt in the dining room.

•

Two weeks later we were killing time before going into the dining room for dinner. Bear and Granger approached me to talk. Both wanted to give me sole credit for the victory, which I modestly but insincerely declined. I was about to walk away when Bear locked his arm around my neck from behind. Granger slammed shut the dorm's double doors, and Gellhorn and Aubert grabbed my arms. Together they wrestled me into the bathroom.

Davidson was at the far end filling a metal trash barrel with steaming hot water from a shower head. I kicked, but Smiley and Yusupov were quickly able to pull off my trousers and underpants and efficiently cinch my legs at the ankles with a belt. Someone else cinched my wrists behind me with a necktie.

I fought and called for help because I was afraid. When they were painting my balls with blue markers, I felt anger and humiliation. The moment they stuffed me into the metal barrel full of scalding water, the ritual alchemy of astringent ink, tender skin and hot water flared into a burn, and I screamed.

They rolled me out into the dorm in the barrel. Cheering faces swirled above me chanting, and everything became a splashing vortex of sharp pain, sound, eyes, mouths, waving arms and prancing knees. The only boy I focused on was Davidson who was jumping up and down, pointing at me and laughing wildly. When I saw him, the fire in my balls flamed hotter, and I laughed harder than I had ever laughed in all my life.

A cold shower and scrubbing with a rag did not remove the blue ink from my balls, but it mainly quieted the burn. I put on a coat and tie and followed the others into dinner.

•

The Schmitzes never reappeared at our table, their place taken by Mr. Zierotin, the math teacher and assistant rowing coach. The balance of the term was uneventful. Beetle and I went out of our way to avoid each other, but, in those few moments when we were unavoidably thrust into proximity, he always stopped, gave an almost imperceptible tip of the head, and saluted me as, "the very dapper Mr. Skaggs." I always gave him a small bow and addressed him as "Mr. Frick, sir."

—

We were at our hotdog stand in Nice. Our meeting was off to a worse start already than the last. She was in her foul blunt mood.

"You never talk about your multiple marriages," she said out of the blue with something like a sneer.

"Only two. Before that, I was engaged once, very briefly to a French farmer's daughter in Aix. I was not yet nineteen, and she was barely eighteen. That did not happen, thanks to the farmer."

"Lucky for you."

"I have no idea. I still see her now once in a while in the market, and she pretends not to know me. I think she's why I am still there."

"Did she look like me when she was young?"

I was embarrassed. "Yes. A lot."

"I figured."

"Oh, did you?"

"Well, Woodrow, I didn't have to be Sherlock Holmes. So who else is on the roster?"

"My first marriage, very ill-advised, was to a crazy girl I knew from Harvard. That was during my hotshot commodities years. The only other marriage lasted a few years, to a lovely woman, a fellow academic. We eventually agreed we weren't cut out for each other."

It was mid-July and a little too warm. The street was dusty. Ellen fidgeted, clinking her frosty bottle of beer on the metal tabletop.

"After all this talk about St. Philips, do you think you learned anything there," she said, "or took anything away from the school that was of value?"

"Some of the values were of value. I think they have stood me in good stead over the years, helped me get through. I learned how to win without gloating. How to lose without whining. How to shake hands at the end of a good fight. The difference between a good one and a bad one."

"Couldn't you have learned those same values somewhere else?"

"Sure. Maybe prison. But I have to say, I never ran into those values much before St. Philip's, and I've seen precious little of them in the world since."

"And those are upper-class values?"

"Tend to be. That's one of the things I find so irritating about the upper classes. Sometimes they're right."

"Are you upper class?"

"Me? No. I'm just a rich guy."

"If you're so rich and you went to school with them and you know how they act, couldn't you be upper class, too, if you wanted to? Is it just because of your lowly birth, your blood?"

I gazed out into the action on the street. A small crew in a city van had pulled up not far. They piled out, three men and a woman, and began examining a badly bent stop sign.

"You know," I said, "it's that but not only that. I still hang out with them some. We're friends. It's more about who and what you are, versus who and what you are not. We're all tiny windblown spores before we're born, and we fall to earth randomly. It's a question of what you do with where you land."

She chuckled softly. "You're very resigned in some ways, Woodrow. So where you land is what you really are, forever?"

"Sort of. So what? Why are you so antsy today?"

"One more question."

"OK."

"Couldn't you just be Jewish?"

"I'd have to check it out. Ellen, what's the matter?"

She shrugged, moped, turned away, mumbled. I couldn't hear her over traffic.

"I'm sorry, what did you say?" I asked.

When she turned back, her eyes were moist—the closest she had ever come to tears in my presence.

"Things are sort of sad. Happy and sad." she said.

"What's going on?"

"All that time I thought he was preoccupied with his practice, with medicine, that he was just a medical nerd and that's why he didn't have time for me."

"Oh, shit," I said. "He was preoccupied with somebody."

"Quite a somebody. Oncologist. Five years my junior."

"I'm so sorry."

"A very hot oncologist," she said.

"I'm having trouble getting a picture."

"Believe me. Very beautiful. The wife of one of our best friends."

"Oh, Christ. I'm so sorry, Ellen. But the brain surgeon is a fucking moron."

"Um. Well. I may be one, too."

A gaggle of schoolgirls pranced by our table, laughing and shrieking like magpies. We watched them swoop and dive into the distance.

"I'm a little confused," I said. "Are you or are you not bereft?"

She made clicking sounds on the table with her perfectly painted nails. "I don't think I qualify as bereft. There has been someone here in Nice. It's why I've been here so much the last couple of years. Someone I'm seeing. More than seeing. Quite involved. Sorry to just drop this on you like a ton of bricks."

"I had surmised."

"Oh, had you?"

"Well, Ellen, I didn't have to be Sherlock Holmes."

She snickered in an impossibly cute way that I found encouraging.

I walked over to the hotdog stand. As a concession to the international trade, the proprietor had agreed to chill his beer in a tub of ice. I brought back two frosty bottles and two fresh glasses. Ellen grabbed a beer and took a long draught straight from the bottle.

"We want to get married," she said.

"Is he French?"

"Yes."

"Where would you live?"

"Here."

"Oh, goody."

She laughed and took both of my hands. "You could move in with us."

"I don't know yet if this guy has enough class for me."

"He's an academic. I think he has some family money. He's not poor. He lives in a lovely apartment. He's smart and handsome and tough and very sweet to me."

"Jewish?"

"Totally."

"Married?"

"Once. His wife died. He has kids, girls, ten and thirteen. I love them to bits. They adore me. His father died when he was young, and he's very close to his mother. She lives with them."

I shook my head gravely. "I'm not the world's biggest fan of mothers."

"Oh, me either, but this one is wonderful, and she's my own biggest fan. She's my advocate. She wants him to marry me."

"Ellen, I am so happy for you. So happy."

"It's just the getting it done. The lawyers. The property. At least there were no kids. I just hate this part of it. I can't imagine how bad it would be if we weren't both at fault. Things are so much easier when everyone is to blame."

"Gosh, that should be written in needlepoint somewhere."

"Oh, Woodrow," she said dreamily. "Where would I be without you?"

"I cannot even imagine."

•

On a Sunday after lunch, I was on the bed in my alcove studying when Compton came in, bewildered.

"Can we go for a walk?"

"It's snowing," I said.

"So what?"

I pulled on galoshes. "Why do you want to go for a walk with me all of a sudden? Are you going to go mental and try to cave in my skull?"

"Only if you pull your fucking Puerto Rican switchblade on me."

"Deal," I said, putting on my parka and gloves.

The snow on the ground was fresh and deep. We skirted behind the Lower along the edge of the frozen pond into the woods behind the New Chapel. The trail was white and fallow, marked here and there by soft hieroglyphics left by rabbit paws. To our right, a deep pinewoods disappeared in gloom, and to our left, the wind dragged long curtains of snow across a gleaming marble floor of black ice. In the distance the boards of the empty hockey rinks rose like a ghost city.

As soon as we entered the trail, thick silence fell over us, broken only by the crunch of our boots and the occasional distant trill of a cardinal. Twenty minutes up the trail, we came to a stone bench on the edge of the ice. Compton swept snow off with his gloved hand and nodded we should sit.

I said, "OK," and sat next to him. "Now what?"

"I need to ask you something."

"What?"

"What is high school like?"

"What?"

"What do you mean what? Public high school. Am I not speaking English here?"

I turned and saw the eyes beginning to dilate. I got up to leave.

"Fuck this, Compton, I didn't come out here to get beaten up. What happened, somebody hit you in the head with a hockey stick or something? You're acting weird as hell."

He caught my cuff. "Don't go."

I snatched my sleeve free.

"This is serious," he said. "Please."

I was stunned. I had never before heard the words, serious or please, from Compton's lips. I sat back down.

"Why do you give a shit what public high school is like?"

"I'm not coming back after Spring break. I have to go to public high school in Queens. I want to know if I can make it there or if I'm just going to get killed the first day by Puerto Ricans."

"Different high schools are different," I said. "You're not coming back?"

"My dad's going to prison."

I stared at him for a long moment. He wouldn't turn to meet my eye. His face was tight.

"I've known about it for a couple years, sort of," he muttered to the ice. "They never told me, but part of it was in the newspaper. Rensevear, Colfax, and Howard got in trouble at Peck for teasing me about it. I'm sure they told everybody in Dorm Three."

"What happened?"

He shook his head. "You know my dad's a big deal Wall Street lawyer, right? Anyway, he got in some crooked deal with a banker about Greek ships or something. I have no idea what it was."

He rose and paced the snow before me. "They've been fighting it all this time, but I always sort of knew it was going to be bad. I heard my parents arguing. My mother kept saying, 'If you're such a hotshot lawyer, why can't you beat it?' That really pissed him off. He'd go into this big thing about look at all the things he's done

441

for this family. I got the picture we were always on thin ice. Now it turns out the banker guy is already in prison for something like twelve years. I think my dad ratted him out. He only has to go to prison for eighteen months. But he has to pay this huge fine to the government."

He turned to me, and his face was ghastly. "We don't even have our farm anymore. It's sold. There are other people living on it already. My mom was already living in some shit apartment in Queens when she came up here to take us to dinner."

He picked up a snow-laden pinecone and skipped it out over the ice. "A friend of theirs got her a job as head of bookkeeping for a hospital."

"Does she even know how to do that?"

"That's what she did before they got married. She only went to college for a year. She was a bookkeeper at the law firm where my dad worked before he went out on his own."

He stood facing me, his lower lip trembling "That's not all. I have to work at the hospital after school. I'll be a bedpan guy like Doc Herter's wife." He slumped to the bench at my side, and I saw a tear starting at his cheek.

"Wait a minute," I said. "Are you crying because you have to work?"

He wiped his cheek with his sleeve and snuffled. "Wouldn't you?"

"No. Not about a job. I've had lots of jobs. I earned my own clothes to come here."

"It looked like it."

"Jesus, Compton, most of the world works. You worked on your farm. I've seen you work on work squad. You know how to work. You're good at it."

442

"That's not the same," he said plaintively. "Being a bedpan guy is like being a wombat."

I hesitated before telling him. "Compton, when my mother came here, she told me, if I flunked out, I couldn't come home. I had to stay here and become a wombat."

"So what?"

"You're sitting here about to start crying like a little girl because you might have to be a wombat. I almost did have to become a wombat, if I hadn't learned how to grind to get my grades up."

"Your becoming a wombat is totally different from me," he said.

"Why?"

"You're already a wombat."

I jumped up. "Fuck you. I wish to hell I did have a switchblade right now so I could cut your heart out and eat it in front of you." I stalked off down the path toward the New Chapel. He jumped up and scuffled behind me.

"Wait a minute, Pontiac. Please. I need to talk to you. I'm sorry. Please."

I stopped but kept my face ahead, not facing him.

"I'm scared," he said behind me. "I need to know if the high school guys are just going to kill me on my first day."

I really didn't want to answer him. I resisted for a long while. But it was cold. I turned around. "Look, Compton, do you feel like you can handle me in a fight?"

"With one hand tied behind my back. Maybe both hands."

"All right. I'm a wombat. I'm a public high school guy. I have galoshes, not L.L.Bean boots. And you're right, you can handle me. You can handle high school guys no sweat. In fact, of all the guys in this stupid school, I would say you could handle public high school guys better than anybody."

He was unbelieving, astonished. "Is that really true or are you just saying it?"

We moved briskly back to the trailhead, Compton clomping along behind me in his L.L.Bean boots. I pointed around to the beautiful pond, the woods, the chapel looming in the distance.

"All this, the buildings, the way they have the sluice all walled in, the ponds, everything, this is all bullshit."

"Fake, you mean."

"Yes. Fake. Rich people fake. Not the real world. This is a post-card. It's a dream world. It's not the real world. It's where rich kids come so they can be protected from the real world. You get that. None of these other guys get it."

"Roosevelt maybe," he said.

"Maybe. But you do. Because you're smart. You're smarter than all these guys. Plus, you're tough. You're the one guy who could make it in the real world. You and maybe Evers. Evers for sure."

When we got back to the Lower, we stopped in the first-floor lobby to stamp the snow off our boots and shake out our coats. I asked him what Queens was like.

"It's horrible, I think," he said. "I've never been there. But it's where people like cops and firemen have to live because they're not smart enough to live in on the Upper East Side."

Back in the dorm, we sat on the radiator bench at our end of the dorm.

I said, "You know your theory about how people like cops and firemen are too dumb to live in the rich part of New York? I'd keep shit like that under my hat for a while when you get to Queens."

"Good information. Check."

444

We went to our alcoves. I wanted to study. I tried for a while but couldn't. I went over to his alcove. He was on his bed, reading. I sat on the end of the bed.

"How do you feel about your dad going to prison?" I asked.

He closed his book.

"My mother thinks I should be crying all the time for the son of a bitch."

"You're not sad."

"I just hate his guts. I think he's stupid. He's the one who should have to go to Queens, not us. He fucked us all up. He acts like such a big shot all the time, like nobody can touch him, like we're so far beneath him. And then, bang. He fucks us. He's in prison. Instead of going to Harvard, I have to go be a bedpan guy for the rest of my life."

I laughed.

He sat up straight. "Are you laughing about it?" He was angry, about to jump off the bed.

"Yes."

"What's funny?"

"You. You're not going to be a bedpan guy the rest of your life, for Christ's sake. A guy like you? Believe me. You're going to go out there, kick ass and get richer than anybody else at this fucked up school, probably richer than anybody from this place ever did."

"How do I do that when I'm a bedpan guy?"

"Keep your eyes open," I said. I gave him a long look, trying not to laugh. "And keep your nose out of the bedpan."

We both laughed.

"Hey, Pontiac," he said. "You did the big thing. You're the one who got to Beetle."

"We all did it."

"Yeah, but you were the one who finished them off. You put the Schmitzes and Beetle over the edge. You have it made here already. It didn't take you that long. Two terms is all. You got your grades up. You stood up for yourself. Guys respect you. You earned it. You're not a mooch anymore."

"I was never a fucking mooch."

"I know, I know. Sorry. Anyway you're not one anymore. If you keep your grades up."

—

Ellen scanned the white boats in the harbor bobbing up and down like sheep in a pen.

"You know what I found myself wondering the other day," she asked. "Did Compton wind up going to Harvard like the rest of you?"

"No. Community college, then NYU for some kind of minor half-assed business degree, then straight out onto the mean streets of Queens."

"But he owns that hospital chain now."

"No. I mean, yes. Compton is the principal in a fund that owns a holding company that owns chains of hospitals all over the world, including the one in Chicago where the brain surgeon plies his grisly trade. Compton never goes public, and he's rabidly private about his own wealth, but I happen to know that he is one of the world's biggest players in private healthcare."

"And you know this because?"

"I see the reports. I've been a major stakeholder from the

get-go. He came to me and Stick early on. He owned a couple of rip-off dental clinics that exploited black people and Puerto Ricans in Queens and Brooklyn. He wanted to buy a crappy chain of small rural clinics in Texas and Louisiana. He'd already been through a bankruptcy. The only people who would lend him money were the Mafia, which he was seriously considering doing and which he may already have done to get the dental clinics. We staked him big-time, but we took a major pound of flesh out of him in terms of our future share."

"And the two of you still have your original stakes?"

"I have mine. He pushed Stick out long ago. It was brutal. They'll never speak again."

"Why not you?"

"He's not allowed to push me out."

"According to what?"

"The vow."

"You mean your boyhood vow in the infirmary?"

"Best vow I ever made."

She sipped her espresso and gazed out over the harbor. "I think I still don't get WASPs. If it's all about blood, about being from the right family tree and so on, why on earth would Compton, of all people, be king of the WASPs now, throwing these lavish parties like the one where we met in Chicago, and all the rest of them coming in from the far corners. Given the background you've told me about, scraping around with scammy community clinics and borrowing money from the Mafia and all of that, they should look down on him. Right?"

I thought about it. "Right. I know. It doesn't really hold together. But what they really care about is money and then, after that, manners. Compton has both now. His parents almost did. His father was sort of half WASPy, rowed at Yale and so on, but he got de-WASPed when he went to prison. His mother was always a wannabe."

"WASP-a-be," she said.

We both snorted and laughed.

"Compton throws these big shindigs all over the world," I said, "and he pops for the orchestra, the booze, the venue and so on."

"Generous of him."

"He knows what he's doing. He's always raising capital. He tells me he makes out pretty well on most of his parties. Lately he's been bitching that the WASPs are running out of money. He's learning Mandarin."

"You guys are getting up there. Won't Compton get tired of making money and just want to retire and relax?"

"I wish he could relax. I worry about him a lot. I got him to come visit me in Aix, but that was a disaster. He was on the phone every waking moment. We argued. I couldn't wait for him to leave. He's one of those guys who will die in the saddle. I knew another guy like that—family was rich, went bust, lost all their money when the kid was an adolescent. It does something to them. For the rest of their lives, there isn't enough money for them in all the world."

"He throws a nice party."

"He does do that."

•

On the last day of the term when it was time to go, I sat on Compton's bed, trying to find a way to say goodbye. He asked me what I was going to do over Spring break.

"It's not going to be too much fun," I said. "I have to try to get my brother out of juvie."

"Juvie? You mean your bother is in prison?"

"Kind of."

"Christ. What a family." He handed me his most recent bribe box, unopened. "Take it. I don't want it."

I got up, went to my alcove, and put the box under my bunk. When I returned to Compton's alcove, Gellhorn came in, sat down heavily between us, and said nothing.

Compton said to me, "He knows I'm not coming back."

"I have my own problems," Gellhorn said. "I'm not coming down on the train to Boston with you guys. Beetle just told me. My mother is about to show up. She's taking me to Manchester airport in a cab, and then we're flying on a chartered plane to Boston. Then we fly to Chicago and then rent a car and go somewhere out west for a week."

"Why?" Compton asked.

Gellhorn shook his head and was silent for a long while before answering. "I am being taken to meet the great man. My real father."

"Hemingway!" I blurted. "Cool!"

"It's not cool," he said. "At all. It's some kind of emergency because he's sick. I think he's crazy. They're trying to get him not to kill himself. I don't know what the fuck I'm supposed to do about it."

"A guy like you might even have the opposite effect," Compton said.

Gellhorn ignored him.

"Jesus Christ," Compton said. "You have to go out west to meet your loon father whom you've never even met before so you can get him not to kill himself. Pontiac has to go to Pontiac to get his brother out of prison. And I have to go to Queens and become a bedpan guy. We should just stay here."

Gellhorn and I nodded agreement.

Chapter Nine

ELLEN BROUGHT HER MAN TO MEET me in Aix En Provence. I was staying at a hotel while my farmhouse underwent renovation. He was charming, very handsome, and, of course, French. They were on their way to pick up one of his children at a school outside Marseille. He had to get back to their hotel right after lunch to deal with some issue involving the child and travel. Ellen and I strolled the Cours Mirabeau, stopping at the stalls of vendors to survey the spring wares. She wore a blue wool jacket and long white scarf. The eyes of all passing Frenchmen were upon her, and I was proud.

"Where's your brother?" she asked while we walked.

"He's rich. Not as rich as me but rich. Got sent to Vietnam, had a bad time, not like me. He had to fight. When he got home, I got him a job selling used cars in Secaucus for a guy who owed me money. David turned out to be the greatest salesman since Moses. He went back to Pontiac, bought his own lot and then bought up a bunch more lots. He wound up buying every new-car Pontiac dealership in southeastern Michigan. He was all over Detroit TV for years, Big Dave Skaggs, the Pontiac King of Pontiac."

"Are you close?"

"Very. He has a swarm of kids. He takes all of them and his wife up to the farm in northern Michigan a lot, even brought them all over here a few times. We have great fun. I always tell him he's way cooler than me. Know why?"

"He's way cooler than you."

"Yes."

"Do you have children?" she asked.

"One. A daughter."

"Do you see her?"

"We're very close. Now. I didn't see her for the first fourteen years. Her mother died of a drug overdose. Her mother's parents blamed me."

"And were you to blame?"

"Maybe 50 percent. Her father thought fifty-one."

"OK. Maybe we should sit."

We found a stone bench. The day was a little brisk, and the bench was in the sun. A mild breeze brought us scent of almonds and lavender.

"Her mother's drugs didn't start until the child was two years old," I said, "so there was no prenatal damage. The grandparents took her from me the day of the funeral. I was at a bar getting drunk. My father-in-law went to our apartment with a couple goons, barged in past the babysitter, and snatched the kid."

"My god. Did you call the police?"

"He was the police. Worse. He was the US Attorney for the Southern District of New York. Dickie Decherd had been pestering him for a year about some stuff Stick and I were doing with the Hunt brothers and soybeans. My father-in-law had been batting him away like the horsefly he was."

"But all of a sudden your father-in-law was interested."

"Yup. You get away with stuff when they don't want to catch you, not when they do. My father-in-law got together with the IRS and worked up a big file. Our lawyer told us it was enough to send me and Stick to the pen. I stayed away from the kid, and the ex-father-in-law kept the file in his desk drawer."

"So you forsook your own daughter to keep yourself out of prison."

"And Stick."

"Yes, of course, poor little Stick. But then you saw your daughter again. How did that happen?"

I sat watching young French women walk by. Especially in the South, they have a way of walking, a presentation that perfectly marries sensuality with force.

"We were on the hook for both wire and mail fraud," I said. "The years rolled by. Eventually, my lawyer called to tell me the statute of limitations had run. It took me two more years to find a way through an intermediary to meet my daughter without risking criminal charges. I finally arranged to meet her at the Brooklyn Botanical Garden without the knowledge of the grandparents but in the presence of the intermediary. It went fantastically badly. She told me she was afraid of me, she thought I was Satan, I killed her mother, and she never wanted to see or hear from me again. I never got a word in edgewise. God she was mean. And so angry. And so beautiful and full of beans and smart. They did a great job bringing her up, which is amazing because they were such assholes."

"How did the intermediary take it?"

"She thanked me afterward for the worst afternoon of her adult life. It also rained on us and was cold, and an attendant balled me out for throwing down a hotdog wrapper, just to complete the picture. My daughter told her grandfather about the meeting. He was so furious about it that he had a stroke."

"And died?"

"A month later."

"So you killed her mother and her grandfather."

"Notches on my parasol."

"Then what happened?"

"She came to me three years later when she was seventeen. Looked me up. She didn't actually come to see me. She called. She had received an early admit to Stanford. She wanted to do pre-med. Her grandmother had just enough loot left that the Stanford shitheads wouldn't give the kid a good scholarship. So her grandmother sent her to me for the rest of the money, which was a bundle."

"And you told them to go fuck themselves."

"Absolutely not. I told her I would put her through undergrad, med school, residency, fellowship, all of it, nice car, apartment, allowance of a rich kid. But she had to have lunch with me four times a year. She said no way. She just wanted the money. I said no lunch, no money. She called me a bastard and hung up on me. So, you know, count the beats. Two weeks later, she calls me back. Grannie has told her to do the lunches but Grannie gets to come along. I said no Grannie or no money. The kid calls me back the next day, OK, no Grannie, give me the money. So I did. But I piecemealed it, a nickel and dime at a time."

"So she had to do the lunches. How did those go?"

"Horribly at first, of course. She tried to duck out early, but I had a rule that if she didn't stay through at least two courses, I would hold up the money. I would ask the waiter what took the longest to prepare and then order it. She'd take off, so I would slow-pay her money. She called me in fits. She'd scream at me, 'Now you've made me late on my rent and they're calling me from the bank about the car. How could you humiliate me like this?' I said, 'No lunch, no money, Honey.' I made her do do-over lunches to get paid. It was awful for a long time.

"And then, maybe a year into it, we stumble on this amazing discovery, triggered by a guy at the next table who was being racist to a waiter. We discover by accident that we both hate white people."

"She's white."

"As am I. But she's very bright about this stuff. She tells me that white is the matrix and that people who live inside the matrix don't know it's a matrix. Everything she says happens to coincide exactly with things I have thought about in relation to languages. It turns out we have a lot to talk about. It wasn't that we agreed on anything, really, but even when we disagreed on things, we found each other's views interesting. And guess what? We liked each other. She even starts calling me between lunches, always about politics at first, but then she calls me about a boyfriend."

"What on earth could you have told a young girl about a boyfriend?"

"Not shit. I think that's why she called me. Just to run her mouth."

"Where is she now?"

"Austin. She's an eye surgeon. Married to a puppeteer. You tell me, what kind of eye surgeon marries a puppeteer?"

"A really cool one."

"Exactly. And he's cool, too. I love them both to bits. They are my earth, moon, and stars."

"I thought you hated surgeons."

"Brain surgeons, Ellen. I hate brain surgeons. Not eye surgeons. That's totally different."

We rose and walked again, this time out in the street to escape the crowded sidewalk. A cool breeze had picked up.

"You do see her, then."

"Yes. She and the puppeteer have produced two lovely grandchildren for my amusement, a boy and a girl. They bring them up to the farm for the summer."

"And the parents are able to stay in Michigan all summer?"

"Oh, no, they both have demanding schedules. They sort of take turns dropping in and out over the summer. But I stay up there to oversee."

"You take care of two little kids all by yourself, an old coot like you?"

"No, Ellen, obviously not. The children come with their own Department of Child Welfare, poor things, a retinue of nannies and attendants and people I'm afraid to even ask what their fucking jobs are. I have a farmer who farms my land for hay and is also my Man Friday at the house, and he has a college-age son who helps. I hire the farmer's wife and daughter to cook lunch and dinner. I do breakfast. I feel like I'm feeding five thousand mouths at the table. It's very jovial."

"You sit where?"

"At the head of the table."

"Good for you, Woodrow. Wonderful. And you like it."

"I adore it. Every minute. There isn't a bad minute. Even the bad minutes I adore."

"What's the puppeteer all about?"

"He's funny. Warm. Quite brilliant, I think. Mainly he's the greatest dad ever born."

"Does he remind you of yourself?"

"Not in the slightest."

"Well, that's good."

Ellen found an outdoor table at a café and ordered coffee. I ordered hot chocolate.

"Oh, Woodrow," she sighed, "This is such a relief. And a surprise. So this whole grotesque saga of your boyhood comes to a denouement in which you're happy."

She stared hard for a response.

"I balk at the word, 'happy,'" I said. "I think happy is a concept invented by Hollywood to sell soft drinks and popcorn. No one went to America to become happy. People went there to eat."

"God. Fine. Of course. You have to say all that shit, Woodrow, I realize, but would you admit to being just a tad happy in your old age?"

"Dotage."

Our drinks arrived. Stirring sugar into her cup, she said, "Face it, Woodrow, you're happy."

"Are you going to have me committed?"

"Maybe later. Do you think about your grandkids when you're away?"

"All the time. They're going to be very rich."

"That makes you happy."

"No. It worries the shit out of me. The girl will be pursued by hound dogs. I hate the idea of her parents having to tell her all the way through adolescence that no boy really loves her—all they want is her money. I try to think how I can protect her from that."

"Protect her or protect the money?"

"Both."

"Got any ideas?"

"Yes. The boarding schools are mainly co-ed now. I think I'll send to them to one that's full of all rich kids."

"Oh, my God, Woodrow, not really! You of all people. Why would you do that? So they can be snobs?"

"Of course not. I would hate it if they were snobs. I just want them to be kids. A school full of all rich kids is a way of controlling for wealth. If everybody's rich around them, they won't be targets. They can have childhoods. I'll be leveling the playing field for them."

"Shit. Wow. So everything just comes back around and nothing changes?"

"Everything changes. The only thing that doesn't change is money."

She got to her feet, ready to move on. "I think it's wonderful you worry about your grandchildren. Making up for past sins."

I rose and threw money on the table.

"When I die, Ellen, if you get any inquiries from up there (I pointed skyward), be sure to bring this up."

"I'll give you an excellent reference."

"Even if you have to fudge a little?"

"Fudge-city, man."

•

I had been away from home only seven months. It could have been five years. I couldn't even remember who I was when I left. The bus ride from Boston to Detroit was a reprise of the trip that had taken me away from Pontiac—the backed up toilet, the musty cloud of cigarette smoke, mothers scolding, families bickering. There was even a sailor screwing a girl on the backbench. Could it possibly be the same one? In the morning when we pulled into the Detroit depot, he was asleep on the floor.

Rather than have me take a local bus out to Pontiac, my father drove into Detroit to pick me up at the depot. He hugged me warmly and tousled my hair on the way to the car.

"Johnny Wilson called me," he said as we rode out Woodward Avenue from downtown. "He said you're doing real good. Is that just talk?"

"No, Pa. I am."

I explained how difficult my classes had been at first. He frowned and bit his lip. But when I told him how much my grades had improved, he relaxed. When I said that I had been first and second in my class for the last several grading periods, his mouth opened and he smiled so broadly I could see the gaps between his teeth.

"Woodrow, that's somethin'. That's really somethin'. I'm real proud of you, boy."

"Thank you, Pa."

My mother was another story. She did not even come to the door when we arrived at the house. I trundled my suitcase up to the attic bedroom and came back down to the kitchen. She was cooking.

"Hi, Ma."

"Hello, Woodrow." She did not lift her face from the pan.

I spent the first several days alone in my bedroom grinding for the exams that awaited me on my return to school. When I passed my mother in the house, she looked away. I could tell that my father was especially afraid of riling her and that she was carrying some kind of loaded gun for me. No mention was made in the house of David, not a syllable.

At the end of my first week back, I decided to lance the boil. Over lunch, I asked her, "What do you hear from David?"

"Nothing," she said flatly. "I don't talk to him."

My father pleaded with his eyes.

"Don't talk to him?" I said. "Why wouldn't you talk to David?"

"I figured you took care of all that already."

I looked up from my plate. She was coiled to strike.

"How did I take care of it?"

My father muttered, "Susan, please. The boy's just back a few more days."

She sprang to her feet and ripped open a drawer in the kitchen cabinet next to the refrigerator. With a grand flourish she pulled out a crumpled sheet of paper, snapped it in my face and tossed it on the table. "You seen that before, I guess. You wrote it."

I picked it up it. It was my letter telling David he had done the right thing.

"How'd you get this?"

"Don't you no never mind how I got it."

"The juvie give it to her," my father mumbled.

"So David never saw it?"

"No, he never seen it," she hissed. "That's why they give it to me." Her face quivered with anger. "They give it to me so he wouldn't see it. And you ain't allowed to go see him neither, so forget about that if it's what you're thinkin'. They got you on a list of bad influence. I made sure of that."

"Ma, I don't think you understand . . . "

"Oh I understand OK," she cut me off. "I had plenty time here to think about it, sittin' here readin' that letter while we waited on you comin' home. I understand you think it's a fine thing David thinkin' just like them other thugs in the juvie and proud he's got six more months and stayin' in there forever like you told him." She gulped for air. "Because now you're in with the rich people and Johnny Wilson says you can stay up there, well now you'd just as soon David should stay in there locked up forever so's maybe nobody will find out you even got a hoodlum white trash brother like him. If they didn't just but know, he's the one ain't a bastard."

My father let out a moan. My head was down. I didn't look at her when I spoke. But muttered words escaped my lips, words that changed everything forever, words I still hate, words I have never truly regretted.

"I know I'm a bastard," I said. "Did you think you kept that a secret from me? But you know what you are, Ma? You're just a mean bitch and a shit mother who can't even think about anybody but herself."

My father leapt to his feet and shouted. "Woodrow! You get in here!" He nodded toward the living room. "I can still whip your ass boy, you use language like that on your own mother, I will surely not put up with that."

I started to rise from the table, but she said, "Sit down, both of you. Nobody ain't going to whip nobody." She pointed a finger at my father. "This is just what I told you and that goddamn Johnny Wilson. Send him to a smartass rich boy school, all's they're going to do up there is teach him to be even more of a smartass than he was already before he even got sent up there. And now you see what he is, calls his mother bitch."

"Susan you called him a . . . "

"I didn't call him no name, I just said what he is. That's not a name. It's a fact." She turned to me. "Woodrow, I can't keep you from coming home here 'til you're sixteen, but I will tell you one thing. I do not consider this your home, and I do not want you in it. I want you gone as soon as you can manage. Soon as they got a place up there for you fulltime, you grab it, because you ain't got one here no more."

She went into the living room and turned on the television.

My father reached across the table for my hand. I took his hand. "Pa, it's OK. Me and you will always be OK. I'll be OK. I know everything I need to do."

I put the letter in my pants pocket, went to the phone, and called Billy Shirtlift. I pulled on galoshes and a winter coat and trudged through deep snow to his house.

None of us was old enough to get a driver's license, which meant absolutely nothing to Old Man Shirtlift, who had banged together the rotting husk of a pickup truck abandoned years ago behind their garage. He told Billy to figure out how to drive it without teaching him, which, of course, Billy did in about half an hour. Billy needed a vehicle because his father had secured him a late night job as a sweeper and dishwasher in a saloon in Pontiac, also illegal at his age, also not important to his father, who applied all of his son's earnings to his own liquor and gambling tab at the saloon.

I gave the letter to Billy and explained his mission.

He repeated it back. "Jis gothu juvie an give over this'r later to Die-vit. You cain't go cuz yurroner shate lest. Tell Die-vit he cain't leyyer old lie-dee knowt he goddit."

"You got it."

—

On a perfect morning in late May beneath a robin's egg sky, Ellen and her man were married at my lavender farm outside Aix. With a good deal of hired help, my daughter and I served a banquet of too many courses to more than a hundred guests, en pleine air at long, covered tables in a dormant field awash in scent of lavender. A majority of the guests were his people, but Ellen had commanded a sizeable contingent from Illinois, and I even persuaded Compton and some of his hockey buddies to stop by on their way to a game in Moscow. They still played, all over the world. After, lunch my son-in-law put on a Punch and Judy show in French that delighted the children, with just enough cynical double entendre to keep the French adults happy.

At a certain point in mid-afternoon, I was suddenly very tired. By then I was walking on a bad knee with a cane, my back severely stooped, and I fatigued easily. I intended to return to the house, but I only stumped along as far as a now barren table and slumped onto a chair. A short time later, Ellen's man appeared at my side and took a seat. We chatted in French at first. He said my accent was "quite good," which in French means noticeably foreign. But he said my son-in-law's accent was perfect. "And when Punch speaks, it is in the accent of the old Languedoc."

I switched us to English. "My son-in-law is wonderful, isn't he? And listen, I'm so happy for Ellen. And for you, as well. So happy."

"Yes," he said, "We are very happy. And Ellen especially is in a wonderful moment. I don't know which pleases her more, our wedding or her progress with the novel. She says it's finally coming together after such a long struggle."

He saw my surprise.

"I hope I didn't let the dogs out of the bag," he said. "I was quite certain you already knew about her novel."

"Yes. I think so. This is the novel about the woman married to a brain surgeon."

Now the surprise was on his face. "Not at all. She gave up on that long ago. This is the story you told her, about the boy in an American boarding school in the 1960s. She told me that you encouraged her to go back to that idea."

"Did I?"

"I hope you are pleased."

"Delighted. Of course. That's the much better story. It's so good, I just hope some unprincipled bastard doesn't beat her into print with it."

He chuckled. "You forgot you told her to go back to it."

"Yes, well. Getting old." I touched a finger to my temple. "Memory."

"I understand. It is normal. My mother struggles with this now."

"Perhaps you should introduce us."

He touched my arm gingerly. "If my question is not too familiar, what became of your own mother?"

Most of the wedding guests, the ones who weren't staying with me on the farm, had departed for the train station or their hotels in Aix. A soft cloud of laughter floated up from the tennis courts where a few stragglers were lingering.

"My mother died of cancer about fifteen years ago."

"And had you . . . had the two of you made a reconciliation by then?"

"No. We never spoke again after my first vacation home from school."

"But surely you saw her whenever you returned home for vacations."

"I didn't return home, as a matter of fact. I spent the shorter vacations at the homes of school friends, once their parents decided it was safe to invite me. The school sent me here to Aix for a summer to live with a French family. I spent two summers working on a ranch in Montana owned by the family of a schoolmate, and then I came back here on my own and worked on a farm. I stayed here for a couple years."

"In Montana you were a cowboy."

"I was a cowboy's assistant, but even that was pretty heady stuff for a kid from a factory town."

"And your mother . . . "

"My parents split while I was at Harvard. I remained close to my father, as I'm sure Ellen has told you. My brother David looked after our mother. But, no, she and I never spoke again. I never saw her."

"She was very fiercely a woman of her own resolve I suppose."

"I suppose. I think Ellen must have told you that I'm a bastard. Someone in the rich family my mother worked for as a girl got her pregnant. I'm sure she was already very beautiful. There was no wedding, of course. My father rescued her. He loved her deeply, and she was grateful to him. But I think whenever she looked at me, she saw in me something she hated, something in my blood she couldn't get around. She was a product of rural Georgia. People there believe in blood. It's a dangerous place."

"More dangerous than the rest of your nation?"

"I believe so. The only place that might be more dangerous is Arkansas."

We sat silently for a long while watching two bees buzz around spilled honey. He smoked a cigarette.

"Never to speak to your mother again," he said. He did the Compton shrug. "Perhaps it is not my place, but I think this is very sad."

I said, "C'est la vie."

•

I didn't have enough money for the sixteen-hour express bus ride across Ohio and Pennsylvania to Boston, so I had to take the twenty-four-hour ride through Canada to New York State. All afternoon, the two-lane highway across the flat expanse of southern Ontario was a tunnel through walls of snow, broken only by black shadows of passing trucks. The bus horn raged again and again ahead into the white abyss.

Night was falling on Buffalo when we got there. The bus broke down some distance from the depot. The driver ordered everyone off. The streets were deserted, the city a white sepulcher. Black smoke poured from a rear wheel-well. The driver walked across the street into a diner to make a call. The night was wretched cold, and the snow was driving down hard. The driver came out and announced there was no substitute bus yet to pick us up. A truck would come by to collect our luggage. The bus was not safe for us to re-board. He pointed down the street and said we should walk to the depot six blocks away. Someone shouted, "Tell them to come pick us up, asshole." Only a few people took his suggestion and trudged off toward the depot with their heads bent into the solid white wind.

I put on my thick hooded parka and hurried across the street into the diner, managing to get inside in the nick of time. Less fleet-footed passengers had to stand outside waiting to get in, stamping their fleet on the sidewalk and clapping their elbows against their bodies in the universal pantomime for freezing to death. Behind the counter, a harried man in a white cap madly worked the grill while a middle-aged woman in a hairnet took orders and collected money. The windows quickly fogged with human heat. I ordered a hamburger and a Coca Cola. They gave me a hotdog and a milkshake, which I accepted gladly and paid for without complaint. There were no stools open, so most of us squeezed against the walls and ate standing up. The heat and stuffiness of the place were oppressive. When I had finished eating, I looked in vain for paper napkins and finally, not wanting to foul my gloves, wiped my greasy hands on my pants. I squeezed my way back through the crowd and out the door. A crew were handing the luggage up by relay onto a flat-bed truck. The driver was speaking to a knot of passengers. I stood on the rim of the crowd and heard him say a new bus had been sent from Batavia and would come pick everybody up in about an hour. The injured bus was still on the side of the street across from the diner, down on a toe with the engine running. The fire in the wheel well had been put out. The driver allowed passengers to board the re-warming bus while waiting for the new one to show up.

A lighted billboard above a building across the street said, "Niagara Falls, Maid of the Mist Boat Tour," with an arrow. I walked that way down a silent side street that dead-ended into a major thoroughfare traveled by only a few vehicles. On the far side of the thoroughfare were thick woods. I was about to turn and go back toward the diner when I heard something in the distance, a sound almost like the sluice in the forest but deeper and more com-plex, like an immense chorus of voices singing and moaning in the blackness beyond the snow. Watching for traffic, I crossed the bou-levard and entered the woods. There was no path. With each step I had to lift my knees higher to get up out of the snow. The roaring grew deeper and broader, and now I thought I could hear notes of brass and tympany and the braying of animals. When I broke out of the woods, my clothes were powdered white. I came to a narrow park road, which I crossed. A steel fence rose far above my head, crowned with concertina wire. Signs were posted every five feet, warning in large red letters not to climb. She was above.

Lighted by spotlights, the mountainous white Niagara tossed her immense silver mane up into the black ceiling of the night. Clouds of stars roared down out of the brilliant heavens into her churning womb. She sang and shouted a ferocious anthem of power and glory. She sang that she was beautiful beyond my comprehension, that she was aware of everything in all reality and that she was aware of me. She sang that she would allow me to live for now if I worshipped her. I asked if I could pray to her. She said yes but not for small shit. I bowed, turned away in terror and stumbled back across the deep snow through the woods.

On the way back to the bus, I found an open drug store. I purchased a generous-sized bag of grape balls and asked the man at the liquor counter in back if there might be any way he could sell me a pint of apple jack.

"I don't sell no apple jack," he said, "and I don't sell liquor of no kind to kids. But if you go back out and look down that alley next to me, there's a guy back there will come in and buy some for you. Don't let him skin you for more than a dollar."

In the unlighted alley next to the store I found a ragged man cowering inside a lean-to made of wooden packing crates covered with black tar paper. His face in the crack of a canvas curtain was lighted fiendishly by the white flame of an alcohol stove. After negotiation, he agreed to buy me a pint of whiskey for a commission of two dollars. By the time I had consummated the deal and was off to the bus with my booze, grape balls, and several packs of Lucky Strike cigarettes in my pockets, I was down to very little money.

In promising a new bus, the driver must have been joking. The bus from Batavia was a smaller and even more weary vessel, and, because our unscheduled delay had required us to take on more passengers, this replacement bus was now packed to the gills. I was late to board, so I had to go almost to the back. I found a seat next to a very large woman just across the aisle from the toilet. A few feet away on the bench at the back of the bus, the sailor was wetly mouth-popping a girl.

Not too far into the wintry night of upstate New York, an elderly man, bent and stumbling on a cane, came painfully down the aisle toward the bathroom. A young woman whom I took to be a grand-daughter followed close behind him. The bathroom was occupied and locked. The old man elected to stand next to the seats occupied by myself and the large woman. "I need in there real bad," he told her. The young woman behind him shrugged to show us she was helpless. My seatmate stood up, pushed past the old man and began beating on the bathroom door.

"Open up!" she bellowed. "We got a old man out here 'bout to shit hisself."

The door flew open and the sailor staggered out so drunk he could barely walk. He stumbled to the bench and collapsed prone on top of the girl who did not move or make a sound and could have been dead. The old man closed himself inside the toilet from which we heard awful groaning and shitting noise for ten minutes. When he opened the bathroom door to make an unsteady exit, he released a wet shitty smell into the bus, spurring an outbreak of cigar and pipe smoking that did not make things better.

The sailor's girlfriend was not dead. When they began to engage in noisy sexual intercourse, I looked up at my seatmate in despair. She said, "Boy, you need to pull that coat up over your head and go to sleep." She pulled her own woolen coat over her head and we stared at each other, eyes inches apart inside the lit-tle cave of coats we had fashioned. I reached into the pocket of my parka and pulled out the pint, which I offered to her.

"Well you are one smart little white boy after all," she said. She took a deep pull and winced. "But you don't go in for the expen-sive stuff, do you?"

"Nope."

She laughed. We took turns at the pint inside our soft cavern of coats. In the morning, I awoke with my head against her shoulder. The cocoon of coats had fallen away. A metallic white sunlight caromed off high plowed snowbanks along the shoulders of the highway.

The bus smelled better, if a little too much like toilet deodorizing cakes. The sailor was sleeping soundly on the floor again. The girl had crawled up like a child on the bench and was scrawling a pattern with her finger in the frost on the rear window. Ahead of me several rows, the old man had thrown a comforting arm around his granddaughter, whose shoulders shook with silent sobs. Across from me was a Mexican family who must have boarded in Rochester while I slept. They consumed a wordless breakfast of cold refried beans and tortillas—three young children in thin cotton jackets gazing up in worship at their mother who parceled food from a cardboard box while the father stared resolutely out the window at endless fields of white.

In the brittle light glancing off the speeding snowbanks, my seatmate's sleeping brow glittered like polished obsidian. I sank back in my seat smiling and thought, "Home at last. Home at last."

Acknowledgments

This novel would never have happened without the brave hand of Will Evans, my impresario publisher. It is a far better (and quite changed) book thanks to my excellent editors, Michael Jauchen and Linda Stack Nelson. My sincere gratitude to Teimour Amri for reading my French and sparing me (I hope) international embarrassment.

No character in this story is a boy I knew at St. Paul's School, but all of the boys I went to school with are here. It is the wonder of boys that as awful and as marvelous as boys may be, from distant paths and even warring tribes, all boys may join as one in haunting song and pray for the peace of Jerusalem

Biographical Information

Jim Schutze was born in 1946, spent his childhood in Ann Arbor, Michigan, and attended high school at St. Paul's School in Concord, New Hampshire, after which he was an automobile assembly line worker in Detroit for six years. He is retired from a decades-long career as a newspaper columnist writing about local politics in Dallas, Texas. Schutze's book on race relations in Dallas, *The Accommodation*, was pulled from the presses by a local publisher and suppressed in 1986. Re-published thirty-five years later in the wake of the George Floyd murder, it was selected for a citywide reading program in Dallas.